Dudley Bernard Egerton Pope was born in 1925 into an ancient Cornish seafaring family. He joined the Merchant Navy at the age of sixteen and spent much of his early life at sea. He was torpedoed during the Second World War and his resulting spinal injuries plagued him for the rest of his life. Towards the end of the war he turned to journalism becoming the Naval and Defence Correspondent for the London *Evening News*. Encouraged by Hornblower creator C S Forester, he began writing fiction using his own experiences in the Navy and his extensive historical research as a basis.

In 1965 he wrote *Ramage*, the first of his highly successful series of novels following the exploits of the heroic Lord Nicholas Ramage during the Napoleonic Wars. He continued to live aboard boats whenever possible and this was where he wrote the majority of his novels. Dudley Pope died in 1997 aged seventy-one.

CONVOY

DUDLEY POPE

HOUSE OF
STRATUS

For Kay,
with all my love

CHAPTER ONE

As soon as the nurse had filled in the details, hung the board back on the locker and turned to the patient in the next bed, he reached out, unhooked and looked at it. The temperature graph was evening out – the upward zig had levelled off and presumably in a few hours would begin a downward zag, back towards normal after oscillating near the top of the page. The line had been spectacular for a week which was now beginning to fade into a distant haze of pain, brief spells of morphia-induced sleep, and dreams that verged on hallucinations. Curiously enough there was no memory of pain; he now knew one did not remember pain, only the circumstances associated with it.

The hand still throbbed with the pain darting up and down like vibrating toothache or summer lightning in the distance, and seemed to be storing itself in the armpit where, one of the nurses said, there was a gland that intercepted all the poisons being manufactured in that hand.

It was still dark; dawn was an hour or more away. He glanced up at the big clock over the swing doors. An hour to go before they wheeled in a trolley carrying the long white enamel dish full of scalding water and put the screens round his bed. Fifty-four minutes, to be exact. All important clocks seemed to have Roman figures. Then they would lift the arm off the pillow, undo the bandages, remove the dressings, give him a warning glance so that he could brace himself by

1

gripping the top of the bed with his good hand and pressing his feet hard against the bottom, then they would press that stinking purple and green left hand into the scalding water and his world would spin and burst into a red sunflower of pain.

They teased him and told him he always said 'Christ!' as his hand went into the water, and perhaps he did; but the worst part always came a couple of minutes later, when the heat of the water had time to soak in. Eat in, really, like a corrosive acid, but to be fair they were saving the arm. The surgeon had given a satisfied sniff yesterday: to begin with he had brought more of his chums and they had gathered round with long faces and muttered like parsons at their patron's deathbed and there was no doubt they were measuring him up for the saw: should it be at the wrist, across the forearm, at the elbow, or below the shoulder…

After reading the thermometer and putting it back in the glass of antiseptic, she had to reach across the fellow in the next bed to unhook his chart board, and her legs were spectacular, even in those dreary black stockings. One seam was crooked; she would be furious if he mentioned it. Woollen, they seemed, although she said they were made of some mixture. He pictured black silk on those legs, whose calves seemed almost too thin, but which guaranteed she would have slim thighs. Thinking about them eased the pain; even at this time of the morning a few moments' erotic thoughts were more effective than a pain-killing pill, though not so long-lasting.

The charts did not give much away. Edward Yorke, aged twenty-five, five feet eleven inches tall, 164 pounds, had at 0530 on this dark November morning in 1942 a temperature of 100.3, a pulse of 84, and had experienced a bowel movement ('Yes?' That polite smile if the patient nodded, the frown if he shook his head).

Her name was Exton; he had found that out within hours of being brought into the surgical ward at St Stephen's. And she was a member of one of the nursing associations, probably the QARNNS, and no funny jokes about the Queen Alexandra's Royal Naval Nursing Service, which seemed to be a highly efficient volunteer organization for debs who had abandoned the cocktail party circuit to nurse their would-be escorts through wounds and sickness. In peacetime they would be nursing them through hangovers, and their uniforms would be their nakedness, not these starched and rustling dresses out of which black-stockinged legs grew.

She had been off duty for the day or so before his operation – he would never have forgiven her if she had administered the blasted enema – and the septicaemia had begun almost as soon as he had belched and vomited up the last of the chloroform and ether fumes. Then there had been the haze of pain, the rapidly increasing stink of the septicaemia (the stink of his own flesh) and finally one became absorbed into the routine of the hospital surgical ward with ten patients, five in beds along one wall, five opposite, and a desk in the middle at which a nurse or sister wrote up notes (or love letters) at night by the light of a dim, green-shaded lamp, looking like a Whistler painting of Florence Nightingale.

A surgical ward – one could be thankful for that. Plenty of pain but no illness; at least not the sort of groaning illness, like stomach ulcers, where everyone had a long face. In this ward people were cheery enough, except immediately after their treatment, which the clock showed was now due for him in forty-six minutes' time. St Stephen's was old, the plaster of the ceilings was cracked, the lifts creaked alarmingly, but it was standing up well to being a Navy overflow hospital.

She was called Clare; he had discovered that on the second night, when the pain had seemed unbearable and she had stood up from that desk as though sensing the agony and glided silently to his bedside, and whispered: 'Is it really bad, Lieutenant?'

It had been so bad he had only been able to nod, and she had fetched the night sister. After what seemed like a week the sister had come back and whispered instructions to the nurse, whom she had called Clare, and moments later there had been the prick of a needle and, just before the morphia took effect, he had heard the sister hissing some criticism of the way Clare had used the syringe.

Clare Exton. Tiny, black-haired, shy, humorous, with the promise of a body he could (and did) only dream about under all that nurse's uniform, and so officious when necessary, which was frequently enough in a ward of young naval officers who were alternately in pain and bored stiff.

'Lieutenant Yorke,' she was now saying sharply, 'please put that board back on the hook.'

'I can't reach over with my right arm, Nurse.'

'You unhooked it without trouble.'

'The seam of your right stocking, Nurse.'

She was blushing now. 'What has that to do with it?'

'It's crooked, Nurse.'

'That's right, Nurse,' a patient opposite confirmed. 'It twists clockwise. Makes your leg look like a spiral.'

'Like the baldacchino in St Peter's at Rome,' Yorke said, hoping to confuse her.

'The *turisti* never seem to notice they spiral the other way,' she said calmly as she snatched the board, hooked it up with a clatter and then hissed: 'Don't bother asking for a bottle, Lieutenant; I've gone deaf.'

'The quack said I'll be able to get up for an hour today,' he said, a tentative peace offer.

'Just you wait until you try it,' she said. 'Your arm will throb so much you'll think it's going to burst and you'll be so dizzy you'll probably fall over.'

The plump paymaster lieutenant in the next bed said in a stage whisper: 'She's afraid you'll start chasing her round the ward.'

'I shall be off duty when Lieutenant Yorke finds how difficult it is to walk after several days of high temperature,' she said coldly.

Yorke was suddenly conscious of the drone of a German bomber right overhead as a series of whooshes told of a stick of bombs coming down: brief whooshes ending in heavy thuds that warned that the last two or three might hit the hospital, if not the ward.

A dull, deep explosion, then another; sudden darkness as the lights went out, a heavy weight on top of him, the shattering of glass, dust in the lungs…and yet another thud as the last bomb in the stick passed over and, from the noise, landed in the road beyond. The weight wriggled, he felt lips on his face and a hard kiss, and a murmured: 'I'll give you seams! I hope I didn't hurt your arm.'

And then she was gone, flicking on her torch and showing the ward was full of dust like fog. She began checking the blackout screens; and only he knew she had used her own body to protect him when it seemed certain the ward would get a direct hit.

He saw her shadowy figure following the torch beam from window to window jerking all the heavy black curtains back into position and shaking out the broken glass, carefully screening her torch. A few moments later there was a faint vibration as the hospital's emergency generator started up, then the lights flickered on and off once or twice and then stayed on.

'Close,' the paymaster said and was promptly contradicted by a full commander on his other side. 'Bet it didn't even hit the building. Whistled too long – obviously going right over us. You barely have time to hear the one that hits you. Hiss, bang and you're dead. These long whining johnnies – just passing over you. You draw it on a piece of paper and you'll see I'm right.'

The paymaster turned and winked at Yorke. 'You were safe enough,' he whispered. 'I saw in the flashes of the explosions.'

'You know what sister says – shove your head under the pillow to protect your face from glass.'

'Think what I'd miss.'

So now the paymaster was in the conspiracy: not too many winks and sly remarks, please...

'Must have been a late one on his way home, that Jerry. Still, we haven't had the all-clear, Hardly heard him,' the paymaster said. 'You can't mistake those engines, though; not synchronized, that's why they seem to rumble.'

'You sound more like an engineer than a paymaster.'

'Hobby. Not aeroplanes, but motor cars. I've a nice little Frazer Nash down at Portsmouth.'

Yorke remembered the paymaster's right leg had been amputated, and he had just had a second operation; something to do with the nerves being pinched in the first operation and leaving him in constant pain.

'I'm hoping Archie Frazer Nash will fix it up for me after the war so I can drive with one leg. Put in a handle throttle; shouldn't be too difficult.'

'Easy, I would think,' Yorke said, knowing how optimism could keep a man alive; he had only just passed through the dark night of a possible future with one arm. 'A bit of flexible cable and some practice. Like the Bowden cable on the Lewis gun of a last-war fighter.

'Hill climb trials will be out, though; I used to enjoy them. Great little bus for trials, the AFN, plenty of acceleration.' He glanced up at the clock. 'Be glad when they bring the tea urn round; that bloody dust has left me dry.'

Clare was taking the last few temperatures. Broken windows and dust were an almost nightly occurrence; the plaster ceiling looked like a reference book picture of leprosy. Soon the real work of the day would begin: after the glass and dust had been swept up the beds would be made, breakfast served, and then sister's rounds, matron's rounds, and finally doctor's rounds. And today the whole ritual would be punctuated by the cheerful cursing of the glaziers replacing the glass in the windows. But before that, the surgical dressings; in another twenty-two minutes, in fact.

'Any letters to be posted?' Clare asked the ward, and several patients answered and reached into the drawers of their lockers. Yorke held up a letter and as she took it he said, 'It needs a stamp on it, nurse; here's the money.'

She took the coins and glanced at the address. 'You've been writing sweet nothings to your girlfriend, Lieutenant?' she teased.

'Yes, the writing's a bit wobbly because I can't hold the pad steady.'

'She'll understand,' Clare said, and Yorke knew she would, because the superscription on the envelope said: 'Nurse C Exton.'

Sister Scotland put the last of the eleven stitches into the white enamel kidney bowl and then dropped the forceps and narrow pointed scissors with a clatter, as if to signal that the job was done. 'Wipe his face, Nurse,' she said to Clare, who reached for the towel on the rack behind the locker and patted his brow, which he knew was covered with pearls of cold perspiration.

The Sister cradled his hand gently as she wiped the scars with surgical spirit. It was bruised and bright pink with matching pairs of small purplish spots along each side of the long scars where the stitches had been. 'The incisions and cuts have closed nicely,' she said. 'In six months you won't notice anything, unless your hand gets cold. Then the scars will show up white.'

Yorke looked at the hand, remembering when it exuded yellow and green pus; when the putrid smell made him vomit. The hand was still there and he could just move the fingers and the only discomfort was that the skin seemed too tight, as though he was wearing a thick glove which had shrunk and become a size too small. It was still hard to believe the arm was his; it was a strange, alien limb, joined to him only by pain.

'An artist's hand, eh Nurse?'

Clare glanced up. You could never be sure with Sister Scotland.

'I suppose so,' she said warily.

'Aye, and the last of his sun tan's wearing off now.' She flipped up the other pyjama sleeve. 'See? The skin's quite white. But all this – ' she pointed at the left forearm ' – this dark brown will peel off; it's from all the hot water. Scalded, really. It must have hurt.'

'It did; I remember saying so at the time.'

'Aye,' she said, ignoring his sarcasm, 'and I seem to remember your bad language. Now you've got to start the remedial exercises for the arm; otherwise it can wither and leave you with a useless hand.'

Clare glanced at him in alarm: no one had mentioned this before.

'Wither, Sister?' He tried to keep his voice flat but no man faced with that could be a hero in pyjamas.

'Don't be alarmed, Lieutenant; the physiotherapists at Willesborough will sort it out; you'll soon get your grip back again.'

'Willesborough?'

'Down in Kent; we're opening an annexe there in a day or two. An old country house, just the place for convalescence. Plenty of draughts, no doubt; but you'll get a good night's sleep, which is more than can be said for up here, with all the bombing and the guns. And anyway, the surgeons need your bed.'

Clare was staring down at his hand. Had she known about Willesborough?

'And you'll not be escaping from me either, Lieutenant,' Sister said with an arch smile.

'Are – will you be going to Willesborough, too, Sister?'

'Yes, I shall be in charge of the unit. Three staff nurses, two physiotherapists, and six beautiful young ladies to powder your bottoms and make sure you don't get bedsores.'

The paymaster was quick; he seemed to guess Yorke's anxiety and from the next bed said: 'Don't say we're losing Nurse Exton, Sister?'

'Yes – no, rather, because you are coming to Willesborough, too, so Nurse Exton can continue to record your chronic constipation. We'll fit you out with a wooden leg and you'll soon be cadging free pints at the local pub. Anyway, Mr Yorke will need someone to fit his cufflinks and studs and you'll need someone to prop you up for a bit. Jack Sprat and his wife; I can see the pair of you escorting Nurse Exton to the Willesborough church fete. They'll put you in charge of the lucky dip,' she said to Yorke, 'you only need one hand to dip into a bran tub.'

'When do we go?' Yorke asked. 'We might miss the three-legged race.'

'The staff and the first batch of patients go tomorrow. By bus. One of your nice Navy buses, painted grey and with all the seat springs broken. It'll be like a Sunday school outing, won't it, Nurse?'

The bus juddered its way up the long hill and the movement made Yorke wince while the paymaster, lying in a nest of pillows across the back seat, swore quietly and monotonously, trying to steady the stump of his leg. Sister Scotland, sitting in the front offside seat, suddenly stood up, rapped on the window behind the driver and, having attracted his attention, shouted in a piercing voice: 'Change down, you bloody fool!'

The driver obediently dropped into a lower gear, the juddering stopped, and Sister Scotland sat down to a round of applause, which she acknowledged with an airy wave of her hand.

It seemed odd to Yorke to be back in uniform again. The hospital authorities thought they would all wear hospital blue for the journey and found they had seven almost mutinous and certainly truculent naval officers who were in any case not mobile enough to pack their own uniforms and had no intention of admitting that any nurse could, and intended using the whole episode as a reason for not going down to Willesborough in flimsy hospital wear, even though assured the bus had good heating and they would have blankets.

So Yorke sat alone in uniform trousers and half-length mess boots, a white rollneck woollen jersey, his left arm in a sling, and his uniform coat and cap on the seat beside him. He saw Clare and another nurse get up in response to instructions from Sister Scotland and walk slowly back along the bus, talking with each patient. The other nurse sat beside one man, then walked forward again and spoke to the sister before resuming her walk.

Yorke put his jacket across his knees, leaving the other seat empty, and in a few moments Clare sat down, the paymaster at the back telling her cheerfully, 'Leave me to your mate; I've no complaints and I don't want a bottle.'

Clare took his jacket and put it across her knees and, turning back one of the sleeves, ran a finger along the gold stripes. 'You're regular Navy, then. I thought you were Wavy.'

Her eye caught a flash of colour and she turned the coat and pointed to a single medal ribbon, red with blue edges, on the left breast.

'I didn't know you had a DSO.'

'I haven't yet; only the ribbon. Have to collect it one day.'

'Why didn't you say?'

'It's like virginity, one doesn't go on about having it.'

'I would,' she said impulsively and blushed as he looked round at her. 'That medal, I mean.'

She looked down and pointed at his bandaged hand, and murmured: 'Was it anything to do with that?'

Yorke laughed. 'The chicken or the egg! I'm not sure why they gave me the gong; the hand was a piece of something from an explosion.'

'A torpedo?'

'Bombs. Now tell me why a lovely girl like you isn't married. Or engaged.'

'I was married. I'm a widow now.'

'I'm sorry.' He had been clumsy but there had been no warning; no rings. Was Exton her married name?

'He was a pilot,' she said. 'Killed in an accident. It was a long time ago.'

She spoke in a curiously flat, unemotional voice. If she was my widow, Yorke thought, I would have liked her to have

11

continued wearing my wedding ring, even if on the other hand. '…A long time ago.' And obviously the memory still hurt. She was still in love with – well, a ghost. No living man could compete with that; the Rupert Brookes always stayed gilded youths, never to be supplanted, never ageing, or becoming unpleasant, their personalities never changing; flies in amber.

'I'm afraid this is a gloomy conversation, even for a bus,' he said.

'You'd prefer soft lights and sweet music and the air thick with tobacco smoke and night-club prices?' she asked.

'Or sitting on a five-barred gate along a country lane. Or on a rock watching the waves breaking on a shingle beach.'

'Why shingle?' she asked. 'Why a five-barred gate?'

'There are lanes and gates around Willesborough. I like the sound of water rolling the pebbles, and the nearest beach is shingle. At Hythe,' he added. 'Probably with barbed wire on it now, and land mines, but…'

Sister Scotland looked round and Clare caught her eye and got up. 'You know Willesborough?'

'Yes, fairly well. Fine old windmill, one of the best in the country.'

As Clare walked away he did not say that Ashford, into which Willesborough merged, was the railway centre of Kent and one of the Luftwaffe's main targets, and the windmill was white and enormous and the sort of thing a bolting German bomber pilot was likely to aim at, just for the hell of it.

He saw down to the right, through trees now bare of leaves, Leeds Castle sitting four-square like a fairy-tale fortress in a great oval moat. A castle had stood there for more than a thousand years – the first made of wood and built, if his memory served him, at the time of William the Conqueror, and the present one, now a mellow stone, creamy and smoothed by the centuries. Another potential target for a bolting German pilot; a thousand-pounder in the middle of that should kill the gardener and his wife who served as housekeeper, and a dozen ducks; a victory Goering's boys could hardly afford to miss. From up here on the main road the water in the moat seemed calm and a faint blueish-green as though distilled by age.

It was just three months ago; exactly twelve weeks the day after tomorrow. August, long days and short nights, not the time of year for destroyers to be steaming close to the Bay of Biscay, not with Junkers and Dorniers using those French airfields around Brest.They were reckoned to have a range of 1200 miles – five hundred out, two hundred to play with and five hundred back.

Death passed by so smoothly, just as Leeds Castle had slid into sight through the trees. You did not always have to see it; if you were reading a book or had been asleep it could pass unnoticed and touch someone else. The signalman had come up to the bridge and handed the page from the signal pad to the captain who read it and walked over to the chart.

Yorke had seen him glancing at the latitude and longitude scales and then putting an index finger on the chart – on a position well into the Bay of Biscay.

'Number One – here a moment. We have some trouble with the Teds.'

'The Teds' – a relic of the *Aztec*'s recent time in the Mediterranean and her association with the Italians, mainly ferrying them as prisoners. The Italians had no love for their allies, and their word for Germans, *Tedeschi*, provided the Royal Navy with an obvious abbreviation; a change from the usual 'Jerry'.

The captain smoothed out the signal for him to read. It was from the Admiralty and came ten minutes after the *Aztec* had herself picked up garbled signals from a ship being attacked in the Bay.

The captain, Lt Cdr Henry Bascombe, was a deceptive man: at first glance he seemed a ruddy and chubby-faced prosperous farmer dressed up in naval uniform. He smoked a foul pipe (originally, before the charring really got to grips with it, a distinctive Peterson of Dublin) and was given to using seagulls as targets when he felt the need to exercise one of the pair of 12-bore hammer guns he kept cased under his bunk. He did it less frequently since Yorke asked him, with well-simulated innocence, if he had ever used one of the pump guns that were becoming popular with American sportsmen. But, seagulls or not, Lt Cdr Henry Bascombe had been a fine shot.

His orders once he read the signal had been quiet and complete: warn the engine room that they would soon be going on to full speed, alter course now to east, get the navigator up on the bridge, and make sure that all the small-arms ready-use ammunition lockers were full, and have the galley make enough bully beef sandwiches to provide everyone with three – there was no telling when they would have time for a proper meal.

So the *Aztec*, a Tribal class destroyer on passage from Gibraltar to the Clyde on a sunny day in the late summer and with orders to stay at least four hundred miles from the French coast once abreast of Ferrol, increased to thirty knots and steered for a little pencilled X the navigator had put on the chart.

Bascombe was thorough; he had ordered another lieu-tenant to decipher the signal again; he had no wish to have the *Aztec* dashing off to the wrong position. And Yorke guessed that in the Operations Room at the Admiralty the little disc, or whatever they used to mark ships on the big plotting board, and which represented the *Aztec*, would be moved towards this other ship.

The *Aztec* – this one was a mighty warrior, despite the peaceful origin of the name: four U-boats sunk so far, thanks to Henry Bascombe's quite uncanny knack of seeing into a Ted submariner's mind. Or was it the farmer's instinct for outwitting a weasel, or even knowing over which holes to drape the nets before putting the ferret into a rabbit warren? But using a Tribal to hunt U-boats: it was an awful waste of a Fleet destroyer.

The first of the Ju 88s had picked up the *Aztec* some fifty miles from the position given by the Admiralty, and Bascombe had given the sequence of helm orders for evasive action as though he was at the local market bidding for a few ewes in which he was not really interested but knew the seller needed the money for some particular purpose, like paying a doctor's bill. Bascombe would have been that sort of a farmer. Prosperous, cheerful – and thoughtful. Squire Bascombe – that was the nickname he had picked up at Dartmouth many years ago.

The twin-engined Ted had let down its dive brakes – the first time Yorke had ever seen them used on a Ju 88 and they looked like latticed trapdoors opening downwards on the underside of each wing – and tried to line up on the *Aztec* as she jinked below at high speed, probably appearing as a grey dolphin leaving a wide white ribbon of wake.

'Port fifteen, quartermaster,' Henry had said, 'that should do it this time... And now starboard twenty, that'll break some china in the galley...'

But it had turned the *Aztec* into the last of a stick of five bombs which the despairing German pilot had dropped across the destroyer's mean course. The mean course: Henry had been so keen to go to the other ship's help that he had not deviated more than thirty degrees either side of the course at a time when a few circles and figures of eight might have helped to confuse the bomber.

They were small bombs, no more than 250-pounders, but this one had hit B turret, landing on the breech of a gun and just in front of the bridge, blasting up thousands of metal splinters that riddled it like a pepper dredge. The captain, navigator, lookouts, signalmen – every man on the bridge had been killed or badly wounded, and the word had been passed that Mr Yorke was in command – and a fire had started under B turret.

The next four hours had been a nightmare: Yorke could remember nothing beyond standing – crouching, rather – in the wreckage of the bridge smelling burning paint and shouting helm orders down the bent and battered voicepipe, calling engine-room orders to a rating who had managed to rig up a telephone, and leaving the men at the guns to fight as best they could under whichever warrant and petty officers survived while he tried to keep the ship afloat, which meant twisting and weaving like a wounded fox being attacked by eagles.

He had managed to dodge the next two Ju 88s and a Do 217, each of which, after dropping six bombs, had tried to rake the ship with machine-guns, but the *Aztec*'s own light armament had driven them off, a raucous barking of cordite which cheered up the ship's company. The clatter of empty cartridge cases rattling across the deck with every roll was music; the gunners' brass band.

But the only surviving officers were himself and the lieutenant 'E', who was busy down in the engine room trying to deal with blast damage, keep some pressure on the hoses for firefighting, and making sure Yorke had speed in hand.

Soon, as the fire was doused under B turret and casualties were carried below, Yorke retrieved the chart and brought the plot up to date more by guesswork than anything else. The soccer fans among the ratings had the score: twenty-two misses for the *Aztec* – bombs she had managed to dodge – and one hit for the Teds. They were arguing how many points should be scored for a miss and for a hit when lookouts sighted the ship they were supposed to be rescuing – an old Polish destroyer. God knew what she was doing in this corner of Biscay, but enemy bombers were circling her like a swarm of gnats, either ignoring the *Aztec* or because they had not sighted her.

And so he had steered for the Pole; steer for the sound of guns, the fighting instructions said, though presumably Their Lordships in their wisdom had meant 'sight' not 'sound'.

There was no need for radio silence now: that was one of the few advantages of being in direct contact with the enemy. A sighting report to the Admiralty on Fleet wave full power, giving their position, and reporting in cipher the damage and casualties, brought an order in cipher that the civilian passengers on board the other ship must be rescued at all costs. It did not matter that the Ted direction-finding stations could pick up the transmissions and plot the *Aztec*'s position; the bombers knew well enough and must be sending back a running commentary.

The engineer had turned up the wick in a bid for every knot of speed and Yorke was thankful that the stokers, or whichever of the survivors were down there handling the sprayers, were a bit heavy-handed because for a few moments they let in more fuel oil than the furnaces could burn, so that a stream of black smoke poured out of the funnels.

Smoke. He had not thought of it. There was not much wind – a breeze of perhaps ten knots, but every little helped. He took the telephone from the rating and talked to the engineer, and as he spoke he saw two gnats leave the Polish destroyer and head for the *Aztec*.

At the same moment he realized that the Polish destroyer was now stopped, fought to a standstill, and one of the lookouts with binoculars confirmed that she seemed low in the water, although not listing.

'May have low freeboard, sir.'

There was no time to look her up again in the identification books – even if they could be found in this tangle of bent metal. Grab the boys and girls and bolt, said Their Lordships; thank goodness there was no question of taking the Pole in tow.

And here was the first of a new wave of Teds diving down from ahead. Ju 88s, silvery in the sunlight despite camouflage on the upper surfaces, the black crosses easy to see, the reflection of sun glinting from the flat pieces of Perspex forming the cockpit canopy. Was the pilot right-handed or left? That had been Bascombe's last mistake; Yorke was sure that for some reason the commander had guessed the pilot was right-handed, but he had been left.

The plane, dive brakes down, was now beginning a shallow dive towards the *Aztec*, which for the moment was steering a straight course. The Ted pilot did not know before he began his bombing run whether the destroyer would jink to his left, his right – or carry straight on. If she turned to port (to his right) and he was right-handed, the plane's alteration of course to aim his bombs would be easy to make, an instinctive move. Was it any harder to the left? What did their bomb sights look like, anyway? Was it like a car driver pulling out to pass?

'Now!' he shouted at the rating holding the engine room telephone and saw the man's mouth twist into the word 'Smoke!'; then he called, 'Starboard thirty!' into the voicepipe and held on as the *Aztec* heeled violently in response to full effective rudder applied at full speed. He glanced aft through the splinter holes and saw a gush of black smoke streaming up from the funnel; just enough (he hoped) to divert that Ted pilot's attention for a few seconds when he should be concentrating on his bombing run. From aloft, the *Aztec* might look for a moment as if she had been hit by a bomb not yet dropped.

The score went up to thirty misses, though the engineer complained that two of the six had been close enough to start some rivets below the waterline and there were a few trickles of water round skin fittings. And, he grumbled, all this high-speed steaming was raising the engine-room temperatures…

The next was a Dornier 217, and the score rose to thirty-six; the third and fourth were Ju 88s, which dropped only two bombs each and then tried to spray the *Aztec* with machine-guns.

'Only forty – they must have used the rest of the sticks on that bloody Pole,' grumbled the starboard lookout, who had appointed himself scorekeeper.

At that point a petty officer scrambling across the wrecked bridge came up to Yorke, who recognized him despite a grubby and bloodstained bandage round his head.

'The torpedoes, sir: is there any chance…?'

Yorke thought of all that explosive and compressed air sitting amidships – as well as the depth charges aft. The Admiralty seemed very concerned about whomever was on board the Polish destroyer. Were the torpedoes so much extra weight? Would there be a chance to use them? Perhaps to make sure the Pole sank – the Teds might send out tugs, or even a destroyer.

'For the moment, no; but make sure all the depth charges are set to safe.'

The order about the depth charges should have been given long ago; there had been more than one case already of a destroyer sinking and, with her men swimming in the water above her, reaching the depth to which the hydrostatic valves in her depth charges had been set, where they had automatically exploded. Water being incompressible, the men were found unmarked but dead, the shock wave rupturing something inside them (Yorke watched the last Ju 88 turn away to the north-east), the diaphragm, he supposed.

'No Teds over the Pole, sir,' one of the lookouts reported. 'But – yes, two more approaching him from the east.'

It was little short of a miracle that the Pole was still afloat. Judging from the *Aztec*'s losses, when she could still steam and evade at full speed, he dared not think of the dead and wounded in a ship which had been fought to a standstill.

These latest two Ju 88s seemed determined to sink the Pole before the *Aztec* arrived; then no doubt they or their mates would deal with the intruder. They wheeled and dived again, like vultures over their prey and uncertain what to do, greed fighting fear.

The wind was south-east, and he gave the quartermaster a course that would bring the *Aztec* passing to windward of the Pole. The breeze was perhaps ten knots; the smoke should drift about one mile in six minutes although it was impossible to guess if this wind was constant; the *Aztec*, thundering along at over thirty knots, prevented anything more than guesswork. A young man standing up in a sports car tearing down the Brighton road at about forty land miles an hour would have the same difficulty…

One of the Ju 88s suddenly banked away from the Pole, but there were no bomb bursts. Were the Teds just waiting patiently for her to sink? The *Aztec* was vibrating as the engineer tried to get the last knot out of his engines, so that it was hard to see through binoculars.

Now the Ju 88 was darting for the *Aztec* in the same shallow dive from ahead. Was this the Luftwaffe's standard procedure for attacking ships? The pilots were (thank goodness) unimaginative: the *Aztec* was steaming towards this one at over thirty knots and he assumed that the Ju 88 with air brakes down was making 100 knots, so the *Aztec* would pass beneath on an opposite course at a combined speed of 130 knots. But if the pilot came up astern in the *Aztec* 's wake, the destroyer's speed would be subtracted; the Ju 88 would pass the destroyer at 70 knots, giving the Ted bomb aimer more 'time over target' and therefore a better chance. He stopped thinking about it; one could not be sure about telepathy, and anyway, there was no need to walk under ladders any day of the week, least of all on a Friday.

This pilot is left-handed! He's coming down in a gentle curve to his left, a difficult job for a right-handed man. Wasn't it? Wouldn't a right-handed man make a single larger alteration to line himself up, so that he could then approach in a straight line?

'Port thirty,' he snapped down the voicepipe, staking everything on his guess. If the bridge communications hadn't been so badly damaged he'd be reducing and increasing speed too, like a plover shamming injury to lure the enemy away from the nest.

But he might guess wrongly, like Bascombe, and bring a bomb down to shatter the bridge. 'Port thirty' had been enough; five bombs burst in a neat line on the port quarter.

'Forty-five for one,' remarked the signalman as he reported to the engine room. 'Be a while before we get "Bad light stopped play", though.'

Now Yorke could make out the Polish destroyer's outline clearly with the naked eye. The ship had paid off in the wind and sea so that her bow was heading to the north-west.

'She's a bleedin' wreck, sir,' reported one of the lookouts with binoculars. 'Hits on A turret, B turret and the bridge, both funnels riddled, torpedo tubes smashed... No fires though, and no steam neither... Reckon her boilers are out.'

'Any floats?'

A group of lozenge-shaped Carley floats, the simple rafts which were little more than rope nets over wooden frames, would be the clearest indication that the Poles were abandoning ship, and knowing the kind of men they were it would mean the destroyer was at last sinking fast.

'No, sir. Still a lot of tracer going up. Bet them gun barrels is hot.'

Yorke could just see the three or four thin red lines of tracer curling up towards the single plane still circling the stricken ship. It was light stuff; more likely stripped Lewis guns than anything else; guns which could be aimed and fired by hand: no electrics or hydraulics would be left working. And there would be only so many pans of Lewis gun ammunition remaining, however fast they were loaded.

She was now perhaps a mile away. The remaining Ju 88 seemed undecided what to do. The Ted pilot had no bombs left; that much seemed certain. Almost certain, he corrected himself.

Using the *Aztec* to circle the Polish destroyer a mile off, laying smoke, meant steaming round in a circle for just over three miles. At thirty-five knots – that was what the engineer now reckoned – it would take a little over twelve minutes to lay the screen. How many Ju 88s could – would, rather – arrive in that time, a flock of screaming vultures determined to stop the *Aztec* from spoiling their party?

Now a sick berth attendant was waiting to report.

'Surgeon, sir – he says we've eight so badly wounded they won't last, no matter what we do, and fifty-three other wounded.'

'How serious are the fifty-three?'

''Bout twenty bad; the rest cuts and fractures, sir; no amputations.'

'Very well; thank the surgeon. The dead?'

'Twenty-seven, sir. Leastways, them we know about; but there ain't been time to search everywhere yet; the surgeon said to get out the livin' and leave the dead, sir. For the time being, anyway.'

'Quite right,' Yorke said, watching the Polish destroyer now lying like a log on the port bow. The last Ju 88 was heading away north, rapidly growing smaller, exasperated or out of ammunition. Twelve minutes, that was all he needed now. A clear blue sky – that had its advantages because the Ted bombers could not sneak in above clouds and suddenly dive through a gap to bomb. It seemed strange, though, that gulls wheeled under a warm sun while around them men were blowing each other to pieces.

He called to the rating at the telephone: 'Tell the engine room to make smoke.'

He could imagine seamen spinning valves so that more fuel oil poured out of the sprayers than could burn properly, and the extra would – like a smoking paraffin lamp in a draughty room – be sucked up the funnel and poured out in a thick black cloud.

He glanced aft through a splinter hole and saw the smoke streaming astern to lie on the water as an oily black coil barely moving in the wind, a bulging thick snake, writhing slowly, almost languorously.

Senior surviving officer. Only surviving officer except for the engineer and surgeon. Not even a blasted midshipman to lend a hand, run errands, take over responsibility for a part of the ship. And somehow he had to get 'the passengers' off that damned destroyer. Not just passengers, of course, but the whole ship's company. Well, he could do with the men; the *Aztec* was like a ghost ship, just thundering along with a handful of men on the bridge, a few at the remaining guns, some in the engine room, a lot in the sick bay... But the Pole would have few survivors too; she had taken a terrible beating. But if a Pole could crawl he could fight; Yorke had met enough of them to know that.

A few words down the voicepipe to the quartermaster and the *Aztec* began her turn; an Aldis lamp winked from the bridge of the Polish destroyer and Yorke ignored it; one of the signalmen would report the message and he could already hear the metallic chatter showing that the man had found an undamaged lamp and was acknowledging each word.

Now the Polish destroyer was on the port beam and the smoke was hiding a quarter of the horizon; now she was coming round to the port quarter and the smoke cut off half the horizon and was rising slowly.

'Sir, ship says "Thanks for smoking; we've given it up." '

Must be the British liaison officer. Still, it was a good signal; they were still cheerful.

'Signalman, have you a pad? Good, make this: "When smoke covers us am coming alongside stop expecting more visitors so cannot stay long."'

The Aldis chattered away while Yorke continued turning the *Aztec*. She seemed to be towing a great black tail of smoke. No planes yet, but the two ships could not stay in the smoke for ever; the Teds could chase them – the *Aztec* anyway – the moment she came out of it and made for home. That was assuming the smoke hid them anyway: was it rising high enough to hide the tops of the masts? Perhaps the Teds would get short of planes; maintaining a flying circus over a sinking ship three hundred miles from their base must need plenty – a couple of hours out and two back, half an hour or more to fuel and bomb up – say five hours. It would take twenty planes to keep one arriving over the target every fifteen minutes. That was nearly two squadrons by the British measure; twelve planes per Imperial squadron. Did the Teds use the Metric system? By now Hitler might have followed Napoleon's example and invented his own system of weights and measures.

Half a mile to go and then the *Aztec* and the Pole would be snug inside the smokescreen. Suddenly it went dark and he began coughing as he breathed in the smoke, shouting a new helm order to turn the *Aztec* inwards out of the tail of her own screen. Just as suddenly it was bright sun again and the two destroyers were like two wounded chicks inside the rim of a nest, hoping the sparrowhawks would not see them through the leaves of the hedgerow.

The Pole, her ensign flapping sporadically as a gust of wind stirred the cloth, was deep and sluggish in the water: he could now see that her decks would soon be awash and as she rolled the sea sloshed down one side then the other like breakers along a sandspit. Men seemed to be gathered like limpets on the upper deck – her captain would have everyone up from below.

'They've got the casualties ready just abaft the bridge on the port side, sir,' one of the lookouts reported. 'I can see 'em clear. A dozen stretcher cases; the rest can move. Bandaged up, a lot of 'em.'

Very little sea; for once the Atlantic was not pushing swell waves across the Bay, and he was thankful: swell waves were the ones that would pick up the *Aztec* as she stopped alongside the Pole and smash the two ships together so hard they would hole each other.

The wind and sea, what there was of it, was on the Pole's starboard side. He had better come alongside her port side – as the Polish captain had anticipated – so that the breeze would be trying to blow the high sides of the *Aztec* away from the stricken ship and getting clear again would only be a matter of cutting ropes… Everything that saved time would be a help – already the smoke was drifting gradually and perceptibly thinning; the bombers might be back any moment.

And, he thought to himself, it had worked: he had brought the *Aztec* alongside the Pole – it was only in the last few moments of the approach that he realized just how much she was rolling, the result of all those hundreds of tons of water sloshing around inside her, the 'free surface liquid' that caused instability.

As the *Aztec* came alongside, with ratings throwing heaving lines, Yorke guessed the Polish ship was in effect a mirror image of the *Aztec*: her bridge, too, was riddled; it looked like what was often to be seen along a country lane, a can on a stick riddled by shotgun pellets. The rust was there, too; the scorching heat of blast and the impact of splinters left a neglected and rusted effect, burning or chipping off the paint.

That it worked was a tribute to the way Henry Bascombe had trained the ship's company. Yorke spoke into the voicepipe and called to the rating at the engine-room telephone and did very little more than that. One of the lookouts, the one on the starboard side of the bridge, had a strident voice and relayed orders to both ships' companies like a loudhailer fitted with a five-second delay, the time it took for the man to absorb Yorke's orders and repeat them.

The heaving lines were hauled across the narrow gap of water between the two ships, heavier ropes followed and were secured, holding the two ships together. The wounded men, cocooned in the slatted stretchers, were hoisted on board the *Aztec* with the surgeon standing there, white overalls so bloodstained he looked as though he had spent a busy morning in a slaughter house.

The torpedo artificer had taken command of his section of the *Aztec*'s deck, under the surgeon, and the wounded were first put down beside the torpedo tubes.

Now someone was shouting from the Polish ship's bridge: a British voice. The signalman repeated it: 'Gennelman asks if it's all right for the rest of their ship's company to board now.'

Like the Gosport ferry, Yorke thought: 'Yes, if all the wounded are over.'

'They are, sir; they've seen to that.'

'Very well, pass the word.'

The Polish ship's company boarded as though they were a Whale Island team working under the fiercest of gunnery instructors, in preparation for the annual Earl's Court Show. Whale Island GIs were the fiercest animals in Britain not kept behind bars, but they would have found little to criticize in those Poles.

Yorke watched the sky as the smoke thinned round them; the black hedge was grey now, almost transparent in places, like fog or mist dispersing. The whole ring had drifted to the north-west, and the south-eastern edge was only a hundred yards or so from the two ships. Was it worth making more smoke now so that it would blow to leeward, a long black column into which the *Aztec* could dart if the bombers came back? No – the Poles would give him enough men to fight the ship; there was no merit in hanging about: their only chance was a high-speed run from now until darkness.

Was the Polish captain senior? Did he take command of the *Aztec*? Was he rated RN? Hardly. The point had never arisen, so far as he knew. Even the bloody British liaison officer might be senior and want to play silly buggers by commanding the *Aztec* for the trip back to the UK. Well, he was welcome to argue the point; but unless his name was senior in the Navy List, Lieutenant Ned Yorke was taking this wreck home.

The liaison officer, a VR lieutenant, appeared on the bridge, introduced himself as John Wood, and told him the Polish destroyer was the *Orzel* and that the captain would be along as soon as the last man was off.

'It's the passengers,' Wood said. 'They're special people.'

'Where are they?'

'I took 'em straight down to the wardroom, out of your way. Civilians. Your steward's taken charge of them. They're important political refugees; they've had a bad time.'

'What the hell are they doing in the Bay?'

'They'd escaped across Europe to Spain and the *Orzel* took them off a fishing boat near Ferrol. All arranged through the Admiralty.'

'The Jerries spotted you quickly?'

Wood nodded wearily. 'I reckon the Spaniards gave us away because the fishermen were four hours late so we didn't stand a chance of getting clear by daylight. The bombers found us at dawn.'

'At dawn?'

Wood seemed resentful, although it was hard to know who he was blaming. 'Yes, at first light.'

'They must have known where to look, because they couldn't search in darkness. Didn't you take any evasive action? Surely you didn't steer direct for Plymouth from the rendezvous?'

'We did,' Wood admitted. 'At full speed. The captain reckoned the less time we stayed within range of those Ju 88s the better. I suggested we left to the south-west, but...'

Yorke shrugged his shoulders. 'We live and learn.'

At that moment an officer came on to the bridge and Wood introduced him as the *Orzel's* captain. Yorke shook him by the hand. 'You speak English?'

'Some,' he said, looking at the two gold rings on Yorke's sleeve.

'All your men are off?'

'Everyone except the dead, Lieutenant.' Just a faint emphasis on the rank; what the lawyers called 'without prejudice'.

'Is she sinking?'

'Ten minutes at the most.'

'Depth charges set to safe?'

'Yes, of course.'

Yorke turned to the lookout. 'Pass the word to let go fore and aft.'

To Wood and the Polish commander he said: 'Can your chaps man the small-calibre stuff? We're a bit thin on the ground. Once we're out of this smoke we can expect visitors...'

The Polish commander scrambled out to the port wing of the bridge and bellowed a stream of Polish aft along the deck. Wood nodded to Yorke. 'This chap knows his stuff; he fought the *Orzel* out of Danzig to reach England; air attacks all the way across the North Sea. Losing the ship is like losing their home. And they suspect treachery by the Spaniards, too.'

Yorke had watched the *Orzel* draw clear as the *Aztec* drifted to leeward and said to Wood: 'Go down and find the torpedo artificer: he's still alive, the little fat PO with a bandage round his head. He's helping with your wounded. I want two fish put into the *Orzel* the moment we are at the right range.'

'She'll go of her own accord,' Wood said.

'I can't wait around,' Yorke said sourly, 'and Their Lordships would love to hear we left a destroyer afloat in the Bay. You made sure all the confidential books have been sunk?'

'Yes, the captain and I did it together.'

'Good,' Yorke said, and added: 'I'm asking because it'll crop up at the court of inquiry; it'll help you to have witnesses.'

It was the next ten minutes that were all telescoped and confused in his memory: the *Aztec* had drifted clear and he had turned her on the screws to make the Polish ship an easy target for the torpedo artificer. There had been the double hiss as the two torpedoes were fired and the double detonation as they hit, but before the pillars of water had subsided and the *Orzel* began to sink both bridge lookouts had reported enemy planes – 'Red two five…green four five…green two oh…' Five Ju 88s and all attacking the *Aztec* at once from different directions and heights to avoid mid-air collisions: obviously they had been home and put in some practice.

There was hardly time for the gunners to change targets. Wood shouted in a momentary pause, 'Let's hope they collide with each other!'

One bomb burst under the *Aztec*'s bow as she increased speed and Yorke cursed, wishing he had delayed a few moments; the second hit the starboard side abreast the funnel and they were deafened by the safety valves lifting and high-pressure steam screaming upwards. Yorke thought ironically that if he had increased speed a few moments earlier it might have missed astern. The fourth hit the torpedo tubes but by then the *Aztec* was slowing down and heeling to starboard and Yorke saw the Polish commander wrestling with a Lewis gun, obviously trying to transfer it from one mounting to another. At that moment a sudden whoosh like the flight of a bird turned everything black as a bomb burst on the forward side of the bridge.

CHAPTER TWO

The bus was passing through Charing before Clare came back to sit beside him and shut off the memories. The rolling countryside was bleak now in the early winter and the paint was peeling from the signposts that stood at each crossroads, white pillars of wood or cast iron, the pointing arms that once gave the names of towns and hamlets now amputated and taken away, so that the stranger, whether a travelling Briton or a bewildered German paratrooper, remained lost.

They played a game and he knew Clare had sensed he had spent the time while she had been away brooding over the past. She had suggested it. They rated each house they passed with up to ten points. Ten meant they could live in it; one meant it was suitable for a troublesome relative or bureaucrat. Most of the houses they could see from the road rated up to five. Every new and again they would see a white card taped inside a window, 'Stirrup pump kept here', or the 'W' showing where an air raid warden lived.

Suddenly the bus stopped on the outskirts of Ashford and they saw Sister Scotland standing up and glaring at the corporal of Military Police who now climbed on board and asked to see all travel documents. Sister Scotland, more concerned that her patients had enough pillows and blankets, had accidentally left the large brown envelope of documents – including, it now seemed, all the case histories – on her desk.

The corporal took off his cap with its red cover and scratched his head. 'But, ma'am, a Navy bus loaded with men, and entering a restricted zone!' He put his cap back squarely on his head and adjusted his red armband, then looked down at the highly polished toecaps of his boots. His flattened nose showed he was a boxer, but neither the ring nor the training course organized by the Corps of Military Police had prepared him for encounters with irate hospital sisters.

'Forbidden zone fiddlesticks! We're going to Willesborough. These officers are convalescing and due to have physiotherapy.'

'I don't doubt you for a moment, ma'am, but...'

'I should think you don't! Count the number of officers, add their arms and legs, and divide by four and you'll find the answer's wrong because some have limbs missing.'

'That won't be necessary, ma'am, but the only hospital is the civilian one here in Ashford, so...'

'Oh damn and blast it!' Sister Scotland said in a burst of anger, 'we're opening this new place. We're the first – staff and patients. Ruckinge Lodge it's called. Phone somebody and check it – here, I'll write down my hospital number.'

'No one told me, ma'am,' the corporal grumbled, 'and you've no documents, and this is a military area. No one allowed in, civil or military, without a special pass. It's to do with the Germans invading, you see. And it's no good giving me that phone number; it'll be a civil number. It's London, too, and I ain't paying for no calls.'

'The invasion hasn't actually started, has it?'

'No, ma'am, and there's no call to adopt that attitude.'

Yorke leaned forward. 'Corporal, you know as you go out of Ashford on the Folkestone road there's a big house with tall brick chimneys that lies back on the left, almost hidden by the beech trees?'

'With the sort of gatehouse beside the drive, sir?'

'Yes. The gatehouse has diamond panes in the windows.'

'I know it, sir.'

'That's where we're supposed to be going. It's only three or four miles. Why don't you lead us there with your motorbike. Then you can confirm that we're expected.'

'Oh I could do that, sir. I noticed they had builders and removal vans there, bringing in beds and things. That was a week or so ago.'

'Yes, converting it. It's going to be an annexe of St Stephen's Hospital, in London.'

'I'm sure you'll be comfortable, sir. It's a nice house. Bit cold, I expect; them places is usually draughty. Just right far an ospital. Mind you, though,' he said with a sideways glance at Sister Scotland as he climbed out of the bus, "ospitals depend on the matrons.'

Sister Scotland's snort of annoyance was partly offset by her sudden promotion, and she looked suspiciously at Yorke. 'You seem to know this area.'

Yorke shrugged his shoulders. 'Anything that gets us moving. The heating seems to die the minute the bus stops.'

Clare sat on top of the five-barred gate, a picture from a fashion magazine, in a speckled grey tweed suit and black brogues, and as he leaned against it, looking across the rolling fields towards the smooth green folds flecked with white chalk forming the North Downs beyond, she said: 'Now tell me about the medal, and how you hurt your arm.'

'How did you know the columns of Bernini's baldacchino spiral the other way?'

She looked puzzled for a moment. 'Oh, you mean the twisted stocking. Well, I've been to St Peter's. Before the war.'

'Obviously! But you were wrong; they spiral clockwise.'

'Probably. I was contradicting you because I was angry.'

'Angry? What on earth for?'

'No girl likes to be told her stocking seam is crooked. Not in front of all those men.'

'But I was only teasing.'

'I know, but I'd been on duty all night – and…'

'And you forgot that at least one of those men at five o'clock in the morning was sufficiently interested in your legs to notice a crooked seam!'

'Men are always interested in sex.'

'Not before dawn in a hospital ward after a night's bombing.'

'My husband always…'

She broke off and he waited for her to continue, but she ran her hands through her hair and jumped down, smoothing her skirt and twisting her hips to check the seams of the thick, light grey knitted stockings. 'Come on,' she said, 'let's walk.'

Her husband – her late husband, rather – always what?

A blackbird raced along the far side of the hedgerow, raising the alarm, setting the tail of a distant magpie twitching as it pecked at the grass, and starting a plover cartwheeling in the air with its plaintive 'pee-wit'. A gust of wind whipped up an eddy of brown leaves and across the fields towards Ashford a siren began wailing on the same note and finally died after a minute or two.

'The all clear,' Clare commented. 'I didn't hear the warning.'

'The wind's changed. It carries the sound now.'

'You've changed, too,' she said quietly, taking his hand as they walked.

'I've grown older,' he joked, worried at the tone of her voice.

'No, in the last few moments. When I mentioned my husband.'

'Is that surprising?'

'Yes,' she said in her direct way, 'you're simply going for a walk with Nurse Exton, one of the war's widows. She mentioned – or was going to, anyway – her husband.'

'I'm jealous,' Yorke said bluntly. He was conscious that he was wearing old grey flannel trousers, now mud-stained, and a white rollneck jersey that was shapeless, and his left arm was cocked up awkwardly in the sling so that walking was difficult, his body feeling twisted and clumsy. He pictured the smart RAF uniform, wings, the jaunty cap, the wearer slim and moving gracefully, no mark or blemish on him; no distorted arm, no hand that looked as though it had been put through a mincing machine. She would have a framed photograph in her room, probably more than one, and each with some loving message written across the corner.

'You might well be,' she said unexpectedly. 'He was the complete opposite of you.'

They walked another fifty yards in silence except for their shoes occasionally grating on a piece of gravel, before, gripping his hand a little tighter, she said: 'He was taller, with curly blond hair. He had a mouth that women dreamed of, and a laugh that bubbled. He wasn't a serious old stick like you. He lived for flying. Died for it, too, three years ago.'

And, Yorke thought to himself, it would be just my luck that I fall in love with his widow and so many years after the crash I find myself walking along a country lane with my head and heart full of romantic ideas, and this bloody flier appears between us like the ghost of Hamlet's father.

'Are you Mrs or Miss Exton?' he asked and for a reason he could not understand found himself dreading the answer.

'Miss. It's my maiden name. He was called Brown. Mundane. He hated it.'

Another fifty yards. Whoever owned this land had the hedger and ditcher at work early in the season, ready for the winter's rain. The amount of chalk in the soil – washed down over the centuries from the Downs – was shown by that warren, where rabbits had dug white streaks from the topsoil of yellow clay. Stop talking about the husband, he told himself; do not stir up memories or provoke comparisons.

'You shouldn't be jealous,' she said, almost in a whisper, as though talking to herself.

'I know; it's a corrosive feeling. I'm ashamed of myself, but I feel it, and that's…'

'He's dead; there's nothing to be jealous of.'

He stopped and swung her round holding her shoulder with one hand, and before he could stop himself said bitterly: 'He was the first man you loved enough to marry. You have all those memories. Your honeymoon, the private jokes, tunes, places – St Peter's in Rome. Paris? Florence? I have nothing to be jealous about? I'm jealous of all those memories.'

She clung to him now, tiny yet tense; he thought she was tense with anger and instead of silencing him it made him go on and on like a stuck record. 'The man who first shows you the view from the Spanish Steps, who is with you when you first smell Gauloise cigarettes as the cross-Channel ferry berths, who explores the Louvre with you and shows you the treasures in the Piazza Navona, and comments how muddy are the Arno and Tiber, and how the uniforms of the Swiss Guards seem tawdry: yes, I'm jealous, I'm sick with jealousy.'

He managed to stop himself adding that their memories, the memories and shared experiences of Ned Yorke and Clare Exton were, so far, of bedpans and bottles, the bared teeth of pain, the stink of his own suppurating flesh, the clinking of the lid of that white enamel dish which held the scalding water. Those things, and one brief moment as a bomb hissed down towards them.

She looked up at him, white-faced and stricken, and reaching for his face and holding it between her hands whispered: 'Answer me truly, because we've known each other only – how long, a month? Have you really fallen in love with me, Lieutenant Yorke, or am I just an available nurse, a pretty young woman for a wounded sailor to dally with until he goes back to sea?'

He tried to clasp her with the arm in the sling as well as the right arm. 'What do you think?' His voice came out harsh, not at all the way he wanted it to sound, but his vocal cords were suddenly constricted, tightened by unknown muscles.

She looked away. 'Until now I thought – well, you'll soon be back at sea. But when you talk so bitterly of Rome and Paris, I'm not so sure; I'm suddenly confused. Ned, I swore I'd never fall in love in wartime. I'm not afraid of *being* alone; I'm afraid of being *left* alone for ever. You'll never understand that it's the men who get killed who are the lucky ones: the women who are left die thousands of times, at every anniversary, every time particular tunes are played, jokes made… Have you ever thought of *that*, Ned? The bereaved keep on dying; the dead die only once.'

'I know, but it *was* like that, wasn't it?' he demanded bitterly. 'You went to all those places on your honeymoon? Or before, probably. And now, as you say, you die again every time you remember. How can I compete with that?'

'What about you?' she asked angrily. 'How many girls have you taken there? How do you know what it's like? Why should you be jealous of him, and me not be jealous of her – or them? They're still alive – I may even meet them and never know they shared anything with you.'

'There's never been a "her" in that sense; I've been to, all those places, but never with anyone I loved.'

'Never a girlfriend?' she challenged.

'Oh yes, plenty; enough to make me…'

'Make you what?'

He tried to laugh it off, realizing he had talked himself into a comer. 'Make me appreciate a girl with a crooked seam who tried to save me when she thought a bomb was landing close.'

'Oh that,' she said offhandedly. 'A nurse's duty is to her patients. You were the nearest.'

The shock of the remark made him let her go. 'Do you mean that?'

She looked up and smiled impishly. 'Why be upset? You *were* the nearest.'

'Suppose I hadn't been?'

'We'll never know!'

'But…'

'Ned,' she said, arranging his sling and avoiding looking at him, 'why question everything? You were the nearest. I did my duty as a nurse – or I did what I wanted to do as a woman. Why analyse everything? Now,' she said, turning him round and tugging his arm to make him walk, 'tell me how you hurt your hand. And the medal.'

'I don't know what happened with the hand.'

'Oh,' she said impatiently, 'don't sulk, and don't suddenly get modest and understated: it's so boring! I'm curious, nosy like all women. I want to know about you – if only to gossip to the other nurses!'

'I'm not being modest or understated,' he protested. 'I was in a destroyer and we were attacked by bombers. We were hit several times. One bomb burst on the bridge, on the other side from where I was standing.'

'And then what happened?'

'The destroyer sank. Or so they told me. I was knocked out.'

'Oh, Ned, come on! It's you, and I want to know all about it. Do I have to squeeze it out of you?'

39

He stopped and swung her towards him. 'Yes!'

She put her arms round him. 'I can't squeeze too hard because of the sling.'

'That's just about right,' he said, and he could feel her breasts hard through the tweed material.

'I'm waiting,' she said. 'I'm supposed to be squeezing the story out of you, remember?'

'I came to sitting in a Carley float with four other chaps.'

'A Carley float?'

'A sort of small raft made of very light wood, like a square quoit, with a net across the open part.'

'Who were the others?'

'One of the bridge lookouts. A Polish naval officer. A wardroom steward. And a Polish seaman.'

'Why Polish? Were you serving in a Polish ship?'

He shook his head. 'No, we had some on board and some Polish refugees, that was all. Other survivors were also paddling round in Carley floats.'

'How long were you in the float?'

'A day or two. We managed to keep together, and another ship picked us up.'

'And the medal?'

He shrugged his shoulders. 'They usually give one to the senior surviving officer.'

'But surely you weren't commanding the destroyer, were you? You're much too young.'

'I didn't command her to begin with.'

'Oh – but you did at the end. You survived.'

He nodded. A quarter of them had survived; the rest had been killed by the bombs bursting on the *Aztec*, been killed in the water when the bombers had flown back and forth, methodically machine-gunning the survivors, or died of exposure. The Teds had been trying to make sure the Polish civilians died – and ironically every one of them had survived; only their rescuers died.

His arm, particularly the hand, had obviously been slashed by the explosion on the bridge; he had lost a lot of blood in the Carley float, and fuel and lubricating oil had soaked into the wound. And three days later they had been picked up by a submarine, more dead than alive; three days without food had been unimportant; three days without water had been worse. But three days with oil soaking into the wound had been painful and, as it began to swell, grotesque, too.

'A penny?' she said.

'That's an old trick.'

'You should be flattered, Lieutenant Yorke. Miss Exton wants to know your thoughts: she might get jealous, too.'

'If she knew my thoughts at this moment she might also get embarrassed.'

'I doubt it, Clare said. 'You can't shock an old widow woman who's spending the war nursing rough sailors.'

CHAPTER THREE

He was as different as a man could be. With other men he was obviously decisive; the sort that a group looks to for leadership: does not even look, she sensed, just accepts without thought. He was twenty-five. Had a DSO which – so Sister Scotland said – was rare and hard to get in the Royal Navy. And had commanded a destroyer, though apparently briefly and because his senior officer had been killed.

She could love him; did love him, if she was honest, despite her vow; she had known it from the moment she had felt for him in her very womb when she heard those bombs coming and had flung herself on top of him for a reason she had since tried to analyse: was she trying to save him, or make sure that she too died if he did? Were you being brave or cowardly, Nurse Exton? Was that the same sort of question that sometimes made men embarrassed, as Ned was about talking of his DSO? That an action was often capable of having two motives so that one was never quite sure which was which? Yes, she loved him; no, she didn't know whether she had covered him with her body to save him or die with him. But a bomb which killed him, she now realized, would have killed everyone else in the ward anyway, but at the time…

It was all crazy; up to that moment, until the sound of the bombs, they had done nothing more than have routine conversations in that ward, 'Nurse Exton' and 'Lieutenant

42

Yorke', or 'Mr Yorke' for a change. He had (although she did not know it at the time of the bombs) written her a note, a formal note in some ways, but one she had since read a dozen times.

Now, after this afternoon's walk, she understood that note so much better: using a series of almost stilted phrases he was in fact trying to discover if she was engaged – the thought that she might be married, let alone widowed, had obviously not occurred to him. It was a wonder that one of the other nurses in a piece of cattiness had not called her 'Mrs Exton' or 'Mrs Brown'.

Would he, she thought inconsequentially, ever know how lucky he had been not to lose the arm? He did not realize that the surgeons had not dared to amputate for fear of more septicaemia; that the torture of having the arm put in hot water every four hours was a fairly desperate attempt to control it, and it had not worked… He would never know, unless Sister Scotland (or perhaps Nurse Exton) told him, that what saved his arm was that the hospital managed to get a new and experimental drug still known only by the maker's number, M & B 693, and which Ned had called 'horse urine' and disliked because it had to be injected in large quantities into his buttock and was painful, and had a brownish colour more reminiscent of a stable than a hospital ward.

It had made him so depressed – Sister Scotland had warned him that it would – and probably for that reason alone he had hated it so much that he had not realized it was the reason for the septicaemia clearing up and the swelling subsiding as the pus stopped forming. All he knew – and from the pain it caused it was understandable – was that the hot fomentations had stopped, the arm and hand had started healing, and now the whole arm and hand was a livid-looking mess with brown, dead skin which would peel off, and the hand would be normal again one day, crisscrossed with scars but usable.

Luckier, for all the pain and the grumbling, than Pilot Officer Reginald Brown, who had dived a Miles Magister plane into the ground 'while on night operations' three years ago. She had accepted the official explanation until she realized a Magister was a two-seater trainer, and not used for operations. Eventually she had discovered what had happened: Reginald and some of his fellow pilots, celebrating a birthday, had been drunk and decided to 'buzz' the aerodrome. They had taken off without permission in the only three available planes. The Magisters had fooled around until Reginald had flown into a row of trees, killing himself and so injuring his friend in the other seat that he too had died before dawn.

It had been just a drunken party; newly-qualified young pilots trying to behave like seasoned men. It was the time of the 'phoney war'; the favourite song had been that nonsense about hanging out the washing on the Siegfried Line. Before Dunkirk; before the Battle of Britain. War to them then had been a glamorous game: the first those young pilots had known of death had been Reginald's crash. How many of them had since survived the Battle of Britain?

At the time everyone had been so sympathetic towards the young widow; they had not really understood why she had not gone to the funeral – there had been time – and the authorities were still writing to her about the pension. Everyone, she thought as she walked along the lane, had been so understanding, but none of them had understood.

So she had become a nurse. She had struggled through the training, often feeling so faint she finished a class bent over with her head between her knees, breathing deeply. She had studied Gray's *Anatomy* and read the latest reports written as a result of experience in the fighting in France and the bombing – that shock could kill a person as surely as visible wounds. But nursing had sounded more glamorous than it was: a patient might be a hero, but he still needed bedpans and bottles, his temperature had to be taken and his bowel movements recorded. No man was a hero to his valet, they said, and likewise no patient could be a hero to his nurse. Ned was one of the most sensitive patients she had ever nursed: a septic arm was smelly, and it embarrassed him that the nurses had to put up with it – even while he was retching himself.

She looked at her watch. She was on duty in four hours' time.

'We must be getting back.'

'Do you really sleep in the mornings, when you go off duty?'

'I did this morning,' she said, 'even though we had a quiet night. It's so peaceful down here. The birds singing, the wind in the trees…one gets the feeling of centuries passing with no change. There's always such a senseless bustle in London; everybody seems to be hurrying but no one really gets anywhere.'

'No bombing down here.'

'You hear them going over, though, and it's horrible to think they're carrying bombs…'

She watched that distant look come back to his face. A glass screen seemed to slide over his eyes; he went a thousand miles away; a thousand years almost. For moments, minutes even, he became another man obviously reliving memories – of what? Not women, from what he had said; probably something to do with the sinking of the destroyer. He had said the *Aztec* was bombed. A British destroyer sinking amid bursting German bombs was so far from this Kentish lane –

yet perhaps not; at the rate the Germans were sinking the merchant ships, they might yet invade successfully.

She could imagine the hand and arm inside that bandage; she could only guess at the memories inside that head... He was jealous of her memories (what a bitter irony) but deliberately shut her out of his.

'Clare,' he said suddenly, 'you're having a boring afternoon.'

'I'm not, but I shall if you say things like that.'

'But I'm so serious, so dreary. I'm not laughing or making jokes. I'm just rattling on about the war, instead of cheering you up.'

She took his hand again. 'Yes, you are boring,' she said lightly, 'but because you won't rattle on about the war. I've been trying to get you to tell me, but you fob me off as though I was an inquisitive old aunt.'

'But why on earth do you want to hear about all that?' He was genuinely surprised; that much was clear to her and she was not sure whether to be angry or exasperated. Instead she stopped walking, so that he had to turn to face her. She brushed her hair back with a hand.

'Ned – tell me once again, am I just a convenient companion for winter walks while you convalesce, a romantic sort of junior Florence Nightingale who sneaks you a goodnight kiss, or...'

'Or,' he said quietly.

'Very well, give me a chaste kiss now...'

He bent and kissed her, and she said: 'You want to know about me; about what I did before I became a nurse, before I met you...'

'Of course I do; is there anything odd about that?'

'No, but what about you? Didn't you exist until they brought you to the hospital?'

'Of course I did!'

'"Of course"! That's twice you've said it. Can't I be curious about your life before then? About what made you the man you are? Can't I be jealous about the girls in your past? About the places you've been to, the jokes you share with other people, but not with me?'

'But there's nothing. It's all been flat until now.'

'What do you mean by that?'

He shrugged his shoulders and winced at the pain in his arm.

'Well, you've been in love, you've married… You were happy, even though briefly. You have happy memories. My memories don't involve happiness; they involve months of war.'

'Oh Ned, you are so jealous of my late husband. He's dead; he's no rival to you! I've tried to avoid telling you about him because it doesn't matter: you're here and alive and…'

'Yes, but I'd prefer to know.'

Suddenly she stood back from him, her face taut, her eyes narrowed as though she had just made a great decision; she looked incredibly beautiful and, he realized, suddenly distraught and incredibly vulnerable.

'I'll tell you then,' she said. 'I hated him. He married me because I have a private income and because he wanted to stop people talking. I found out on our honeymoon that he was homosexual. The pilot killed with him was his lover. He joined us in Rome for the honeymoon. Our married life lasted four days. I was too embarrassed to divorce him, so I was still legally "Mrs Brown" when he was killed. Now you'll hate me because I disgust you: I was a homosexual's alibi, but I didn't understand.'

He took her in his arms as she began to sob.

'Oh, it was so disgusting… I'm still – oh Ned, I'm a married woman but I don't know – I mean, I'm still – oh…'

47

'I know what you mean,' he said, 'and I've been incredibly stupid and clumsy.'

He held her for two or three minutes, until she stopped sobbing, and with both of them realizing there was nothing more that needed saying, they continued walking along the lane, hand in hand.

As the lane turned gently to the right, rising slightly to give a better view over the fields, Clare nodded towards a clump of half a dozen trees forming the corner of a meadow. 'Those large lumps in the top branches – what are they?'

'Magpies' nests.'

'So big?'

'They're made of mud and sticks and so thick that you can stand underneath with a shotgun and the pellets won't penetrate.'

They stood for a few moments looking across the meadow and Clare said: 'It looks as though there's been a paperchase through here!'

'Large pieces of paper – there's a bundle of it over there, caught in the bushes.'

Before he could stop her she had run a few yards along the lane to a gate, scrambled over it and walked across to the nearest piece of paper. She stared at it and then went over to pull the bundle from the bushes. She came back and gave him one of the sheets. The paper was poor quality, greyish, the kind used for newspapers. There was a message printed on one side.

He read it, half unbelieving, half amused. 'We've lost the Battle of the Atlantic!' he said. 'It says so here.'

'I know, I've just read it. Who…'

'German planes dropping leaflets. That bundle – the chap forgot to cut the string so the whole thing dropped. The rest must have fluttered down during the night. Better than bombs!'

She shivered. 'These figures – millions of tons of shipping sunk by the U-boats. Are they true?'

'Certainly not true, because pamphlets are only propaganda. But they're sinking quite a few ships – at the moment we're certainly not *winning* the Battle of the Atlantic.'

'Will we?'

'We have to,' he said grimly, 'otherwise we'll starve.'

'But here,' she waved one of the pamphlets, 'the Germans say they're sinking more merchant ships than we're building. Surely that means eventually...'

'Exactly! Unless we stop the sinkings and increase our building.'

'Can we?'

'We can't; not Britain alone. But now the Americans have come in – just wait until they get going.'

'How long will that take?'

Yorke shrugged his shoulders. 'Your guess is as good as mine, Nurse. Still, there'll be a few more cuts in the meat and cheese ration before the extra ships are launched, you can be sure of that.'

'But a week's cheese ration is only the size of a matchbox now!'

Yorke looked her up and down without smiling. 'It suits you. Two matchboxes and you'd be plump.'

'No, seriously, Ned.'

Seriously, Nurse. No one's starving.'

'But we're losing a lot of ships.'

'Yes, and the Germans are losing a lot of bombers over Britain, and tanks in the Western desert. And U-boats in the Atlantic, too. Don't forget that.'

'What do we do with these pamphlets?' she asked.

'Take some back with us – the others will love to see 'em. You can offer the bundle to this boy coming along on a bicycle – he can probably get a penny each for them at school.'

'Should we, Ned? Isn't that what the Germans want – everyone to read them?'

Yorke laughed and waved the paper. 'I hope everyone does: it's such blatant propaganda, so strident… It's written in such a shrill and hectoring way that even if it was true, no one would believe it.'

Clare was far from convinced. 'Then why do the Germans drop them?'

'Because they don't understand the British for a start. Tell us we're beaten and we start waking up and trying. But if the Germans *were* winning the Battle of the Atlantic, why bombard us with pamphlets? Why not save paper and wait for us to starve? If all this was true,' he tapped the bundle she was holding, 'we'd have to surrender by Easter or starve to death.'

Finally she smiled. 'Stop looking at me like that. I've been putting on a little weight, but it's all the potatoes.'

'So you won't be surrendering by Easter?'

'Not to the Germans,' she said, and waved the boy on a bicycle to a stop. She held out the bundle. 'German pamphlets. The man in the bomber didn't cut the string. There are plenty more in the fields over there. Are they any good to you?'

'Cor!' the boy exclaimed, snatching the bundle excitedly and inspecting it with the eye of an expert. 'I just found a dozen or so sheets over in Nicholson's fields, but I didn't realize others drifted this far. Must have been the wind. 'Ere, lady, can I really 'ave this lot? I get a penny each at school and Mrs Rogers – she runs the Red Cross – is on at me to give 'er some to sell to buy bandages and things. She charges tuppence. Promised she wouldn't undercut me. These ain't damp, neither. Them I got last week was useless – it'd rained for hours before I found 'em. In Hatch Park they were, and I reckon some poacher got a good picking first.'

By now Clare was holding Ned's hand again and smiling. 'Very well, you can have the bundle, and there's a trail of them across those fields. But make sure Mrs Rogers has as many as she can sell.'

'Oh, yus, miss. It's the bandages, you see; they're very expensive.' He caught sight of Yorke's hand in the sling. 'I bet you know that! You must have a bob's worth on that hand. 'Ere, mister, are you one of the chaps from the new place they've just started in Willesborough?'

Ned nodded and the boy grinned. 'I 'ear they've got a smashing lot of nurses there. My dad works for the electricity, and he had to go there yesterday to read the meters. Made my mum jealous, he did, the way he went on about them. Anyway thanks for these!'

With that he turned his cycle round and pedalled back the way he came, riding without hands and clutching the bundle to his chest, the trail of loose pamphlets forgotten.

'Don't tell me,' Clare said. 'A few more leaflet raids and we could make enough money to build a new hospital.'

'And I'll be the recruiting officer who chooses the "smashing nurses"!'

Sister Scotland wore what Clare usually referred to as her 'official face'. Standing beside Yorke's bed, she coughed and said: 'Mr Yorke…'

'Yes, Sister?'

'About that arm of yours.' When Yorke raised his eyebrows, startled by the ominous tone in her voice, she said: 'It's not really responding. The physiotherapist is very worried by the limited movement in the wrist.'

'It should move more by now?'

'Yes, at least, we had hoped so.'

'And the fact it doesn't means?'

'It means either the muscle is more damaged than we thought, or you aren't concentrating on your remedial therapy.'

'There's no much else to concentrate on,' Yorke grumbled.

Sister Scotland stared at him. 'I thought you were concentrating on long-distance walking. I've been expecting Nurse Exton to tell me the Admiralty had started patrols over the North Downs, collecting German pamphlets.'

'Oh, you've heard about them?'

'A small boy called at my office this morning – he came with his father, who works for the electricity company – asking if any of the patients had found any more pamphlets. It seems his first consignment came from you – he described you as "the gentleman with a bob's worth of bandages on the left hand" – and he's sold them all.'

Yorke looked out of the window, where a weak sun shone through fast-moving patches of cloud. 'If we hear any German bombers tonight, perhaps you'll let me go for a walk tomorrow, Sister?'

'Of course, of course, Mr Yorke. You are walking so well there's no need for a nurse to accompany you.'

'No,' Yorke agreed, smiling, 'but you know how risky it would be for patients to wander round these lanes alone. Nurses, too – they might be hit by a bundle of propaganda leaflets.'

'One has been already,' Sister Scotland said dryly. 'I'm very worried about her.'

'The diagnosis was made yesterday,' Yorke said quietly. 'The prognosis – that's the correct word for the future, isn't it – is excellent.'

The Sister looked down at him, silent for a few moments, obviously considering what he had just said. 'Yesterday, eh?'

'Yesterday afternoon.'

'The specialist took his time,' she commented gruffly. 'A month, almost six weeks.'

'He didn't have all the papers in the case.'

Sister Scotland nodded and as she moved away said quietly, 'Work on that arm; it's touch and go, but now you have an extra incentive.'

As he watched her moving among the other men in the room, pausing beside each bed to chat, he thought of Clare. Somewhere in this old house, in one of the bedrooms, probably in one of these same iron-pipe beds, she would be sleeping, because she was still on night duty. It was tiring for her but gave them the most time together: she was allowed out for a couple of hours in the afternoon; she spent the whole night on the ward. She would be sitting at the small table over there, in the middle of the room, a tiny figure in a tiny halo of light thrown by the green-shaded lamp. She would be in profile. She would, during the night when she thought he was asleep, look round at him. And while she worked on the pile of papers and wrote reports, he would watch her without her realizing it. Childish, romantic, pointless – yes, all of these, and yet so important.

'Mr Yorke...' He looked up to find the physiotherapist waiting. She was a tall, bony woman in her early thirties, mousy-brown hair bobbed short and her face having the well-scrubbed, fresh look of a games mistress...'has Sister told you?'

'About the extra exercises?'

'Yes, two one-hour sessions. It'll be tiring but it might make all the difference.'

All the difference, she did not add, between spending the rest of your life with a withered arm or an ordinary one which is badly scarred but useful.

She took the exercise instruments from the trolley and gave him first the little device for improving his grip; two pieces of wood shaped to fit his palm on one side and his fingers on the other, and separated by several small compression springs. For the next ten minutes he had to grip the exerciser and keep on squeezing.

'The Spanish Inquisition was never like this,' he grumbled.

'It probably was, but I'm sure the victims didn't complain as much. After all, this is for your own good.'

'And that,' Yorke said, grunting as he squeezed, 'is exactly what the Inquisition said. They put their victims on the rack to save their souls.'

'I'm not interested in your soul,' the woman said with mock viciousness, 'it's your body I'm trying to save!'

He continued squeezing. It seemed to take an age to reach a hundred; finally at four hundred she said: 'That's ten minutes.' She took the grips and began the series of exercises for his wrist.

'The postman's been,' she said unexpectedly. 'I have some letters for you. Three. You get them when you've finished your exercises.'

'Anything interesting?'

'I'm sure I don't know. I don't pry. There's a long one in a manilla envelope. On His Majesty's Service. From the Admiralty, I think. Two handwritten ones, a London postmark and a local one.'

'Local?'

'Willesborough. Here. The little sub-post office is only just up the road. Whoever wrote it could have saved the price of a stamp and delivered it by hand.'

For someone who didn't 'pry', Yorke thought to himself, the physiotherapist was well informed about the letters. All the other patients were due to have exercises, so presumably they too would get their mail afterwards, like giving a horse a sugar lump after a difficult jump.

'And your name's in the newspaper,' she said. 'In the list of people who've been given medals.'

'Oh, they've Gazetted it at last.'

'I don't know about that,' she said, 'but don't you want to see the paper and find out what you've got?'

'I know already.'

She was clearly disappointed. 'I'd have thought they'd keep it secret until they put it in the paper; a sort of surprise.'

There was no point in explaining that for security reasons the names of people getting awards were often not Gazetted until months after the awards were made: German intelligence officers could not then work out from the officers and men receiving awards the activities of individual ships. Sometimes, when it was known that a particular ship had been involved in a battle, the names were listed together; but when the Admiralty wanted to keep secret a particular loss, the names were scattered.

'What did you get it for – the DSO?'

He shrugged his shoulders. 'Being a good boy. I made everyone eat up his porridge. The Admiralty are very keen on porridge. Gives your stomach a warm lining on a cold day.'

'My boyfriend is serving in the Tropics.'

'The porridge packet says that in the Tropics it's for external use only.'

'I'll write and tell him. Might help keep his privates cool.'

Yorke laughed. 'Yes, a sovereign remedy for avoiding hot privates.'

'Don't be vulgar, Mr Yorke,' she said severely. 'My boy-friend's a sergeant; he worries about his men. They're privates. It's infantry, you see.'

The exercises changed and his arm ached; the whole forearm felt as if it had been pummelled with a mallet. 'The bandages are chafing.'

'They're bound to, but the skin's too soft to exercise without them; your hand would blister.'

If only Clare was the physiotherapist. No, that was not fair on either woman: Clare would not be tough enough, and this woman certainly knew her job. More important, she knew how to make her patients do the exercises without bullying them.

'There!' she said, putting the various exercise devices back on the trolley, 'That's it for this morning. I'll be back this afternoon. And here are your letters. And the paper with your name in it. They seem to know all about you. Quite a story, eh? Didn't know you came from these parts.'

He knew which letter he would open last, because he wanted to savour it, but which first? He tore open the Admiralty letter. Pale blueish-grey paper; the usual formal introductory sentence. Then the orders: as soon as he was discharged from the hospital as being fit for active service he was to report to the Admiralty, and in the meantime indicate when that was likely to be. There was a room number and a four-letter initial, ASIU. What department was that? It must be new; the usual ones were familiar enough – DNI for the Director (or Department) of Naval Intelligence, DOD for Operations Division, and so on. This must be some new and crackpot department which allowed the Second Sea Lord (who dealt with appointments) to find quiet jobs for deserving wrecks like Lieutenant Edward Yorke, DSO, RN – providing he had two arms that functioned. If his left arm seized up then he would be invalided with a pension and one of the large silver lapel badges called 'The King's Badge for Loyal Service' (presumably intended to stop old ladies giving you white feathers) and turned out to graze in civilian clothes with the assurance that the King and his various helpers could now beat Hitler without Lieutenant Yorke's one-armed assistance.

There was a great future for a one-armed man of twenty-five who had been trained only as a naval officer, especially one who had specialized in navigation, so that a dagger sign followed his name in the Navy List. The world was waiting with open arms for unemployed dagger navigators; they were needed to help old ladies drive their cars through the centre of London, making the best use of the petrol ration.

The letter from his mother was, as usual, a calm note which ignored the existence of Hitler, the Luftwaffe, rationing or bombing, and which was a measure of her personality since she was living in the town house in Palace Street, only a few hundred yards from Victoria Station. She described how she had been able to find some 'artificial boarding' to cover up a few broken windows – no mention that the glass was shattered by the blast of bombs – and the loose tiles had been replaced. She was more concerned lest she had said the wrong thing to newspaper reporters who had called to find out details about him. 'The fact was,' she wrote, 'that they seemed to know a great deal more of the interesting part of your life than I did; I was able to tell them only that over the years the men in the family had tended to go to sea. There was an amusing moment when we found out that one of the reporters, who was a bit tipsy, thought I said "tended to go to seed", but a colleague of his, a nice young man who had lost a leg in the Western Desert (trod on a landmine, I think he said), seemed to watch out for that sort of thing.'

Then, with her usual forthrightness, she commented on his reference to Clare. 'I was interested to read about your beautiful young widow – you seem to prefer small women. But beware of widows in general. The advantage is that they have few illusions left about men; they have learned all the lessons and if they fall in love with you it is likely to be both genuine and without any illusions. The disadvantage is that if they loved their first husbands, then the new husband is competing with a ghost and will always lose. He might in fact be a much more satisfactory husband, but he will never be certain because he'll never believe his wife's assurances. If you love her,' his mother wrote, 'then trust her and dismiss from your mind that there was ever a predecessor. You wouldn't be jealous of an earlier lover – in this modern age most young women have had one – and a brief marriage differs from a brief affair only in the legal aspect.'

Yorke folded the letter and put it on his locker with the manilla envelope from the Admiralty. Clare, whether as Miss Exton or Mrs Brown, was welcome at Palace Street. He wished his father had still been alive to meet her; but on the other hand the last few months of the war would have broken his heart: with Winston Churchill he had tried in the House of Commons to warn the nation against Hitler and persuade it to rearm; but like Churchill he had been howled down. Peace had been the fashion, the Labour Party was against rearmament and the Conservatives against taxation, and the majority of the people had been prepared to pay any price as long as it cost nothing. Well, the bill was now being presented – not just their sons' lives but, in the bombed cities, their own as well.

The third letter…the writing small, educated, by a woman with a strong personality who had studied Greek. She had written it the second night after telling him about her husband.

'I am sitting here at the desk in the middle of the ward looking at you sleeping. The lamp is so shielded that you are just a shadowy figure. The four other patients are snoring but you aren't. You don't snore. I don't know if I do. I wonder if you are dreaming. Dreaming of your loved one is, I believe, a myth; I'm told (by a doctor specializing in psychology) that however much two people are in love, they usually dream of other people, and if the dreams are erotic, then they are almost never of the ones they love. Are you having an erotic dream at this moment? Who is the lucky girl? Who has flown into your sleeping thoughts and roused you in a way I cannot because I am Nurse Exton, on night duty in Ward BI? I hate her; I am jealous; I want to walk over and shake you until you wake up, so that she has to go away, because I know she exists only while you sleep and no matter what you might try to do to keep her, she will vanish the moment you wake.'

He continued reading the letter slowly, picturing her at the desk – which was now empty except for the lamp with the green shade which looked like one of the first electric lights ever made – and thinking of her watching him as he slept.

'You were jealous of the memories you thought I had of my previous (unhappy) existence, but I wonder if you realise how many *happy* new memories I have already even though Lieutenant Yorke and Miss Exton have known each other such a short time? Just think of yesterday – the look of shock, amazement and then relief on your face when I told you how it had been: I knew then that although you might have a girl in every port, I am the important one. And then finding the German leaflets. How right you are, about the Germans not bothering to drop them if they were really winning. Anyway, I have put one of them among my few treasures, to look at again when I am an old lady.

'Then, already surprised how well you knew the countryside here, I suddenly realized the coincidence of your name and the name of the big house we can see in the distance, so I cycled over there. Yes, the old gardener finally broke down under fierce interrogation by Nurse Exton, even though he felt loyalty to the family meant he should say nothing about anything to anyone.

'So that was your home until the war began. How your mother must have hated giving it up "for the duration". And you grew up there. I still can't picture you as a small boy. Did you collect birds' eggs and have a catapult? Did you get measles and have to stay in bed and eat jelly and blancmange? And, my darling Ned, all those paintings that are boarded up in various rooms (the gardener let me see the house) – are they portraits of your forebears or dreary landscapes, where the varnish has darkened so much that high noon over the Weald of Kent now looks like midnight in Limbo? Don't tell me, and I liked the mystery as I walked through what I suppose was the dining room and saw those rectangles of bare wood, the size of picture frames. I realize they must protect paintings on the actual wall, or set into the plaster. Perhaps some long-dead Yorke commissioned Rubens to cover the walls with chubby pink and naked cherubs.

'How I wish I could have shared those early years there with you. And yet had I done so they would not seem so intriguing now. The fun is *speculating* about the boy Ned; *knowing* might be disappointing! It is better to imagine rather than to see a small boy with measles sitting up in bed counting his birds' eggs and repairing his catapult and then feeling sick because he's eaten too much blancmange.'

CHAPTER **FOUR**

Walking round the south side of Trafalgar Square with the clouds streaming in low from the west, a scud warning of rain, he felt almost a stranger in London as he headed for Admiralty Arch. Six weeks at Willesborough, with almost daily walks along the lanes skirting the rolling fields at the foot of the Downs, no acute pain to keep him awake at night, and Clare within a few yards every day, had pushed the war into the far distance; a memory no stronger than a film seen last year. Ironic, come to think of it, because but for the war Clare would never have been at Willesborough and he would never have met her; nor, for that matter, would his left forearm and hand look like a pink walnut. This damned cold and damp weather brought a sharp-yet-dull pain to the muscles and was as good as a barometer; no wonder old folk can forecast the weather by sciatic twinges.

The last time he had walked across the top of Whitehall and under Admiralty Arch into the Mall – the other way, rather, because they were all going to Charing Cross Station to catch the Dover train – had been with Clifton and Jeffries, and both of them had been killed within a few weeks. Clifton was lost in a corvette; Jeffries had been commanding his own flotilla of MTBs out of Felixstowe but was late back from one night patrol when several German fighters caught him after dawn somewhere off Smith's Knoll. Although his riddled boat managed to get back without her petrol tanks exploding, she was, they said, like a seagoing hearse.

Salute, salute, salute…rarely ten paces without a salute. The Poles seemed most frequent and were a smart crowd; even the privates had taken their battledress jackets to decent tailors for a good fit. All the American soldiers looked like officers and even the lowliest private, obviously freshly arrived in Britain, the hayseed still in his crew-cut hair, seemed to have two or three medal ribbons, although from what he had heard they received medals where the British would have been lucky to get an arm badge – marksman, and so on; even a medal for being in Britain, which they considered a war zone. Judging from the sandbagged doorways, signs pointing towards air-raid shelters, boarded-up windows and bombed buildings, perhaps they were right.

Even the pigeons had a military gait, perhaps more Nazi than Allied; strutting, almost goose-stepping, and always beady-eyed, like Guards drill sergeants or Navy gunnery instructors. All that each one lacked was a respirator slung over the shoulder; a standard Service-issue one but with stiff cardboard or plywood inside, front and back, to make the bag square, in the best Guards style. Guards? Put a telescope under a wing and each pigeon was a strutting midshipman or flag lieutenant on the quarterdeck as the admiral loomed in sight. They were blasé about bangs, too; a taxi backfiring a few yards from one group of a dozen put up only a single bird which fluttered a yard or so and then, Yorke was sure, looked ashamed as it strutted back.

Under Admiralty Arch, with the ammonia whiff of the pigeons who lived up there, and then he could see Buckingham Palace sitting at the far end of the Mall, four-square and reassuring, the double row of trees stark now, stripped of leaves for the winter. The Palace was in fact the symbol of yet another family who weren't moving out because of the Ted bombers. And there, just inside the Arch and beyond the bronze statue of Captain Cook, was the 'Gingerbread', officially the Citadel, the huge brown concrete box, nearly new and housing, many feet below ground, the operational heart of the Royal Navy. Down there officers juggled with markers and charts and sent fleets to sea or tracked Ted U-boats as they converged on some convoy unlucky enough to have been spotted by Focke-Wulf Condors, or seen by a single U-boat which raised the alarm...

Yorke walked into the entrance and explained his business to the ancient messenger sitting in the booth just inside the door.

'ASIU, sir? Any particular person? Captain Watts? If you'll just wait a moment, sir, and fill in this form?'

While Yorke wrote in the details, the messenger spoke on the telephone, and by the time he had put it down and torn off the top sheet of the form another and slightly younger messenger, like the first one obviously a retired former petty officer, was waiting.

'Take this gentleman to Captain Watts in ASIU, Room 103.'

Yorke followed the messenger, whose row of medals included most of the last war.

'Submarines, sir?'

'No, destroyers.'

'Sorry, sir, 'ope you didn't mind me asking. Most of the gentlemen calling on Captain Watts is submariners.'

'I expect you know them?'

'Yes, sir,' the messenger said, turning to grin at Yorke. 'Joined me first boat in '17, took me pension in '38. Wouldn't let me sign on again on account o' m'eart. Give me a pension and this job.'

'You saw some changes between the wars.'

By now they had turned off the corridor of the old building with its marble mosaic floor and gone through thick steel and concrete doors into the Citadel itself, with its faint hum which Yorke assumed was a form of air conditioning.

'Yes, sir. You never saw the M class, I suppose?'

'Only three built, surely? One had a big gun – twelve inch, wasn't it? And another carried a seaplane in a tiny hangar…'

'That's 'em, sir. Big boats all right. I was in M 2. Ah, here we are.'

Captain Henry Watts looked as if he had been lifted straight out of a Noel Coward war film and put behind a desk: he had the build of a rugby player, black wavy hair and features that were only just a little too heavy to be handsome in the film-star style. Two ribbons on his left breast showed that although Watts might enjoy his pink gins at the Senior, he had been put in charge of ASIU to do a proper job, not because the Admiralty were trying to find him employment. Next to the DSO was the ribbon of the DSC, and Yorke knew that Captain Henry Watts, DSO, DSC, was one of the most successful destroyer flotilla commanders in the Navy, who was himself credited with sinking four U-boats.

He shook Yorke by the hand: 'Welcome to ASIU. How does the job appeal to you?'

Watts spoke briskly and clearly was not a man to waste words. Yorke saw no reason to dissemble.

'I don't know anything about it, sir – not even what the initials mean – but I'd prefer to go back to sea.'

'That makes two of us, but Their Lordships in their infinite wisdom think we can outwit the crafty Jerries in their submersible sausage machines by using our brains, instead of just hurling depth charges at them. Not so noisy. And ASIU stands for "Anti-Submarine Intelligence Unit". It was formed six weeks ago.'

'I'm sorry you've got stuck with me, sir; I'm not much good on anti-submarine work. Not the theory, anyway.'

'I didn't get stuck with you,' Watts said, 'I asked for you. Lesson number one for success, my lad, is never get stuck with people you don't want because they'll sink you. I want a good crew, but don't think you'll get back to sea by making a balls of it here; my failures will get happy jobs like deputy assistant NOIC in Massawa with the temperature 110° in the shade on a cold day.'

'I can make a good pot of tea,' Yorke said.

'That'll be useful because since we've only been in existence six weeks, all we've got so far is a Wren, kettle, teapot and some black-market tea. I'm still fighting to get typewriters and files. If you're wondering what we're supposed to be doing I'll quote from Mr Churchill's memorandum creating us and dated two months ago. The original is locked in someone's safe, but he ordered the First Sea Lord to form "a group of specially skilled young sea officers who will devise new and cunning methods of outwitting Admiral Doenitz by detecting and destroying his U-boats".'

'New and cunning?'

'Their Lordships would settle for old and crude, providing we sink the bloody Jerries. Oh, I see what you mean. No, we're not expected to invent new weapons – we leave that to the Underwater Weapons boys. No, Their Lordships assume the Boss had tactics in mind. And having seen from the bridge of a destroyer and from this desk the pathetic tactical methods we rely on, while I run this shop it's going to be tactics and intelligence that we're buying and selling.'

'You mean the mathematics of attacks, sir?'

'How do you mean?'

'Well, how many depth charges to ensure destroying a U-boat within a given area; the most effective patterns; the sinking rate of depth charges…'

'Christ, no! All that's supposed to have been worked out by the boffins before the war began – slide-rule stuff; quite beyond me. No, as I see it our job is just to out-think these buggers. Out-think Doenitz and out-think Oberleutnant Hermann Schmidt who is just doing his first trip in command of one of Hitler's latest boats. Use any intelligence we can get that lets us build up a picture of Doenitz's methods.'

Yorke had instinctively leaned forward: whether or not Their Lordships, otherwise the Lords Commissioners of the Admiralty, let Watts run ASIU as he wanted, the job would be interesting while Watts lasted.

'How does it interest you?' Watts demanded unexpectedly, as if reading his thoughts.

'The out-thinking bit sounds interesting, but I've no real anti-submarine experience.'

'Let's call it outwitting the bastards: "out-thinking" sounds a bit pretentious. "Outfox" is even better. But don't make any mistake, my lad; we haven't much time to find answers; the outfoxing has to start yesterday. We're in trouble, in case you didn't know.'

'I saw some leaflets a few weeks ago, dropped by Goering's boys. Seems we're losing the Battle of the Atlantic.'

'Don't make any mistake about that,' Watts said sharply, 'we *are*. I don't have to remind you about the Official Secrets Act, but what I'm going to tell you now explains why ASIU has been formed and why we have to get cracking. In the first full year of the war, 1940, we lost four million tons of shipping. Four million, remember that figure.

'On the German side they can claim they had not yet perfected attack methods; on our side we can say we hadn't got the convoy system sorted out. So let's look at the next year's figures. Well, in 1941 we lost four million tons, the same as 1940. So you could say it was a sort of stalemate, the Germans not improving their attack methods, we not improving the convoy system.

'Now we come to this year, or rather the eleven months that have passed so far. We'll have lost eight million tons by Christmas. Double last year's and more than 650,000 tons a month.'

'How many boats do we reckon Doenitz has in service?'

'He started off the war with about sixty, according to the Intelligence boys. Now he has about four hundred, as far as we can tell – by inspired guesswork, air reconnaissance of the building yards, and intelligence work, mainly breaking ciphers. Four hundred boats means a hundred actually patrolling on the convoy routes, quite apart from those on their way there and back, and being refitted.'

'Mostly operating in packs, sir?'

'No, they seem to search alone. Then, as soon as a boat sights a convoy it signals U-boat headquarters at Lorient to drum up business and they blow the whistle and Doenitz assembles enough nearby boats to form a pack.'

'We can DF the first U-boat's transmission?'

'Oh yes, usually we know the moment a particular convoy has been sighted, but that doesn't help much. Take SL 125 coming home from Freetown last month. Spotted off Madeira, Doenitz assembled a pack of nine boats and attacked every night for a week. Escort three or four corvettes, thirteen merchant ships lost. The worst non-Russian one so far – but probably not for long. We just don't have the escorts, and corvettes are beaten by really bad weather. They can stay at sea but they can't attack. I'm just waiting for the SL 125 boys to get in to have a chat with them.'

'Where do we start, sir?'

'Well, the rest of my lads have already made a start, but they haven't got very far yet.' He stood up and headed for the door. 'Come and meet the rest of the family.'

The family, as Watts always called his staff, comprised two lieutenant commanders and four lieutenants, six officers sharing five DSCs, one DSO and four mentions in dispatches, and not one of them physically complete: all had been wounded and would normally have been invalided and given a pension, but in wartime their knowledge and experience made them too valuable to lose. Three wore the straight gold bands on their sleeves showing they were regular Navy; the other three wore the wavy bands that Watts called 'the sine wave' Navy.

The room they worked in was small, the upper part of the walls lined with piping and ducting, like the cabin of a ship, carrying hot water, cold water, sewage, air conditioning and electrical wiring. It would save time and effort, Yorke thought sourly, if they ran a tea pipe into each room, collecting coupons once a month. Dark cream walls with dark green at the bottom, the room was an improbable cross between the cabin of a ship and a school classroom.

The three regulars Yorke remembered from Dartmouth; the RNVR lieutenants were strangers. All but one of the six had one thing in common – they had been serving in escort destroyers, chasing U-boats, until wounds had put them on shore. The sixth man had been serving in submarines; his last boat had sunk eight ships. Now, as Watts said in his breezy introduction, the poached, rather than the poachers, were turning gamekeepers, and Yorke was the seventh and last that Their Lordships would allow ASIU.

Each of the six, Watts explained, was specializing in a particular aspect of sub-hunting. One of the lieutenant commanders was working on convoy attacks by single submarines, the other on pack attacks. A lieutenant was investigating U-boat attacks on single ships – those merchantmen which could maintain fifteen knots or more and often sailed alone. The fourth man was a signals expert – Watts said jokingly that he was also good at repairing torches or radios, but rather expensive – and was by now one of the Admiralty's experts on the German Navy's radio procedure and responsible for the evaluation of much of the U-boat HQ's intercepted orders to its boats and their reports back.

The fifth man, whose desk was beside a large table on which an unusual-looking chart of the Atlantic was unrolled, with the Channel, North Sea and the waters up to the North Cape of Norway included, was introduced by Watts as 'the Croupier'.

'He's supposed to keep track of every U-boat from before it sails. He cheats at times by cribbing from the Operational Intelligence Centre and the trade plot.'

'Why keep several plots going?' Yorke asked.

The Croupier pointed at the chart of the North Atlantic and Yorke realized that it was heavily-gridded and, with a gothic style typography that looked German, had numbers and letters of the alphabet forming the horizontal and vertical sides, not the degrees and minutes of latitude and longitude. The whole chart was crisscrossed with thin lines drawn in with coloured pencils.

'Trends, habits, systems, methods...' the Croupier explained. 'We track the boats on their way out to their operational areas and we track 'em back. Or we try to. Some of the coloured lines represent only two aircraft sightings of a U-boat and a report from some bloke in the Resistance standing on a cliff near Lorient watching the boat come back or leave.'

'The chart?'

'German – we captured it. Very secret, too; they still use the same co-ordinates in W/T trafiic.'

'You're hoping to find a pattern?'

'Yep: patterns or habits. Everyone develops habits, but not just captains or boats. I'm watching to see if and when Doenitz's operations boys start sending out the boats on regular routes – or fetching 'em back.'

'Any luck?'

The Croupier shrugged his shoulders and looked up at Captain Watts. 'I call it deduction and the Director calls it luck; but we've jumped a few when we could cadge a Coastal Command plane, or beg a couple of frigates. Easier on their way home because we've usually identified them by then and found out if we know any of the CO's quirks. I've a file on those captains we know. But homeward-bound means they've also done the damage, too. Harder to spot 'em on the way out – usually they keep radio silence now until they're well out in the Atlantic and sight something.'

The sixth man in the ASIU's team, wearing the ribbon of a DSO and the tiny bronze oak leaf of mention in dispatches, was the submariner, a regular whom Yorke remembered from Dartmouth days. His jerky movements and the nervous twitch of his head betrayed the months of tension that made up a submariner's life in the Mediterranean and caused the tic.

Watts called him 'Jemmy' but Yorke was not sure if it was a play on 'Jemmy Twitcher', the nickname of the Earl of Sandwich who was First Lord of the Admiralty in the days of Samuel Pepys, or the character in *The Beggar's Opera*.

'Jemmy,' Watts said, 'is our fake Jerry. He's supposed to dream up ways of attacking our convoys by using and beating our zigzag diagrams. He's a bit of a mathematician, and when a convoy zigs he tries – at nine knots or so – to get to the zag point so he can attack, fire a few fish and dive deeper below a convenient layer of cold water so that the escort's Asdics bounce off.'

'What's the object of the exercise?' Yorke asked. 'Improve our zigzag diagrams or improve our methods of attacking the attacker?'

'Both,' Jemmy said, giving a violent spasm that seemed likely to dislocate his neck. Yorke was wondering whether to look him in the face or look away when the lieutenant said matter-of-factly, 'Ignore this bloody tic. I knocked myself cold with it last week. I was standing with my back to a brick wall and gave such a monumental twitch that I bashed my head and woke up flat on my face on the pavement. Two agitated old trouts were kneeling beside me trying to wrestle the top off a bottle of smelling salts that one of them had in her handbag.'

'Tell the rest of the story,' Watts said.

Jemmy grinned. 'Well, I sat up with my head throbbing and the old trout who owned the smelling salts suddenly began to feel faint, so I had to wrestle the stopper off the bottle and give *her* a whiff or two to get her back on her pins.'

'If Hitler knew the diabolical cunning and intrepidity of his enemy,' Watts said in imitation of Churchill's rolling tones, 'he'd surrender tomorrow.'

'In the meantime we have to get through today,' said Jemmy, 'and I'm getting some good leads on six boats trying to form a pack ahead of QB 173, which is eight days out of Halifax.'

'Is that a Clyde or Liverpool convoy?' Watts asked.

'Clyde,' Jemmy said, 'if it ever gets that far. Doenitz has put Kohler in command of this pack, and he's good. He usually outguesses the zigzag diagrams.'

Watts took Yorke by the elbow, pointing to the vacant and well-worn desk in the far corner of the room. 'This is your berth. Every one of these pipes,' he pointed to the wall, 'gurgle, belch and fart at irregular intervals. Unnerving at first; but useful as an alarm clock if you doze: off. Dozing is not encouraged in ASIU; we're supposed to stay wide awake to fight the King's enemies.'

Yorke raised his eyebrows. 'And my role in this unremitting battle, sir?'

'Ah yes, your job. Well, first of all don't let those pipes get you down. At first Jemmy was inclined to bellow "Dive, dive, dive!" when they gurgled and vibrated, but he's settled down. Well, your job is to apply your unsullied young mind to a very new problem which so far has defeated the rest of these dumb buggers. They don't admit defeat, of course; they simply write me brief memos each day which I assume say they are too busy on their own problems to tackle this one. I don't read the memos, you understand. My tame Wren secretary tells me they simply retype the last one with the new date on it, using the same split infinitives.'

'And my job, sir?' Yorke reminded him.

'Hmm...well, it's something which has equal priority with what these chaps are doing, but we've only just discovered it. You have to read all the dockets and pick the brains of the others (and use your own, too) and then come up with a convincing explanation of how, *without any warning whatsoever*, a U-boat can torpedo our ships from *inside* the convoy. No one knows how he avoids the escorts and gets into the middle, nor how he gets out again. But at the moment it's the Germans' latest trump card. It's a new card and one which so far is a winner. The others will tell you how to get up the papers on the attacks so far from Records. If you drop a neatly typed solution into my In-tray in a week's time, I'll see you get a bottle of gin in yours. But I warn you, if you listen to these fellows you'll end up blaming voodoo, poltergeists, Wagner, the Indian rope trick, the Stewards of the Jockey Club or the Ministry of Fuel and Power. I can assure you,' Watts said with a straight face, 'they've all been investigated by NID and cleared of any complicity.'

CHAPTER FIVE

Staying at his own home in Palace Street and working at the Admiralty should have been a young naval officer's dream, with a pleasant walk to the end of the street, a right turn into Buckingham Palace Road, passing the Palace on the left, and making the big decision of the day – whether to walk through the trees and bushes of St James's Park or along the Mall itself.

He usually chose the Mall and often let his mind slip back a few centuries as he walked. The park had once been a marsh, and Henry VIII had drained it to make it into a deer park beside his new palace of St James's. And as Yorke walked towards Admiralty Arch he often imagined the lonely Charles I almost three hundred years earlier taking his last walk across his path, under guard and bound from St James's Palace to his execution in Whitehall.

Slipping back in time was not difficult for Yorke: he might be dressed up in the modern uniform of a lieutenant, Royal Navy, gloves in hand, respirator over the shoulder, shoes polished and heels clicking on the paving stones along the great boulevard of the Mall, with its double row of trees, or more quietly among the paths of the park, but on several mornings there was a smell of smoke, as though bonfires had been burning among the trees, autumnal and making one think of charcoal burners at work in past centuries, when coal was an expensive luxury.

Only it was London that was burning now, not charcoal. The night's bombing usually left enough blazing buildings for the reek of smoke and charred wood to last long after dawn. Occasionally, as he skirted the Queen Victoria Memorial in front of Buckingham Palace, he could see the individual fires linked by a smoky haze, and occasionally a big blaze nearby which had gone out of control still billowing smoke like a destroyer laying a screen.

On his first day's walk to the Admiralty he found the Mall roped off, with an Army lorry with red mudguards parked nearby – a bomb had landed halfway along it. Don't know if it's a delayed-action job or a dud, sir, the steel-helmeted police constable explained. 'Won't do much damage even if it does go off, and the bomb disposal lads are busy.'

On the third day, after a night's raid, he chose the Park route and found that forty or fifty incendiary bombs had landed on the green grass and only a few – those which had glanced off trees – had ignited: the rest had landed on ground which must have been too soft to set off the impact fuses, and they stuck up vertically a few inches above the ground, their fins painted green, slightly darker than the grass, and the bombs even smaller than the cardboard tubes used to protect calendars and other such things when sent through the post. One of the ancient park attendants was walking among the trees, stabbing pieces of paper with a stick which had a nail protruding from the end. As he removed a piece of paper and stuffed it into the big bag slung over his shoulder he saw Yorke looking at the incendiary bombs.

'Look like 'eads of celery, don't they? Make yer think they oughter be earthed up!'

York nodded towards a blackened patch of earth at the foot of a tree where one of the bombs had burned.

'Yus, they burn bloody 'ot, and no mistake. They say it's haluminium hoxide. Still, only scorched one side of the bark and the grass'll grow again.'

'Best place for them to land,' Yorke commented. 'The earth must be soft there from all the rain.'

'Yus. Not like the two that hit our 'ouse."

Yorke knew that a man needed to tell his bomb story again sometimes, and, although this old chap must be over seventy, he spoke with a mixture of pride and modesty, as if referring to winning the darts championship at his local pub.

'Yus, we got two. One ledged in a beam in the attic, the other landed in the lavatory pan. We 'ad a stirrup pump and a couple of buckets of sand, but me and the old lady couldn't do much – she gets the screws in 'er back somefing chroninc. So up it all went. Lived there forty-three years we did, ever since we was married. Mum wasn't arf mad, I can tell you, sir. We're living with the married daughter now – 'er hubby's gone for a sojer, the London Scottish, and she's glad of the company, and the extra money and coupons 'elps with the 'ousekeeping.'

Yorke chatted for a few minutes. The old man needed no sympathy; the loss of his home after forty-three years, with the mortgage long since paid off, did not worry him: he and mum were alive to tell the tale, and all he asked was an occasional sympathetic listener.

As he walked the last hundred yards to the Citadel, reminded by its shape from this angle of desert forts and half expecting to see a French Foreign Legion camel patrol trotting out of a hidden gateway to meet the lurking Tuaregs, Yorke was thankful that the filters in the air conditioning, intended to take out any poison gas, would also remove the stench of charred wood and smoke which, from the wind direction, must be from some gutted building at the St James's Palace end of Pall Mall.

'London Bridge is falling down'… The old nursery rhyme came back to him. London was enormous; it might take fifty years of nights for the Ted bombers to flatten it, but only five years would reduce it to a city without character. Nelson's column, the old Banqueting Hall, Somerset House, the Admiralty and Horse Guards buildings in Whitehall, Downing Street, St Margaret's, and the Abbey…these still stood. Parliament was damaged – the Commons, anyway – but Big Ben was there. St Paul's remained amid flattened office buildings: one could really see it for the first time: he hoped that when peace came the City Fathers would prevent crude property profiteers building new and ugly office blocks to hide it once again. But all over London, in quiet squares and busy streets, the Queen Anne, Georgian and Regency houses were being smashed down by high-explosive bombs or gutted by incendiaries, although ironically some of the modern monstrosities like the Lever building, Adelphi and Savoy seemed to have a charmed life, their very ugliness apparently making them bombproof.

Would London eventually become a shell inhabited only by starving starlings and pigeons? How did a U-boat get into the centre of a convoy without being picked up by Asdic? The two questions were related.

Jemmy was already at work with parallel rules, protractor and dividers, plotting a particular zigzag diagram on the back of an old chart. Like all such diagrams the long legs and short legs, the zigs and the zags, were so designed that after a set distance on each one the convoy would at the end of a certain time be back in a position it would have reached had it steered a direct course.

Jemmy's 'Good morning, Ned,' was half-strangled by a twitch but he was in a good humour. 'Just look at this bloody diagram!' he said cheerfully. 'The man who designed it must be a traitor in the pay of the *Kriegsmarine*. Look – you get ahead of the convoy or find it coming towards you, so you park your U-boat either here or there.' He pointed to two red crosses he had drawn in. 'Now, no matter which zig or zag come up next, it takes the convoy within a mile one side or other of you. A browning shot into the middle of the covey from all the forward tubes and dive deep... God, if only the Teds had sailed Mediterranean convoys using this diagram...'

Teds, Yorke thought to himself; the one word that showed a man had served in the Mediterranean, or anyway near the Italians. 'What do you do now?' he asked curiously.

'Show it to Uncle,' Jemmy said, waving towards Captain Watts' office. 'Then he'll go and raise hell with someone in Trade Division and then escort commanders and convoy commodores will be told not to use this particular diagram. My third double-top, incidentally.'

'Third what?'

'Third diagram that I've shown leads the convoy right into the wolf's arm, or legs, or jaws.'

'Mr Zig or Mr Zag is going to end up hating you.'

Jemmy shrugged his shoulders and gave another twitch. 'The buggers ought to be jailed. That's the trouble with the Admiralty and the Civil Service. No one ever gets a real kick in the backside. He can kill a hundred men and all he'll get is a "displeasure" letter from Their Lordships. My last CO had twenty-three of them framed and hung up in his lavatory. He also had a VC DSO and a DSC, plus five mentions. But the fool who designed these three diagrams – if anyone does any-thing about it, which is unlikely – won't get a kick: no, he'll be told to draw up three more diagrams to replace 'em. The brotherhood will cover up.'

'The brotherhood isn't as bad as that!' Yorke exclaimed.

'It's worse,' Jemmy said quietly. 'Every bloody profession – trade, too, probably – has its own brotherhood. The Navy, the Admiralty civilians, the brown jobs in the War House, lawyers, accountants… Same with the Civil Service. Look how they refused to let Wrens work here until recently. "A civilian establishment" – Christ, don't the Civil Service Union know there's war on? Have you ever heard of an incompetent doctor being jailed for killing a patient by negligence? Or a lawyer made to pay his client damages for ruining his case? Or a firm of accountants struck off for giving wrong advice and ruining a client's business?'

The lieutenant's face was white now with perspiration which was breaking out along his upper lip and his brow just below the hair line, and Yorke realized he must have seen some great injustice done – or perhaps he knew of too many mistakes that sank merchant ships and drowned men in the winter wastes of the North Atlantic.

'The aristocrats of impregnability,' Jemmy continued, 'are the highest permanent civil servants in a ministry. They are the safest – they can gang up on a minister, but no one can gang up on *them*: they can't be sacked – unless they're pinched on a criminal charge – and all they need do is sit still, avoiding decisions, supping their char (in better quality cups as they get promotion), and then collect their pension. The temporary civil servants come next – the cream of the war dodgers, they are. What a future they have when the war ends!'

'Don't be so bitter at this time of the morning, Jemmy,' Yorke said.

'B-b-bitter!' Jemmy stammered angrily. 'I'm the only survivor from my last boat because of these bureaucratic buggers, and they gagged me at the court of inquiry. Too bloody secret to be talked about, so the president said. I was so angry they ordered a couple of Marines to march me out. Somehow Uncle heard about it and asked for me. Probably saved me from a court martial. Anyway, I got away with "an expression of Their Lordships' displeasure".'

'The first of your collection?'

'Yes. Uncle paid to have it framed by a Bond Street firm and gave it to me as a present. We had a formal presentation last month. Christ, it was a riot: he sent invitations to the Board Secretary, all the Board Members (including the Civil Lord) and that fellow Aneurin Bevan – who didn't come, incidentally. He'd have had a fit if he'd known what he was missing!'

'But Uncle...' Yorke said lamely. 'It's a wonder they didn't make him naval-officer-in-charge, Freetown, or Aden, or even liaison officer with the Russians in Archangel!'

'They daren't,' Jemmy said, cheering up. 'For a start he's brilliant and Winston knows it: Uncle is under orders to trot along to Winston once a month to report direct, with copies to the Board. When the First Sea Lord, old Dudley Pound Cake, made a moan about my presentation, Uncle said he was concerned that the gravity of the affair should be brought home to me, hence the ceremony!'

'Uncle must be quite a lad!'

'Uncle is quite a lad. Either he's a future First Sea Lord, or he'll be pensioned off the moment Winston stops being the PM. There's no in between. If you want a cuppa, incidentally, Uncle's Wren secretary arranges it. She's mine, by the way.'

'Congratulations,' Yorke said, remembering the girl with honey-coloured hair and a ready smile.

'I just thought I'd mention it.'

Yorke grinned and saluted: 'You may safely dive to periscope depth.'

The folders sent up from Records and now stored in the safe comprised a pile of eleven dockets, each one of which contained all that was known of eleven convoys attacked by single U-boats which suddenly appeared in the middle, undetected by the escorts.

Yorke spent the morning skimming through them all before carefully reading the first one, which was outward-bound. There seemed to be no pattern in the attacks, no pattern in the times except that they were always at night. The advantage of Uncle's arrangement of ASIU was that in one room were experts in many aspects of anti-submarine warfare, and after lunch Yorke sat on Jemmy's desk, seeing if the submariner had any ideas.

Jemmy, his face grim, put his hands flat on the desk and said in a low voice, 'I've seen some of those dockets. What Uncle didn't tell you, and I will now reveal for the good of your immortal soul, is that there's been a colossal bog-up. The first of these attacks was more than a year ago. The first time the ASIU saw those reports was two weeks ago.

'The trouble is simple. Over there, on your desk, you have eleven dockets; eleven folders containing all the reports about each of those eleven convoys. But let me assure you, that ain't the way the Admiralty got them in the first place. Uncle is now fighting to get the system changed because he's been to see the Air Ministry boys to find out how they get all the information out of hundreds of air crew after a big bombing raid. Not only get it, but get it within a few hours, sort it out and if necessary act on it. They have a system of "de-briefing" where everyone who flew in a raid is questioned immediately his plane lands by intelligence officers. They can spot any weakness in the Ted defences immediately, or any weakness in our own planes, as well as assessing the success of our bombing.

'Well, my old mate, that's not the way the Navy and Merchant Navy have been doing it where convoys are concerned… Take as an example a convoy from the UK to, say, West Africa. The senior officer of the escort sees the merchant ships into, say, Freetown, Sierra Leone. He writes his report, hands it in to the local port admiral, and eventually, whenever there's a ship coming back to the UK, the report is forwarded to the Admiralty.'

'But that could take weeks!' Ned interrupted.

'Exactly, my lad, and that's why Jemmy is telling you this parable. The commodore of the convoy also writes his report and that wanders along "the usual channels", from one "In" basket to another. Losses, on the basis that bad news travels fast, get signalled to the Admiralty as soon as the convoy escort arrives at the destination. So already you have a separation of weeks between the Admiralty knowing that Convoy X lost Y ships, and then getting the SO's report of what happened and eventually the commodore's report. And here at the Admiralty the poor devils are swamped with paperwork, anyway.'

'But hellfire, Jemmy, all this has cost dozens of ships and hundreds of lives,' Ned said angrily.

'Yes,' Jemmy said quietly, 'and that's why, the minute that someone suspected there could be an "insider" – it was only an idle rumour; gossip at a club bar – all the papers were got together and bunged over to us. That was last week. This department isn't yet six weeks old. Now you have all the dockets on your desk. All you have to do is find out what the Teds are up to, and write a memo to Uncle… Easy isn't it…?'

Suddenly Ned felt trapped; caught between his own knowledge of the sheer exhaustion of escort officers, and the demands of Admiralty planners. Equally suddenly he knew that Jemmy's twitch would never be cured while he was doing his present job; he was driven on to find flaws and answers because he knew, from bitter experience, that men's lives depended on his wits.

You, Lieutenant Edward Yorke, he told himself, are caught up, too; you know the senior officer of an escort arrives at the convoy's destination worn out with the actual voyage, but the minute the ship is anchored new orders arrive on board telling him to escort another convoy… No rest, no relaxation: the ship has to be fuelled and provisioned; men have to be given a few hours' leave if possible; calls have to be made on port admirals; dozens of reports have to be written or checked and signed. Say that four ships were torpedoed – no SO wants to admit a U-boat managed to get through his screen, so probably he blurs the details in his report, never suspecting for a moment that the U-boat managed to get inside by some trick, rather than the SO's faulty screen.

If, Ned warned himself, it was a trick and not inefficiency. He looked down at Jemmy's drawn face. Jemmy was ruthless – with himself and others. And, Ned realized, it was the only way. So start with Uncle: Uncle had said that ships were being torpedoed by U-boats that managed to get inside the convoys, implying it was by some new invention or a clever trick. But supposing it was simply that the SOs of eleven escorts had been inefficient, or that the whole system of convoy defence was badly organized, or… There were dozens of possibilities. He could only hope, he realized, that the answer was in those eleven dockets, the contents of which had been so tardily assembled.

Delay, delay, delay... It had already killed so many men and lost so many ships, yet could anyone really be blamed? Could every escort commander's report, and every commodore's report, be sent by wireless to the Admiralty the moment a convoy arrived? Obviously not – the Admiralty's entire wireless capacity would be swamped. And for most of the convoys arriving it would be unnecessary.

He realized Jemmy was watching him.

'Now you see you've got a problem,' the submariner said without malice. 'It's easy to say that a complete report on every convoy should be sent to the Admiralty immediately on arrival – and there's no reason why it isn't when a convoy arrives in the UK – but how can it be done for the convoys arriving in Canada, the USA, West, South and East Africa, India, South America... Ned, my old mate, Uncle was wrong when he said you shouldn't blame voodoo: it's the only explanation I can think of.

'I've seen some of the dockets,' Jemmy continued, 'but let's go over it from the start. If I remember correctly the first that anyone in the convoy or escort knows is when one or two ships go up with a bang, often followed by others?'

'Yes, with the torpedo always coming from somewhere inside the convoy.'

'So there's absolutely no doubt the Ted boat is in there among the merchant ships – actually inside the perimeter of the columns, in other words?'

'None at all. Not in these eleven cases, anyway.'

'You realize what this means, Ned?'

'Well, there's little or no chance of the escort detecting or attacking a U-boat which is actually inside the convoy: the heavy propeller and engine noises of the merchant ships themselves mask the U-boat, which is running silently on its batteries.'

'Oh yes, we can take all that for granted,' Jemmy said, 'and it won't matter a damn if the U-boat attacks submerged or on the surface. No, you're missing the vital point, mate.'

'Surface and tell me, then.'

'Every one of the escorts must be deaf. A Ted boat *did* get into the middle of each of these convoys, and to do that he must have passed close to one or other of the escorts, but they heard nothing. Not a single return ping on a single Asdic…'

'The Ted could have been down deep with motors stopped.'

'Oh yes, but every time he had to be in exactly the right position so that the convoy's next zig or zag brought it right over him, so he could surface in the middle. Bit of luck, eh?'

'But you've just found a diagram…'

'I know, but your nine convoys were all using different diagrams: different from each other and different from mine. I checked the numbers, and they didn't include the three.'

'So you don't think a Ted boat could be lying in wait ahead for the convoy to pass over?'

'No,' Jemmy said bluntly. 'At least, it could be but wasn't in these cases. But let's have another chat when you've gone through the rest of the dockets. Incidentally, you're probably new to dockets,' he added, a bitter note in his voice. 'Don't take any notice of the minutes written on them by various directors: most of them are just trying to impress each other with their wit, not win the bloody war at sea.'

Yorke went back to his desk and reached for the second docket, a convoy from Freetown to Liverpool. Dozens of reports by everyone ranging from the escort commander to the skipper of an ocean-going tug that found a lifeboat from one of the torpedoed ships, full of dead men. He glanced at the dates. They had been written over a period of nine weeks; they had been received at the Admiralty one by one and up to three months later, so that no one ever read all the reports together, and that was the weakness – unavoidable, of course – of the system.

Forty-two merchant ships had rendezvoused in the great almost landlocked bay at Freetown, ships from other ports on the west coast of Africa like Takoradi on the Gold Coast and the open anchorage of Accra, Lagos and Apapa, the twins on either side of the same river in Nigeria; and from Port Harcourt. Some of the ships had come from South America, crossing the South Atlantic in a small convoy.

They had weighed anchor and then formed up outside Freetown, seven columns of six ships each, like chocolates in a box, with an ocean-going tug forming a little tail and steaming at the end of the fourth column. The tug was intended to be the rescue ship because no merchant ship was allowed to stop to pick up survivors from another which had just been torpedoed. The order had at first seemed harsh to the Merchant Navy – until it realized that when a pack of U-boats was attacking it was easy for a particular U-boat to torpedo a merchant ship and then stand by her as she sank, waiting for the next astern in the column to stop for the survivors – presenting another and perfect target, without the U-boat having to manoeuvre. Before the order was given, there were cases of three ships lying torpedoed within a hundred yards of each other, victims of the same U-boat.

Yorke sat for a few minutes, staring unseeing at the badly typed reports but picturing the convoy forming up. All the ships would be painted grey, the famous 'crab fat grey', and many would be rusty, particularly those just arrived from the South American ports of Buenos Aires, Montevideo, Santos or Rio, and carrying cargoes from all three countries of meat, hides and wool. The meat ships with their refrigerated holds were usually modern-looking, but the rest of the convoy ranged from one of the new American ships to old coal-burning tramps, ancient enough to have been in convoys trying to dodge the Kaiser's U-boats in the Great War. Coal-burners – a nightmare to escort commanders because from time to time they suddenly erupted black smoke from their funnels; one could imagine the bells ringing the stokehold to start the stokers shovelling and the smoke lifting over the horizon into the field of vision of a U-boat captain…

The ships from along the west coast of Africa: they had come out with bombs, shells and small-arms ammunition in the holds and crated aircraft on deck, enormous rectangular boxes almost as high as the bridge, creating a frightening amount of windage in a gale. These planes, uncrated and assembled in West Africa, would fly diagonally across the great continent to join the RAF in Egypt. Now the ships were going back to the UK with an almost bewildering mixture of general cargoes – palm nuts to be made into margarine or soap, palm oil in those few dry cargo ships also fitted with tanks that could be heated (because the oil had to be kept at a certain temperature), dehydrated bananas (which looked like sunbaked dog droppings), copper, bauxite, cotton…

With the exception of the Elder Dempster Line, which operated regularly in peacetime to West Africa and built fine-looking ships, the West African run seemed to a cynical young naval officer to be a godsend for every struggling shipping company that in peacetime would have gone to the wall: they could charter their miserable ten-knots-maximum, six-knot-convoy-speed rusty wrecks to the Ministry of War Transport, which provided crews from 'the Pool' and DEMS gunners (who were volunteers from the Royal Artillery and the Navy and received their name from the description Defensively Equipped Merchant Ships), and complete cargoes. And if a ship was sunk by enemy action, the Ministry provided a new ship as well…

Paint blistered from the tropical sun, the officers and men yellow from the Mepacrine antimalarial tablets or with their heads buzzing from the bitter quinine, and sometimes still pale and shaky from the malaria that often defied all precautions... And all the ships preparing for the strict blackout once again after several weeks on the coast in ports far from the enemy where there was no blackout; on the contrary, unloading and loading continued through the night using powerful arc lamps. And those damned lamps – Yorke could remember when dining on board merchant ships how frequently one heard the bulbs bursting as huge stag beetles, the size of large walnuts and harder, dazed by the light, crashed through the wire screens and into the big bulbs, breaking them in a cloud of sparks which produced the bellow, 'Where's Lecky?' He seemed to remember the ship's electrician was usually on shore or sleeping off an overcharge of palm wine.

Most of the men were glad to be leaving the tropical heat. Well, perhaps the high humidity rather than the sun's heat, although the engineers suffered badly, having to eat salt tablets to make up for the salt lost in perspiration.

The commodore's ship would steam out into a clear patch of ocean, with all the other ships milling around – chugging, in many cases – each flying the four-letter flag hoist of her registration letters that identified her. The leaders of the columns would get into position abreast the commodore, three on each side in this case. One of them, commanded by an experienced captain, would be the vice-commodore, and he would take over if the commodore's ship was sunk. A third captain would be the rear-commodore.

The seven ships would be the leaders of the seven columns and each of the forty-two ships had been given a position – third ship in the fifth column, sixth in the first column, and so on. Slowly and warily – for the masters of merchant ships disliked manoeuvring near other vessels, having spent a life in peacetime worrying about collisions and insurance claims, underwriters and average adjusters – the ships would form into columns, with the escorting destroyers and corvettes (most likely only corvettes and perhaps a frigate: destroyers sailed with only the most important convoys) staying outside the throng, biting their nails with impatience perhaps, but knowing that a harassed master became mulish and probably abusive when, doing his best, he was chivvied by one of the escorts. There was little love lost between the Merchant and Royal Navies, and none between masters (with twenty years' sea time and more) and the young officers commanding a corvette, a type of ship little admired by the masters because it was slow and, in anything of a sea, pitched and rolled too much to operate its Asdic, fire guns or drop depth charges.

Yorke focused his attention on the commodore's report. The convoy of forty-two ships had formed up and steamed off in good order at 1635 on the 23rd instant escorted by His Majesty's ships – and the names were listed, a frigate and four 'Flower' class corvettes. The Ship Names Committee deserved to be hanged one at a time for calling such tough little ships 'the Flower class' and then giving them names culled from their grandmothers' gardens – peony, pansy and so on. Many tough seamen after weeks at sea, most meals eaten out of bowls because of bad weather, were not too pleased at being referred to as 'a Pansy', or 'a Peony'.

The forty-two ships, the commodore had noted in his report, comprised three tankers and thirty-nine dry cargo ships. Two were Norwegian, one French, four American and one a neutral, a Swedish ship. The rest were British. All the masters had attended the convoy conference in Freetown, each had copies of the zigzag diagrams, 'Mersigs' (the book of

Merchant Navy signals) and various instructions. It was, in other words, a routine sailing with an escort of four corvettes and the escort commander in a frigate (which was due for repairs in the United Kingdom but could not be spared to make the voyage home on her own).

The rest of the commodore's report was brief: eleven nights out of Freetown, with no U-boats detected, the fourth ship in the fifth column was hit with a single torpedo and sank in eight minutes. The wind was westerly, force six, with a moderate to rough sea. Moon in the first quarter, three-tenths cloud... Ten minutes later the fifth ship in the fifth column, which under standing convoy orders had moved up to take the lost ship's position (and her next-astern had also followed) was hit with a single torpedo and sank half an hour later.

The next night saw a repeat performance: the third ship in the fourth column and the sixth in the second column. Three ships were sunk the third night and another reported sighting the phosphorescence of a torpedo track from the port side which just missed astern. Three more ships were lost the fourth night and two the fifth.

With twelve ships lost in five nights and the convoy zigzagging the whole time, a corvette steaming up and down between the columns just before darkness fell, the commodore admitted that he considered dispersing the convoy: with an average rate of two point four ships lost a night, it would take only thirteen point three nights for the remaining thirty-two ships to be sunk...

Yorke was intrigued by the precision of the commodore's mathematics but even more so by the position of the torpedoed ships in the convoy: they were all in the middle section: none of the leading ships nor the last in any column was hit; nor were any of those in the outside columns.

The commodore had not thought of – or, rather, did not mention in his report – re-forming the convoy into a broad rectangle of eight columns each of four ships, or a narrow one of four eight-ship columns. What effect would that have made on the U-boat? Four eight-ship columns would have made it easier and quicker to zigzag: the problem with any convoy altering course was that it was like a big wheel – the ships on the outside of the turn had to increase speed while those on the inside had almost to stop (and became very difficult to manoeuvre). It was hard enough in daylight; on a dark night it was a nightmare.

Increasing the convoy speed of six knots was impossible in this case because four of the ships had been unable to guarantee a sustained speed of more than six knots. Again, neither commodore nor escort commander could do anything about that, even though the Admiralty suspected that in dozens of cases the speeds announced by certain masters were not the best speeds they could maintain but their ships' most economical speed: the one which would save fuel and give the ships' owners that much extra profit on the voyage. That such parsimony could cost men's lives seemed not to bother them: a benevolent Ministry of War Transport replaced the ship and men if they were lost… Yorke turned over to the last page of the report. The attacks had stopped suddenly on the sixth night, by which time one more ship had been lost.

The report of the escort commander told Yorke little more. The master of the rescue tug merely listed the numbers of people he had saved from each ship, and to which ships he had transferred them at daylight. He had picked up a total of 272 men, some of whom had been torpedoed two or three times as their new ship was hit. He could not give a total of killed or missing because in several cases the captains and pursers, often the only ones who knew how many had been on board, were lost.

Afraid that he would miss some too-obvious clue, Yorke drew the convoy on a sheet of paper, forty-two dots in seven rows of six ships, and wrote in the names of those that had been sunk, marking where ships astern had moved up to fill the gap and, in several cases, then been hit themselves.

He glanced up to find Jemmy looking down at the drawing.

'Most interesting, Ned. I'll tell you one thing, and it'll cost you a gin.'

'Consider the gin ordered and paid for.'

'That Ted was inside the convoy every time he attacked.'

'That's not worth a gin; I'd worked that out myself.'

'All right. Are these numbers against the ships the nights they were hit?'

'Yes, "1" means the first night; "2" the second, and so on.

Jemmy traced the sequence of numbers with his index finger, giving an occasional twitch. He reached the last ship and sighed.

'It'll cost you two gins.'

'I hope it'll be a better-quality pronouncement than the last one.'

'It is. First, he stopped the attack eventually because he'd run out of torpedoes. He must have been carrying a full load when he found the convoy. Second, in any one night's attack, he never moved more than the distance between two columns.'

'I'd spotted that, too; but I'll count the "full load" as a separate piece of information.'

'What about the other convoys? The ones you asked me about. Are you drawing them out?'

'I think so. I can picture it better.'

'Wise man. One picture, to borrow the Fleet Street phrase, is worth a thousand words. Pity the Navy ever gave up drawing for writing. In Nelson's day the artist Rowlandson could tell it all in one sketch.'

With that Jemmy ambled back to his plan in a series of twitches and jerks, and a moment or two later the Croupier went over and perched on the edge of the desk, no doubt to see if Jemmy had any ideas on the U-boat movements which were being so carefully plotted.

At that moment Yorke realized how clever Uncle had been in the way he had organized ASIU. Half a dozen experts each working in separate rooms could very easily become pundits or prima donnas – or just plain lazy. Each would be working in a separate, isolated compartment. All in one room, they were eager to 'try it on the dog', going over to another man's desk with an idea or a problem and inviting criticism or an answer.

Jemmy, with his cheerful cynicism, obviously had a very shrewd mind as well as an intimate knowledge of submarines. Anyone spending so long attacking enemy ships in the narrow and often shallow confines of the Axis-held Mediterranean coasts had to be clever beyond all permutations of chance. Jemmy's twitch showed the price he had paid; but his mind was alert, a violin string. And, Ned thought, in this imperfect world where jealousy had more to do with promotion (or the lack of it) than most people would admit, Jemmy was lucky to be working for Uncle, who was obviously making good use of him. The same went for the Croupier. And for himself, he supposed, providing he produced results.

Results. One docket which had been read and digested, a large pile so far only skimmed, and a diagram. Now Jemmy and the Croupier were coming towards him.

'Lock up all that bumf for the weekend, Ned,' Jemmy said. 'It's six o'clock and my friend here, who's the ASIU union shop steward, says it's gin time on a warm Friday evening. I owe him a gin so you can buy him one of the two you owe me.'

Ned was due to telephone Clare at seven to see if she had been able to get a short weekend's leave, coming up on the ten o'clock Saturday morning train from Ashford after night duty. His mother had produced a rabbit from some butcher's hat to augment the meat ration and she had made up a bed for Clare in a guest room next to his own. She slept on the ground floor now the bombing was heavy, having been persuaded to turn what used to be a study into a bed-sitting room. Nothing had been said; the guest room had been prepared, and if Ned had teased her about it being next to his she would have looked blankly and said that she had no intention of putting a guest in a third floor room with only tiles and some plaster and laths to protect her from bombs and fragments of anti-aircraft shells. Mother was sophisticated in – well, a kind and practical way. It was up to Clare (whom she had not yet met, and Ned; she had prepared a guest room; it was up to them what they did.

Outside the Citadel it was dark; the dank November night air was still heavy with the smell of charred wood overlaid with the improbable wet straw odour of sandbags which had been treated with some smelly green substance intended to stop them rotting. The sandbags, Jemmy observed, brought out the worst in St James's Park, whose earth had been used to fill them and below a certain depth still retained its marsh smells which Ned thought inconsequentially might date from Henry VIII's day.

'Stirrup pumps will be worn,' the Croupier announced in a stentorian voice as they passed under Admiralty Arch, startling two hurrying civil servants. 'Pub or club?'

'Pub,' Jemmy said promptly. 'I'm bored with seeing our gallant brother officers fighting the King's enemies in the celibate splendour of their clubs. Let us to an alehouse until night-club time, and hope to find some big-breasted Land Girls who'll lead us to pastures green.'

'Land Girls in Whitehall pubs?' the Croupier exclaimed. 'You're a couple of hundred years too late. In good King Charles' golden days, when lechery no harm meant, I'm sure there were dozens, handing out syllabubs to the thirsty and lecherous soldiery; now you'll be lucky to find a couple of venereal strumpets.'

'It's splendid the way the Croupier lapses into this twentieth-century Elizabethan jargon when he's thirsty,' Ned commented to Jemmy. 'Just listening to him takes my mind off the smell of the pigeons; I swear I'd never hear a siren if he was neighing a sonnet.'

They walked into a public house at the top of Whitehall, carefully slipping between the blackout curtain, and Ned ordered the drinks. The barman guessed they were from the Admiralty. 'Plymouth or Gordons, sir? Can only let you have one round.'

'Gordons for me,' Ned said quickly, regarding Plymouth as being an expensive substitute for petrol.

At a few minutes before seven Ned left the other two men after getting ten shillings' worth of change from the barman, and went out into the blackout just as the air raid sirens began wailing, the disembodied howling echoing along the streets as though coming from the black sky.

Charing Cross Station was one of the easier targets for German bomber pilots to find: like Cannon Street and

Victoria, it was at the end of a shiny grid of railway lines and just over the Thames. As Yorke walked to the telephone kiosk he was thankful not to be sitting in one of the trains waiting to huff and puff out into the night in a cloud of steam and sparks and slowly cross the long bridge to the south bank of the Thames.

He was lucky: he had put the money into the box and was pressing Button A after only seven minutes; the phone had rung, Clare told him, at exactly three minutes past seven. And then they had nothing to say to each other.

'I was so excited waiting for the call I didn't think…' Clare admitted.

'The sirens have just gone; I was afraid there'd be hours of delay.'

'How is the new job, Ned?'

'Interesting – challenging, in fact.'

'You're not going back to sea?' she asked in sudden alarm.

'No – and'…he paused, knowing he must sound like a nervous schoolboy but finding himself almost terrified that the answer might be no…'are you – er, can you get away this weekend?'

'From you?' she teased.

'From your other boyfriends.'

'It's wonderfully peaceful down here. Just a few bombers going over at the moment – heading your way, I imagine. But walking along the lanes, even though the trees are bare…'

'Did you get the weekend off?' he asked stiffly.

'Yes,' she said innocently. 'Until night duty on Monday, which means 6 p.m.'

'Are you coming up to London?' His heart was thudding; his palms were wet with tension and he felt he ought to be ashamed that a girl on the end of a telephone line could make him jumpier than a diving Ju 88.

'I *could* do,' she said coolly, 'but no one's asked me.'

'What do you mean?' he flared. 'Dammit, I – '

'Asked a bit of crumpet up to Town for a dirty weekend!'

'Clare!' he said angrily. 'I've asked you to stay in my house. Meet my mother. Do – '

'You haven't, you know! You've taken it all for granted. In fact all you said when you left was that you hoped I'd come to London on my next leave.'

'Well, you knew perfectly well what I meant,' he said sulkily.

'I'd, darling Ned, but you've no idea how nice it is to have someone get angry – '

'There are the pips: wait, I've plenty of change!'

He put in the coins requested by the operator and pressed Button A. 'Go on, you were saying…'

'I feel all warm and snug because you are getting angry at the idea you might not see me this weekend. It does me good. I feel all woman.'

'But you know I love you!'

'Oh yes, Ned; but it's wonderful to hear you getting jealous, even if your rival is only a country lane.'

'I'm jealous of everything and everybody. Ten o'clock train?'

'Yes, eleven forty-five at Charing Cross.'

'I'll meet – '

He dropped the phone and dived out of the kiosk, clear of the glass partitions, as he heard the whistling hiss of a bomb. It burst with an earth-shaking thud beyond the station, among the network of railway lines. He stood up and sheepishly groped for the receiver, hearing Clare's alarmed voice calling: 'Ned! Ned!'

'I'm here. Sorry, a visitor seemed to be coming.'

'You're all right?'

'Yes, in fact it was a long way off.'

'I love you, Ned.'

'Takes a bomb to get you to admit it.'

'Takes a bomb for you to appreciate it.'

They paused for a moment, each considering the other's remark, then she said: 'The pips will be going in a few moments. Let's say goodbye now, before the operator interferes.'

'Until tomorrow, then. Your room is ready.'

'A bed in the attic is all I need.'

He thought a moment. 'You have a large room next to mine.'

'Your mother's choice?'

'Yes. There's an attic if you prefer it'

'No, I'll trust your mother's judgement.'

As the first pip sounded she said, 'Good night, my darling,' and hung up.

Ned walked out of the station and down the slight slope of the forecourt quite unaware of the crackling barrage of anti-aircraft fire and the occasional distant whistle of falling bombs. He could hear only her voice, slightly distorted by the telephone line, and his feet hardly touched the ground.

CHAPTER SIX

Both Jemmy and the Croupier were in the Citadel next morning with such bad hangovers that Jemmy yelped every time a twitch jerked his head. Ned, who had walked home down Whitehall and Victoria Street after telephoning Clare, had spent a couple of hours in front of a fire which flickered with all the ferocity of two lumps of coal and one of slate, alternately glancing at the four pages which comprised the evening newspaper and trying to think of U-boats.

Here he sat within half a mile of Parliament and Downing Street in his own home, inconvenienced only by the noise of bombs and anti-aircraft guns outside. But out in the Atlantic on this November night, between 300 and 3000 miles to the west, there were many convoys under way, some heading south towards the sun, some steaming north from the Tropics, but the majority steering east or west, bringing arms and supplies to Britain from the New World, or returning for more. How many of those convoys had sufficient escorts, and how many were being decimated nightly by U-boats attacking without warning from inside the convoy? Decimate was the right word; one in ten was about the proportion. A thirty-ship convoy losing three ships a night was being decimated. In ten such nights it would be destroyed.

A piece of coal cracked and then fizzed as a pocket of gas ignited. It gave little heat but in common with most Britons on a winter's night, Ned wore warm clothes and regarded a small coal fire as a spiritual rather than a physical comfort.

He had slept fitfully, a night when the sudden drum-rolls of an anti-aircraft barrage interrupted thoughts of Clare which in turn merged into sleep. Camp coffee and scrambled dried eggs on burnt and dry toast (they were hoarding the butter and margarine ration for the weekend) made a depressing breakfast and he thought he would go in to the Admiralty and read another docket, although Uncle had made it clear that no one was expected to work on Saturday mornings: with a decent night's sleep impossible and his staff recovering from various unusual experiences, he wanted five good days' work from each man; the weekends, he said, were for charging batteries and picking up the ideas that tended to float in through the French windows or, he said with a lewd wink, emerge from between a lissome tart's bosoms.

'That gin,' Jemmy whispered. 'It was the first step on the road to Sodom, or Gomorrah. When you deserted us we went along and met Uncle's Wren at the point of no return – in this case the number nine bus stop at the end of Piccadilly, whence she had travelled from her Wrennery in Earl's Court, and, in response to an urgent phone message from me, she had brought company for my loyal shipmate the Croupier.'

At that the Croupier groaned. 'Soaks up booze like a cruiser's main suction line, makes love with the thrust of a 16-inch gun's recoil, laughs the whole time, and is called Sandra.'

'Are you complaining or boasting?' Ned inquired.

'I'm not sure,' the Croupier said shakily. 'I'll tell you later. What doesn't ache is sore; what isn't sore is trembling.'

'When do you see her again?'

'This afternoon. And with a bit of luck we'll go straight to bed and stay there for the weekend and I'll be here making the same complaints on Monday morning.'

'If you keep off the booze you might conceive some ideas by then,' Ned said unsympathetically, unlocking the safe and taking out his next docket.

'If it's only ideas,' the Croupier said. 'I think Jemmy has died. A corpse with a twitch. Ought to be preserved in formalin.'

'Don't think so loud,' Jemmy said, 'I was just watching Ned taking that docket from the safe. The second convoy, eh Ned? And there's another of Doenitz's boys in the middle of it like Neptune's jack-in-the-box, ready to jump up as soon as it's dark and shout, "Booo".'

At that moment Captain Watts' Wren secretary, Joan, walked in with four cups of coffee on a battered tray. 'No sugar left and yesterday's milk has gone sour,' she said, putting the tray down on Jemmy's desk. 'Here, this may help.' She took a cup herself, sat down at one of the nearby desks, and groaned.

Yorke then noticed that she was pale, with dark rings under her eyes, and remembered Jemmy's comment a few days earlier, 'She's mine.'

'Poor Joan,' the Croupier murmured sympathetically. 'Do you want some aspirins?'

'I've had three already. I ache all over and I feel sick.'

'Never dive with a submariner,' the Croupier said. 'I warned you. They've six hands and a rampant periscope.'

'I know all about that,' Joan said crossly. 'And he has all the subtlety of a German sausage seller.'

'Don't listen to her,' Jemmy said quickly, knowing there was no stopping her once she began grumbling.

'This – this desiccated Neptune's idea of being romantic is to shout "Up periscope" as he begins to make love. It's funny the first time, if you like a joke in bed, but not *every* time.'

'You can always shout "Down periscope" at the appropriate moment and see what happens,' Ned said.

Jemmy sipped his coffee. 'I don't know what she's grumbling about. Six sightings in one night.'

'Six?' Joan was outraged. 'One and he falls sound asleep. He dreams the rest.'

'It is not the custom of the service,' Jemmy said, 'to discuss one's sex life with one's brother officers.'

'Joan's a sister officer,' the Croupier pointed out. 'The Wrens work under a different set of KRs and AIs.'

'They bloody well don't,' Jemmy said. 'The King's Regulations and Admiralty Instructions apply to everyone. Like the Bible. Everyone in naval uniform, I mean.'

'I imagine that neither officer was in uniform at the time,' Ned said dryly.

'Not unless you count socks,' Joan said. 'He complained his feet were cold.'

Ned coughed and Joan said: 'We've shocked the lieutenant. It's an old Yorke family tradition that a gentleman takes off his socks.'

'It is,' Yorke acknowledged, 'but this particular lieutenant finds it hard to study dockets in an atmosphere thick with concupiscence.'

'Thick with the stale memory of concupiscence', Jemmy corrected. 'But you're right. To work. Joan, is there more coffee?'

An hour later Yorke had read the details of yet another convoy attack. Thirty-seven ships sailed and eleven were sunk in seven days; two of them each hit with two torpedoes. The convoy had started with an escort of four corvettes but once the attacks started they had been reinforced by two frigates, whose presence made no difference: sinkings went on at the same rate. Thirteen torpedoes. Although no other tracks had been sighted, the U-boat had probably missed with one and begun the attack with a full outfit of fourteen. Then the U-boat had presumably left the convoy, transmitted a brief score-board report in cipher, and headed for home, which most likely would be Lorient. British direction-finders would have picked up the transmission, plotted the position and perhaps broken the ciphered message, but none of that helped; the U-boat's route home didn't matter a damn – as far as Ned's problem was concerned – and the number of ships she had sunk was hardly a secret…

Six hundred and sixty men had died in those eleven merchant ships. The lucky ones were killed by blast from torpedoes. The rest were drowned as their ships sank, died suspended in the water by their lifejackets, or died of exposure in lifeboats. Ten masters had died – and they were the most irreplaceable part of a convoy. More than ninety DEMS gunners, men of the Maritime Regiment of Royal Artillery or seamen from the Royal Navy, all volunteers, had died. And all of them, ships, cargoes and men, recorded only by a few dozen pages in a manilla folder.

He glanced at the cargoes lost and totalled some of the figures: 1595 lorries, 550 tanks, 66 fighters, 24 bombers, 44 thousand tons of mixed cargo… All sunk by one U-boat in a convoy which included British, American, Norwegian, Dutch and French ships belonging to the Allies, and a neutral, a Swedish dry cargo ship. It must be nerve-wracking to be in a neutral ship sailing in an Allied convoy. Still, quite a few did; it was better than taking the risk of sailing alone and being sunk by a U-boat captain who did not believe that navigation and accommodation lights by night or a neutral ensign by day were anything but a trap.

Once again he drew a convoy plan, marking in the positions of the thirty-seven ships and the names of those sunk. Once again none of the victims was in the two outside columns, nor among the leaders or the last in the columns.

A pattern? Not really. On a night when two ships were sunk, they were usually in adjoining columns, but in two cases on the next night the third ship in a particular column had been hit, followed by the fourth, and the U-boat had obviously waited after the first hit and fired at the next ship to pass.

The coffee and Nature's own resources had restored Jemmy, and Yorke walked over to him with the convoy diagram. 'Another picture – can you tell me a story to go with it?'

Jemmy examined it for several minutes.

'The victims are more concentrated than those in the last convoy you showed me.'

'Which means the U-boat didn't move around so much.'

'You're learning, Ned. You're not sure what the lesson is, but you know you're learning something!'

'Tell me, then.'

'Handwriting, Ned; everyone writes differently. Driving a car – everyone has some mannerism which might be difficult to spot but is there all right. Taking soup: everyone slurps it up differently. Understand?'

Yorke nodded. 'Two different Ted skippers. This one is cautious, doesn't move far from his first victim to his second, probably because he fears detection by Asdic. Seems not to have missed, although the previous chap missed at least once. And he seems content to shut the shop for the night once he's sunk two ships.'

'Exactly,' Jemmy said, mustering a grin. 'Now bear that in mind when you plot the other convoys.'

'But I can't expect to find two different convoys attacked by the same skipper.'

'Of course not. You might over a long period, but it wouldn't help much even if you did because he'd show the same style. Now, what you should be doing – if you haven't a fearful hangover like mine – is getting into the minds of several U-boat skippers. Eleven, in fact, and discovering eleven different ways of torpedoing a number of ships from inside a convoy. I don't know the total number of ships sunk in all those convoys but say one hundred. One hundred attacks by eleven boats. Shake that up inside your skull and then you should be better able to dream up ways of stopping it.'

'Poachers and gamekeepers.'

'Exactly. Brother Doenitz and his gipsy orchestra have thought up a way of penetrating a convoy with a single U-boat; now Brother Watts and his string septet have to find out how they got in and mend the fence. In fact Brother Ned has the job, and I don't envy him.'

'Do you think they've worked it out, or just that in the beginning one boat did it more or less accidentally, and U-boat Command have put it in the drillbook?'

'Worked it out, I'm sure. Worked it out at a desk in U-boat Headquarters in Lorient or the *Seekriegsleitung* in Berlin.'

'Why not discovered it accidentally?'

Jemmy looked up at Ned, his eyes narrowing as he held out the convoy diagram to return it. 'Ned, my old chum, do you feel strong enough to hear Jemmy's Epistle to the Heathens?'

Ned nodded. 'As long as you're strong enough to preach it.'

'Well, Ned, you don't seem to realize it, but Uncle has given you ASIU's toughest problem to solve. Not just ASIU's, but the Navy's.'

Ned laughed, misled by Jemmy's tone, but the lieutenant gave a spasmodic twitch and held up a warning finger. 'I'm serious, Ned: let me explain. The Battle of the Atlantic is simply the battle between our convoys and Doenitz's U-boats.

We'll win it in the end because we've got to – we're within months, if not weeks, of starving. The Teds are sinking more ships than we're building and that quite simply means we're losing. You can draw graphs, juggle statistics, make speeches in secret sessions of the House of Commons, puff a Woodbine or wave a cigar, but the Teds are bound to win the war if they can go on sinking more ships than we build.'

'Don't forget the Americans.'

'I'm not. They've been in the war only a few months, and up to now their Navy is not affecting convoy losses: even when you toss in their shipbuilding capacity – not very impressive at the moment – the Teds are still sinking more than we and the Yanks are building. So we're losing. It's like trying to fill a bucket with a hole in it.'

'What about the pack attacks?' Ned asked. 'They're sinking scores of ships but my "insider" Teds are only sinking dozens. What's the importance of these inside-the-convoy boys compared with the packs attacking from the outside?'

'That's easy to answer. Beating the pack attacks means quite simply having more and bigger escorts and maybe – once we have enough – letting loose packs of frigates or destroyers to hunt down the Ted boats. Unless Doenitz has some surprises in store, we'll beat the packs once we have more escorts. That's oversimplifying, but basically we and the Yanks just have to build more.

'But even when (on a morning like this I think it's "if") we get enough escorts to smash the packs, we still have your problem, or rather the single-Ted-boat-in-the-middle. The insider. We'll be losing five hundred ships a year, working on the present number of our merchant ships at sea and the losses. But to win the war we've got to have double or quadruple the number of merchantmen. Unless you produce some answers, Ned old boy, we're going to double or quadruple our losses, too...'

'Why pick on me?' Yorke grumbled. 'Christ, I'm no A/S specialist, nor a submariner like you!'

'And that's why Uncle chose you. He had a hell of a fight with the Second Sea Lord's office – they wanted to send you off in another destroyer.'

'But why me?' Yorke persisted.

'You are a bore, you know,' Jemmy said amiably. 'All the other days in the week when we could discuss this, and you have to choose a morning when my brain is raw. Well, the anti-submarine boys think their bloody Asdics and hydrophones give them all the aces. It's quite useless to show 'em the figures of losses and ask 'em what happened. They say too few ships, a bad winter with too much rough weather, the summer too fine so the Teds use planes to hunt the convoys. They say we should never have given the French the secret of Asdic, then the Teds wouldn't have got it when France fell.'

'And the submariners?' Yorke prompted.

'They're just as bigoted. They say that if they had as many boats as Doenitz and as many convoys at sea as we have, they'd sink the lot. In other words, the A/S boys and the submarine boys all have axes to grind. Uncle, for reasons not clear to me in my present befuddled state, thinks you have four virtues.'

'Only four?'

'As far as he's concerned, four are enough. You aren't an A/S specialist, you're not a submariner, you're reasonably experienced in escort work, and you hate the Teds.'

'What makes hating the Teds so important?'

Jemmy sighed. The Innocent Abroad... The strongest motives that drive men – which means they'll plot, scheme and work overtime to achieve them – are lust, greed, jealousy and hatred. There may be others, and you can juggle the order, but Uncle reckons (and I agree) a good whiff of hatred for the Teds clears the mind wonderfully.'

'It's not doing much for you this morning.'

'I was sabotaged last night by my friends. Here, take your bloody diagram and buzz off for the weekend. The Croupier over there is about to go, Joan and I have plans, and she has to lock up the shop.'

Clare snuggled back in the deep, wing-back armchair, the flames in the fireplace flickering to light the comfortable sitting room and make her black hair seem a deep purple. Dusk in central London on a Saturday afternoon – boring, peaceful, cheerful or the dead end of the week: it could be any of these things. There was a faint smell of hops from the brewery on the other side of Palace Street; occasionally a distant train gave a whistle as it came in over the Thames bridge into Victoria Station, as though it was the railwayman's equivalent of touching wood in case a bomber lurking in the clouds made an attack.

She was happy and at peace. She wore a corn-coloured dress of wool, cunningly cut so that although it appeared a normal fit, her body moving inside it seemed to be nude; dark but sheer silk stockings (the first time he had ever seen her in anything other than black uniform stockings or thick woollen country-wear ones that matched comfortable brogues) which revealed, almost flaunted, slim legs that invited him to speculate about the thighs above the hem of the dress.

It was hopeless, he realized; he had not heard her few sentences because, from the comfortable depth his own armchair, he had let his imagination speculate about her body. In hospital it was always sheathed in the sexless nurse's uniform; on their country walks it was hidden in tweed suits or heavy coats.

'...Do you?' she asked.

'...Do I what?' he mumbled. 'Sorry, darling, I was daydreaming.'

'So I noticed. You'd even put the dress on a hanger.'

'On a hanger?'

'Yes, after taking it off me.'

'Oh dear, was it as obvious as that?'

'Yes.'

'I'm sorry.'

'Don't be; it's very flattering for a girl just up from the country.'

'Warms the room, too.'

'How is the arm, darling?' The question was sudden and, he realized afterwards, deliberately so.

'Getting better. Hurts in the cold. The muscles feel as though they're a fraction of an inch too short.'

'What about the grip?'

'Improving. I wouldn't want to be hanging on the edge of a cliff using only that hand, but it seems to belong to me now.'

'Sister Scotland and the physiotherapist want me to do tests before I go back.'

'Are they worried?'

'No, just interested. They loved mothering you.'

Yorke looked startled. 'I'd prefer being mistressed to being mothered.'

'By Sister Scotland?'

'Well, maybe not.'

Her nose was slightly hooked, her lips full, her skin golden, as though she still had the early-autumn remainder of a good summer tan. He knew her eyes were brown but by firelight they were black, large and emphasized by the high cheekbones.

'You're off again,' she said.

'No, I'm examining your face. Dictating notes to a lot of spotty medical students who need the obvious explained to them. "Now this patient, female, has two eyes, a mouth, nose and two ears, one on each side of her head…"'

'Professor Jepson at Charing Cross Hospital: you sound just like him. A wonderful surgeon but a fearful bore. The patient has no defects for you to point out, Dr Yorke?'

'If lack of height is a defect, I should point out five feet one inch is not Amazonian. The bust measurement is not stated, nor waist and hips. Legs slim, quite acceptable where examined. Feet small, elegant in court shoes, when they – the shoes – have not been kicked off… Temperature normal, pulse normal – '

'In fact the pulse is "elevated",' she interrupted. 'That means it's beating faster than usual.'

'Why? You're not feeling ill, are you?'

She laughed at the alarm in his voice. 'No, but a girl's pulse is allowed to beat faster when she's alone in a strange man's house and about to meet his mother for the first time. What a dragon!'

'She's not! You'll like her.'

'As far as nervous girlfriends are concerned, all men's mothers are dragons at the first meeting. They may improve as time goes on.'

Yorke nodded. 'Yes. I wonder why they usually start off so badly?'

'They don't always, of course. If it is obviously just a mild flirtation, mum is charming. If it is more serious, mum breathes smoke and flames or is as bright as a glacier on a sunny day.'

'But why? Jealousy?'

Clare held out her hands towards the fire, as if to warm them. 'Jealousy? Yes, I suppose so, but of a very involved sort. Being protective, I think. Even though the son is ten feet tall and twenty-five years old, he's always a baby to the mother, who sees him becoming involved in another womb... She's afraid of losing him, feels the girl can't be worthy... One of the oldest stories in human relationships.'

'The more polite mothers control their feelings. Put on a mask. Go through the drill.'

'I know. It's hypocrisy, but it's more pleasant.'

'Most of the world runs on hypocrisy. One has to work with a number of people one dislikes. But there have to be smiles and handshakes and so on.'

'The social conventions,' Clare murmured.

'Exactly. Machinery needs oil to make it run smoothly. It'd work very briefly without the oil, and then seize up. Society is the same. So are the social conventions hypocrisy or society's lubricating oil?'

She shrugged her shoulders and said: 'The rebels call it hypocrisy but I prefer the lubricating oil.'

'This is a hell of a conversation to be having on our first real afternoon together,' he grumbled.

Clare looked at her watch and said, a practical note in her voice: 'Your mother is due home any moment, and I have nothing to deter me from my duty, which is to put on the kettle and prepare some bread and butter.'

'I'll help.'

'I can fill a kettle and slice a loaf without help, but you can come and admire me.'

She watched him stand up. 'I've seen you in pyjamas, uniform and uniform trousers and a heavy jersey. I've never seen you in proper civilian clothes before.'

'You've seen me naked too. Half and half, rather, when I had those blasted blanket baths.'

'Yes, and I'm not sure who was the more embarrassed.'

'I was. I was afraid I'd...'

'Quite, but you didn't. Men usually don't, as a matter of interest. Shyness is very inhibiting. Anyway, there's only a dinner jacket left. And tails and topper.'

'You're still ahead of me, anyway·

'How do you mean?'

'I've seen you in nurse's uniform, country tweeds, and now an ordinary dress.'

'Well, that's – ' she paused and blushed. 'I see what you mean.' She nodded towards the door. 'I'll start preparing tea. You had better pull the blackout curtains, otherwise a warden will be banging on the door saying we're showing lights.'

'It might be a noisy night,' he said. 'Half moon, broken cloud, not much wind...'

'I've been in London since the blitz started,' she reminded him. 'Willesborough is a new experience.'

They both heard the front door opening. 'Damn!' Clare exclaimed. 'I wanted the kettle boiling when your mother arrived!'

Both women were secretly pleased to find that their original fears had been groundless. Mrs Yorke had quickly realized that Ned's latest girlfriend was far from being a grasping young widow thirsting (lusting?) for a quick wartime romance and some good jewellery in payment, and Clare had found that Ned's mother was gentle, decisive, well able to look after herself and certainly, not (as Clare had once feared) attempting to interfere in Ned's life.

They were nibbling at some dried-up and bright yellow fruit cake made with powdered egg when Clare had realized that Ned was the head of the house: he owned the house (and probably everything in it) and his mother lived there as – well, guest, housekeeper, mother, châtelaine. It was obvious neither of them ever thought about it – the house near Willesborough was closed up and likely to be requisitioned 'for the duration', so Mrs Yorke quite naturally lived here in Palace Street, with a small oil portrait of her husband on the wall in the dining room and a photograph of him in a silver frame beside her bed. One day Ned would marry and Mrs Yorke would move out to leave the house to the new Mrs Yorke, but that was usual: these were the rules by which people like the Yorkes lived their lives.

Ned had – at Clare's request – taken her into the room to show her the photograph of his father. The similarity between the two men was almost alarming, yet now she had met Mrs Yorke she saw that Ned had her smile, her chin, and her rather dry humour. The three Yorkes must have been an affectionate, closely knit family, and Clare had (inquiring about some other portraits on the dining room wall) discovered the Yorkes had been shipowners until the First World War, They had flourished – according to Mrs Yorke, who seemed to view them with affectionate irony – in Nelson's day, continued to run their ships profitably during the Crimean War, started to find profits were becoming sporadic at the time of the Boer War, and finally gone under at the end of the Kaiser's War.

The various members of the family had not starved but Clare sensed that Yorke House and the Palace Street house represented all that was left of Ned's share: death duties, a need to adapt a Bentley attitude to an Austin income, meant that they had learned from experience that it was better to have a few of the best rather than a lot of the second best; they would never come to terms with Bakelite and chromium plate but they understood the decline that Gibbon was describing.

She was surprised – startled and frightened in an odd sense she could not explain to herself – to find Ned was the last of the Yorkes: in one war the family had been all but wiped out. Four of five Yorke sons had died fighting in the Kaiser's War, and the fifth had been Ned's father. Only two of the four had been married; only one had a child, a girl, who was Ned's first cousin, a don and a spinster at one of the women's colleges. So from five Yorkes the family had been mown down – Clare was satisfied with the phrase; it summed up all its dreadful tragedy – from five brothers to one son.

Because she was a woman with her normal sensitivity heightened by a new and unexpected love, Clare looked across at Ned and wondered if in fact the family was not already as good as wiped out. She could see him lounging comfortably in grey flannel bags and a tweed sports jacket, the left hand held awkwardly, almost askew, because he still had not become accustomed to it. Although the uniform, the DSO, the war, the Battle of the Atlantic, were for the moment ignored, away to the westward was the broad sweep of the Atlantic, torn by torpedoes and bombs. Ned knew all the time and accepted it, and so did his mother, but Clare suddenly realized with a shock that was almost physical that within months of going back to sea he would probably be killed: that was simple mathematics, not cowardliness or heroics. She realized at that moment that Ned so accepted it as his duty that he never even hinted at it, and that was his mother's attitude. She could see her son depart for the war and death, and accept it as duty: his duty to go; her duty to have had a son who was available to go if the need arose.

It was not blind acceptance of fate, though; Clare needed only to remember the ribbon of the DSO, and Ned's determination to get his left arm working again. A functioning left arm and hand meant returning to sea, going back to his beloved destroyers. It was a miracle that had saved his arm – and as far as she was concerned another that had just given him an appointment in the Admiralty. It must be an odd job and presumably would not last long, and she was slightly irritated that he would not talk about it. She knew him well enough to understand he was not being deliberately reticent to disguise the fact he had been given a glorified clerk's job because of his arm. No, he was not talking about it because it was something secret and something which had made him preoccupied, almost tense, since he left Willesborough. Well, anything that kept him on land was welcome. She was being selfish – or was it protective? Men fought for their country; women fought for the men they loved.

Mrs Yorke spoke that pleasant shorthand used by intelligent and self-assured people. Clare sensed, after only a quarter of an hour, that this woman with prematurely white hair, aquiline nose, finely carved features and the hands of a pianist already saw (and accepted) her as a possible daughter-in-law, and while it was still on the 'Miss Exton-Mrs Yorke' level she had said, casually, 'Any relation to Charles Exton?'

'Yes, he was my father. You knew him?'

The woman seemed to go away for a few moments and then come back as if she had left briefly to glance back over a wall into the past. She gave a slow smile. 'Yes, quite well. He went to school with my husband; they served together in the same battalion in the First World War. He was one of the most handsome men I ever met.'

Ned sat up, startled. 'Good heavens mother, I didn't connect...'

'There's no reason why you should: we always referred to him as "Charles". I doubt if you ever heard us using his surname.' She turned to the girl. 'He must have died when you were quite young, Clare.'

'Seven. But he'd…'

Mrs Yorke nodded. 'I know. Your mother behaved splendidly.'

'She didn't have any choice.'

'Oh yes, she did, you know,' Mrs Yorke said mildly. 'Any woman whose husband deserts her can always comfort herself with drink, a series of lovers, or a mild affair with the gardener. Or she can remarry.'

'Which is what my mother did.'

Ned, puzzled, asked: 'What happened to your mother?'

Guessing the girl would prefer not to explain it herself, Mrs Yorke said quietly, the sympathy quite evident in her voice: 'Clare's father ran off with another woman, and Clare's mother married again. Happily, I believe?' When Clare nodded, Mrs Yorke said: 'Her new husband, Clare's stepfather, was badly wounded and captured at Dunkirk. He was not a young man, naturally, but the Germans refused to include him in the exchange of prisoners. I believe that he was in a special camp with others that the Germans might try to use as hostages. Anyway, he died last year.'

Ned tried to remember the details of Dunkirk, but all memories of people, of accounts heard later and wardroom gossip, were blurred by the overpowering memory of smoke over the beaches and the rows of hopeful faces up to their chins in water and shaded by steel helmets as the soldiers waded out to boats which ferried them to the waiting rescue ships. The insane scream of dive-bombers, the raucous chatter of the destroyer's guns… The dash back each time to Harwich with the decks so crowded it was hard to distinguish the ship for khaki-clad men, all cheerful once they were sure they were on board a British destroyer. Then suddenly it came to him who Clare's stepfather was. As he glanced up and caught her eyes he realized that the only remarkable thing was that they had never met before.

'How do you do,' he grinned, and from her chair she mimed a curtsy. Then, unexpectedly, she turned to Mrs Yorke and said: 'I was married. My husband was killed in the RAF.'

Mrs Yorke nodded. 'Your mother told me all about it before she died. We had met at a WVS reception. You know how old women gossip.' There had been a faint emphasis on the 'all'.

Clare had noticed it and said: 'You're not old; but I'm glad you gossiped. It saves me having to explain.'

'When people meet and fall in love,' Mrs Yorke said, a hand going up instinctively to make sure her hair was tidy, 'there's nothing to explain. Perhaps to fill in some answers for Donne, but only with affection.'

'Donne?' Clare asked. 'You mean John Donne?'

'Mother is a romantic,' Ned said, and quoted:

> ' "I wonder by my troth, what thou, and I
>   Did, till we lov'd? Were we not wean'd till then?
>   But suck'd on country pleasures, childishly?" '

Clare smiled and, watching Ned, said: 'I can only answer, kind sir,

> "Stand still, and I will read to thee
>   A lecture, Love, in love's philosophy." '

Mrs Yorke stood up and looked affectionately at Ned and said 'Another line of Donne is also appropriate – "Go, and catch a falling star" – and I'll go and put that scrawny rabbit in the oven: dinner is going to be late.' Just then the rising and falling of the air raid sirens cut through the night. She looked at her watch. 'Hmm, they're late, too.'

CHAPTER SEVEN

On Monday morning as Ned walked through St James's Park it was not until he saw the Citadel – in much the same way that a marauding band of Tuaregs would see a French Foreign Legion fort in the dark of a sandstorm – that he thought again of the Battle of the Atlantic. The charcoal-burner's oven smell of charred wood still hung over the city after another night of heavy bombing and left a layer of haze. It was one of those unexpectedly mild and cloudless November mornings when a pale-blue sky brought a few hours' life to the skeleton parade of leafless trees and emphasized the peeling paint of the buildings. Nurse Clare Exton was having breakfast in bed. In Clare's own bed, or rather the one in the lower guest room, served by his mother.

It was a situation which had its funny side and he suspected both women knew it. Clare had arrived at Palace Street nearly exhausted by a long spell of night duty, and at Willesborough she had gone for walks with him in the afternoon when she should have been sleeping. Then her weekend in London had been exhausting for her, but in another way: two nights when, as he remembered them in detail only a few hours later, they had made love with the desperation of a couple knowing they would soon be parted, or that the next hissing bomb could kill them both, and it was a desperation which left them exhausted yet, because of the possible ultimatum, not sated.

However, as a smiling Clare had commented when he had kissed her goodbye before setting off for the Admiralty, although it left dark rings under the eyes it did wonders for the complexion. She was glowing with love – and shivering with it, too, because she had gone back to her own room after getting Ned some breakfast, and found the sheets cold. Mrs Yorke had insisted that as Clare was not due back in Willesborough until the evening she should spend the day at Palace Street, sleeping as much as she could, doing any shopping she needed, and catching the latest possible train back.

Ned smiled to himself as he pictured Clare curled up in her bed, now wearing a nightdress and sleepily and pleasantly bewildered by the physical effects of making love. But there ahead was the Citadel, the towers and cupolas of the old Admiralty building beyond emphasizing the eastern atmosphere – almost Byzantine, except that the cupolas lacked the Byzantine boldness and colours.

He collected his dockets, notes and diagrams from the safe and went over to his desk. The room was empty and still chilly, the pipes round the walls gurgling and rattling as if they were doing their best to rouse the building after the brief weekend. He had just arranged the papers on his desk when Jemmy came in, his head jerking with the usual twitch but looking surprisingly rested. 'Morning, Ned, nice weekend?'

'Fine, and you?'

'Went to bed Saturday afternoon, got up this morning. Feel all the better for it. A few aches but the old brain is clear. Joan will be in with some coffee,' he added, the train of thought all too obvious. 'Don't tease her; she's in a wonderful mood. She should be, too, so let's make the best of it.'

Within five minutes the Croupier was spreading his gridded German chart of the Atlantic on the table like an Arab carpet seller displaying his wares and the other four officers were at their desks. Ned took out the docket on the third of the convoys. It was almost a rubber stamp version of the others. Nine ships sunk, five others saw the torpedo tracks of near misses because of abnormal phosphorescence – the German electric torpedoes left no wake of compressed air.

Once again he drew a convoy diagram of the eight columns and marked in the ships which had been sunk. Yes, there was the same pattern – all the ships hit had been in the centre, the third or fourth ships in the third, fourth or fifth columns.

He reached for the next docket and read the details. The brief, almost illiterate accounts of some of the survivors picked up later and interrogated, the terse report of the rear-commodore of the convoy (both the commodore and vice-commodore had been killed when their ships were sunk), the clipped wording of the report of the senior officer of the escort… No one complained, everyone did his best to explain what he saw or did, but it added up to five nights of horror. And, to be fair, the captain of the U-boat must be a brave man.

The convoy had sailed from Halifax, Nova Scotia, forty-four merchant ships, with three frigates and four corvettes as escort. The convoy commodore was a retired vice-admiral who had volunteered – as had so many other retired officers in their late sixties and early seventies – to 'serve at sea in any capacity'. The senior officer of the escort was an RN two and a half ringer who had a reputation of being one of the best.

By the last day of February the convoy was close to the southern edge of the Grand Banks as a gale come up astern: a gale verging on a storm. With massive following seas the ships had kept their positions, and Yorke could visualize the corvettes being more like half-tide rocks. Gradually the weather had eased to a near gale with a biting cold wind sweeping down from the north-west, chilled as it came over the icecap. Then the attack had started: two ships the first night, three on each of the second, third and fourth nights and two the fifth. Then a pack had taken over, and surprisingly enough they had sunk only two more ships before the escorts, with improving weather, sank two U-boats. The single U-boat inside the convoy had sunk thirteen ships; the convoy had finally lost fifteen.

But this convoy was different from all the others because during the first three nights of bad weather the insider U-boat had attacked on the surface. First sighted between the third ships in the fourth and fifth columns, stopped and athwart the convoy's course, it had then apparently fired one torpedo from its bow tubes at the ship ahead and one from its stern tube at the target astern, and both had hit. The nearest merchant ships had immediately opened fire on it – just a black shape on a swirling black sea – with machine-guns and Oerlikon 20 mm cannons, and it had submerged. Probably not, the commodore noted, as a result of the gunfire but because its night's work was completed.

On the second night it had been sighted on the surface near the head of the convoy. There had been a flash as a torpedo hit (and sank) the vice-commodore's ship, and a sharp-eyed lookout in another ship had spotted the great black whale-like shape. Almost at once the tanker which had been the vice-commodore's next astern was hit as she passed the sinking ship, unable to alter course in time to pass on the other side and so use the sinking ship as a shield between herself and the waiting U-boat.

No one had sighted it on the third night – the first anyone knew of the U-boat's presence had been the hollow 'bong' of a torpedo exploding in a merchant ship hull. Then, after five nights, the pack had arrived. And – was this significant? –

from then on the U-boat in the convoy had not attacked again: with thirteen ships to claim he had left it to the pack. And, just as Jemmy had said, the escorts could deal with pack attacks...

Yorke reached for the fifth docket, but then decided that first he would draw out the convoy diagram of the fourth to see if he could plot the U-boat's track for the first three nights. The escort commander's comments on putting a frigate inside the columns were succinct and correct – there was little or no roam to manoeuvre; dropping depth charges risked having them explode as the next merchant ship steamed over them... The only chance would be for the frigate to ram, should she manage to spot a U-boat on the surface. More important, he pointed out that a surface attack by a single U-boat (even in the bad weather of the winter when high seas made it difficult to use the periscope) was very rare...

He folded the finished diagram and put it in the docket. It all made a packet less than a quarter of an inch thick: all that was known – and a good deal more than most people cared – about one of hundreds of convoys which had been attacked, with ships sunk and men drowned and cargoes lost. Even as he put the docket back on the pile he thought of those euphemistically called 'the next of kin'. By now they would, after a great deal of arguing with the bureaucrats, be receiving meagre pensions and no doubt the minute the war ended the politicians would cut the rate of the pension and in many cases abolish it altogether. Wars were fought by men who could be killed or disabled, but wars were administered by sycophantic civil servants lurking in ministries at the dictate of politicians who converted fighting men's patriotism into cheap victories in the Parliamentary voting lobbies. The last piece of irony was that in the dockets the dead men were not even recorded by name; they were merely totals under the

'Dead', 'Wounded' and 'Missing' columns next to the names of each ship.

In all the bureaucratic war there had been one victory for the fighting men, he recalled with a tinge of bitterness. Although the Admiralty was a fighting headquarters in the way that the War Office and Air Ministry were not, the Civil Service Union insisted on regarding it as an administrative headquarters, so that to begin with all the clerical staff had to be civil servants. Yet from here, from the Admiralty building, ships of war of every type and size were dispatched hither and yon by naval officers, who sometimes found themselves directing the battle. The Submarine Tracking Room was just along the corridor, marking the position of every known U-boat, while the Trade Plot gave the positions of all the Allied convoys at sea.

The Air Ministry did not exercise direct tactical control over its aircraft in this way; fighters were controlled from different sector headquarters while the Army was administered from various commands scattered throughout the world. The War Office did not tell a distant battalion to march from place A to place B, yet the Admiralty, by direct wireless signal, did tell HMS A to 'proceed' to position B to carry out operation C. But at last the Civil Service Union had been persuaded there was a war on; that out there in the Atlantic beyond Bath, beyond the reach of buff official envelopes, beyond letters drafted in that bureaucratic language which is only one remove from illiteracy, there was indeed a war being fought and men were dying by the hundreds, and Wrens were needed inside the Admiralty, highly intelligent and specially chosen girls, many of them university graduates, excellent linguists, mathematicians... Above all, more than willing to work long hours and stand watches.

All of which had little to do with finding out how U-boats attacked from inside convoys. Yet in a way it did; cheating seamen (any servicemen for that matter) out of their pensions, laying down arbitrary bureaucratic rules from Bath or some such safe evacuation centre, going on strike as the dockers had done, refusing to unload the cargoes brought in by the merchant ships, were things that were kept secret yet were none the less shameful. The next of kin of those in the 'dead' and 'missing' columns might wonder for what their men died, while those disabled and even now lying in bed in some hospital, missing an arm or a leg, an eye or whatever, while doctors and nurses tried to mend them, must at times wonder whether they would have been wiser to volunteer for some safer wartime task, same clerkship in the Ministry of Fuel and Power, some post in the Ministry of Food. The best thing if you were of military age and likely to be called up was, of course, to stand for Parliament: Members of Parliament were not called up. By some strange logic (an instinct for self-preservation?) it was considered to be war service, and several sturdy young men with MP after their names making stirring speeches about the conduct or misconduct of the war were duly reported in the newspapers. No one turned round and said that with more than 600 Members of Parliament, the task of the political government of the country could be left to the older men – many of whom, ironically, had volunteered or were on active service. The younger Members were obviously intent on building up reputations that would secure their political advancement after the war, although the way the Battle of the Atlantic was going (if the pile of dockets was a true indication) it would be hard to find a bookie who would give even reasonable odds about the 'after'.

The fifth docket was of a thirty-one-ship convoy from Freetown to Liverpool. There were many pages of paper which were simply epitaphs to eight of its thirty-one ships sunk by a single U-boat inside the convoy. Once again he sketched out a diagram and saw the eight ships had all been in the centre. Again, no pattern – although perhaps the attacks in the centre ought to be regarded as a pattern.

Eleven ships in this convoy had crossed the south Atlantic to Freetown from various South American ports in a small convoy and not seen an enemy. At Freetown they were joined by four American, two Norwegian, one Swedish and three Dutch ships: a cosmopolitan bunch carrying every sort of cargo from frozen meat to palm nuts, with several of the ships which had passenger accommodation (usually for a dozen or so people) bringing back Service officers or, in the case of the ships from South America, men and women volunteering for the Forces. Four such ships had been sunk; of fifty-two passengers, only eleven had survived. Forty-one had died before seeing the shores of the Britain they intended to help defend.

He read through the reports referring to the eight ships and noticed that five of them had each been hit with two torpedoes while the other three had been hit with singles, so the U-boat had certainly fired a total of thirteen.

Yorke picked up his diagram and walked over to Jemmy who glanced up and combined a twitch with a grin when he saw who was standing beside him. 'Solved the riddle, Ned?'

'No, I just want to peer into the devious mind of a submariner. Look, eight ships sunk by the same U-boat. Five are each hit by two torpedoes, but three others get singles.'

'Ten fish expended on five, plus three, makes thirteen fired. Any misses seen?'

'No, not one. No phosphorescence.'

'Thirteen…and a U-boat carries fourteen, so either he missed with one fish that no one sighted, or he kept it in reserve for the trip home. Or one was defective. What do you conclude from all that?'

Ned shrugged his shoulders. 'That convoy was like all the rest of them: when the U-boat joined in he had a full outfit of torpedoes. Which means, I suppose – ' it hit him like an almost physical blow, ' – yes, that it's definitely not chance that puts a U-boat into the middle of a convoy. Every U-boat up to now has had a full outfit of torpedoes. So old Doenitz is planning it in Lorient. Kernevel, rather – or wherever he has his headquarters.'

Jemmy's eyes narrowed and he seemed to be staring at a far horizon. 'Ned, keep on talking...'

'Well, I'm not too sure of that, come to think of it. Most of these convoys are homeward bound, which means they're loaded down and also sailing from places thousands of miles from Lorient. Halifax, Nova Scotia, New York, Freetown and so on. Each convoy I've checked so far was attacked by a U-boat which fired at least a dozen torpedoes. That makes me wonder whether each of these U-boats sighted a convoy by accident, as it were, and somehow got into the middle and attacked until all its torpedoes were used up, or whether the U-boat was there with a full outfit of torpedoes to attack a particular convoy: whether it was sent out from Lorient full of fuel and fish with orders to wait for convoy number so and so in a certain position.'

'You mean, the Teds know when our convoys sail. Or at least the ones that are attacked. Is that likely, Ned?'

Yorke shrugged his shoulders again. 'I'm only thinking aloud. But isn't it too much of a coincidence that the first five "insider" convoys I check were all attacked by U-boats with full outfits of torpedoes? If you command a U-boat what would you reckon on your chances of sighting a particular type of convoy before you'd fired any torpedoes?'

'Pretty good,' Jemmy said. 'After all, most attacks are on convoys, not single ships. But the chances of staying with that convoy are not so good, so I might then find a second convoy with only half my torpedoes left. But Ned, keep thinking on these lines…this last convoy: the chances of a U-boat with a full outfit of fish picking it up just after leaving Freetown does seem a hell of a coincidence. There are so many single ships running along the West African coast – between Freetown, Takoradi, Accra, Lagos, Calabar, Port Harcourt – that…well, it's surprising, to say the least.'

'And the ships hit with two torpedoes, Jemmy?'

'That's either definite orders from U-boat Headquarters or this particular Ted captain thinks a bird in the hand is worth two in the bush.'

'I don't follow you.'

'Well, you have fourteen torpedoes. In theory you should be able to hit fourteen merchant ships. In fact we know from experience and radio intercepts that usually a U-boat is lucky if it sinks four ships on each trip, even when part of a pack. That probably means ten fish missed. Most captains dread running out of fish – they're sure the enormous target of a lifetime will loom up the moment they've used the last one. So even though a captain knows he should fire two fish at every target – which could give him seven ships sunk – he usually tries to get away with firing one. So the Ted attacking your convoy was either acting under orders or he was a realist, an experienced skipper who knew it was better to be certain of one ship for every two fish rather than gamble on one for one. Sensible chap.'

'What would you have done?'

'What I always did, Ned my lad: if it is worth the risk of getting into a firing position, which means farting around at periscope depth, dodging escorts, it's worth firing two fish to make certain of one sinking – after all, you're risking your whole boat and crew. Mind you, occasionally you find a target where all the conditions are perfect and one fish is enough: your Ted found three like that in this convoy, but he wouldn't gamble on the other five.'

Yorke took back the diagram and said ruefully: 'All we've learned from that lot is that a U-boat usually has a barrowload of fish when it meets a convoy.'

'That a U-boat going to attack from *inside* has a barrowload.' Jemmy corrected.

'I'm beginning to dislike submarines and submariners,' Yorke grumbled. 'Why don't you tell me all about 'em? Ted ones, I mean.'

'Right,' said Jemmy, 'grab a notebook and make some notes while I deliver my "Meet the Ted U-boat" lecture. I start off with this gesture – ' he gave a thumbs down sign ' – which means: "We who are about to be torpedoed say ta-ta to the tarts in Trafalgar Square."

'Now, at the moment we reckon Doenitz can keep between 200 and 250 boats at sea at all times. His headquarters are at Kernevel, which is a small town near Lorient. His Atlantic boats can refuel at six places – Brest, St Nazaire, Lorient and Bordeaux, La Pallice and La Rochelle.

'Now for the boats themselves. Various types, so I'll describe the. latest we know about. Commanded by an *Oberleutnant* (occasionally a *Kapitänleutnant*) with a first lieutenant (responsible for torpedoes and gunnery), a second officer (radio and ciphers) and an ensign (similar to a sub-lieutenant) who is the navigator. The engineer is a lieutenant.

'There are signs that Doenitz is getting very short of really experienced captains – we reckon we've sunk about a hundred boats in the last twelve months. We captured Kretschmer, and two of the other aces, Schepke and Gunther Prien (the chap who sank the *Royal Oak*), have been killed. Still, Doenitz has the pick of the German Navy's men, even if he has to promote 'em fast to keep up with new building and losses.

A typical boat – well, 770 tons, 75 metres long, six metres diameter. Twin diesels, of course, which give it nineteen knots on the surface and charging batteries at the same time. Generally they have to recharge every twenty-four hours. Submerged speeds? Well, according to the information we have, they can make a maximum of nine knots submerged for an hour; after that their batteries are almost flat. Or they can chug along submerged at one or two knots for three days – by which time the air is nearly solid.

'Depths? Again, it varies with the type of boat, but the latest we know of can dive safely to 120 metres, which you can call sixty fathoms, or more than 400 feet. The newest boats can probably double that by now.'

Yorke sensed that Jemmy envied and admired the German boats. 'What armament?'

'Fourteen fish, with electric drive, so there's no trail of compressed air bubbles to give 'em away. You'll only spot tracks when they go through patches of phosphorescence. Four tubes forward and one aft. They can fire four in quick time. They're discharged by compressed air, so on the surface in daylight you might spot a few bubbles. Enough to say "Boo" to. So much for fish. In the bang department they have an 88 mm gun – that's the flat trajectory job that's bashing up our tanks in the Western Desert – and a couple of 20 mm cannon for anti-aircraft stuff.'

Yorke finished scribbling notes and then said: 'I know British and German subs are different, but use your imagination and describe what it'd be like in a Ted submarine while she's making an attack. What the skipper is thinking, what happens if she's depth-charged. I want to try to get into the skin of a U-boat commander. Maybe that'll help me working out how he thinks.'

'I can do that,' Jemmy said, 'and better than most because I've been in a U-boat. It's secret that we've ever captured one, so keep your mouth shut, but it's one of the reasons why I'm on this zigzag diagram lark: I'm supposed to be a specialist in Ted submarine tactics.

'Okay, then. You could get the next bit from the Croupier, but I know it and he's busy, so I'll give it to you. You've seen the big gridded chart he's got. The Teds don't use ordinary ocean charts with latitude and longitude – for U-boats, anyway. The charts are gridded, letters of the alphabet in pairs one way and numbers the other. This system probably changes a lot. Anyway, our U-boat surfaces for its night's battery charging and picks up a radio transmission from U-boat Headquarters at Lorient. The message might be something like: Emergency, All U-Boats With Torpedoes Proceed Full Speed To Grid Square AB 64 Where Convoy Expected Pass Six Knots On Course E S E.

'That signal would come over in cipher and the second officer would be called to crank it through the cipher machine. If we had torpedoes and if we could reach AB 64 within a reasonable time, we'd go up to full speed on the surface. If we picked up the signal soon after darkness on a winter's evening, don't forget we can be more than 200 miles away by dawn.

'Once we get to AB 64 we search and if we sight the convoy we might try a daylight attack if we are in the Black Pit, outside the range of Allied planes. Most probably we'd shadow at extreme range until before nightfall, and making sure we're in good attacking position by then.

'We'd shut down the diesels and go on to the electric motors, diving and rigging the boat for silent running. Four fish loaded in the forward tubes, one in the after tube. Motors turning at something between sixty and eighty revolutions. We'd have plotted the convoy's course and speed by now and I'd have had a guess whether they're on the leg of a zigzag or not. I'd be watching the sea water temperature gauges, too, looking for cold water layers. The Teds were lucky. When they captured French warships at the fall of France they captured the Royal Navy's biggest secret – one we should never have shared with the Frogs. They found our Asdic... The magic ping that bounces off the Ted boats and comes back up and registers as a bearing. They also found what we'd long known and kept secret – that the ping won't go through a layer of cold water. All this you know well enough, but I'm like a gramophone record, I have to start at the beginning and go on until the end.

'Anyway, I'd be watching the gauge to see if there's a convenient cold water layer around in case I want to hide underneath it, like a bomber dodging under a cloud to hide from a fighter above, with the difference that the fighter can't come down through the cloud!

'I'd pop up to periscope depth for a few moments every now and again, just to check the convoy hasn't zigged and to try to plot where the escorts are. One might even come towards me and I'd dive deep and shut off everything and no man would move. We'd hear the ping of the Asdic impulses, high-pitched, like a wasp sending dots in Morse. We'd all be breathing shallowly – pure nerves. Then maybe the escort would think she was getting an echo on the Asdic. She might stop, so her own turbines didn't interfere with her hydrophones. If she stops reasonably near we'll be hearing the ping-ping-ping of the bloody Asdic, and the whine of her auxiliary motors and pumps – fantastic how sound travels through water, and anyway our ears are working overtime.

'We'd hear her starting her turbines and there'd be a slowish swishing noise as her propellers started turning. Then maybe we'd hear a single splash, a double and then a single… Which would mean, Ned my old chum, that the escort has dropped a diamond pattern of four depth charges.

'If they explode too near us the boat will groan as though someone is twisting the hull like a dry cigar. There'll be same noisy banging overhead as the pressure waves make deck plates jump. Inevitably the glass of some dials will break – hardly surprising; the jerk you feel from the explosions will loosen your teeth, too – and the inevitable leaks will be reported: propeller shaft packing leaking, valve seats and gaskets letting water trickle in… The main thing is that if there isn't too much water we don't pump it because pumps mean noise and, like the mouse, we know the cat is up there waiting and listening.

'That's about all there is to an attack on the boat. One gets to know the noises well enough – the pounding of the cylinders of a triple-expansion steam engine, the fast drumming of diesels, the singing of steam turbines. They make noise; so do you. The chap with the best ears wins! But the skipper's morale – if he's anything like me – is likely to be more affected if he's been through a long spell of bad weather – North Atlantic winter sort of stuff, when every time the hatch is opened half a ton of beastly cold water crashes down and drains into the bilge, every man comes off watch soaking wet and frozen, trying to dry his clothes, and the humidity down below gets so high it is nearly precipitating into rain in the wardroom. There's condensation streaming down the bulkheads, the damned charts get soggy like blotting paper and when you move the parallel rules across them, the rollers stick and the edges take bites out of the paper, and if they're the sliding sort they won't slide. Everyone's snappy, everybody seems to be farting, and the atmosphere gets vile. The weather's far too bad to keep the hatch wide open...it's the sort of time when you pray for the ammeters and voltmeters to hurry up and show the batteries are charged so you can dive to get out of the rolling and pitching – but diving won't reduce the humidity...'

Yorke smiled as he said: 'I'm sorry when it happens to you, Jemmy, but I'm glad it's hell down there for those Teds! Anyway, I get the picture. Let's say we've attacked and sunk some ships. What do we do now?'

'Well, assuming we've no more fish, we surface at night and transmit a ciphered report to Lorient – something brief like Convoy Grid Square CD 32 Course 090 Six Knots Sunk Three Ships 18000 Tons All Torpodoes Expended Returning Base. That would go off to Lorient, Doenitz would rub his hands, and any other U-boats in the area who didn't pick up the original report on the convoy position would turn up the wick and hurry to grid square CD 32.'

'This would be in U-boat cipher?' Ned asked.

'Yes. Pretty simple stuff because of course as far as the Germans are concerned the Allies know how many ships they've lost in that convoy, they know where it is, and they know U-boats are round the convoy so using direction-finders on the transmission doesn't help much. The route our boat takes back to Lorient can vary by 500 miles north or south of a rhumb line.'

Jemmy waited until Ned had finished writing. 'Any questions? I don't seem to have told you much. You've chased enough U-boats in that destroyer of yours. In fact as far as I am concerned, destroyers are the enemy, no matter whose they are!'

Ned thanked him and went back to his desk, picking up the next docket. The sixth convoy had been attacked five weeks after the fifth, thirty-seven ships bound from Halifax to the Clyde. Five sunk and one more damaged but taken in tow, although finally sunk by the escorts. Five had each been hit with two torpedoes, while the sixth had been hit by one but had seen another miss ahead. Twelve torpedoes definitely fired for a score of six merchant ships, probably two other misses.

He looked at the list of ships and their positions. Fourteen American, sixteen British, three Norwegian, one Dutch, one French, one Swedish and one Greek. All those sunk had been in the centre columns. Weather reasonably good, the attack lasting only four days. No further attacks after the sixth ship was hit, and no pack attacked, although the Submarine Tracking Room report in the docket said there had been a pack passing to the south which subsequently attacked another convoy. He drew the convoy diagram more out of habit than anything else and glanced up to find Joan standing at the side of his desk. 'Uncle would like to see you,' she said. 'Nothing alarming – he just wants to hear how the detective work is going.'

Ned grunted and Joan, glancing at her watch, misunderstood and said: 'Are you meeting her for lunch? It won't take more than fifteen minutes – unless you talk a lot.'

'Thanks for the kind thought, but we said goodbye this morning.'

'Did you have a nice weekend?'

'Yes,' Ned said and without thinking added: 'You look as if you did, too.'

Joan smiled and said, 'Yes, it does wonders for the complexion.'

And, Ned thought to himself, realizing that although Jemmy still had a king among twitches, he seemed much more relaxed in the last few days, it must be good for overworked submariners, too.

Uncle was relaxed like a tiger in the shade after a good meal: comfortable, tractable and cheerful, but ready to spring at a moment's warning.

'How is it going, Yorke? Anything interesting turned up?'

'No, sir. They're all alike. The ships are sunk in the middle of the convoy. From the fourth convoy onwards it seems Doenitz ordered them to fire two torpedoes at every target.' He thought for a moment. Did Uncle want to chat about it all, to throw ideas back and forth, or was he interested only in specifics? Well, there was no harm in mentioning it. 'I've been totalling up the number of torpedoes fired against each convoy, and it seems that every U-boat had a full outfit of fourteen torpedoes on board when he began his attack, or certainly never less than a dozen.'

'Have you mentioned it to Jemmy?'

'Yes, sir: he thinks it is a hell of a coincidence, particularly in cases where the attacks began a day or two out of Halifax, or Freetown. And a hell of a long way to go with a full barrow of fish.'

Uncle picked up a pencil and balanced it across the index finger of his left hand.' A hell of a long way unless your orders were to attack that particular convoy and no other…'

'That's what Jemmy and I thought. But being ordered to attack a particular convoy implies the Ted knew it was due to sail. Which means spies – or else they've broken some of our ciphers.'

'Local spies, most probably. Once ships began to collect it's difficult to keep it secret that a convoy is about to sail. Someone watching in Liverpool or the Clyde, Halifax or Freetown… An agent familiar with ships and even half sober should, from his own observation, be able to estimate the time of sailing within twenty-four hours, probably less. All he needs is a decent pair of binoculars. Or even grandad's old telescope.'

Just how much did one contradict Uncle? He would soon know. 'Yes, sir, but would even forty-eight hours' notice be enough for a U-boat? Supposing the agent could get the warning to Lorient, for example. It means that a U-boat with all its torpedoes would have to be within forty-eight hours' steaming of the port, or the convoy's track, which it would have to know. The later ones can make nineteen knots on the surface, but 450 miles in twenty-four hours isn't…'

Uncle nodded thoughtfully. 'Yes, a fully-equipped U-boat waiting off each of the major ports from here to the New World and to West Africa. Well, that rules out agents with binoculars and mathematical wizards breaking our ciphers. Which seems to leave us ouija boards, black magic, voodoo, telepathy or politicians' promises.'

'I've only gone through five of the eleven convoys so far, sir.'

Uncle shook his head gloomily. 'Unless there are eleven coincidences, there must be a pattern, and that pattern must be in the first five as well as the last six.'

'If there's a pattern if must be like marriage, sir; if you take fifty couples who seem ideally suited to each other, you'll be lucky if you find twenty-five of them are really happy after a year of marriage.'

'You mean there was a pattern for the fifty but it broke down?'

'Not exactly. There *seemed* to be a pattern for fifty but in fact it was valid for only twenty-five, so we have to be careful we don't grab at some pattern just because it *is* a pattern.'

'My dear Yorke, how right you are – about marriage anyway. I've been divorced twice and my third marriage goes through the divorce court mincer next month.'

'I – er, I'm sorry, sir, I – '

'Don't be, my dear fellow; I only mentioned it as proof of your pattern theory. My first wife was quiet, very county, mad on horses; my second was half French, very chic, very animated and loathed the country and all but the most obvious form of sport; my third is a very shrewd businesswoman, runs the estate very well, was a very good rally driver until the war put a stop to all that…no pattern except that for me the path of marriage leads to the divorce court.'

Yorke thought to himself that there was indeed the beginning of a pattern – a county wife mad on horses sounded as though she might be frigid, as did the 'very shrewd business woman', and the pattern was broken by the half-French woman who loathed all but the most obvious form of sport but who didn't stay the marriage course either…

Uncle looked at him from under bushy eyebrows, his eyes twinkling. 'That's the way, Yorke; I want you looking for patterns in everything. And by the way,' he added casually, 'I have to report on our work to the Boss this afternoon.'

'The First Lord, sir?'

'No, I have to go round to Number Ten.'

'"Fraid my contribution doesn't amount to anything.'

'Can't be helped, but it's these inside-the-convoy attacks that are troubling him. He says – and he's quite right – that we'll beat the packs as soon as we get enough escorts because it's simply a question of enough dogs to chase the foxes. But we could beat the packs and still lose an enormous number of ships unless we find out how these insiders operate.'

Yorke suddenly had a mental picture of that chubby pink face with the hooded but sharp eyes looking across at the Citadel from Downing Street as he listened to Uncle's report. Surely he would expect half a dozen men working in watches trying to solve the problem.

'Does the Prime Minister – er, know that...'

'Know that Lt Edward Yorke, DSO, RN, is the only person working on the problem?'

'Well, yes sir,' Yorke said lamely.

'An honest question which deserves an honest answer, but don't let it scare you. Yes, he does; in fact it was his idea. You realize this isn't a new problem: it began eleven convoys ago. It's just that only recently did they spot the "insider" aspect. That's when the Boss started getting angry.'

'He must be raving by now, sir,' Yorke said bitterly, wishing he was back at sea.

'No. From what I know of him and the little experience I have of his methods, he's a queer bird. You know he writes books, histories. Well, it seems he does an enormous amount of research, and then does nothing for ages: he says after the research his mind is like a muddy pool, and he has to wait for the mud to settle. Once the water is clear the ideas come swimming to the surface.'

'Where do I come in, sir?'

'Well, the Boss' idea is that when you have a problem you swot up all the facts without any previous prejudices or ideas – you start off with an open mind, in other words, which in this case the previous chaps who are supposed to study every convoy attack didn't have because they were all anti-submarine specialists with their own prejudices. One of them used to beat a drum for Asdic, another had an idea for faster-sinking depth charges, another wanted faster escorts, and so on. So the Boss quite rightly set up ASIU to deal with the *whole* anti-U-boat question. Just after that, the "insider" was spotted. Finally the Boss told me to look around for one person whose brain he was proposing I should muddy up on the insider problem, with the proviso that when the water cleared some ideas surfaced.'

'And I was that one person?' Yorke asked incredulously.

'Yep. I told you when you arrived that you'd been selected. Don't think you were chosen from the whole Navy List, though. You were available and have seen service. "Smelled powder", as the Boss calls it.'

'So I ought to be living like a monk in a cell, just reading dockets and thinking hard.'

'Not bloody likely. I want seven or eight hours of your time during the day. The rest you can spend as you wish, providing you're creating the state of mind in which, once the water clears, the ideas pop up. The Boss seems to keep going on brandy, cigars and cat naps, late nights and a patient wife. Have you got a girlfriend?'

When Yorke nodded, Uncle asked: 'Where is she? What does she do?'

'Nurse at a hospital down in Kent.'

'Met her while you were having that arm fixed?'

When Yorke nodded, Uncle said, 'Does that mother of yours approve of her?'

'Yes – apparently her family are old friends. I didn't know them, though. I didn't know you knew my mother, sir.'

'I don't really. Met her at various cocktail parties though. If she approves, you must have found yourself a fine girl. What's her name?'

'Clare Exton.'

'Oh yes,' Uncle said, picking up a pen and writing on a pad. 'Must be old Bunko Exton's daughter. And where's the hospital?'

'At Willesborough in Kent, beyond Ashford. An annexe of St Stephen's. But why…?'

'Don't you wish she was up here at St Stephen's, rather than the other side of Kent?'

'Why, of course, sir, but perhaps she…'

'As far as winning the war is concerned, my lad, it's far better that she's up here holding your hand, or whatever, than being in the Weald of Kent. However, you'll register suitable surprise when she tells you of her transfer back to town. Now, anything more to report?' When Yorke shook his head, Uncle stood up and said: 'I estimate we have a month to six weeks left. By then we'll have to see our way to getting enough escorts to break the packs, and we'll have to know the secret of the insiders. Otherwise we'll have lost the Battle of the Atlantic and we'll face starvation and maybe not surrender but – well, that's when I switch off thinking.'

CHAPTER EIGHT

When Clare arrived back in her room at Willesborough annexe later on Monday afternoon she found that the village a couple of miles away where Ned had spent his childhood had taken on a new atmosphere or, rather, that she felt a part of it. Ned and his mother had told several stories of happenings there, of disasters at Yorke House when they had given fetes in aid of local charities, of the day an elephant from a passing circus lumbered through the gate and sat down on the lawn, sucking water from the ornamental pond and squirting it out of his trunk at his distraught trainer who rushed round picking up the goldfish.

Of Ned as a little boy running out 'to smell the traction engine' – two breweries still used the coal-fired steam engines for delivering barrels of beer to local public houses. And how he was always excited by the red Trojan van which had solid rubber tyres and a chain drive and belonged to a tea company. And the ting-a-ling of the bells of the tricycles belonging to two rival ice-cream companies, and the tension for Ned as to whether he could get some money from his mother before the ice-cream man had pedalled past. A penny for an Eldorado vanilla, Ned had remembered, or twopence for a Walls choc ice. A jolly fat man had the Eldorado tricycle and always opened and closed the lid of the icebox between the two front wheels with a cheery bang, and occasionally let Ned climb up and peer in at the mysterious white block which smoked inside – solid carbon dioxide, the man had told a disbelieving Ned, who had never heard of 'dry ice'. The red Post Office van still passed the house at half past seven in the evening, as it had years before, indicating the time by which Ned had to be home, and the trouble there was the night when Ned, having climbed a difficult tree a mile away to get at a magpie's nest, had been too terrified to get down because a branch had split – too terrified, that is, until he saw his angry father approaching through the gathering darkness. That, and the knowledge that it must be ten o'clock, had made him brave the branch–which did not break. The trouble was, Ned had added ruefully, that the crack was on the upper side of the branch and could not be seen from the ground, and his father had not believed his story.

There was the village shop, Mr Wilkinson's, that sold Barrett's sherbet dabs for a halfpenny each, a thin tube of liquorice sticking up from the yellow cylinder, and on one wall was a big poster advertising a blend of tea and showing 'Peter the Planter', a handsome man heavily sun-tanned and wearing a rakish topee. 'Not a drop of perspiration on his face,' Ned had commented, 'and in the tropics now no one wears a topee, except certain regiments, and Peter the Planter's type of topee blows off in anything over a five-knot breeze.'

Mr Wilkinson's shop was so tiny that three customers had to stand with their elbows tucked in and be careful their shopping baskets did not upset the advertising display cards the old man could not resist, lodging one behind the other on the shelves so they looked like thin gravestones in a crowded cemetery.

Rheumy-eyed, with flowing hair and an immense white walrus moustache stained brown on the left side from the Woodbine that perpetually smouldered, rather than was smoked, Mr Wilkinson treated small boys with the utmost gravity as they came in with their pennies, starting the bell fixed to the top of the door by a short piece of leaf-spring steel tinkling merrily. 'What can I get you, young sir?' he invariably said, looking over the top of tiny, rimless pince-nez, the Woodbine giving him the air of a raffish Mr Pickwick.

The whole shop always smelled of paraffin, which he stocked (few houses had electricity at that time) and sold from a leaky can, along with lamp wicks, complete Valor stoves and Aladdin mantles.

The shop was still there – Clare had visited it half a dozen times – but 'T H Wilkinson, Prop., Licensed to sell Tobacco', was long since dead and so was the angular woman he always referred to as 'the wife' and summoned with a stentorian 'Bella' when the shop became crowded and he needed help. Only Mrs Fox (who ran the little sub-post office) knew that when letters arrived for 'the wife' they were addressed to 'Miss Bella Morrell', and Mrs Fox made a point of never revealing the secret to anyone from another village; people, she had once said, did gossip so.

Sherbet dabs, Liquorice Allsorts, along with Sharp's toffees, aniseed balls and gobstoppers still sold from tall glass jars which lined a high shelf – the memory had been vivid for Ned when he described it over dinner in Palace Street, and Clare had confirmed that they were still there.

Then there had been the local forge where a curious Ned, aged perhaps five or six, spent hours watching Mr Ludgate, the blacksmith. A farmer would bring in a great carthorse and Mr Ludgate, a tall and painfully thin man with arm muscles that stood out below rolled-up shirt sleeves like heavy rope wound round a stick, and wore a waistcoat but never a jacket, would tie the halter to an old worn post and then shove against the horse's flank until its rump was near the fire. Then he would bend and lift up a hoof, one after the other, and inspect the old shoes. Clare could not remember the exact sequence, although Ned's word picture had been vivid enough. The great pincers would remove old nails and shoe from a hoof, and the worn shoe would be inspected before Mr Ludgate, giving a non-committal sniff, would toss it with considerable skill halfway across the forge to a corner where it joined an imposing pile.

Then out would come the paring knife and with the horse's hoof held securely against his knee, hard against the leather apron, the blacksmith would pare away some of the hoof, shaping it for the metal shoe. When he started on the last hoof, Ned would move forward a step or two, to make sure Mr Ludgate remembered he was there, and the smith would look up and nod, saying 'Give 'er a blow then, lad.' Ned would rush to the long handle of the bellows and work it up and down, watching the fire change from a dull red pile to a bright red glowing mass as the draught from the bellows roared through it. And then the banging started as Mr Ludgate heated the shoe, hammering and finally slapping it on to the hoof amid smoke and the smell of burning glue. And then the nails would be driven home and each time Ned found it hard to believe it did not hurt the horse, even though the animal stood there quietly enough.

Clare put a match to the fire which had been laid in her room and sat down in the single armchair with her coat on until she was sure the fire had caught. The single bed was Spartan, the blankets of the grey drabness that could only be produced to a Government specification, but the room was large with low ceilings and the uneven oak-planked floor usually found in old houses.

Would Ned ever see Yorke House again? Would she ever see Ned again, or would the Admiralty suddenly send him off to join a ship? She tried to shut off the racing thoughts with the memory that less than twelve hours ago she held him in her arms; she had circled his body with her arms and legs and felt him secure inside her. Secure – for two nights. One day, perhaps, Mrs Yorke would telephone her, or send her the official telegram, and they would be alone again, two women, one a childless widow, the other a mistress without a lover. Maudlin thoughts, but war widows were a commonplace these days and it was impossible to believe that having met Ned the war would leave them alone.

At that moment she saw a buff envelope on the small table, secured against random draughts by an ashtray. It was addressed in handwriting to 'Nurse Exton' and she opened it to find a brief note from Sister Scotland saying: 'See me when convenient, JMS'. She glanced at her wristwatch. It was only five thirty so now was a 'convenient' time. She checked the blackout curtain, put the wire guard in front of the fire, picked up her torch and went along the corridor to Sister Scotland's room.

The smile was neutral. 'Ah, Nurse Exton – you had a pleasant weekend, I trust? And how is Lieutenant Yorke's arm – he's still doing the exercises, I hope?'

There was no point in telling Sister that the scars were now in his mind; that the pink and purple bands and white lines lacing his forearm and hand left him embarrassed; he had seen too many young women look and suddenly glance away; he had heard too many young and old women gush and sympathize in stereotyped phrases. Embarrassed? She had the feeling that he was nauseated by it, with all the horror an otherwise completely healthy person had for a deformed limb. Not that there was any deformity; simply that Ned could not (or would not) understand that within a year the flesh would return to its normal colour; that by then scarcely anyone would notice it – and even if they did, what did it matter: had he not seen the terrible facial scars of aircrews?

'Yes, Sister, he's doing his exercises and there seem to be no adhesions. He wished to be remembered to you, by the way.'

Sister Scotland nodded in acknowledgement as she walked over to the table which served as a desk. 'Matron telephoned from London late this afternoon. Did you meet anyone from St Stephen's while you were in London?'

The question was casual – too casual, Clare realized. 'No, I spent most of my time with a former patient and his mother!'

Sister Scotland smiled. 'It doesn't matter – it's simply that Matron gave instructions for you to return to London tomorrow and be ready to start day duty at St Stephen's on Wednesday. I was afraid that – well, that you had run into some kind of trouble, but she assured me all was well. She was suitably mysterious as to why Nurse Exton's services were so urgently required, but she did mention that a request had come from outside the hospital.' A request, Sister Scotland had guessed from the tone of Matron's voice, though she did not mention it to the nurse standing in front of her, that had both impressed and puzzled Matron.

'I shall be sorry to leave here.'

'And I shall be sorry to lose you. I don't envy you going back to the bombing, but you'll be able to see more of Mr Yorke.'

'I hope so, Sister, but his new job at the Admiralty takes up most of his energies.'

'Is it a secret, or can one ask…?'

'Secret – he's never hinted to me what it is.'

'Well,' Sister Scotland said grimly, 'at least he's not at sea. He's done his share.'

At noon on Tuesday, just as the London train for which Clare was waiting on the platform of Ashford Station slowed

146

down after passing the signal box at Smeeth, Ned Yorke looked at the eleven dockets piled in front of him. He had gone through them all, and no revealing pattern had emerged. At what point, he wondered, did he report to Captain Henry Watts, DSO, DSC, that he had no ideas? It was all right for the man at Number Ten, Downing Street, to talk to Uncle about mud settling and ideas springing up through the clear water, but solving the problem of the convoy insider was not like waiting for the inspiration to write a book. He had never written a book, but he was sure it bore no relation to checking through dockets – more like plodding police work, surely?

Jemmy had twitched his way through all Ned's diagrams showing the position of the ships in each convoy when they were torpedoed; he had gone over each zigzag diagram with Ned. They knew on which leg of which zigzag diagram each convoy had been when the attack started. They had examined carefully the fact that no convoy had zigged or zagged while an attack was in progress and both he and Jemmy had agreed that it would have made no difference; zigzagging a convoy at night was like trying to get a herd of blindfolded elephants to do the Palais Glide; they were keen to oblige but lacked the finesse.

'It's position that matters, not speed…' The phrase from the Admiralty's current Fighting Instructions came to mind and although it had been proved wrong time and time again from Jutland onwards and most recently in the sinking of the pocket battleship the *Graf Spee*, did it have any relevance for these convoys?

Position…his own diagrams had shown the position of the torpedoed ships. They had been torpedoed at random, it seemed, within the limits of being more or less in the middle of the convoy. The middle of the convoy…who chose which ships were to be in the middle? Usually it was a matter of chance; only the leaders of the columns were specially picked, ships whose captains were known to be steady men and good station-keepers, because in gale or calm, fog or the darkest of nights, they were expected to keep the ship on course with the leaders of the columns on either side usually two hundred yards away. That distance, a cable in seamen's language, normally governed a convoy's life: each ship was a cable astern of her next ahead and a cable from the ships on either side. So the insider's victims were chosen at random – chosen, that is, by the commodore of the convoy and the escort commander, who drew up the convoy plan, with the ultimate selection being made by the Ted captain of the U-boat, the ghost who could materialize in the middle of a convoy with a dozen or more torpedoes under his arm.

Cargoes – were the victims carrying particular cargoes, like tanks or planes? He could check by going through the dockets again, but it would be impossible for a U-boat to pick out specific ships during the night attack. Yet…

There was one last thing he could do, which was to draw up a table giving all the details of all the ships in each convoy, and marking those that were torpedoed. It was the last chance of noting a pattern and he would include apparently irrelevant things like whether a ship was a motor ship or coal-fired; single or twin screw…

Jemmy was humming to himself as he worked at ways of beating the zigzag diagrams; the Croupier was sharpening a pencil before drawing in more bearings on his gridded chart. The other four officers were at their desks, absorbed in their tasks. The pipes running along two sides of the room gave an occasional gurgle; in the distance there was a sporadic whoosh as a message carrier sped along the pneumatic tube. A man who had used this desk at some time in its long life had a habit of resting a burning cigarette along the edges so that in places the wood had blackened, scalloped sides.

He walked over and cadged an old chart from Jemmy: the back of it would provide a large enough area for him to draw out the spaces for the entries in his list. Now, what facts did he want? Nationality? Hardly important, since they were all sailing in an Allied convoy, but the information was given in the dockets so he might as well include it. Tonnage – gross, net registered, and deadweight. The length wasn't given but he could get that from Lloyds Register. Steam or motor. Single or twin screw. Cargoes – no need to do much more than differentiate between one ship laden with tanks, guns and lorries and another bringing home grain. Which zigzag diagram the convoy was using at the time of the attack (Jemmy would never forgive him if he omitted that). Details of the escort. Total torpedoes fired in a complete attack, with the number of hits and misses (misses where the torpedo tracks were sighted of course). When, where and how the U-boat was sighted during an attack (it had happened only three times, all during bad-weather attacks at night, when the U-boat could not use its periscope effectively because of the height of the waves). Weather conditions during the attacks – including the amount of phosphorescence when any was present. Date on which the convoy sailed and the port. The identity of the Ted U-boat skipper where the Submarine Tracking Room had been able to discover it from his signals, ciphers or other secret methods. Whether or not the ships and escorts used parachute flares to light up the convoy – this was occasionally done when attacks were made on the surface. He continued noting down headings and then drew out the diagram.

This, involving clearing his desk to spread out the chart, brought Jemmy and the Croupier. 'Spring cleaning?' inquired Jemmy, 'or wrapping up Christmas presents?'

'Don't tease the lad,' the Croupier said, 'he's run out of ideas.'

Ned glowered at him. 'How did you guess?'

'You have that sort of trapped look, as though a girl just phoned to say her period is four days overdue...and you know you were only doing her a favour. We all get it, lad, it's part of working in ASIU – and having girlfriends.'

'It'll pass,' Jemmy added. 'Usually they find they made a mistake in their diary. Girls I mean. I'm not so sure about U-boats. Come and have some lunch.'

Yorke shook his head. 'I want to get on with this.'

'Don't overwork that tiny brain,' Jemmy said. 'It'll overheat.'

'No,' Yorke said, 'I want to get this diagram drawn out while the idea is fresh in my mind.'

Clare found an empty carriage and climbed in, hoisting her suitcase up on to the rack after taking out a book to read. She tucked her ticket in the top pocket of her grey tweed suit, ready for the ticket inspector who would soon amble along with his clippers and probably want to pause for a chat. 'Charing Cross, madam? Pr'olly be a few minutes late...' and on it would go from there because today she would welcome it.

Standing on the 'up' platform of any station should cheer a person surely because the mere fact it was 'up' and not 'down' meant the trains coming to it were bound for a more important destination than the ones going the other way. She had previously heard the ancient porter over on the 'down' platform calling the destinations for the train due from London, his Kentish accent broad as he started off with

'Smeeth, Westenhanger, Sandling Junction…' and finished up with a triumphant '… Walmer, Deal and Sang-wich!'

But he had most fun with the little two-carriage waiting on the other side of that platform for passengers. It went to Canterbury, calling at Wye, Chilham and Chartham (whose first two letters were pronounced as they were in Chatham and Chiswick), but the porter was already having his regular joke, crying out to the few people on the platform that the little train was for 'Why kill 'em and cart 'em to Can-ter-bury…' Clare had a feeling that the old porter and the joke dated back to the opening of the branch line.

Stations on the line…nameless, cold and draughty, the waiting rooms of some lit with weak electric light bulbs, others depending on hurricane lamps. She glanced up as the engine gave enormous huffs and puffs and the train started moving, doors slamming as porters swung those left open by thoughtless passengers. The posts which once were topped by boards proclaiming Ashford were missing; like the signposts on the roads they would have helped German parachutists if (or was it when) England was invaded. The train began chattering as it passed over the points and gathered speed so that in a minute or two it would be clear of the terraces of houses and out into the gently rolling countryside of the Weald, passing within a few yards of farmhouses and so familiar that hens pecking in the grass did not look up and a sheepdog scratched itself, unconcerned at the roaring giant: both knew the giant never moved off the rails; it passed like the sun and the moon and with the same regularity.

Suddenly Clare felt alone; not just lonely but terrifyingly alone. Two months ago, before chance brought a patient called Edward Yorke to St Stephen's Hospital, she had been alone. As Nurse Exton, a war widow, she had neither husband nor parents. There were a few distant relatives whom she knew but rarely saw, but she had never felt alone or lonely. Her marriage, she realized, had been such a shock that she had quite deliberately made herself self-contained. She had stayed away from people, keeping them at a distance whoever they were: polite but aloof and risking being thought a cold woman. She had surprised herself one day when she realized she was quite unconcerned about what people thought: other nurses were nice enough but more concerned with finding supplies of lipstick and silk stockings and ways of getting back into the nurses' quarters after the door was officially locked at midnight. The men patients tried to flirt and because most of them had been wounded in action she was pleasant, but she always made sure it remained a nurse-and-patient relationship: she would do shopping for them during her time off, post letters, even meet elderly parents at the station and bring them to the hospital for special visits, but it had stopped there – until Ned Yorke had arrived, and the time came when she had seen his eyes watching her, had seen the distress in his face when she had pretended to be angry over the teasing about the crooked stocking seam. Then the stick of bombs had started falling and she was certain one would hit the ward and kill them all, and she had in a second suddenly known that she wanted to die with him and had flung herself across his body in the bed.

Since then – well, 'the courtship had run its normal course', but suddenly, on this train, in this compartment decorated with sepia prints showing the peacetime delights of resorts served by the Southern Railway and the warning that pulling the communication cord ('Improperly', a piece of jargon that always made her want to giggle) would cost five pounds, she felt both alone and lonely.

Why now, of all absurd times? In London – not five hundred yards from Charing Cross station, in fact – Ned was working in the Citadel; half a mile beyond him in Palace Street was Mrs Yorke who had, in a dozen delightfully subtle ways, showed that Clare Exton was a welcome addition to the family… Yet Ned and his mother might be the reason for this feeling. Before she had met either of them she had been self-contained; she had nothing to lose and therefore nothing to fear. She had given no hostages. The German bombers came nightly, the Battle of the Atlantic went on as a vague, grey and frightening rumour, the war was being fought in the Western Desert and caught all the headlines, but apart from a hatred of war because of the misery it brought, she had nothing more to lose.

She went through the polite motions when someone sympathized at her losing her pilot husband (people tended to think he must have been a Battle of Britain hero), and she knew that by now she would have been suicidal had he lived and insisted on her playing at the farce of being his wife. No, she had nothing of value to lose then; her family jewellery was stored in a bank; the inherited family portraits and some other paintings were being kept by a distant cousin whose house was in the depths of the country. With nothing of value to lose she had nothing to worry about. Her house in Norfolk was rented on a long lease to people who looked after it, and anyway it meant very little to her now. Or, rather, it had meant very little to her then. Now she began to think of Ned ambling through the familiar rooms in an old jersey and a pair of grey flannel bags, boots muddy and grinning with pride over some gardening triumph.

Suddenly, since she had met Ned, she had possessions; she had things to lose, or from which she could be parted. Separated from Ned, she felt lonely. If – she forced herself to think about it – anything happened to him, she would be *alone* in a way she could never previously have experienced.

Losing something, in other words, meant first having something to lose. This was the price one paid for falling in love in wartime: the danger could heighten the bliss of being together but it could also mean a parting for ever. She had not got just something to lose but everything, so that the words 'bombers' and 'torpedoes', for instance, took on new and terrible meanings.

The train hurried through Charing as she forced herself to think on, hoping the ticket collector would come and chat for a few minutes, long enough to leave her willing to start reading her book. Supposing something happened to Ned – and it could: his escape this last time must have been a miracle, and she now knew him well enough to understand that his refusal to talk about it told her more than any words could about the loss of the *Aztec*.

Be thankful for what is rather than fret about what might be, she told herself; he's been appointed to the Admiralty. Presumably such appointments are for at least six months, so they (she, anyway; Ned probably took the 'I could not love thee dear, so much...' view, and unfortunately she both understood and accepted it) had that much time. Those leaflets dropped by the German bombers had said categorically, 'The Battle of the Atlantic has been lost by the British...' Ned had read one and laughed, but she realized now that he had laughed to reassure her because she had found the bundle of leaflets in a field, not because the words were absurd and therefore funny. The Battle of the Atlantic, she saw, *was* being lost; the sinking of Ned's destroyer was but a symptom, like the cheese and sugar ration being cut. And the bombing: people were used to it now (just as well, perhaps) but it went on night after night, gradually battering down London. People said all the big factories were out in the suburbs of London and other cities, and the Germans always bombed the centres and thus missed the factories, but it was hard to believe the Germans could be that silly.

Ned killed, London burning, the Germans invading – in a panicky moment of fantasy she knew she would then take a scalpel and open a vein... And this was Tonbridge: the engine shuddering as the metal brakes pressed against the great wheels. And the face of an old woman appeared at the window, grey hair topped by what was obviously her best hat. Clare lip-read the request to open the door and then realized the woman was holding a battered old case in one hand and a large bundle wrapped up in a counterpane in the other.

'Room for me, dearie?'

Clare helped her in and swung her baggage up on to the rack. The old woman sank down with a thankful sigh after reassuring herself that she had her back to the engine. 'Frightens me to see where we're going' she commented. 'With my back to the engine I don't think about it.'

As the train started pulling out of the station the woman glanced up at her case and package and said conversationally, 'It's me daughter, that's why I'm going to London. Lost 'er 'ubby a month ago, 'e was in the artillery in the Eighth Army. She don't know what 'appened yet; just the telegram from the War Office. But 'er next is due in two weeks – it's 'er third; you'd never think I was a grandma, would you? Anyway, I'm going up to be with 'er when 'er time comes. Going to 'ave to bundle up a bit, though; a bomb took 'arf the roof orf last week. The council 'ave put a tarpauling over it, but it means the spare room is no good – window gone and the ceiling down, and mortal cold with just a tarpauling above. And that shrapning, or shrapnel, or whatever they call it from the anti-aeroplane guns, well, it'd go through the tarpauling like an 'ot knife through butter. Leastways, that's what Betty says, and this is the second time. Lost the whole house last time –

council had to dig 'em out. They got this new place – and now the roof's gone.'

The woman sighed. 'Betty's own bleedin' fault,' she said crossly. 'She won't 'vacuate, see? The council would send her down to the country because of the kids and her expectin', but Betty won't go. I've told 'er a hundred times to come down to me. I got a spare bedroom, but she knows 'aving those kids yellin' and cryin' round the place makes me nervous. Very 'ighly strung, I am; never think it to look at me, would you? But she's too free and easy wiv 'em. I'd give 'em a back 'ander when they play up, but Betty uses the modern method. Very modern she is; just lets 'em yell and scream. I don't 'old with it; a good slap didn't 'arm our Betty.

'Breast feed 'em and slap their bottoms; that's the secret, take it from a grandma. My old man thinks the same. 'E's staying down 'ere on account of there's no room up at Betty's, and we got the two cats, and he wants to get the allotment dug over while I'm away. He gets 'is boots so muddy the 'ouse'll be a pigsty when I get back, but I can't complain; never lifted an 'and to me, not in twenty-seven years of marriage. Well, once, but that was my fault; I was a bit flirtatious when I was a girl – ' her hand went up to make sure her hat was straight, 'not that my 'ubby left me much energy in those days.'

Clare smiled at the woman because there seemed nothing to say; in a matter of three or four minutes the woman had, quite matter of factly, told such a tragic yet heroic story without a word of complaint and obviously without exaggerating, that the only word that came to mind was 'undefeated', and there were millions more like her.

CHAPTER NINE

Ned Yorke closed the last docket, put it back on the pile, and then stared down at all the entries he had made in the big form drawn on the back of the chart. Recorded there, in his own handwriting, was everything of any consequence known about the eleven Allied convoys which had been attacked by U-boat insiders. If no clue emerged from the figures and words he had written in so carefully, then he could see no way of ever beating the insiders, except by putting corvettes and frigates among the centre columns, and with the danger of depth charges exploding beneath Allied merchant ships there was no chance of doing that, even had the escorts been available.

The story told by the bare statistics on the form was frightening: eleven convoys with an average of thirty-three ships – a total of 363. Of those, eighty-eight had been torpedoed by insider U-boats – enough ships to make up two and a half averaged-sized convoys had been sunk, killing 2,376 men (and some women too, passengers coming to England to join the Forces). The lost ships totalled 554,000 tons deadweight.

He looked under the column headed 'Cargo carried' and saw there was not the slightest pattern. Tanks, guns, ammunition, fighters, bombers, fuel oil, high-octane petrol, grain, hides, palm nuts, cotton bales, ingots of copper, steel and aluminium, great reels of newsprint… Cargoes which were vital – but only vital cargoes were ever loaded.

All the zigzag diagram numbers which had been used by the convoys from the day before the first attack until the day after the attack ended were listed. Again, no pattern. Yet where an attack had lasted, say, six nights, the U-boat managed to stay with the convoy despite zigzagging. Even though the underwater speed of a U-boat was only a few knots, the Teds had not been shaken off. No U-boat could make six knots submerged for twenty-four hours, but no U-boat captain, snatching a quick look round with his periscope, could possibly know which particular zigzag diagram the convoy was going to use. The ships themselves had only a brief warning – a flag hoist from the commodore giving the number, followed by another hoist giving the time the first turn would be made…

There was an average of three neutral ships in every convoy; a total of thirty-two had sailed in the eleven convoys and mercifully only four had been hit. He ran his eyes down the list again and realized some were not in fact neutrals now: thanks to some of Hitler's more recent activities, they were Allies: Denmark and Norway, for example. Only two neutrals had been hit, in fact. For a moment he thought of Sunday evenings before the nine o'clock news on the BBC – it had become the custom to play the national anthems of the Allies – France, Belgium, Holland…then more had been added as Hitler overran Europe and the Japs had finally brought the Americans in. Now it took nearly a quarter of an hour to play all the anthems…

The telephone on his desk rang. He made sure the switch was not on 'Scramble' and lifted the receiver. 'Yorke here.'

'Exton here,' Clare said with a giggle. 'Is this a bad time to talk?'

'No, of course not – but is something wrong?' Pleasure struggled with alarm in his voice.

'Don't sound so frightened, darling; I just wanted to hear your voice.'

'You didn't phone last night.'

'I told you I wouldn't. It's a long walk to the kiosk in the village, and it was raining.'

'I know, you're forgiven.' He looked at his wristwatch. 'Hmmm, you should be sleeping. Or is night duty less arduous?'

'I'm on day duty now.'

'Thank heavens for that. Listen; the pips will go in a few moments – have you plenty of change?'

'Don't worry about that,' Clare said airily. 'Now, how is the arm? Any pain?'

'No, just a dull ache. But I told you – I hardly notice it, except on a cold, damp day.'

'And you're doing the exercises?'

'You know I am. Hell, you were watching me the day before yesterday. I say, we're getting a long three minutes, aren't we? And it's a very clear line.'

'Yes,' Clare said, 'very clear. Your mother says dinner is at eight-thirty, so don't be late. Two plump partridges for three.'

'Three? Partridges? What – '

'You'll never make a detective, darling! I'm phoning from Palace Street. Old Walter poached the partridges from somewhere – in fact they're probably your own – and gave them to me when he heard that I was going up to London again.'

'And why, Nurse Exton, are you in London?'

'Because, Lieutenant Yorke, for reasons I don't understand but certainly don't question, I've been ordered back to St

Stephen's. Apparently Willesborough can function without me but St Stephen's can't.'

Ned suddenly recalled a comment of Uncle's made yesterday morning; a remark which Ned had not taken very seriously. Uncle knew which strings to pull, although Ned would have thought it easier for an RN captain to get a destroyer moved halfway round the world than have a nurse transferred. Still, Uncle was also a regular visitor at Downing Street and had obviously picked up a few tricks.

He was bending over his desk holding the receiver, his elbows resting on the big form on the back of the old chart, and as they talked – quite freely because Ned was thankful the rest of the ASIU team were still out at lunch – he found his eyes resting on the entries under the 'Neutrals' column. Only one neutral country had a ship sailing in every one of those convoys.

Eleven times the word 'Swedish' appeared, making not just a pattern but almost a spinal column.

'Ned! Ned! Are you still there?'

Clare's voice came from a long way off and it took a conscious effort to pull himself back to his desk at ASIU in the Citadel: in his imagination he had been watching the pale ice-blue and yellow flag of Sweden streaming out in an Atlantic breeze.

'Sorry darling, yes I'm here again. When do you have to report for duty?'

'Tomorrow, for duty the next day. They are giving me a day or two of leave.'

'Does that mean…?'

'Your mother has been kind enough to invite me to stay tonight.'

'Me too,' Ned said. 'I must go now. I'll be back by six.' He put the receiver back too quickly to hear her say: 'I love you,' and he ran his finger down the column once again, in case his eye had jumped and there was in fact a convoy without a Swedish ship in it which had been attacked. There was none.

Jemmy and the Croupier were still having lunch so it was probably too soon to take the diagram in to Uncle. He pushed the chart away and pulled the pile of dockets towards him. Who owned the Swedish ships? Were they sailing for their owners or were they on charter? He flipped open a notebook, picked up a pencil, and leafed through the first docket until he found the three pages of typing, held together by a rusting paperclip, giving the owners and managers or charterers of the ships in the convoy. Most British ships were under charter to the Ministry of War Transport; the Americans were owned or chartered by the US Maritime Commission. He found the Swedish ship was registered in Stockholm and under charter to another Stockholm company. Six thousand nine hundred tons and twin screw – unusual for a ship that size. Sultzer diesels, as one would expect. He added the details to his big diagram, drawing in extra columns.

The next docket was thicker but he soon found the list of ships and owners. Eight thousand seven hundred tons, twin screw, different owners but same charterers. The Swede in the third convoy was roughly the same size, owned by the same company as the first – and was under charter to the same Stockholm firm. But single screw – did that show the fact that the first two were twin screw was just a coincidence? But the same charterer for the Swedish ships in the first three convoys – was that a pattern?

Quickly he worked his way through the remaining dockets, noting down all the details, until finally his notebook and diagram showed that the eleven Swedish ships were owned by four different shipping companies, most were twin screw (although three were single), all were motor ships, none was smaller than 6,500 tons and none bigger than 9,500. All were chartered by the same company. All had been in the third, fourth or fifth columns and were usually fourth or fifth in a seven-ship column. In other words the convoy commodore and escort commander had always given them the safest positions. And, of course, not one had been lost.

That set off another train of thought, and Yorke referred back to his other lists. Yes, not one of the neutral ships lost was Swedish.

He went through his convoy diagrams, where the positions of torpedoed ships had been marked. He picked up a red pencil and on each convoy diagram he put a red ring round the Swedish ship and then checked the position in relation to it of the ships that had been torpedoed. There was no particular pattern; a few were ahead or astern, though most were to port or starboard. None was far off, but most of the insider victims were close to the centre of the convoy anyway.

The time had come for a quick walk in St James's Park to ease the anger mounting in him and clear his head so he would be ready for all the questions that first Jemmy and the Croupier would raise, and then Uncle. He would need to think hard during the walk; it was possible that he had found a pattern – there was no doubt about it in fact. What mattered was whether the pattern had a damned thing to do with U-boat insider attacks. Was it significant or just a coincidence?

As he locked up his papers before leaving the room he found the exhilaration and anger which had been sweeping him along for the past fifteen minutes were vanishing; like a sailing dinghy slowing down as the gust of wind died and the wave crest passed on ahead, he realized he had done nothing concrete towards beating the insiders; he had merely found a possible pattern. A possibly significant pattern rather. He had been struggling so hard to find a damned pattern that he had made the mistake of thinking that finding one would reveal the answer.

A pattern...a pattern...a pattern...he kept repeating to himself as he climbed the stairs up to the ground-floor level in the old building next to the Citadel and, showing his pass, went through the main door and up the few wide steps past the Captain Cook statue, turning left along the Mall and leaving Admiralty Arch behind him, buried under its layers of soot and bird lime.

Swedish owners, all motor ships, mostly twin screw, and all chartered by the same firm. The patterns were thus – first, Swedish; second, same charterers; third, all motor ships (but these days most modern ships were); most were twin screw – which was unusual in these smaller sizes. They were definite threads in the pattern – even individual patterns in a whole design. Less definite (the thing that Uncle might well decide was mere coincidence) was that no Swedish ship had ever been torpedoed in one of the convoys.

There were a couple of dozen other men in uniform striding about St James's Park, and a few civilians. Half a dozen of them seemed to Ned to be men with unsolved problems waiting on their desks. Another half-dozen were clearly keep-fit fiends who made it a rule to walk twice daily around the Park. A red-tabbed and red-capped brigadier with two rows of medal ribbons, including most of the tough ones from the First World War, was clearly hoping a brisk walk would help him sober up, He looked shocked and sad rather than harassed and puzzled, and Ned wondered if he had been using his club bar to drown some private sorrow; a son killed on some distant battlefield, perhaps, because the man looked like a link in what was often called a 'military family'. He might have a son of thirty who could have spent the last year fighting in the Western Desert, and whose luck had at last run out...

There were half a dozen whores, middle-aged, but perky and bright-eyed even though the night bombing obviously affected trade and cost them their beauty sleep. Their dresses were clean, but frequent ironing was leaving a shine not intended by the makers of the fabric. So far, Ned reflected bitterly, he had speculated about a possibly bereaved Army brigadier and a few game old whores, one of whom winked as he went by and another who smiled wryly and said: 'You ain't on leave are you, Jack?' He had walked nearly half a mile and not thought once about the Swedes and the convoys.

What was there to think? Sitting in an underground room in the Citadel was not going to find any more answers. The eleven dockets had been drained, squeezed and stripped of every fact, pattern or gobbet of information that stood any chance of answering the question of how the insider got into the convoy in the first place and managed to stay there until it had used up all its torpedoes and left, transmitting to Doenitz its number of kills and then making for Lorient or Brest, where leave, French wine and pliant women waited...

Piles of large leaves, gold and brown, swirled round the trees along the Mall; two Guardsmen saluted smartly; Buckingham Palace and its trees formed the western horizon behind the Queen Victoria statue. Farther to the west, hundreds and thousands of miles beyond, there was probably a convoy plodding its way across the grey wastes of the North Atlantic winter, bound for Liverpool or the Clyde, with a U-boat like a rapid cancer in its midst and every man in every ship knowing that as soon as it was dark the insider's torpedoes would start to run... Equally, a U-boat captain was perhaps glancing at the convoy every hour or so, confirming its course, perhaps choosing his victims for the night.

Supposing that somehow the Swedish ship in every convoy was in fact the key to the insiders – what then? Would the Government refuse to allow Swedish ships to sail in British convoys? They would need plenty of hard evidence before making such a decision: they were treading very lightly with the Swedes as it was, trying to ensure they could buy the vitally needed Swedish ball-bearings, and knowing the Swedes allowed troop trains to pass back and forth through their country carrying Germans to Norway. The Germans and Prussians were traditional friends of Sweden and the cynic might say that with Britain apparently on her knees and Denmark and Norway occupied, this was no time to expect the Swedes to turn on her old friends.

How to prove it? And, having proved it, what to do about it? He found himself walking along Birdcage Walk knowing that, for all the good he was doing, he might as well walk the extra few hundred yards to Palace Street and see Clare. Army dispatch riders, Air Ministry cars, the wide tyres noisy on the road… He turned left to cross Horseguards Parade and fifteen minutes later was back in the ASIU room two floors below ground level in the Citadel.

Jemmy and the Croupier were busy at their desks and Ned unlocked his papers and spread the old chart face downwards on his desk, so that the enormous form could be read. He opened his notebook, and then called to the two other men. When they came over he gestured at the form.

'That shows the guts of the material in the dockets.'

Jemmy sniffed like a pointer testing the wind and ran a finger across the headings. 'Jesus,' he said, 'who *cares* who owns the bloody ships, and what does it matter what they're carrying? They all get sunk!'

'Read out the entries to him,' Ned told the Croupier crossly, irritated by Jemmy's manner. 'He gets tripped up by words of more than one syllable.'

The Croupier was already scanning the columns and he remained silent for two or three minutes reading the entries, while Jemmy huffily lit a cigarette. Finally the Croupier sighed. 'The bloody Swedes… All this time they've been shitting on us from the sanctity of a neutral flag. Has Uncle seen this?'

Jemmy, startled, bent over the form. 'I was looking at the zigzag numbers. Nothing of interest there.'

Ned shook his head in answer to the Croupier. 'No. I only spotted it when you were both out at lunch, and I took a turn round the Park just to sort out my thoughts.'

'You've checked all this?' Jemmy asked. 'I mean, you've gone through the dockets again just in case there was one convoy without a Swede in it?'

'Yes. I did that straight away. I was hoping there was one,' he admitted. 'Their Lordships are likely to shoot the bearer of bad news.'

The Croupier gave a short and bitter laugh. 'No, TL will be delighted. But don't accept a drink from anyone at the Foreign Office because it'll be poisoned. It was the Foreign Office (in its infinite wisdom, of course) that insisted we allow neutrals into our convoys. I once saw an FO minute on the subject. Said letting in neutrals like the Swedes – yes, they damned well mentioned the Swedes as an example, come to think of it – would "create a good impression". Well – ' he ran his fingers along to the total under the 'losses' column, 'it looks as though they were right: an "impression" on eighty-eight ships.'

'We ought to get this in to Uncle right away,' Jemmy said. 'You have the facts in your noddle, not just written down?'

When Yorke nodded he added: 'I warn you, Ned, that when Uncle starts questioning he sounds like the prosecutor in a murder trial. He's going to make damn' sure he's got a case to take to – hell, I wonder who?'

'He reports direct to Number Ten on anything important, with the carbons to the Director of Trade Division and the Assistant Chief of Naval Staff, U-boat Warfare and Trade.'

'Come on then,' Jemmy said impatiently, 'don't forget there are convoys at sea while you two girls gossip. Now, tighten your brassiere straps and bring that form and your notebook. Lock the bloody dockets up in case one of those security chaps comes snooping round. Let me get my stuff put away.'

As Ned waited for the other two he saw Jemmy take a docket from a drawer and noticed it had "Secret" in red letters on the front. Jemmy placed it squarely on the blotter and then came over to Ned. 'Ready?'

'What's that?' Ned asked, pointing at the docket.

'Oh, that's Jemmy's Revenge. One of the security chaps had me hauled up before Uncle for leaving some low-grade nonsense on my desk. That docket has nineteen pieces of toilet paper in it, each sheet marked top and bottom "Medicated with Izal Germicide" and with my signature in red pencil in the middle. It's like a fisherman setting night lines,' he added miserably. 'So far the bloody fish have stayed at the other end of the river.'

The arrival of three of his 'boys' warned Uncle of an emergency. Chairs were pulled up, Joan was sent off to find tea or coffee, and then Captain Watts glanced at Ned.

'How do they do it?'

Ned shook his head. 'No idea, sir But I think I've found a starting point.' He handed over the folded chart with the form drawn in on the back. 'If you'll look at this a moment... It is all the data in the dockets of the eleven convoys put down in tabulated form.'

Captain Watts was no longer Uncle; he was a man who had won a DSO and DSC in action, had several mentions in dispatches, and commanded the Anti-Submarine Intelligence Unit responsible direct to the Prime Minister. The three young lieutenants watched as his eyes locked on a heading and slowly went down the column below it. Would he spot it? Ned wondered. Would it be best to mention the Swedes now, so that Uncle would not be embarrassed if he did not spot it? He caught Jemmy's eye and saw his head move a fraction, a negative shake, before it was overtaken by a twitch. Jemmy knew Uncle better than most...

Uncle's eyes went over column after column and Ned's heart sank. The nationality, owner and charterer columns were at the beginning on the left hand side of the form, and now he was reading the last column on the right. Then he dropped the chart on his desk and looked hard at Ned and said: 'Checked and double-checked?'

'Yes, sir.'

'No chance that there's even one convoy which didn't have a Swede?'

Ned shook his head. 'Nor one case of a Swede being torpedoed.'

'How many ships altogether in the eleven convoys?'

'Three hundred and sixty-three.'

'Torpedoed?'

'Eighty-eight.'

'How many neutrals sailed in these convoys?'

'Sixty-nine. Only four were torpedoed.'

'Charmed life for neutrals, but they're given the safest positions. Fair enough – they can't sail alone...'

'Damned if I know why not, sir,' the Croupier grumbled.

'They'd be all right at night, all the accommodation lit up and navigation lights, but what about daylight, eh? What U-boat is going to waste time manoeuvring close to see what flag she's flying? Painting a great flag on each side doesn't work either – shadow from the sun or a position ahead and you can't see it through a periscope. Bad enough checking them at the beginning of the war from a surface ship, when the Americans painted a big Stars and Stripes on each side and thought it'd be a talisman. I was commanding a destroyer at the time and it took ages checking if they were up sun, or it was a hazy or foggy day. What do you reckon, Jemmy?'

'I agree, sir. In daylight if I saw a juicy merchant ship steaming towards me I'd fire two fish. Farting around, "up periscope, down periscope", is just asking for trouble – air attack, being spotted by an escort, being spotted by the target herself. The point is one isn't *expecting* a neutral.'

Captain Watts tapped the chart. 'These Swedes – eleven of 'em, but different owners, I see.'

'Yes, sir. Several different companies, but – '

'Yes, I've noticed: every ship under charter to the same firm. Know anything about it?'

'No, and there's no clue in Lloyd's. I was thinking that Naval Intelligence could ask our naval attaché in Stockholm...'

'Yes,' Uncle said shortly, 'I wasn't proposing to send you there for a month's leave among the Nordic blondes. But so what, gentlemen? What does it all mean? Every convoy has a silver lining in the shape of a Swedish ship, and every Swedish ship is under charter to the same charterers. Then what happens?'

'The charter company is operating for the bloody Germans,' Ned said bluntly.

'Obviously,' Uncle snapped. 'And even if there'd been eleven different companies chartering the ships, you can bet your last fiver that all eleven would be owned by or working for the Jerries. That's a fact of life with the Swedes – but,' he said quietly, enunciating every word clearly, 'that still doesn't put a U-boat in the middle of a convoy and it doesn't keep its batteries charged so it can stay submerged for days and continue firing away until it has no fish left…'

'You think it is just a coincidence, sir?' Jemmy asked miserably.

Captain Watts shrugged his shoulders and waited while Joan came in and handed round cups of tea. Watts inspected his cup. 'Why do I always get the chipped one? I'll bet you've given Jemmy a good one.'

'Yes, sir,' Joan said matter of factly. 'When I complained about the same sort of thing at Euston Station buffet the old trout serving tea told me there was a war on.'

'Wren officers aren't supposed to drink tea in railway buffets.'

'At five o'clock in the morning after an all-night journey standing in a corridor I'll drink tea anywhere, sir – with respect – and anyway, that was before I was commissioned.'

'The quality is going down,' Uncle remarked conversationally to Ned. 'Not like it used to be. Much lower standard…weaker…not so sweet. I mean tea, m'dear,' he said to Joan, 'but by Jingo, you've a guilty look on your face.'

When Joan had left the room, Captain Watts said: 'I'll get NID to make some inquiries through the naval attaché in Stockholm about that chartering firm. I can guess the answer – just a shop front for the Jerries. Still, the NA in Stockholm is a bright lad; in my term at Dartmouth.'

He sipped his tea and made a wry face. 'God, war is hell… Now, supposing all the answers are yes: yes, the charter firm really is Jerry, yes, of course the Swedish ships get all the secret papers (Mersigs, zigzag diagrams and so on) – where does that get us? A copy of merchant ships' signals may have "Secret" printed on the cover, but what the hell, it gives flag signals which won't help a U-boat. Zigzag diagrams might be helpful–what do you think, Jemmy?'

Jemmy shrugged his shoulders. 'Might help U-boat Headquarters in Lorient when instructing fledgling Jerry navigators, but a U-boat skipper could be clutching a copy in his hand as he attacked and it wouldn't help – not at the underwater speeds we know about. Even add five knots for something fancy, and it still doesn't help.'

'We seem to be back at square two,' Watts said heavily. 'We've passed square one with the throw about the Swedes. We can't pass square two until we find out if there is any link between the Swede and the U-boat inside the convoy. I'm not a communications wallah, but I'm certain our escorts would pick up any chitchat on the wireless between the two, even if the Jerries have some exotic frequencies. Anyway, I'll have a word with our experts. Any ideas?'

The Croupier said: 'We need to know if the U-boat stays inside the convoy during the day.'

'She has to surface for several hours to charge her batteries,' Jemmy said, 'so she can't even if she wanted to. So she has to leave and then rejoin the convoy. Christ, that's what puzzles me.'

'So if the convoy zigged or zagged during daylight, she'd have a long run on the surface to charge batteries and catch up,' Uncle said.

Jemmy shook his head. 'That's easy. I can tell you how I'd do it and that's the way the Jerry would do it, because it is the only way. Blast away in the dark firing fish like a run-amok Billingsgate fish porter starring in a Western film, then dive deep, preferably under a layer of cold water so the Asdic can't penetrate, and wait for everyone to pass, particularly any escort coming up astern after acting as a rescue ship.

Then, with the convoy a dozen miles ahead – two hours' steaming – I'd surface, start charging, and follow the convoy. A set of zigzag diagrams wouldn't help because once it was out of sight I wouldn't know which zigzag it was using but a bit of high-speed steaming on the surface around teatime would find the convoy – there's always smoke, or some bloody fool commodore doesn't realize how dark it is getting and rips off a long signal using an Aldis lamp. Even those little blue signal lamps can be seen a fair distance. And on a quiet night if the wind is blowing from the convoy, you can smell the diesel exhaust fumes. Yep, I know that's hard to believe, but don't forget the Jerry skipper and his mates have spent the whole day in the fresh air and their own diesel fumes are also blowing astern... Anyway, by the time the stewards are mixing the cocoa ready for the night-watch men, the U-boat has sneaked up astern on the surface, ready to dive the moment an escort is sighted...'

Watts pulled the chart towards him and ran his finger down the column giving the positions of the convoys when they were attacked, and even as he did it Ned realized he had not thought of one perhaps vital factor, the one that had obviously just occurred to Uncle.

He mumbled figures and then pushed the chart away. 'Every attack was made in the Black Pit... Not one attack started while the convoy was still within range of our planes.'

Jemmy coughed. 'I didn't bother to mention that, sir: no U-boat would dare belt along on the surface if there was any risk of a Sunderland or a Liberator – or even those weird-looking Catalinas – thundering down, dropping death and destruction and making Hans upset his *Stein* of good *Tedeschi* beer.'

'Very well,' Uncle said, 'since we can invent our own rules for this game we'll call that square two passed: all attacks made outside the range of air cover.'

Jemmy protested, 'I deserve a square, sir, for my description of the boat dropping astern to charge batteries and then sneaking back.'

Captain Watts looked doubtful. 'Well, Jemmy, it sounds likely enough, but your story gets a bit weak at the end. With the convoy ahead there comes a point when the U-boat has to dive to get back into the middle of it. With such a low underwater speed and endurance and the convoy making six knots, if the U-boat can only make seven or so and had to dive six miles astern of the convoy, it'd take her hours to get abreast of the rear ships. By that time her batteries would be flat and we know the attacks usually start within a couple of hours of darkness.'

Jemmy gave a double twitch and wriggled in his chair. Ned knew that Jemmy was thousands of miles away, surrounded by the whine of electric motors, peering out at the horizon through a submarine's periscope for a brief glance at a world measured horizontally and vertically by the range graticules on the lenses. He was trying to think of a way of getting back into the convoy, wondering if the Swede could help, and knowing that the Royal Navy escorts would be crossing the wake of the convoy, guessing that the back door of the convoy, as it were, represented the best way of returning to the hen run.

Finally Jemmy sat up straight and reached out for his cup. 'Christ, she can't make tea,' he grumbled after a sip. 'Still...well, I've no ideas at the moment, sir. So we stay on square two?'

'We stay on square two,' Captain Watts said firmly. 'I'm not trundling my barrow out of the Admiralty building until I've got a better load of rubbish to sell. We'll start looking at the fruit market in Stockholm, but…'

Ned suddenly heard his voice saying: 'There's only one way of finding out, sir, and that's to sail in a convoy close to a Swedish ship chartered by this same firm. Her next ahead or next astern; maybe one on her beam. A powerful pair of glasses, a radio operator and an all-band receiver, and a transmitter to talk to the senior officer of the escort. Board the bugger if necessary. We can use the DEMS gunners as commandos.'

'You want to go?' Uncle asked.

Ned shrugged his shoulders. 'They say those chaps eat well in merchant ships. Would you ask the Director of Trade Division to let us know when the Swedes next apply for a convoy?'

Uncle nodded and then said doubtfully: 'What about that arm and hand of yours? I wangled the transfer of that nurse on the basis that you were a specialist officer who couldn't be spared but needed special medical treatment…'

'I'm the only one who can be spared.' Ned said, gesturing at Jemmy and the Croupier. 'These two beachcombers still have a lot of paperwork to finish…'

CHAPTER TEN

Liverpool in early December with a noontime drizzle that had been falling on its soot-stained buildings for three days had all the gaiety of wet sticks of charcoal planted in a pile of damp grey ash, but the taxi driver was cheerful and Yorke's train from London, delayed for hours by an unexploded bomb on the line ten miles short of the city, had arrived in daylight so that he could join the ship. The taxi had to detour round streets barricaded and blocked because bombs had toppled a building or two across them in untidy piles of rubble or the trestles were hung with the familiar red notices:

DANGER – UNEXPLODED BOMB.

Finally, through gaps in the streets which were like missing teeth in grey gums and showed the damage from two years of intensive night bombing, Yorke saw a few masts. They were stumpy because merchant ships had removed their topmasts to lower their silhouette. Long gone were the coloured stripes or bands on funnels showing the different companies; instead they were all painted a uniform grey, the 'crab fat grey' which in daylight or darkness provided the most camouflage.

'Queen's Dock you said, guv?' the driver said conversationally.

'Yes, number two, Queen's Dock.'

'That's the other end from the entrance we use. You'll need some paper to show the coppers at the gate. Uniform ain't enough these days. Some of these foreigners look like commissionaires so the coppers is tightening up. 'Fraid someone'll go in and drill an 'ole in one of the ships, I s'pose.'

Finally the taxi swung into the great gateway to the dock, an entrance that owed its size to the need to admit heavily-laden lorries rather than a desire to impress. Ships alongside the quays were sharply-angled examples of perspective, their harsh lines in the dull light making the whole scene look like an old print, the paper dulled and foxed, the illustration lacking only the square-sail yards and furled sails to slip back a century or two with ships about to sail in other wars, yet the crews facing the same threat, death. The taxi stopped by a small office at the gate and a policeman came out and saluted.

'What ship was you wanting, sir?'

'The *Marynal*.'

'Ah, the *Mar-ie-nal*,' the policeman said, as if correcting Yorke's pronunciation and certain it rhymed with 'urinal'. 'You have papers, sir? You just visiting her – an inspection?'

'No, I'm joining her.' Yorke avoided speaking the name, which sounded like mariner, and handed over two papers which the policeman read quickly and handed back.

'Thank you, sir: she's the third ship, just abreast the burned-out warehouse. Have a good trip, sir.'

The taxi moved off. Quays in busy ports looked the same the world over, the only difference being the weather, the presence or lack of bomb damage, and the colour of the dockers' skin. Piles of small crates alongside the first ship were being loaded on to large flat metal trays before being hoisted on board by the ship's derricks and two lorries were obviously waiting to unload whatever they carried direct into cargo nets or trays.

Mooring warps curved from stem and stern, their great spliced eyes looped over stone bollards and holding the ship.

Each rope had a circular disc of thin metal lodged halfway along it, like the spinning coloured disc of a child's toy. Rat guards were compulsory and although ports insisted on them being used to prevent rats, perhaps infected in some tropical port, from immigrating into Britain, they also stopped rugged British rats from climbing on board a ship and stowing away for a warmer climate where there was no rationing or bombing. A stick of bombs or a few hundred incendiary bombs on a warehouse, Yorke reflected, must play havoc with a rat's personality.

The wreckage of a small crate which had been dropped, with the black printed exhortations 'Use No Hooks' and 'Stow Away From Boilers' still visible on pieces of the deal boards, had been kicked out of the way. Again, on any quay there would be such wreckage, and if the contents had been edible or saleable, they would vanish like smoke in a high wind.

The second ship was loading tanks and lorries, the sandy-coloured camouflage paint betraying their destination, although many a ship, merchant or war, had ended up in the tropics just after all the crew had been fitted out with thick woollen Arctic underwear and heavy clothing. The ship was also beneath one of the few big cranes left standing, and Yorke saw several large crates close against the wall of the warehouse: aircraft in crates, probably fighters to be stowed on top of the hatches, so big that one on each hatch completely changed the silhouette of a merchant ship.

"'Ere you are, then,' the driver said, pulling up at the gangway of a modern-looking ship, turning the car round a pile of crates and a swinging cargo net. A group of a dockers looked up incuriously, saw an officer in uniform getting out of the taxi and, noticing two gold bands on each sleeve, assumed he was the second officer or one of the engineers – they were too far off to distinguish any coloured stripes between the gold. And Yorke knew that apart from the basic uniform, the insignia of rank and cap badges in the Merchant Navy usually varied, depending on the company. Some favoured straight gold stripes with the regular diamond instead of the curl used in the Royal Navy. Every large company had its own cap badge; the smaller ones made do with the regular Merchant Navy cap badge.

As the taxi driver took Yorke's case out of the boot, a Royal Navy seaman came hurrying down the gangway, hair untidy and wearing working clothes.

'Mr Yorke, sir? I'm Watkins, been fitting the radio gear. Let me take your case.' His eyes rested for a moment on the medal ribbon before he grabbed the luggage.

With the taxi paid off, Yorke followed Watkins up the gangway and paused for a moment at the top. The *Marynal's* decks looked as though every available length of loose rope, empty cardboard carton and cigarette packet had been emptied over them; at least three welding torches spurted eerie blue tongues and showered sparks, twentieth-century dragons huffing and puffing to frighten the enemy.

The convoy was due to sail the day after tomorrow and it seemed the *Marynal* could never be ready in time, but Yorke had seen enough warships in port for a few hours, hurriedly getting stores on board and welding repairs to action or heavy-weather damage, or putting in new equipment that needed extra fittings, to know how soon it could be cleared up.

'This way, sir,' Watkins said, holding the suitcase in front to clear a path through the seamen and dockers. 'Your cabin's all ready sir. One of the two passenger cabins, so you have a choice. If you don't like the one I got the chief steward to prepare, you can change, but it'll be the coolest in the tropics.'

A bed, not a bunk; a big, double-bladed fan fitted to the deckhead above, obviously the slow-turning type that moved a lot of air, plenty of polished mahogany – wardrobe, built-in chest of drawers, two easy chairs, a small writing desk.

Yorke sniffed. 'O-Cedar, from the smell of it.'

Watkins grinned and looked round the cabin with pride. 'That's the stuff, sir; best there is to bring out a good shine. Me and a couple of the lads nipped in yesterday with a can and some rags and gave things a polish here and there.'

'Thanks. Looks more like an admiral's day cabin.'

'Cor, you wait 'til you start on the grub, sir; I'm tellin' you, they eat well, these Merchant Navy chaps. Regular Ritz, this ship is. She called in South America on the last trip and stocked up with plenty of meat. Steak fer dinner tonight, sir. Now, you'll be wanting to see the Capting, but 'e's gorn on shore until four o'clock. Convoy conference ten double oh tomorrow morning, and the ship has a shore phone and – ' he opened the top drawer in the desk and took out a slip of paper, 'I've written the number down here. Will that be all for now, sir?'

'Where are you berthed?'

'Aft, with the DEMS gunners, sir. Nice and snug down there.'

'Out of sight, out of mind, eh?'

'Well, sort of, sir,' Watkins admitted with a grin, 'but I got all me radio gear rigged in the Marconi cabin. That's one deck above you and just abaft the bridge.'

'The DEMS gunners,' Yorke said. 'How many of them?'

'Eight brown jobs, six HO ratings, and a hookie what's Regular, sir.'

'All quiet down there?'

'Their third trip together, sir. They play a wicked game of uckers.'

'Very well,' Yorke said, 'you can vanish until nine tomorrow: I may want you to come with me to the convoy conference.'

With that he hung up his heavy coat, put his hat on a hook and sank into one of the easy chairs. The DEMS gunners were not directly his responsibility, but if he needed them the *Marynal*'s captain had been told he had the authority to take them over as a unit. The eight soldiers, Watkins' 'brown jobs', were of course volunteers from the Maritime Regiment of the Royal Artillery, and the six 'Hostilities Only' ratings with a regular leading seaman in charge, should be useful – particularly because they had already done three trips together and still enjoyed playing 'a wicked game' of ludo. Clearly they were a happy crowd, and that usually meant efficient, too.

By now Watkins would be aft and reporting to his mates what he had been able to glean about the new officer who had unexpectedly entered their lives, along with Watkins himself, another operator and their radio sets. Fourteen DEMS gunners who had been going along quietly with a leading seaman in charge had probably 'got organized', with a good supply of duty-free cigarettes, pipe tobacco and liquor stowed away. Well, as long as they did not smoke on deck at sea after blackout time and did not go on watch 'in liquor', as the charge usually worded it, he was not going to interfere: the *Marynal*'s chief officer, the equivalent of a warship's first lieutenant, would keep an eye on them. Lieutenant Yorke, as far as the *Marynal*'s captain was concerned, was 'on special duty' with Watkins and another operator, and although Yorke had not seen the letter from the Assistant Chief of Naval Staff, the *Marynal*'s owners had been told under conditions of secrecy that the 'special duty' concerned the 'insider' attacks, and that the captain should be told as much as the owners thought necessary to avoid any difficulties. In other words, while not interfering with the Captain of the *Marynal's* authority and responsibility, if Lieutenant Yorke asked him to steer the ship straight out of the convoy, turn three circles and then rejoin, the Admiralty backed him and the *Marynal's* captain was expected to comply.

Yet Yorke knew that for all the Admiralty letter to the owners, conferences between the owners' marine superintendent and captain, and discreet explanations, much of the success of this voyage might depend on the impressions that the *Marynal's* captain and Yorke formed of each other in the first minute or two of their meeting. The job would be twice as difficult with a touchy master, although if it became too bad Yorke could always arrange with the commodore to transfer to another ship.

It was almost exactly an hour later that Watkins knocked on the door and Yorke was embarrassed to realize that he had dozed off in the armchair, uncomfortable as it was. An overnight rail journey these days made anything softer than a plank seem a sybaritic extravagance, and the distant hum of the *Marynal's* generators was restful.

'The Captain's back on board, sir,' Watkins reported. 'Sorry I woke you but I guessed you'd want to see him. And the DEMS leading seaman is asking if you wanted to see him.'

Yorke stood up and walked over to the handbasin, then turned away when he realized he had not unpacked his washing gear. The DEMS hookie obviously wanted to have a look for himself. 'Is he there now?'

'Yes, sir, Leading Seaman Jenkins.'

'Tell him to come in.'

The leading seaman was smartly dressed, freshly shaven, hair carefully combed, the anchor badge on his sleeve showing his rank and providing the Navy's nickname, hookie, for a leading seaman. 'Jenkins, sir. I was wondering when you wanted to inspect the DEMS gunners, and the guns, sir.'

'Good evening, Jenkins,' Yorke said sleepily. 'If you think an inspection is necessary I'll make one, but I'm nothing to do with the DEMS organization. As far as you're concerned I'm a passenger on this trip, unless,' he added cautiously, 'there's an emergency. So you carry on as before. To whom do you normally report?'

'Well, the Chief Officer, sir. Then when we get into port usually an officer from the DEMS organization inspects us and we draw more ammunition if we've expended any. And – ' he gave a conspiratorial grin, obviously knowing that Yorke had just come from a destroyer, 'occasionally they bring us a new secret weapon. We're getting quite a collection.'

'Secret weapons? What have you got in the way of ordinary weapons?'

'Well, there's the 4-inch aft, made by Vickers at Elswick in 1917, according to the plate on it. Then two 20-millimetre Oerlikon cannons. They're in good nick, sir; well mounted and we've plenty of ammo. Then we got twelve machine-guns in twin mountings. They're right bastards, sir, if you'll excuse the expression; known in the trade as 'Orrible 'Otchkiss.'

Yorke frowned. They must be American and by now would be an old design, probably stored after the First World War, like the 4-inch. 'We have to be thankful for what we've got,' he said. 'You've reported all this to – well, whoever you report to in the DEMS organization?'

'Yus, sir,' Jenkins said sourly, 'but it's the same answer: every ship that has 'em is complaining. "Try the projector", they say; and "What about using the parachute-and-cable". My bleedin' life, sir, these things scare me but they won't scare the bloody Germans!'

'The projector? Parachute-and-cable?' a puzzled Yorke asked.

Jenkins shook his head sadly, like a father despairing of delinquent sons. 'New inventions they are, sir; leastways, that's what they tell us. Some madman chained up in a cellar at the Ministry of War Transport, or one of those places, is inventing these things. The projector is a sort of – well, like a length of drainpipe poking up on a tripod. You feed in compressed air – there's a pressure dial – drop an ordinary Mills hand grenade down the spout (you're supposed to take the safety pin out, of course, tho' I don't advise it) and when the Ju 88 comes rushing past you open a valve and the compressed air hurls the grenade up in the air, the safety handle's released, and if he's quick enough the German pilot catches it and chucks it back…leastways, that's how it seems to me.'

'You haven't tried it out, then?'

'Not yet, sir,' Jenkins said, adding darkly: 'But I've 'eard tell of what's 'appened in ships where they 'ave…'

'What happened?'

'Well sir, you can imagine a Mills grenade with the pin removed popping out of this diabolical weapon, landing about thirty feet away and just rolling down the deck like a black orange. There's a five second fuse, and then it makes an 'orrible bang, and the welders repairing the 'ole always scorch the deck paint, and the captain gets ratty and – well, it's best to leave 'em in the packing cases, sir. The captain of this ship,' he added, lowering his voice so that he sounded like a black marketeer in Oxford Street offering silk stockings, 'keeps showing an interest in it, but so far…'

'What about the parachute-and-cable thing? How does that work?'

'The PAC? Well, sir, no one knows really. We've got four fitted, two each side of the monkey island and fired by wires coming through tubes to the wheelhouse with toggles on the end. I could show you the manual if you're interested,' he added without enthusiasm.

'Just give me a rough idea.'

'Well, sir, same as before: a Ju 88 galloping down out of the clouds and you pull the toggle and a rocket goes rushing up from the monkey island trailing an 'undred feet or so of thin flexible wire with a small canister on the end. Once it reaches a certain height the rocket bursts and out pops a parachute. The canister at the other end goes pop, too, and out comes another parachute. Now you have – so says the manual – one 'undred feet of very strong wire suspended 'orizontuallily between the two parachutes. If the German pilot is *very* clever, he can hit it all and wrap his plane up in silk and wire and float down into the sea on the parachutes, surrender to one of the escort, and spend the rest of the war in England as a POW eating dried egg and drinking weak tea and listenin' to Vera Lynn singin' *We'll meet again*... Sorry if I sound a bit 'pertinent, sir, but all these toys are just a waste o' materials and factory time. But...' his voice dropped even lower, so that he sounded like an over-enthusiastic conspirator in a touring Shakespearean company, 'I think this ship's captain wants to play with 'em, which might get some of us killed, so if...'

'You don't fancy doing a high wire act between two parachutes, eh?'

'Well, sir,' Jenkins said with a grin, 'I wouldn't want to take advantage of the fack I'm senior rating if anyone else wants to try it first.'

'I hope the 4-inch is all right,' Yorke said.

'When it was last inspected in Freetown they told us we should use it only in an emergency, sir, except for firing a couple of practice rounds every six months...'

'Apart from the Oerlikons, what have we got that works without the need for prayer?'

Jenkins' face lit up. 'A couple of stripped Lewis guns, sir. They're on single mountings on each side of the poop. They're in good nick. Best guns ever designed, I reckon. Oh yus, sir,' he added contemptuously, 'the brown jobs have got rifles and bayonets in case the Germans drop paratroopers on us, *and* topees what look like coppers' 'ats.'

Watkins nodded his head in confirmation, and Yorke said: 'If the worst comes to the worst, we can always frighten the Germans by putting on the topees back to front. Still, I know the sort you mean; very reminiscent of a policeman's helmet for some people.'

'Me for one,' Watkins said with a grin. 'Still, I never did time.'

The mention of the word reminded Yorke of the reason for Watkins' visit. 'Right, you two, carry on; I must call on the captain.'

Captain Edward Hobson was a Yorkshireman, born in Bingley and very proud of it. He was within a few days of his fiftieth birthday, though most people would guess at forty because his face was just plump enough to keep away wrinkles and his wavy black hair had only a few random grey strands. He was a quiet man without being dour, and had the same contempt for the engineers that they had for the *Marynal*'s deck officers. It was a tradition going back to the earliest days of steam and as much a part of the Merchant Navy as the fact that most ships' engineers came from Newcastle. With his homely North-country accent and smart appearance, Hobson would have commanded one of the company's smaller passenger ships in peacetime: he had enough of the social graces and the physical presence to reassure old ladies in a storm and on quiet days have them giggling over an endless stock of mildly funny stories.

He glanced up as Yorke came into the cabin, his eyes catching the single medal ribbon. He stood up and held out his hand: 'You'll be the Mr Yorke they've been telling me about.'

It took Yorke only a couple of minutes to realize that the directors of the Western Ocean Shipping Company had made a good choice of captain in their effort to help the Royal Navy. Yorke sat down, shaking his head at Hobson's offer of a drink and a cigar.

'You're regular, then,' Hobson commented.

Yorke nodded. 'Like you, though not as much sea time!'

'That's a DSO, isn't it? I'm not up on ribbons, but they don't give 'em away. What did you get it for, eh?' he asked with disconcerting directness.

'I was left in command of a destroyer.'

'And then?'

Yorke realized that Hobson's questioning was not idle curiosity but simply part of weighing up the newcomer; he wanted to know more about the young man – half his age – who might want him to risk the safety of the *Marynal*. With the question not prompted by curiosity, the answer could hardly be boasting.

'Air attacks for hours. We didn't dodge enough bombs, and we were leaking so badly the sheer weight of water was slowing us down. Finally we sank.'

'A lot of men lost?'

'Most of them.'

'That's where you got your hand messed up?'

Yorke nodded. Hobson's blue eyes did not miss much.

'That DSO – was it for something special, or the whole operation?'

Yorke shrugged his shoulders. 'You know how vague citations are... I think it was for the time after the captain was killed and I was left in command.'

Hobson had obviously made up his mind about the young naval officer sitting opposite him. There was a silence for a minute or two as Yorke looked round the cabin – this was obviously the captain's day cabin, large enough to hold twenty gossiping people should he care to have a party, with plenty of light from six portholes and two square windows facing aft, a floral pattern cloth sewn on to the inside of the heavy blackout curtains.

No admiral in his flagship, even a battleship, had so much room and light. Nor were there the yards of steam pipes, electrical conduits and the like masquerading as thick macaroni that always ran along at least two of every four bulkheads in a warship cabin. Hobson's day cabin was as tastefully furnished as a country-house sitting room; instead of the derricks of ships astern, one might have expected to see trees through the two windows. There was even a fake fireplace, complete with a mantelpiece around the edge of which ran low fiddles to prevent things sliding off when the ship rolled. In one corner Yorke was intrigued by a small deal table – a work bench, in fact – over which a blanket had been thrown, obscuring several bulky items. Wires ran from the table to an electric socket in the bulkhead.

Hobson saw him looking and said, 'That's my hobby corner. Come and see.' He pulled back the blanket and revealed a small jeweller's lathe, tray of small tools, vice on a turntable, drill press removed from its stand and, clamped down in the middle of one side of the table, a beautifully made brass model of a locomotive, the famous Flying Scot, perhaps a foot long. Most of the wheels had been fitted; four more, small and presumably for the bogie in front, were in another tray.

'I should have been a train driver,' Hobson said wryly, 'but making a model like this is a good way of passing the time on some of these convoys. Six weeks at sea…a man can brood, or turn to drink. I prefer modelling.' He replaced the blanket carefully and motioned Yorke to sit down again.

'A merchant ship isn't like a warship – that sounds obvious, I know. What I mean is, the main job is to keep your position in the convoy. I like to be on the bridge just before dawn, but I've no need to be there again until I take my noon sight. I do that only for practice; the second mate's the navigator, of course, and I like a couple of the cadets to take sights and work them out. And I'm up there at dusk too, just in case. So apart from being there for a turn if we're zigzagging, I'm the spare man at the wedding; the chap who gets the blame if anything happens.

'It's a good job – I work for a fine firm, have comfortable quarters, and can look forward to a good pension. The job's a sight more interesting in peacetime, of course; now the worst crisis – apart from being bombed or torpedoed – is to have the chief steward reporting a week out that half the crew have the clap, or everyone's got crabs. Or the potatoes are going rotten – last trip we had to buy yams in Freetown, and that's where I discovered the lads don't like sweet potatoes. Anyway, I'm prattlin' on. What do you want me to do?'

'Well, I hope you'll be able to forget I'm on board: I'll try and keep out of your way. Once or twice a day one of my signalmen might need to send a message by lamp to the commodore or the senior officer of the escort, but he can use the monkey island to keep off the bridge.'

Hobson held up his hand. 'Use the bridge as much as you need. Don't forget that merchant ships aren't like warships.

There'll be a quartermaster in the wheelhouse, a mate on the port side of the bridge and a cadet on the starboard, and that's it. In foggy weather there'll be a lookout up in the bow, and at action stations the DEMS gunners are all over the place. So the mate on watch and the cadet will be glad to see you. Four hours is a long watch, and we don't use dog watches; a straight four on and eight off...and too bad if there's a five-hour action stations during your eight off. The third mate has the eight to twelve, the second the twelve to four, and the chief officer – the Mate – the four to eight.'

'The wireless operators...?' Yorke prompted.

'Three, all employed by the Marconi Company, as I expect you know. Chief, second and third. Only the chief has any real sea time; the other two are pretty new. The third sparks was a monk this time last year. He thought he ought to do his bit but didn't want to kill anyone, so he joined the Marconi Company. Plucky sort of thing to do – the lads tease him a bit.'

'My two signalmen...'

'Oh, they're already fixed up. They arrived a couple of days ago and worked with the chief sparks to fit their sets. They're berthed aft with the DEMS gunners, as you probably know. I gave 'em the opportunity of berthing near the wireless cabin, but they preferred to be aft. Probably like a game of uckers with the other lads.'

'What radio watches do your operators normally stand, captain?'

'Just listening watches. They could just as well be doing embroidery because every ship keeps a watch on the call and distress frequency and there's usually nothing to listen to, but the convoy instructions say listen, so we listen. Four on and eight off, just reading thrillers in the warm...'

'My two lads will have to keep a continuous listening watch,' Yorke said, 'so – '

'What, you mean two on and two off, or four on and four off? Bit hard on them, isn't it?'

'We didn't think you'd welcome too many extra men,' Yorke said.

'Well, unless it's all very secret, I know what I'd do: put a mattress down in the radio room for one of your lads, and have a word with the chief sparks: there's no reason why my chaps can't listen to two receivers at once, and if your set starts playing music or whatever it is, he can rouse your man.'

'You think the chief will – '

'He'll be only too glad; those poor buggers get bored stiff just listening to static. Why, their big day is when the BAMS receiver breaks down!'

'BAMS? What's that?'

'Oh, that's our own Merchant Navy radio station. "Broadcasts to Allied Merchant Ships", a fixed frequency thing – apparently the Germans can detect someone twiddling a receiver through the frequencies. Anyway, these BAMS sets just receive the one station. The programmes aren't much. The news, Monday Night at Eight, and Vera Lynn on Forces Favourites is about all I ever hear. That Tommy Handley, I like him.'

'The convoy conference tomorrow,' Yorke said. 'I'll be coming with you. Do you wear uniform?'

'Not bloody likely! Leastways, one or two captains do, and some of the foreigners, but most of us wear civvies. Why?'

'I should have thought of that, I don't want to draw attention to myself, but...'

Hobson looked him up and down. 'I've got just the thing for you. A lightweight, single-breasted I had run up in Rosario on this last trip: never worn it, except for a couple of fittings. Want to borrow it? And a mac. Not very formal, these convoy conferences – except for your chaps.'

CHAPTER ELEVEN

The room was high-ceilinged like an old-fashioned church hall, with rows of cheap chairs (whose single coat of varnish was wearing off) facing a small table which had three more chairs behind it, as though waiting for the vicar and his wife and the guest speaker.

A naval rating at the main door carefully pointed out the chairs to the motley crowd of men now beginning to come into the room. They could have been prosperous farmers attending a branch meeting of the local National Farmers' Union, Yorke realized: most had a suntan, the resulting colour depending on the type of skin. One auburn-haired master, plump and blue-eyed, had a face so red that he might have been verging on apoplexy, and the man he was talking to was a leathery brown, as though he had spent a lifetime following the plough, tanned by sun and wind. Few of them, with the exception of Hobson and one or two others, looked comfortable in civilian clothes. Obviously they were so used to the shape and relative tightness of uniform that the easy fit of civilian clothes made them seem like men wearing suits a size too large. All, he noticed, carried small attaché cases or leather dispatch cases and several had bowler hats. All looked shrewd men.

The Swedish captain was in every way an exception. He was one of the youngest of the masters; his blond hair, brilliantined and combed back flat on his head without a parting, looked like a skull cap made of omelette; his face just missed being thin and had high cheekbones; his nose seemed fleshless but too large to match the rest, and his ears stuck out. But his tailor was a craftsman and the material of his suit could not be bought in wartime Britain, despite the black marketeers: it was a loosely-woven blue, almost like linen, which kept its shape perfectly. The overcoat over his arm was a charcoal grey; the hat he carried in the other hand was a light tan with a wider brim than was fashionable in England. The briefcase under his arm had the rich mahogany brown of good leather; a young barrister starting out for his first day in chambers would have been glad if his wealthy Aunt Jessica had given it to him as a present. Despite the blue suit, Yorke noticed, the man's shoes were brown.

With the Swedish captain was one of his officers of a type at the other end of the obviously Nordic scale: his hair was so blond it seemed almost white, skin so pink and dead he might have been an albino, no eyebrows noticeable at ten yards, hair cut *en brosse* – the American forces, Yorke remembered, called it a 'crew cut' – and he had an unfortunate tendency to what gunnery instructors at Whale Island called 'bleedin' camel marchin' ' – swinging an arm in time with the leg on the same side. The officer's face was crude and cruel; his captain's face was – bland? Yes, bland to the point of seeming smug. And smug almost to the point of sneering, as though he and his ship were above all this lowly crowd; that convoys – well, he was taking part under protest. The two Scandinavians marched to chairs, sitting on two near the back.

'Choose seats a couple of rows behind our Swedish friends,' Yorke murmured to Hobson.

Hobson glanced round. 'The Swedes interest you, eh? They stick out like sore thumbs, don't they? Making a rare profit out of the war and they know it. Treat us all like poor relations.'

Five minutes later, with all the masters seated, three men came through the door and went to the table. The door was shut, with the naval rating obviously standing on guard outside. One of the two naval officers, a lieutenant commander wearing the ribbon of a DSC, took the middle chair with a distinguished-looking white-haired man in civilian clothes (a well-cut but obviously comfortable old tweed suit) on his right and a Royal Navy lieutenant on his left.

The masters stopped talking but several continued puffing their pipes while others opened their cases and took out notebooks and pencils. The lieutenant commander stood up, a slim, almost angular young man whom Ned had known for years and who probably had more experience as an escort commander than anyone else afloat. His name was before the Honours and Awards Committee for a DSO and his wife had just left him because – so gossip had it – she could not stand the strain of knowing that he was at sea month after month and dreading a telegram. She was said to be living with a squadron leader in the RAF Regiment, a man responsible for defending airfields and who spent every night in bed – her bed.

If the Swede was bland, then Jonathan Gower was blithe; he had the self-assured but friendly manner usually associated with the better Harley Street specialists. Gower whispered something to the old man on his right and then stood up.

'Good morning, gentlemen. I am Lieutenant Commander Gower and will be the senior officer of your escort. I shall be in the *Echo* frigate. The Commodore…' he turned slightly to his right to indicate the old man, 'is already known to several of you, Vice-Admiral Sir Sydney Shaw, who came out of a well-earned retirement to get back to sea.' He turned to the other officer. 'Lieutenant Knight commands the second frigate, the *Argo*, and is therefore my deputy in the case of any mishap.

'You should all have received your sealed orders,' he looked round for any wave of dissent, 'which give your positions in the convoy. There are thirty-five ships and we'll be in the usual seven-column formation. We'll probably have an ocean-going tug with us, and she'll act as rescue ship. I must repeat the order, gentlemen, that no ship, except the tug, is to stop for survivors. Most of you know that in a pack attack it is standard procedure for a U-boat to stand by a ship she has just torpedoed and wait for someone else to stop for survivors, presenting a perfect target, so that then we have two sinking ships…

'We shan't know exactly what escort we have until to-morrow because two corvettes are being cleaned up and refuelled and reammunitioned, and it is not certain they'll be ready in time.'

'Why is not the sailing postponed for the whole convoy?' a precise voice demanded, and Yorke saw that the Swedish captain was speaking without bothering to stand up. 'An extra two corvettes is important.'

'This isn't the only convoy sailing or arriving,' Gower said evenly.

'It seems to me – but I am only a neutral, of course – that sailing without a proper escort is asking for trouble.'

Yorke and Gower, in a last-minute conference at the Admiralty before leaving for Liverpool, when allocating the positions for the ships, had anticipated this line of questioning, just as they had invented the delay for the corvettes and the fictitious reason that Gower was now going to give.

'One must expect trouble in wartime, Captain Ohlson, but I think the corvettes were delayed getting here because they went to the rescue of a neutral ship – Swedish, I'm told. A nasty air attack, I believe, with many casualties.'

Yorke watched Captain Ohlson glance round sharply at the other Swede with him. Ohlson had gone white and was now whispering to the other man. Gower was waiting politely, and Ohlson said abruptly: 'What is the name of this ship? What was her position?'

Gower shrugged his shoulders. 'I'm sorry, I've no idea; my only concern was for the corvettes.'

'But this is a *Swedish* ship; I must…'

'Captain Ohlson, many British and American ships are being lost every day. I regret every sinking. But this conference is about our particular convoy; no doubt your government will take up the matter with Berlin direct…'

Ohlson flushed at the implication of Gower's words and resumed whispering to his companion, who seemed to Yorke either to be hard of hearing or not very bright. Gower continued giving details for the forthcoming voyage, with the masters taking notes. Finally he handed over to the commodore.

The old admiral spoke crisply. 'Position keeping, gen-tlemen: please do your best. I know what it's like having to ask an engineer for only one more revolution or one less, but if he grumbles point out the alternative might be a torpedo bursting right where he's standing. One revolution of a ship's screw a minute can make all the difference between a straggling convoy and one in good formation. You've all seen what happens when it is necessary to alter course with a straggling convoy…there's usually a U-boat waiting to pick off the odd ship.

'Now for signals. You all have copies of Mersigs, and remember the only way I can communicate with you is by signal lamp, flag hoists, or, in an emergency, blasts on the siren. I trust the siren will stay quiet, so flags and lamp mean it is essential you always keep an eye on the commodore. Noon positions will be hoisted at 1215 – and hoist 'em dead on time; don't wait to see what the commodore is hoisting so you can copy him. We can all make mistakes, and I'm no exception. I see Captain Hobson sitting over there. He probably remembers sailing in a convoy with me. Forty or more ships. I hoisted my position at the same moment he did. They didn't coincide. All the other ships had the same position as me. Thirty-nine to one. Some odds. I had him called up by lamp and asked to check his figures. He answered at once that he did not need to. Seemed a bit saucy at the time but I checked mine. I (and every other ship in the convoy but the *Marynal*) was wrong and Captain Hobson right. Obviously all the others hadn't made the same mistake; they had just waited until I hoisted my position and hoisted the same – except for Captain Hobson. So remember – hoisting positions isn't a game of housey-housey.

'Lights. Watch your blackouts. I must ask you to punish severely any man caught smoking a cigarette on deck. A glowing cigarette can be seen a considerable distance. No Aldis lamps to be used after sunset – if you use one to call me, remember there might be a U-boat in the distance beyond me who can see a pinpoint of light when he might have missed the low silhouettes of the ships, and thus find the convoy. You have the low-powered blue signal lamps, so use them, even if it means passing a message to me via another ship. And those ships using cadets as signalmen – please make them polish their Morse… That's all, gentlemen; I wish you luck and let's hope we have an uneventful trip.'

By the time Yorke arrived back on board with Captain Hobson, the *Marynal* was beginning to look more like a ship than a rubbish dump. Odd pieces of timber, dunnage, used to secure cargo in the holds by wedging or separating, were being thrown down on to the quayside; seamen with hoses were washing down the decks; the welding gear had been put away and the welds were dark patches surrounded by bubbled paint. The boatswain was talking with the chief officer at number two hatch, where the thick hatchboards were already across and the canvas hatchcover stretched over, and men with mallets and large wooden wedges were preparing to secure them. Number one hatch had already been battened down, number three was still being loaded, and the two hatches aft were also battened down.

Captain Hobson grunted contentedly. 'The lads get a move on when there's a need...'

Yorke realized the remark was both a boast and an apology; for various reasons a Merchant Navy seaman was not subjected to the same rigid discipline as a man in the Royal Navy, and as this was his first experience of the Merchant Navy system, Yorke was prepared to wait before he passed judgement. So far he could see that a dozen Merchant Navy men worked quite happily without any petty officers keeping an eye on them. Whether or not it was necessary, a similar number of Royal Navy men would have had at least one petty officer standing there.

Hobson said quietly: 'I know it's not your job, but I think the DEMS gunners would like you to make an inspection this afternoon. Just have a look at their quarters and walk round the guns with that leading seaman, and the Army lance corporal. Lance bombardier, rather. The chief officer tells me that this morning early they were after him for a couple of new mops, another bucket, a gallon of O-Cedar and a dozen tins of Brasso, and I saw one of them coming out of the engine room with enough cotton waste to make a nest for a family of albatrosses.'

'When is your regular inspection?' Yorke asked.

'Ten o'clock on Sundays. That's what I mean: today is only Wednesday!'

'Maybe they think it's Christmas Day tomorrow', Yorke said with a grin, but he could guess what was happening: as they were leaving for the convoy conference, Leading Seaman Jenkins had been very casual in asking if Yorke would be on board this afternoon.

In his cabin sprawled in an easy chair, dark hair uncombed, eyes still bloodshot from the night journey in the train, nerves tautening as he thought of the forthcoming voyage – he always had this tension, like Nelson and his seasickness – Yorke felt curiously out of place. He had a sense of not belonging to the *Marynal*, and he tried to work out why. She had a fine old name, the ancient word for a mariner. She was a modern ship, launched almost exactly a year before the war began and built for a reasonably prosperous firm, so there were no signs of penny-pinching. Perhaps it was the cabin – he was not used to large portholes, through which he could see the quays of a bustling port which, although pitted with bomb craters, was still obviously in business. A warship alongside in naval dockyards would hear none of the sounds that now welled up round the *Marynal*, with dockers and stevedores alternately cursing and joking, taxis hooting and weaving among lorries and ropes to deposit officers and seamen at their ships after well-deserved leave. Half a mile of quayside surrounding rectangles of oily water, and not a Royal Navy uniform to be seen; just cloth-capped dockers and stevedores, an occasional Merchant Navy man, and piles of crates and rubbish... This was the land of 'Use No Hooks' –

and where a fight could flare up in a moment between a couple of dockers, who would not hesitate to attack each other with the hooks which, like extensions of their hands, were used to haul sacks and crates. The most noticeable similarity with the naval dockyard was that all fire hydrants were marked in bright red and yellow paint, while here and there sandbagged positions gave shelter for air raid wardens.

The *Marynal* herself, of course, bore no resemblance to a warship: this cabin was palatial and there was not the jumble of background noises he was accustomed to in a destroyer. Probably fewer generators running, because a destroyer used a vast amount of electricity even when at anchor or alongside. Many fewer men and therefore much less shouting and pounding feet. And no Tannoy…the public address system in a warship attracted men to its microphone like wasps to a picnic, as though nothing could be true unless bellowed over the Tannoy. And of course a merchant ship was so damned big, even a single-screw motor ship like the *Marynal*. Comparing her to a frigate (let alone a destroyer) was like putting a charabanc alongside a racing car.

The wardroom – the *saloon*, he corrected himself, finding it hard to get used to the different usages in a merchant ship – was considerably more luxurious than anything a warship had to offer. Two long tables, dark mahogany and highly polished, ran along each side; there were curtains at the large portholes which could be pulled back to allow the heavy deadlights to swing over the glass ports and screw down tight; paintings – landscapes and seascapes – in narrow, black frames were screwed to the bulkheads (and they were good oils, not cheap prints). A recent addition just outside each door – the saloon could be entered from a passage on either side –was wire racks to hold the lifejackets that officers were required to carry at sea when going on watch. With the watches changing at eight, twelve and four o'clock, they could eat before going up to the bridge or just as they came off – breakfast, for example, was served for an hour.

A discreet question to Captain Hobson had revealed that the engineer officers had their meals in the saloon only when the ship was in port, and even then often preferred eating in their own mess room. 'It's a company rule – and one I enforce very strictly – that anyone eating in the saloon must be in uniform. If an officer can't be bothered to change, then he's free to miss a meal. It's different for the four cadets – they're not allowed to miss a meal. The engineers, though – well,' Hobson explained, 'the company lets them have their own mess, and the chief engineer can make his own rules. If they are doing some very dirty job, for example, he might let them sit down to a meal wearing flannel bags and a jersey. I don't know; the mess room is the chief engineer's responsibility, and in a merchant ship he's second in command, as you probably know.'

At dinner the previous evening Yorke had been introduced to an almost bewildering number of officers, ranging from the chief radio officer to the senior second engineer, from the electrical officer (always known as 'Lecky') to the chief steward. Several of the officers had their wives staying on board – they were all going on shore today, in anticipation of the ship going out into the River Mersey tomorrow. They were an odd collection of women, ranging from the perky yet homely wife of the chief radio officer, who called everyone 'luv' and genuinely seemed to mean it, to Lecky's wife, a sulky young woman whose features seemed too small for her face, her mouth puckered up in a perpetual discontented sneer at her husband, and whose hair had the startling red that could only come from a bottle. The women, Yorke decided, ranged from the girl next door who had waited for years for her man to 'get his ticket' and with the necessary Board of Trade Certificates to obtain a steady job, to a trollop who suddenly found herself pregnant and needed a husband.

Arriving in the saloon early for breakfast, Yorke found his guess had been right, the married men with their wives on board would be eating as late as possible. The only person there was the chief engineer, a stocky and bald man nearing sixty who was a self-proclaimed bachelor. He had a noisy habit of eating crisp, dry toast with his mouth open but was a cheerful man who had been with the ship, he told Yorke, 'from the day the builders took delivery of the engine'. For a whole year before the war the *Marynal* had acted as a cargo liner – the chief engineer was careful to emphasize the *liner*, a ship carrying cargo or passengers on a regular route or line and thus not a tramp (which went from port to port touting for cargoes), with a tap speed of sixteen knots.

'Mind you, the owners never let us make passages at sixteen; our economical speed is just under twelve. But I remember the day we did our speed trials with all the builder's men on board. Aye, that was a great experience, watching the revolutions creeping up and up, until we were making sixteen… But now it's six-knot convoys for us. The engines are barely turning. Injectors sooting up, too. Suddenly the bridge phones down on a dark night complaining that the funnel is spouting sparks. Of course it is! Soot from weeks of slow speeds. Now I try to blast it out in the daytime. I did it once with a following wind and the mate had just had the fo'c'sle painted – you should have heard his language; he thought I'd done it a' purpose. The fore part of the ship looked as though it had black measles.'

Yorke made sure he was in the saloon promptly at noon for lunch, hoping that the wives would make their husbands late as they primped their hair and tidied up their lipstick: there had been signs that one or two of them had learned from their husband that the naval officer on board had been serving in destroyers and if he was not careful meals for the rest of the day would be prying sessions.

He was lucky; again the only man there was the chief engineer. 'You'll go far, young man,' the chief said. 'You watch points. That's what you've got to do to get on, watch points.'

Yorke was puzzled by the phrase but the chief added: 'Them bloody women – you've got to get in quick when we're in port: it's the only time those wives get waited on and they love humbugging around, sending the stewards off for more glasses of water and complaining the toast is overdone. Overdone! Well, *that* tells you the kind of women they are. Anyway, watch points; nip in quick a'fore those female vultures descend on the feast table. Still, we'll be rid of them by this evening. The Old Man says we move out into the river early tomorrow; the tug's booked for seven o'clock. That means my little sewing machine will start warming up at six. And with a bit of luck she won't stop for another six weeks or so.'

Yorke, finding the easy chair in his cabin grew hard lumps in odd places after half an hour, was just about to get up when there was a knock on the door and Watkins appeared with letters, two in official buff envelopes, one in the particular blue that Clare used, and another addressed in his mother's handwriting.

'Oh, by the way, Watkins, I was thinking of having a look round the DEMS quarters later this afternoon. Will you send Jenkins along to see me?'

An hour later Yorke found himself climbing down the vertical ladder to the DEMS gunners' accommodation under the poop deck. What had once been a storage area had been divided into some medium-sized cabins, with one large cabin used as a mess. Tall, grey-painted lockers lined a bulkhead, showing where the men kept their clothing. There were four circular Players cigarette tins on the table which had been burnished on the outside so that they seemed to be made of stainless steel. Yorke picked one up and saw that instead of the usual fifty cigarettes, it was half full of sand. A safe kind of ashtray, but…

'Where do you get the sand – firebuckets?' he asked Jenkins.

'No sir, there's a tub of sand up in the forepeak to use in the firebuckets, and we can use it. The Mate's scared stiff we'll brew up a fire down here, with all those ready-use shells in the rack round the 4-inch just above us, so we can have all the sand we want. We usually bring him back a couple of sandbags full when we can get a swim on a nice beach in the tropics.' He gave a shiver. 'Times like this, sir, I don't believe the tropics exist.'

Jenkins led him to the various cabins, where the men had their uniforms, blankets and cleaning gear laid out neatly, the soldiers sticking to the Army way and the seamen to the system they had been taught in the Royal Navy. The most impressive equipment, Yorke thought, was the Army topee, looking just like a light tan version of the London bobby's helmet and about as unwieldy. He remembered seeing old coloured prints of British troops in India and in the South African war wearing such hats. Obviously the War Office had not changed the design for a century, although the troops in the Eighth Army went bareheaded whenever possible, something which even a year before the war would have been reckoned an invitation to the sun to send them mad, or at least start the process of frying their brains. Army-issue shirts still had buttons for spine pads of felt, though no one used them now.

Yorke's days as first lieutenant of a destroyer were only a few weeks behind him, and he could remember all too well the quick inspection which preceded the captain's inspection on Sundays. Well, Jenkins and his men had been working hard, polishing with O-Cedar whatever wood took a shine, rubbing away at metal with the Brasso. Handrails had Turk's heads in white line at top and bottom, with canvas wrapped round in between and the seam carefully sewn in a sailmaker's stitch, or for shorter lengths there was some good fancy work which had been scrubbed clean – probably with a couple of mugs of Parozone bleach in the water.

It all pointed to the men taking a pride in their quarters. In turn that meant they were proud of their ship and happy in her. All of which was a credit to Jenkins and the lance bombardier, the chief officer, and finally the captain. Keeping DEMS gunners happy must be the devil of a job because their normal duties were dull – in port it meant cleaning quarters, oiling and greasing guns, and scrubbing and restitching canvas covers. At sea there were long waits and occasional brief action stations…watches spent huddled in what little cover there was around the 4-inch gun when sailing alone. Off watch meant sleeping, playing uckers or cards, smoking, reading Wild West stories, looking once again through tattered copies of *Razzle* and *Men Only*…

Inspection of the guns took half an hour. The Vickers 4-inch mounted on the poop was indeed an ancient piece but Tenkins obviously loved it, and so did the lance bombardier, with the affection young men had for a peppery grandfather. The shells sticking up like a row of stubby thumbs in a circular rack going right round the poop were well painted and then lightly greased. The 4-inch, Yorke could tell, represented a 'proper gun' to the men; something that might do some damage to the enemy. When he reached the monkey island above the bridge and found the canvas covers off the two Oerlikon 20 mm cannons he sensed these too were guns the men liked; weapons that could be trusted not to jam or play tricks. And they were, of course, very effective against low-flying aircraft; a well-aimed burst could bring down a four-engined Focke-Wulfe Condor or Kurier. There were twelve Hotchkiss to inspect in twin mountings, and it was clear that they found no favour in the heart of Jenkins or the lance bombardier. But they were well cared for; each small armour-plate shield, shaped like the window of a Gothic church, was well painted; the guns were lightly oiled; the canvas covers, neatly rolled and stowed at the rear of each mounting, were scrubbed and the stitching was firm.

For a moment Yorke thought of asking to see the grenade projector, and the PACs, which were obviously Heath Robinson devices, but he had glimpsed the rectangular green boxes (in which PAC cables were probably stored) on either side of the forward end of the monkey island, each with a rocket canted up beside it, and decided that DEMS gunners' pay ought to be doubled if they were expected to handle such ludicrous but dangerous toys. He tried to picture the secret committee which had thought of, made, run trials and persuaded someone in authority to approve production of such devices for merchant ships.

Finally, back in his cabin, Yorke took off his jacket, loosened his tie – the laundry in London had put too much starch in the shirt collar and it made his neck sore – and started to read his letters. It was a game, a test of willpower, but he liked to see how long he could wait to read a letter. The two buff OHMS letters he could keep for a week without much trouble; but – he looked at his watch – an hour was long enough to wait to read what Clare had to say. He decided to leave hers until last. The first buff envelope told him that he had been overpaid 9 1/2d a week for nineteen weeks and would he take immediate steps to refund the money; the other told him when he was to go to Buckingham Palace to receive his decoration. On that date, he noted, the *Marynal* would be in mid-Atlantic and, with the rest of the convoy, starting the swing southwards towards the tropics.

The letter from his mother was short, humorous and newsy. Clare came to see her when she was off duty, and they went to various places that they had wanted to see for ages but had never managed to fit in before. They had heard two debates in the House of Commons and, she commented, several young Members were trying to score runs by attacking the way the war was conducted when any other Member with any guts would have asked them why they were not helping fight it, leaving the older folk to do the grumbling. 'We shall no doubt hear a lot from these young gentlemen after the war,' she wrote sarcastically, 'because they are very glib. And, if the casualties increase, they'll be the only young survivors.'

Clare began by giving news of patients he knew at St Stephen's. Two surgical cases had recovered enough to be sent down to Willesborough and Sister Scotland, on the telephone last night making arrangements for them, wished to be remembered to him. The man now in his bed on the night the bomb dropped – as he read the words he could feel her body pressing on his – was a paymaster with a hernia and who had a terror of getting haemorrhoids. The rest of the letter, written the night he had left for Liverpool on the early train, was of the kind that made a man fold it carefully and put it in his wallet, and take it out in the lonely days before the next delivery of mail, and read it again and again.

A knock on the door startled him. It was one of the *Marynal*'s four cadets. The Navy and a few shipping companies called them midshipmen; most called them cadets; some referred to them as apprentices, which was the most accurate if not the most prestigious phrase: they were apprentice officers, even though all too frequently a third-rate company and a ruthless chief officer used them as cheap labour and made sure they never received a minute's instruction in mathematics, navigation, cargo work or ship construction. From what he had heard, Yorke knew that such youngsters had to pick up what they could in their off-watch time, poring over the standard text books.

'Blackout, sir' the cadet explained. 'I'm supposed to shut the deadlights.'

'Don't worry; I'll do them.'

The boy did not move; instead he looked embarrassed. He was, perhaps, just past his seventeenth birthday. From the nicks in his cheeks had to shave once a week and today was the big day. But he was smartly dressed even though his nails showed he had spent the day hard at work, probably in overalls; doing a seaman's job. 'I'll do them if you don't mind, sir. You see, I have to report to the Mate that I've seen them all secured, and you won't want me standing here watching you.'

Yorke grinned and said amiably, 'All right, you do that one and I'll do this.'

He swung the deadlight – in effect a second port, only made of solid metal – across the glass one and screwed down the clips. The cadet had done the other one and said: 'Thank you, sir. Are – are you coming with us this trip?'

Yorke nodded, and the boy took a deep breath. 'Is it true you won a DSO in destroyers, sir? And was wounded?'

Yorke nodded again, and then said: 'There are hundreds like me, you know!'

'Yes, sir, but you've come on board with a lot of secret equipment and two wireless operators. If you're doing a special job and need someone to help, well, sir, I'd be only too glad to do it when I'm not on watch.'

'What's your name?'

'Reynolds, sir. You see, I'm hoping to transfer to the RNR soon as a sub-lieutenant. I can when I've got two years' sea time. Well, providing I pass the Admiralty selection board. I've got all the papers because I wrote to the Admiralty and they gave me all the details.'

'How much sea time have you put in up to now?'

'Just over a year, sir. And a year at nautical school. You can take your second mate's ticket after only four years now – it used to be five. Then you can serve as a third mate. You're always one behind your certificate you see, sir, until you get your Master's ticket. Then you serve as Chief Officer for a few years, and get a command if you're lucky. And it's a good idea to take an Extra Master's ticket, too.'

Yorke was interested in the youngster's keenness. 'Why transfer to the RNR then? Surely you'll lose sea time as far as the Merchant Navy is concerned? Then when the war ends you won't have a ticket and I'm sure no one will want to employ ancient ex-cadets!'

'You think the war will last another year, sir?'

What a question… Another year of war and the boy could apply for a selection board to be appointed a sub-lieutenant, RNR. If the war was over in a year it would mean Britain had lost; if she could hold on more than a year she would probably win, but the war would then last – well, how long? Two, three, four years?

'At least another couple of years, I should think.'

The boy looked at Yorke, sensed the reply was an honest one, and grinned. 'Well, that's all right then, sir. In a year I can transfer. Two years in merchant ships and there'll be no sitting for a second mate's ticket because I'll be dead: ships are being sunk so fast. The old *Marynal* is running out of time, you mark my words, sir. She had five sister ships. Only one of 'em is still afloat.'

'Is that why you want to transfer to the RNR?'

'Oh no, sir, you stand more chance of getting killed in the Navy. No, I'm just sick of being attacked by these U-boats and bombers without being able to shoot back with anything that can do any good. Harm, rather. My mum and dad, you see; they lived in Croydon, right beside the old aerodrome; and the house got a direct hit, so I'm an orphan – well, my dad's sister, Aunty Lily, she's still alive, but she's getting old and is always tipsy. She didn't recognize me when I last went there.'

'Where do you go for your leaves?'

'Well, if one of the other cadets asks me home I go with him; but often as not I stay in the ship.'

'Very well,' Yorke said, 'if I need an assistant I'll ask the Captain for you.'

Now that the cabin was lit by electric light, the cork insulation covering the bulkheads and deckhead was emphasized; the whole cabin had the effect of a house cement-washed with tiny pebbles or gravel and then painted white. The cork chips stopped condensation in cold weather and were supposed to help keep it cool in the tropics. The hell of being in a cabin like this at night was that you couldn't have fresh air and light; opening the door tripped an on-off switch and put the lights out – a blackout precaution, when the ship was at sea, against someone suddenly opening a door before the lights were switched out.

He looked at his watch again. Two hours before dinner, and probably about the same amount of time before the raids started. The Germans would have to be asleep not to notice that the Gladstone and Queen's Docks in Liverpool were packed with fully-laden ships. The Luftwaffe was probably alerted to stage a big raid, U-boats were no doubt soon to be warned once the convoy had sailed – they would not attack within 500 miles of the coast because of Coastal Command. He suddenly felt tired and decided to go to bed.

It had taken two hours for the *Marynal* to get clear of the Queen's Dock and out into the River Mersey, a process which at times seemed like trying to lead a willing but large elephant out of a small but sharply-angled maze. The tug had pushed and pulled; Captain Hobson had used the propeller skilfully and mercifully there was very little wind, just the grey of a chilly drizzle, mixing with smoke from fires still burning after the night's bombing. The Mersey seemed to suck down the grey from the clouds and blend it with its own muddy brown water which contained more dead cats and dogs, contraceptives, soggy cardboard boxes and cabbage leaves than Yorke had previously seen in a waterway.

She had anchored for a tide and Yorke, used to the Royal Navy, where there were always plenty of seamen available (because many extra were needed when a warship went into battle), was startled by how few men were needed. The third officer had been on the bridge with Captain Hobson and a cadet. Then Yorke had seen the chief officer, strolling up to the fo'c'sle, where he was joined by a man he later discovered was the carpenter. The second officer had gone aft to the poop.

Captain Hobson had from time to time given orders to the cadet, who swung the indicator of the engine-room telegraph, and occasionally called a helm order to the quartermaster at the wheel. From inside the wheelhouse he could only see forward, and then through narrow horizontal slits in the blocks of armour-plated material which looked like grey-painted nut nougat and which were bolted on the front and sides of the wheelhouse, so he preferred to stand outside on one or other wing of the bridge, giving his orders quietly in his pleasant Yorkshire accent.

Finally he had the ship stemming the tide, which was just beginning to ebb. One order stopped the propeller turning; then he picked up the telephone which linked him to the chief officer on the fo'c'sle. 'Just about here, Mr Metcalfe; we're in eight fathoms…'

The chief officer waved to the carpenter, who turned the brake-wheel on the capstan and with a roar the chain started running out of the locker below as the anchor splashed into the river. The chief officer turned his head away from the cloud of rust and the carpenter spun the wheel again, so that the chain slowed down and eventually stopped.

Finally the ship was satisfactorily anchored, but even lying out in the river motor launches brought out men – Customs officials, port officials, company officials. The marine superintendent came on board to say goodbye to Captain Hobson and meet the naval lieutenant travelling in the *Marynal* and, more important, he confirmed that there would be no more passengers: the remaining passenger cabin would be empty for the voyage.

By late afternoon the *Marynal* was under way, surrounded by thirty-four other merchantmen. Each had her name board down – this, a large hinged plank usually fitted on either side of the bridge, was normally stowed folded up, hiding the name, but now, when the two frigates and three corvettes trying like sheepdogs to get the ships into convoy formation needed to be able to shout instructions (or threats) over the loudhailer, the name boards came in useful. Once the convoy was formed up the name boards would be folded again and each ship would be grey and anonymous, her name at bow and stern either removed or painted over.

Finally seven ships were steaming abreast of each other on the northern side of Liverpool Bay, the leaders of the columns, and the rest of the ships beginning to manoeuvre to get into the right column. 'The fact is,' Hobson said to Yorke, 'every master has spent his whole working life keeping his ship as far away as possible from any other vessel: in peacetime another ship close by means the risk of a collision. Now, in wartime, we're expected to back and fill quite cheerfully yards from someone else like a pregnant woman scurrying through the Christmas sales looking for a bargain. You chaps are trained right from the start to operate in squadrons, or flotillas, or whatever you call them, so you don't have patience with us old fogies.'

'True enough,' Yorke agreed, 'but Johnny Gower has only an hour's daylight left to get all these ships in position and steaming on the convoy course... If a U-boat sneaks in to attack with them scattered all over Liverpool Bay, it'd be Johnny's neck on the block because there's no way his escorts could do anything about it.'

Hobson watched as the chief officer manoeuvred the *Marynal* to pass astern of a ship in the fourth column and begin the turn to get into the fifth column, the next astern of the Swedish ship. The Swede was the third in the column, the *Marynal* the fourth, and the fifth and last in the column was an ancient three-island coal-burner with a tall, thin funnel; now getting into position like an old dowager joining a funeral procession.

Captain Hobson saw Yorke looking at her. 'One of the "Starving Stevens" – a tramp in peacetime. The owners have a dozen or so ships and a long history of underpaying crews and cheating them out of their grub...the kind of owners that give shipping a bad name and the reason why the lads sometimes need a strong union. And that particular one, the

Flintshire – she's a "smoker". The commodore'll be calling her up every day and telling her to make less smoke.' At that moment, as if to confirm it, her funnel erupted a stream of oily, black smoke which then curved astern and flattened out as the ship moved forward from under it.

Yorke looked ahead at the commodore's ship, leading the next column to port, but Hobson said: 'They'll leave her to smoke for today, just to give her stokers a chance to get their muscles back into trim. But you can bet her captain is on to his chief engineer already – the last time I was in convoy with her she smoked so badly the commodore ordered her to quit and she had to finish the trip on her own. Luckily we were bound for Freetown: if we'd been homeward bound she'd never have made it through the U-boats.'

By now the *Marynal* was beginning to pitch as she met the swell waves rolling in across Liverpool Bay from the north-west, and the bow of each of the ships occasionally spurted a white moustache. The *Marynal* vibrated because like all motor ships she had a critical speed, a narrow band at which she vibrated. Most captains and chief engineers hurried through it but occasionally, like now, they were forced to stay in it. Down in the galley stewards would be cursing as all the crockery and pans rattled. He pictured the table laid in the saloon for dinner and the glasses and cutlery vibrating their way to the edges, and the stewards wondering how long it would go on, trying to decide whether or not to fit the battens round the edges, the fiddles that stopped objects sliding off in heavy weather.

Hobson cursed and finally strode into the wheelhouse, picking up the telephone to the engine room. A minute or two later the *Marynal*'s speed dropped a knot or two and the vibration stopped. From now on all speed orders to the engine room would be given over the telephone; the big brass pillars of the engine room telegraphs on each wing of the bridge would not be used while she was in convoy. From now on it would be the 'up two revolutions...down one...up four...' about which the chief engineer had complained but which would keep the *Marynal* in position.

Night fell and the ships all round the *Marynal* merged into the darkness. Yorke was thankful there would be no zigzagging until they were out in the Atlantic: as they headed north-west they were in effect going towards the narrow neck of a funnel, leaving the Isle of Man to starboard and due to pass the channel between Northern Ireland to port and Scotland only twenty miles or so to starboard – Scotland seeming here to be a series of peninsulas dangling down like fingers reaching out for Ireland – the Mull of Kintyre, and then the Mull of Oa. Not far away to the west a country was at peace: in Eire there was no blackout, and no welcome, and the German Embassy was doing its normal business in Dublin. The bases in south-west Eire which could swing the balance in the Battle of the Atlantic were denied to the Royal Navy.

Yorke felt lost: being in a ship at sea with no duties was disturbing, giving him a vague feeling that he had forgotten something but was not quite sure what. Nor was it being at sea in normal circumstances: instead of the steady whining of steam turbines there was the drumming of diesels, more like a heavy lorry or a charabanc coasting down a hill.

He picked up a pair of binoculars and focused them on the Swedish ship, which was now just two hundred yards ahead. She had a good profile, a slight round in the bridge section giving a streamlined look, the funnel low and wide without seeming squat. All the accommodation was amidships, the fo'c'sle small and probably used only as storage for paint and rope. The poop was almost non-existent; being a neutral ship she carried no 4-inch gun there.

She was pitching, her cruiser stern lifting slightly in seesaw unison as her bow dipped. At this slow speed her propellers – he remembered that like most of the rest she had twin screws – left a distinctive wake of even whorls on the surface of the water. The smoke from the funnel was almost imperceptible; a series of tiny pulses.

Up to now a Swedish ship in an Allied convoy had been for him just a reference on a sheet of paper: the entry '(SW)' after a ship's name on a long list. There had been eleven such convoys and eleven such dockets, all locked up now in Uncle's safe at the Citadel, along with a twelfth, a new one which Yorke had started, giving every detail he knew up to the time the *Marynal* sailed from the Queen's Dock. If anything went wrong that docket would save his successor a lot of work.

But what had seemed a certainty back in the Citadel, in the curiously tense atmosphere of the ASIU room, seemed rather remote out here at sea. Looking at it on paper and noting that a Swedish ship had been the only common factor in each of the convoys, it had seemed not just suspicious but halfway towards solving the mystery of the insider U-boat. Such a fine clue, such a brilliant deduction, he jeered at himself, that he did all he could to persuade Uncle to let him get to sea in the next convoy that had a Swedish ship, leaving Clare, and for that matter a whole lot of remedial exercises for his hand and arm, which was now becoming very painful, to find out precisely what was happening and put a stop to it.

A sort of seagoing Sherlock Holmes, he sneered at himself, except that out here in the convoy, with a Swede just ahead, he was beginning to feel like the Toytown policeman on the BBC's Children's Hour. How could a Swedish ship sailing as number three in the fifth column possibly have anything to do with insider attacks by U-boats? If the ships were all sunk on the same bearings from the Swedish ships one could guess the Swedes were fitted with torpedo tubes. In fact all they had was the smug attitude of a neutral selling materials to both sides without even attempting any of the humanitarian work that Switzerland carried out. Yet one should be fair, he told himself; Sweden had the Russians on one side and the Germans on the other; she had seen two of the other nations in the original 'Three Crowns', Norway and Denmark, invaded by the Germans. Yet, yet...*why* was Sweden spared by the Germans? There could be no humanitarian reasons; having Sweden neutral gave Germany no advantage. She had to send her troops by the trainload through Sweden to occupy and garrison Northern Norway – indeed, the Free Norwegians regarded Sweden's permission as the ultimate stab in the back. It could only be Sweden's old and close friendship with Germany that saved her.

Whatever the reason, it didn't matter a damn out here; the convoy was under way in the proper formation; the three corvettes had managed to refuel and reammunition and join in time; it was getting damned cold as night fell, and there was absolutely no reason why he should stay on the bridge, particularly with a warm cabin and a pile of books and magazines waiting for him. And by now, with the door left open for so long, the smell of the O-Cedar might have gone away, and the Brasso, too. If the price of freedom was eternal vigilance, the price of a polish was an eternal odour, or so it seemed.

CHAPTER TWELVE

Four days later Yorke stood with Captain Hobson in the *Marynal*'s chartroom on the after side of the bridge and looked down at the North Atlantic chart, eastern section, where Hobson had just pencilled a light X and the date and a time and then, taking the dividers, measured the distance back to Londonderry. 'Just over five hundred miles,' Hobson said. 'We're not making bad time, considering how the weather has deteriorated.'

'We're on our own now,' Yorke said, and when he saw Hobson's eyebrows rise questioningly added: 'Well, we're beyond the range of air cover. For the Sunderlands and Catalinas, anyway, because their maximum range is under 500 miles' radius – less with these strong westerly winds up aloft. The Liberators can get out about 800 miles, but we've so few of them they concentrate on the incoming convoys. We're in The Black Pit, as it's known at the Admiralty.'

'Using those Liberators to meet only incoming convoys seems daft,' Hobson grumbled. 'After all, we're taking out supplies for the Eighth Army. We're just as important.'

'It seems different when you're sitting in the Admiralty. The Government's first priority is feeding the people in Britain. Don't forget that even the weekly cheese ration is down to the size of a matchbox.'

'Aye,' Hobson said wearily, 'you'll have to bear with me. But the fact of the matter is we never see *any* bloody aircraft –

except German ones – when we come back, so I don't really believe the policy. Sounds to me more like propaganda.'

'You see the German planes because they want to be seen,' Yorke explained patiently. 'But if you can see a Coastal Command aircraft it probably isn't doing its job properly – any German U-boats searching on the surface for a convoy or making for a rendezvous will be miles away, and it's out there that Coastal Command is looking.'

'You're probably right,' Hobson conceded, 'but you said yourself, we're on our own now.'

Yorke cursed to himself: his loose tongue meant a casual remark was now being given far too much importance. Yorke knew that to Hobson he represented the Admiralty in all its wit, wisdom and stupidity. Although the Yorkshireman had no certain idea why he was on board the *Marynal*, he was already beginning to notice that Yorke had a particular interest in the Swedish ship: one could look at the same ship with binoculars only so many times in a day before some wit asked if there was a beautiful Nordic blonde sunning herself naked on the poop. And the answer 'I'm waiting for the sun to come out,' would soon begin to wear thin.

'Beyond air cover, yes,' Yorke agreed.

Yorke thought for a few moments and then made up his mind. There was no point in keeping it secret, although there was no need to tell too much, either. Yet the men seeing the Swede all the time, if not actually watching her any more than was necessary to keep in position astern of her, were the mate and cadet on watch on the bridge. And, for that matter, there was no reason why he shouldn't have a DEMS gunner on the bridge as well…

'It's that Swede, isn't it?' Hobson commented. 'Something funny about him?'

Curious how foreign ships were usually called 'him'. Still, no reason to deny it now. 'We're keeping an eye on the Swede, but we don't know for sure he's up to anything.'

'They usually bring trouble,' Hobson said, as if stating a well-known fact.

'What sort of trouble?' Yorke asked curiously.

'Oh – people say there's usually a Swede in the convoy when a German submarine attacks solo.'

'Who are "people"?'

Hobson shrugged his shoulders. 'Other masters – you know, people. Last time I heard it was a few days ago in the bar at Euston Station when I met an old chum o' mine commanding a tanker. He'd just come in with a convoy that had lost a lot of ships from this one U-boat that got inside. Why, haven't you heard this latest gossip about the Swedes?'

Yorke nodded knowingly and Hobson winked. 'Thought you had,' he said. 'You coming to the convoy conference, and wanting to sit behind the Swedish master, and then me finding the *Marynal* is stationed next astern of the Swedish ship – I guessed what was up.'

Dismay, that was what he felt, and Yorke admitted it to himself as he rubbed his left arm, which was beginning to throb. Up to now it had just been a word, but now dismay was a definite feeling which he could describe in detail. Yorke with all the facts at his disposal – not to mention the resources of the ASIU, and indeed the Admiralty as well – had taken eleven dockets and several days to spot that there was always a Swede in a convoy attacked by an insider, but Merchant Navy masters had noticed it a long time ago – at least, when the attack was by a single U-boat. To them it was such a commonplace that they gossiped about it over a pint of mild and bitter in the bar at Euston Station. Gossip...for there was one thing about the Merchant Navy men: more than most people they were security-conscious; more than most people they knew it could be very easily their lives. So it was clear enough that the Swedish business was sufficiently commonplace now to be gossiped about... But the gossip had never reached the Admiralty.

It said something for the trust the Merchant Navy had in the Royal Navy that someone like Captain Hobson was only too willing to accept that the Admiralty knew and was fighting it; giving the Royal Navy the credit for having a complex problem to solve, and also accepting that Lieutenant Yorke (and presumably various other Lieutenants Yorke) were now about to do something about it.

Finally Yorke decided that if Captain Hobson had known (in company with many other masters) that the common denominator of each of the attacks (which neither Hobson nor his fellow captains realized was by an insider) had been a Swedish ship, he deserved to be told more. Then a moment later he realized that there was not much more to tell...

'I'd be glad of some help, Captain,' Yorke said. 'We are a bit short-handed, as you mentioned, but thanks to your chief sparks, my two signalmen are working decent watches, instead of watch and watch about. But for the time being I'm damned if I know what kind of help I need.'

'Well,' Hobson said tactfully, 'you just tell me what you think I should know, and no more.'

Yorke shook his head. 'It isn't that! We don't *know* much. I'm here just to keep an eye on this particular Swede. When the next Swedish ship applies for a convoy, another naval officer might be on board her next-astern – that is, if I haven't...'

'I see. Well, what's all this radio business for, then?'

'So I can keep in touch with the senior officer on frequencies neither the Swede nor the German are likely to be using.'

But you haven't used the sets yet, have you?'

'There's been nothing to say! Wait until the insider starts – if he does.'

' "Insider." Aye, that's a good name for him; come to think of it, he usually attacks from inside. Do you reckon we'll get one?'

'From your point of view, I hope not; from mine, yes!'

'Do you think this Swede is – well, controlling a U-boat? Telling him when to attack?'

'No – how would he do it? He's not using his radio – we know that for sure. How else could he pass a signal?'

'By Aldis lamp in daylight?' Hobson asked. 'If he knew where a U-boat was steaming on the surface – out on one of the quarters, for instance – he could use an Aldis to pass a message. If he signalled down a long tube, aiming it accurately, no one would see it unless he was directly in line.'

Yorke had to admit it was a possibility, but a slender one: the chances of the U-boat being in an exact position – and relying on getting the message when there might be a British escort in between – was slight. But Hobson's idea could not be ignored. Right at the moment Yorke knew he would be prepared to accept that the Swede wrote a message and put it in an empty cherry brandy bottle and slung it over the side for a U-boat lurking astern to find and read.

'We've no idea,' Yorke admitted, 'and that's why we must watch the Swede day and night for anything that's even slightly unusual. I'd be glad if you'd tell your officers, especially the cadets, who have less responsibility while on the bridge, to call me for the slightest thing. And I'd like to have a DEMS gunner on the bridge too, doing nothing else but watch. The point is a DEMS gunner doesn't know enough about the routine in a merchant ship to spot anything out of the way, and the mate of the watch and the cadet might have other things to do. Still, between the three of them – and myself some of the time...'

'And me too,' Hobson said.

'Thanks. Well, between us we should be able to keep an eye on them, and I'd like you to have your people call me immediately there's anything.'

'You could move up here,' Hobson said, pointing to the settee running athwartships across the after part of the cabin, between two large sets of drawers in which charts were kept. Above the settee was a large, glass-fronted cupboard in which a dozen or so rifles could be seen clipped to a rack. 'They'd be more inclined to pass the word about something if you were near. They might be a bit chary of sending down to your cabin. Or you can use the settee in my day cabin. You're more than welcome to that.'

Yorke shook his head. 'Thanks for the offer but sending someone down one deck to your day cabin is only slightly less trouble than going down one more deck to mine, so I'll use this settee, at night anyway. Then whoever it is has only to stick his head into the wheelhouse and call.'

'Good,' said Hobson, 'and I'll warn the chief steward. Cocoa,' he added when he saw Yorke's puzzled expression. 'The stewards leave out mugs of cocoa already mixed, so that in the middle of the watch the cadet nips down, adds hot water and brings the mugs up to the bridge. But he can't carry four mugs, so we'll keep mugs up here and the stewards can leave out jugs of cocoa.'

'Such comfort!' Yorke joked, but Hobson shook his head.

'A cold man is an inefficient man. A shivering man can't keep a sharp lookout. All he's thinking about is getting to the end of his watch and the warmth of his bunk or hammock. Put something warm in his belly and he realizes that if he misses seeing a U-boat he'll be cold and wet in no time!'

Hobson had been twiddling with the dividers and finally put them back in the rack, his eyes following the kinks in the line that showed the convoy's zigzagging course so far.

He looked up at Yorke, catching his brown eyes watching him. 'Tell me, what happens when we find this Swede's a wrong 'un?'

'If, not when. Well, I'm damned if I know. Depends what he's doing. It might be us or it might be the escort that has to do something.'

'I'll ram him if need be,' Hobson said quietly. 'I'd need to catch him on the quarter. Those Baltic ships,' he explained, 'often have their bows strengthened for the ice. Hit him in the quarter and I'd probably throw one of his propeller shafts out of alignment so he could manoeuvre only on one screw, with his rudder hard over. Or I can really wallop him amidships and tear him open so he sinks. You just say. But don't expect me to go back for survivors.'

Hobson's voice was so low that Yorke knew he was speaking under a considerable emotional strain. Then he realized that officers and master in the Merchant Navy had much the same kind of bond, or brotherhood, that knitted the Royal Navy: as boys, many of them had started off together at one of the nautical training colleges, like Pangbourne, Conway or Worcester; they had over the years met in distant ports, knocking back strange drinks in smoky bars, come together again for the few months spent at nautical school to swot before sitting for a higher certificate of competency. Obviously there were friendships going back twenty or thirty years which people like Hobson had seen cut short when a ship was torpedoed and sunk, drowning men he had known since his teens.

He watched Hobson make an entry in the log and a minute or two later the second officer poked his head round the door. 'All right if I wind the chronometer, sir?' he asked, and Hobson nodded. The man went to the varnished mahogany box, opened the lid and took out the key. He counted to himself carefully as he wound, then put the key back and carefully shut the lid. The day's ritual of winding the chronometer was over, and the fact would be recorded in the log, along with how fast or slow it was.

The cloud was thickening now and getting lower; another depression coming up fast. The swell pushed ahead of it was already low, making the ship roll. Tonight would be very dark with a cold, lumpy sea. Good conditions for an insider to attack? Marginal, judging from the previous attacks, except for the few U-boats which had attacked on the surface in much worse weather. But if the depression kept south, passing near the convoy instead of turning up to the north-east, tomorrow night would probably be too bad even for a surface attack. So if the insider was already inside the convoy, the first attack would be tonight.

Yorke saw that Hobson had unlocked the safe to one side of the chart table and taken out an unbleached canvas bag which had brass eyelets round the opening and through which ran a thick cord. Hobson undid the knot, slacked it off and opened the bag enough to slip the big log inside. 'The secret papers – just in case,' he said. 'Not that we have many – Mersigs; zigzag diagrams, and the log for good measure. And a six-pound lead weight to sink it all...'

Hobson looked at his watch. 'Would you like to join me for lunch? After that I'm going to get my head down for an hour or two; the way things look, it might be a long night.'

Yorke was on his second copy of *Blackwood*'s when Cadet Reynolds knocked at the cabin door and came in with an excited: 'Captain's compliments, sir: that Swede, the *Penta*, is making some funnel smoke and talking to the Commodore by lamp.'

As Yorke grabbed his duffel coat and cap he asked: 'Much smoke?'

'No, sir – course, she's a motor ship. Before the signalling Captain Hobson called the chief engineer up to the bridge to look and he says it's probably just sooting up because we're only making six knots. We'll be doing the same in a few days, he says, unless we work up to full speed for a while to blow out the carbon.'

By now they had reached the bridge and Captain Hobson handed Yorke a piece of paper.

'That's what the commodore said in reply; of course, we couldn't read what the *Penta* was flashing.'

Yorke read the hurriedly written words, jotted down letter by letter as someone, probably the third officer, read out the Morse letters flickering out questions from the Aldis lamp an the commodore's bridge: 'Is it serious… How long for repairs… Rejoin convoy before darkness, if necessary on one engine.'

Hobson saw Yorke glancing ahead to the Swedish ship. 'I don't know what's wrong – she's smoking a bit, but I had the chief engineer up – he's still in the wheelhouse – and he says the smoke is about what you'd expect at this slow speed.'

'He can't give us any other clues?' Yorke asked impatiently, irritated by what seemed to be a superficial, shrug-of-the shoulders comment.

'No, says we'll be as bad ourselves in a few days. Sparking at night as well. It's happened before; we just leave the convoy for an hour and work up to full speed: that blows the muck out.'

Cadet Reynolds said: 'The *Penta*'s moving out, sir.'

And she was turning a few degrees to starboard so that she was soon between the columns of ships and obviously slowing down to let the *Marynal* and *Flintshire* overtake and leave her astern of the convoy.

'I suggest we don't seem too curious,' Yorke said to Hobson, who nodded and led the way into the wheelhouse.

'We can see all we want from in here,' Hobson said, watching with his binoculars through the narrow horizontal slits which were like letter box slots cut in the armour plating. 'Not that there's much to see. A couple of mates on the bridge this side. Smoke about the same. They're just keeping steerage way. Nice-looking ship. She's got a couple of 40-ton jumbo derricks at number three hatch. That 20-tonner we have is useless, but the owners won't change it'

By now, the *Penta* was getting close, and Yorke could see she was well painted: she spent the end of a voyage in a Swedish port with no war, no blackout, and no shortages. There would be plenty of paint and plenty of painters – and plenty of profits to pay for the labour. The other ships in the convoy looked like the poor and ugly sisters – rust streaks because quick turn-rounds did not leave enough time for a ship's company to get over the side and chip, scrape and paint: there's a war on, mate...

Soon the *Penta* had dropped so far astern that she was on the *Flintshire*'s quarter, and Watkins came into the wheelhouse looking for Yorke. 'Talk, sir, between the escorts, but nothing for us,' he said, obviously being discreet. Yorke walked out of the wheelhouse with him and round to the after side of the bridge.

'Just "Lancaster" telling "Cornwall" and "Kent" – the corvette on each quarter – that the *Penta* (they didn't mention her name) was dropping astern to make some repairs, sir.'

Yorke nodded because it was all so routine. 'Lancaster' was Johnny Gower's radio code name (chosen as a partner to 'Yorke'), while the escort was generically known as 'Cantab' although each frigate and corvette had her own individual name. On this occasion the Commodore would have made a signal to the senior officer of the escort, Johnny Gower, that a merchant ship was leaving the convoy for a few hours, and Johnny would have told the corvettes and no one would mention the word 'Swedish'…and they all knew that Yorke in the *Marynal* was listening. There was nothing to arouse anyone's suspicion; no signals were being made to the *Marynal*. There was no deviation from the normal routine – that was something he and Johnny Gower had discussed in detail. If the Swede was up to something, there must be nothing out of the ordinary to put him on his guard. Likewise in case it was not the Swede but something else in or around the convoy, it was essential that she or they should not know that a special lookout was being kept from the *Marynal*. People might do something (with the escort three miles away or the commodore across the convoy) if the ships close round them – ships like the *Marynal* – were believed to be normal merchant ships.

Watkins went back to the hot cabin packed with radio gear – the glowing valves kept it pleasantly warm in a cold climate, but he would be grumbling about the heat long before they reached the Tropic of Cancer. Still, Yorke thought unsympathetically, he could not have it both ways. At that moment he saw the Swedish ship had stopped and her bow was gradually paying off as the wind pushed her round. In a minute or so she would be lying athwart the seas and rolling heavily. Curious…

'That's odd,' Hobson said from just behind him. 'Not making it any easier for the engineers, are they… If they'd keep one screw turning they'd head into these seas. I can't believe they have trouble with both engines. Maybe once she starts rolling there'll be complaints from the engine room and the bridge will let 'em keep one going.'

Yorke said nothing and Hobson, who had obviously been thinking aloud, said: 'Don't take any notice of me; obviously her captain wouldn't do anything without talking it over with his chief engineer. So they must have trouble in both engines.'

'It's a pity we can't spare one of those corvettes to stand by her,' Yorke said crossly, pulling his duffel coat tighter: it was bitterly cold out here with the wind eddying round the wheelhouse.

'Aye,' Hobson said, chuckling, 'a sort of chaperone, eh?'

What were the chances of two engines breaking down? Two engines might carbon up at the same time – indeed quite naturally they would, but according to the *Marynal*'s chief engineer, all they needed was to be run under load for an hour. Contaminated fuel? That would affect both engines, but each had its own series of filters, and it would be unusual to shut both engines down to clean both sets of filters at the same time. Clean one set and then clean the other. But…but… Supposing a nasty old lady put round the word that the vicar was up to some nonsense which she refused to describe: then people would watch him secretly, and if the poor man paused to stare into a hedgerow, they would never consider that he might be looking at a bird's nest; an innocent peering into the hedge round a neighbour's garden could become a peeping Tom…

'It's a right bugger, isn't it?' Hobson commented. 'There's nothing to get your teeth into.'

Almost exactly six hours later Yorke stood with Captain Hobson at the same place on the after side of the bridge, watching the *Penta* astern. It would be dark in half an hour; already the cadet of the watch was going round the various cabins making sure the deadlights were closed and screwed down tight.

'No, I can't explain it,' Hobson said, 'but it's like what you were saying about the vicar looking over the hedge: he might be looking at Mrs Buggins' hollyhocks, but he might also be looking at Mrs Buggins undressing in her bedroom beyond the hollyhocks.'

'And you agree the *Penta* was making fifteen knots when she came into sight over the horizon?' Yorke asked.

'She must have been. Just about her maximum, I'd say – why with the glasses you saw her bow and quarter waves.'

'And how far off was she when she slowed down?'

'Four miles? You said something at the time but I was too busy watching her through my glasses.'

'I said that I reckoned she was between three and four miles.'

'You want my confirmation, eh? I'll put it down in the log if you like. Would that help?'

It's worth logging,' Yorke said, looking at his watch. 'We might need evidence one day. And she slowed down an hour and fifteen minutes ago.'

'As much as that? Maybe she has engine trouble again. On one screw, perhaps.'

Yorke shook his head. 'She's stayed exactly on course. One propeller trying to push her round in circles against the rudder would keep the quartermaster busy; he'd never hold such a straight course.' Yorke gestured astern at the *Marynal's* wake. 'The Swede's keeping as good a course as us.'

'Maybe he's nervous – look!' Hobson gestured as a small blue pinprick of light showed on the *Penta's* bridge. Yorke hurried round to the foreside of the bridge and was in time to meet Reynolds who reported excitedly: 'Commodore calling up the *Penta*, sir!'

'Read the signal and the *Penta's* reply,' Yorke said, pulling out a notebook and pencil.

Reynolds spelled out the words of the Commodore's signal while Yorke watched the *Penta* for the long dash, T, showing the word had been received. 'Take up original position,' the Commodore ordered, and then asked: 'Are all repairs completed?' He too was obviously puzzled by the *Penta* suddenly slowing down.

'Temporary repairs completed and hope final tomorrow,' the *Penta* answered, finishing with 'AR' signalling the end of the message' and to which the Commodore gave a brief 'R'. The exchange of signals was over. Did it mean anything?

'What was all that?' Hobson asked, and when Yorke read him the two signals he commented, 'He can make full speed on temporary repairs...yet he'll be dropping astern again tomorrow... It'll be interesting to see if he goes out of sight again.'

'More interesting to see if we get an attack tonight', Yorke said, then found himself startled by what he had said, as though the words had been spoken by a stranger.

Hobson stared at him, his homely features becoming taut, as though just given proof of his wife's unfaithfulness. 'Like that, is it?'

CHAPTER THIRTEEN

The dull red flash over on the port bow was like a great furnace door flung open for a few seconds and then slammed again. It made a deep reverberation, rather than an explosion, and Yorke looked at the luminous hands of his watch. Eight twenty. One torpedo. The insider had started.

'Second ship in the fourth column,' Captain Hobson said. 'In the next column to us, in other words, and she is on the *Penta*'s port bow. I wonder...'

He broke off as a second red glow dead ahead silhouetted the Swedish ship for a few moments, signalling that one of the leading ships in the *Marynal*'s column had been hit.

'That could be the leader of our column,' Hobson said.

'No, it'll be the second. The U-boat probably fired a bow tube at the first ship and the stern tube at the second.'

'Has he time to reload that stern tube and fire at us as we go past?'

'I don't think so,' Yorke said, 'but it might be the other way round, and he has his bow heading this way. Anyway you'll be leaving the sinking ship to port so she'll still be between us and the U-boat.' It was a tactful way of making sure Hobson took the *Marynal* the right way, but the Yorkshireman was already calling a helm order through to the wheelhouse and looking astern to see if he could distinguish the *Flintshire*.

'The *Penta*'s beginning to swing out to starboard, sir,' the cadet reported and Yorke recognized the voice of young

231

Reynolds. 'And I can see torches flashing about on that torpedoed ship – she looks heeled over, the best I can see with the glasses, so they're probably abandoning – Jesus!' he exclaimed as another red flash lit up everyone on the bridge and for a moment Yorke saw all the ships on the starboard side of the convoy.

'Another one in about the same position as the first,' Hobson said. 'Must be the third ship in that column hit while she was passing. That German reloaded fast!'

'No, that was from his bow tubes.'

'You think it's an insider, not a pack?'

Never forecast the result on the day of the race – Yorke remembered a journalist giving him that advice years ago. 'Yes,' Yorke answered. 'No one's been hit on the wings of the convoy.'

'Flames, sir,' Reynolds reported urgently. 'That last ship – I saw some round by number two hatch, as though they're coming up the ventilators.'

By now the Swedish ship was swinging well out to starboard to clear the torpedoed ship ahead of her and Hobson was passing another helm order to the quartermaster in the wheelhouse. Yorke called up to Jenkins, the leading seaman who was standing on the monkey island above the bridge, the microphone of a Tannoy system in his hand, waiting to pass fire orders to his guns.

'Jenkins – tell your fellows to train round to red seven-five: there's just a chance you might spot this submarine on the surface, beyond the torpedoed ships. Open fire at once if you do – the tracer might make the Jerries keep their heads down.'

As he finished speaking he was just beginning to distinguish Jenkins' figure standing up against the night sky, wearing a steel helmet and hunched over the microphone, and he realized the slight flicker was because the whole ship

– all the nearby ships in fact – were being lit up by the flames suddenly coming from the last ship to be torpedoed.

'That's the *Florida Star*,' Hobson said. 'I hope she isn't carrying ammo. And just listen…'

Above the gentle rumble of the engine and the whine of the wind, Yorke could hear a weird, distant moan, deep and distressed, the sound of some great mechanical object in agony.

'Her siren's jammed,' Hobson said. 'Often does that when a ship's hit. A derrick or something breaks adrift and swings across the lanyard leading to the siren. The noise is deafening; no one can hear orders.'

Yorke glanced over his shoulder at the long wire lanyard leading from the after side of the bridge to the *Marynal*'s funnel. 'Ought to stow it during attacks!' he said. He meant it but made it into a joke; Captain Hobson's whole life at sea had been spent with the blast of a siren only a quick tug away, to be used in fog and to signal the ship's intentions to another vessel – one blast meant she was turning to starboard, two to part and three that her engine was going astern. But Yorke, seeing how control would break down entirely if the roaring of a siren prevented any orders being heard, reacted from a different background: in an emergency during a convoy attack it was more important to control your men than signal to another ship…

Hobson, watching the *Florida Star* burning, seemed hypnotized by looking at the fire, the seaman's worst enemy. The whole forward part of the ship was blazing now with flames leaping as high as the bridge, but because she still had way on, her own forward movement against the wind created a roaring draught sweeping the fire aft. Through binoculars Yorke could see black figures dropping from the after side of the bridge down on to the deck thirty feet below, risking injury from the jump to escape the flames rolling aft like jagged waves and enveloping the whole bridge and wheelhouse.

Yorke trained his binoculars on the *Penta*. With the wind on the port bow she was rolling like the rest of the ships, but there was no sign of anyone out on the wings of the bridge. The Swedes must be inside the wheelhouse. Curious (or was it natural for frightened men to seek cover?). In a ship men tended – hmm, he remembered he had seen frightened men bolt below, and he had also seen frightened men scurry up on deck, scared of being trapped below. But…he shrugged his shoulders beneath his bridge coat: he had seen very few frightened men, and they had all regained control in a few minutes, indeed, a few moments, usually more scared of anyone else noticing than of death itself.

The *Penta* seemed like a bulky black ghost sliding on into the darkness, turning just enough to pass that black mound on her port side that had, until a few minutes ago, been her next ahead, and was now a steel shell filling with water pouring in through a great hole on her port side. A black ghost she might seem, but the *Penta* was doing nothing that a neutral ship would not be expected to do in the circumstances: haul out to avoid the casualty ahead and increase speed to fill the gap in the column – it was all in convoy orders, just as the *Marynal* would in a few moments increase speed to fill the gap left by the *Penta* moving ahead and the *Flintshire* too would have to move up. With the difference, he thought grimly, that an untoward shower of sparks tonight would make the coal-burner a perfect target…

Out there astern, until now a figure of fun to the *Marynal's* cadets, was the tug. She was tiny compared with the merchant ships (even though she could tow any one of them across the Atlantic if the need arose) and as the swell waves had come up with the approaching depression she had looked absurd as she seemed to chug up one side, flip over the crest like a seesaw and then chug down the other side into the trough, like a toy tugged on a string across a rippling pond. It was obvious that after a good gale the tug would be lucky if she had a single whole piece of china left on board but, as the second mate had remarked in his dour Sunderland accent, no hungry man baulked at eating a hot meal from an enamel bowl. Tonight, though, they had to try and rescue the men from three ships. Three so far.

Yes, there was Hobson going into the wheelhouse to call the engine room on the telephone. They would have heard the three dull but heavy rumbles coming through the water above the din of the engine and generators. Obviously torpedo hits. Yorke could never understand how during an attack engineers stayed sane down in their brightly lit engine room with a noise that prevented any talking, watching dials that varied in diameter from a saucer to the face of a church clock, and knowing that any moment a long steel tube about twenty-one inches in diameter and loaded with explosive might crash through the side of the hull... And above the noise the heat, so hot that even though there might be ice and snow on deck, down there men would be perspiring in the equivalent of the Tropics, many of them dressed in nothing but an oily pair of shorts...

Now the *Marynal* seemed to come alive as her propeller speeded up, and then Hobson was standing beside him again, his face pink in the flames from the *Florida Star*, which was now lying on the *Marynal*'s port beam. Hobson was calm enough, even though he knew quite well it needed only a moment to transform the *Marynal* from a well-run merchant ship to a flaming wreck like the *Florida Star*.

The DEMS gunner who for the whole watch so far had been watching the ship ahead with his binoculars said to Yorke: 'The Swede's hauling round to part now, sir, like she was getting back into the column.'

'Very well,' Yorke said, and was thankful that the far side of the *Marynal's* bridge and the wheelhouse were now beginning to obscure the furnace that was the *Florida Star*. The flames had a horrible, almost magnetic attraction – and he was glad to see that the DEMS lookout not only did not sneak a glance but kept his hands cupping the eyepieces of the binoculars to prevent the fire reflecting into his eyes and completely spoiling his night vision.

And her siren. Along with a bell buoy tolling in a calm on a black, foggy night, it was the eeriest noise he had ever heard at sea. Kempenfelt at Spithead and Sir John Moore at Coruña...toll for the brave...nor a funeral note.

Suddenly beside him one of the signalmen appeared, direct from the radio cabin. ' "Lancaster" is calling "Cantab", sir. Passed the word "Andrews".'

'Very well.'

So Johnny Gower was telling all the rest of the escorts that the attack was by an insider; no pack was involved. It was a routine message sent by low power, although presumably the insider would send off a report to Kernevel as soon as he had time, to tell Grandpa Doenitz how easy it was.

Should he go into the radio cabin and tell 'Lancaster' that 'Yorke' was asking for a 'War of the Roses down the middle', which was the phrase they had agreed on should Yorke think it was worth a frigate making a sweep down one of the columns? Or up – he had to specify which, and there was quite a difference. A frigate down between two columns at, say, ten knots would be meeting ships coming towards her at six knots, so they would be passing at sixteen knots. But going up the column, from astern to ahead, she would be passing at their speed subtracted from her own, at four knots in other words, the speed of a dawdling bureaucrat with his sandwiches in his briefcase.

The answer was no, just as he and Jemmy and the Croupier had agreed it probably would be as they drew sketches in the ASIU room at the Citadel. Supposing a frigate managed to get a contact over there, between the columns. Even if it was in the middle, the lines of ships would be only one hundred yards away on each side of her, and if the U-boat bolted – as it certainly would – the risk of chasing it and dropping depth charges with their delay would be too great: half a pattern might explode directly under an oncoming merchant ship which had steamed over them as they sank, breaking her back, and doing the U-boat's work. Even worse, as far as the long-term safety of this convoy was concerned, the frigate might collide with a merchant ship and receive damage so that the escort was reduced either in size or effectiveness. No War of the Roses, in other words. Not tonight, Josephine, but it may come to that in the end.

The *Florida Star* was drawing astern now as the *Marynal* passed and through the binoculars Yorke could see a group of men huddled right aft, as far away from the flames as they could get. Then his stomach turned as realized the flames had swept aft so fast there had been no time to get to the rafts and the lifeboats were still hanging from the davits – the two on the starboard side, anyway. The forward rope falls of one had burn through so it hung vertically; the second was burning like a bundle of kindling, still held by the gripes, which would be wire or chain. In the distance, right astern, he saw white flecks and for a moment thought of a U-boat pursuing on the surface and then realized it was the tug coming out of the darkness and looking like a halftide rock, shipping green seas right over the bow as she raced to get to the *Florida Star*. With thirty or forty men gathered high up on the stern of a blazing ship, it was going to take superb seamanship to get the tug's bow or stern under the after overhang so that the survivors could drop to safety. But of all seamen, the tug skippers and mates were among the finest, and they were lucky that the *Florida Star* had an old-fashioned stern that stuck out like an aggressive dowager's chin and under which they could probably manoeuvre.

Hobson said quietly: 'I should think we're past now, aren't we?'

'Depends where the U-boat was when she fired: no certainty she was abeam of the *Florida Star*. She might have been fine on her starboard bow, and that would put her on our port beam now...'

'You're a comfort,' Hobson grumbled good-naturedly just as the DEMS gunner turned from the bridge rail to report to Yorke.

'The first ship that was hit is now on our port bow, sir: red three-oh. Down by the bow with a heavy list to starboard.'

'Can you see any boats?' Yorke asked.

'Thought I saw two this side, sir, but those flames from the *Florida Star* make funny shadows with the crests and troughs.' He resumed looking through his binoculars and then added: 'Both boats are gone from this side; I can see the empty davits.'

Any innocent questions, answers or reports helped pass the time; the time it took the *Marynal* to get past the insider. Yorke imagined the German torpedomen over there, sixty feet or so deep in their metal cylinder, heaving and grunting and cursing as they slid new torpedoes into the tubes. No doubt the *Oberleutnant* commanding the boat was trying to make them hurry as new targets passed across his bow and, while petty officers cursed, seamen probably suffered the usual crop of nipped fingers and bruised arms. Of course, Yorke had forgotten to ask Jemmy an important question: how long did it take a submarine to reload four tubes?

He could see the dark shape of the first casualty and she was now abeam, her misshapen silhouette showing how much she was listing – it seemed that in daylight they would be able to look down her funnel, and her masts were like stunted fishing rods poking out from the river bank. Then suddenly the black shape seemed to be surrounded by a bubbling, whitish-green collar.

'She's going!' Hobson exclaimed.

The ship slowly turned over, capsizing with an ever-increasing flurry of white water as though some enormous sea anemone was sucking her down: the air pressure hurled up hatchcovers like a box of matches emptied in the wind.

Hobson was nudging him and he saw much closer, lying dead in the water and now revealed by the Swedish ship's turn, the second ship hit that night, the second ship in their own column and the one whose position had been ahead of the *Penta*.

Yorke, resting his elbows on the bridge rail, swung his binoculars in a circle round the ship. Two lifeboats and four rafts in the water; a third lifeboat being lowered even now because, by luck, the ship was settling upright. A ship heeling as she sank usually meant only the lifeboats on the low side could be launched because those on the high side would not fall clear of the davits without hitting the curving bilge of the ship.

The Board of Trade, now called the Ministry of War Transport, had over the years loaded the dice against the merchant seaman: starting off with the fact that none of the lifeboats for a merchant ship had to have a motor – which meant that in a gale of wind they would be lucky if one boat in four managed to get away – the Board of Trade had specified a type of lifejacket which ensured that most of the men who failed to get into a lifeboat and had to swim would die anyway.

First there had been the scandal (except that of course the Ministry officials made sure that censors stopped it appearing in the Press) of the cork 'BoT' lifejackets. These had by law to be carried, but no bureaucrat had ever tested them properly, so that when a particular troopship was bombed and started sinking rapidly at the time of Dunkirk, hundreds of soldiers donned their lifejackets, lined up on deck and obeyed the order to jump over the side. Within minutes the sea was covered with dead soldiers – men with their necks neatly broken. They had dived in feet first and quite naturally their bodies should have gone under the water for a few feet before they surfaced – as anyone who had ever attended a swimming pool would know. But the big cork blocks in the BoT lifejackets, at the front and back, had stopped that – and because they were not secured between the men's legs, the blocks floated the moment they hit the water and jammed hard up against the jaw and the back of the head so that the plunging men's own weight dislocated their vertebrae as effectively as if the lifejackets had been hangmen's nooses.

The men at the Ministry had then designed a new type of lifejacket, a cross between a waistcoat and a jacket without sleeves. The jacket, made of a light brown material, was filled with kapok, like the quilted coats worn by Chinese labourers. Kapok was cheap, light, buoyant and warm, so that men on watch could wear the lifejacket in cold weather and it helped them keep warm. Altogether it seemed a splendid design – except that apparently no one had tested it properly.

When a motor ship was torpedoed, usually the surface of the sea was covered with diesel fuel, one of the most penetrating liquids in general use. Into this oil – there need be only a thin film of it on the surface of the sea – drifted the hapless seaman wearing his new lifejacket. Unless he was picked up he would sink in twenty-four hours, because the lifejacket soaked up diesel like a wick and it destroyed the kapok's buoyancy. Because a drowned seaman did not return to haunt the gentlemen from the Ministry, it took a long time for the defect to be discovered – Yorke noticed the *Marynal's* men still had the old type. The Royal Navy's blue tube, inflated by mouth, might look crude by comparison, Yorke thought, but it kept men afloat…

Now they were past the last of the torpedoed ships: the dark shape ahead was the Swede; ahead of her would be the leader of the column. The commodore led the next column to port – a column which now had only three of its original five ships left. The *Flintshire* was, to his surprise, in position astern; she had increased speed to keep up with the *Marynal*.

'Do you think that's it for the night?' Hobson asked conversationally.

'Your guess is as good as mine, Captain. I'd guess it is.'

'Me too; that German lad has plenty more nights left. Any road, there's time for some cocoa. Can you spare our lookout? No, don't worry, young Reynolds can get it. Here, lad, now listen. Find another jug down there in the galley and see how far you can stretch it all with hot water. Don't drown it, though. And if you hear any more torpedoes out there leave it and come straight back to the bridge.'

Yorke walked across to the radio cabin, banged on the door to warn that he was going to open it and put the cabin in darkness until he had closed it again, and went in. Watkins was sitting at the chair in front of his sets, concentrating on a paperback book which had been read by so many people that the picture of a long-haired blonde girl with heaving bosoms (barely covered by a black lace brassiere being subjected to strains undreamt of by bridge builders and constructors of harbour breakwaters) was nearly worn off. The second signalman appeared to be asleep on the mattress, his head cradled on a Merchant Navy lifejacket, although his own RN one was beside him, with his steel helmet. The chief radio officer was on watch, too, and listening in on the call and distress frequency.

Watkins jumped up when he recognized the muffled figure as Yorke. 'Bit noisy out there, sir!'

'It's quietening down now. Anything else interesting being said?'

' "Lancaster" 's just checked with "Charlie" (that's "Tail End Charlie," the tug, sir) to ask if he's got the chaps off the flamer.'

'Has he?'

'Five women passengers, sir. The crew put ropes round 'em and lowered 'em down into the tug, cutting the ropes as soon as the tug chaps signalled they could catch each woman. Saved all five…'

Yorke knew what Watkins was going to add, and was thankful the *Marynal* had no passengers at all.

'…But it took time, and the last eleven had to jump into the sea, else the flames would have got them. Five women and twelve men saved.'

'And the other two ships?'

'One of the corvettes is being sent back later to help, but in the meantime the tug will do what she can, sir.'

'That's all?'

'Yes, sir; quiet night apart from that,' Watkins said without any conscious irony. 'One thing about these insiders – they give the escorts much less rushing about than a pack…'

Yorke nodded and thought to himself: *they sink damn nearly as many ships in each attack, though.* He looked at the second signalman, who was still fast asleep. The capacity of a British seaman to snatch a zizz, as he called it – a word derived from the 'zzzz' used in the speech balloons of strip cartoons – was phenomenal. Here was a ship at action stations and only minutes past a fairly savage U-boat attack, but Telegraphist 'Stripey' Bennett could be put in peril of his life by a zealous officer. It was a very fine point indeed whether Bennett was off watch (since he was doing watch and watch about with Watkins) or at action stations, like every other man in the ship. If he was off watch, then certainly he could sleep. If he was at action stations, then his present doze made him guilty of one of the most heinous crimes in the naval calendar, sleeping at action stations.

Ordinary Seaman Bennett, however, had already achieved some fame serving with the commodore in a merchant ship which had a Chinese crew. He had fallen out with the Chinese boatswain. Going to sleep on deck in the Tropics one day wearing only a pair of shorts, he had woken to find that while he slept the Chinese had painted him in narrow red, white and blue stripes and in the process given him a nickname he would never lose for the rest of the time he served before retiring with a pension after twenty-one years' service.

Yorke left the radio cabin and stood outside for a few minutes waiting for his night vision to return. Gradually the *Marynal* took shape round him; soon he could see the ship in the next column to starboard. He walked forward and then climbed the ladder to the monkey island. Jenkins, who had obviously been watching him, was waiting at the top. 'Jerry's gone home for the night, eh sir?'

'Looks like it,' Yorke said, sniffing suspiciously.

'Cold night,' Jenkins said quickly. 'Cup o' kai would be welcome, I expect, sir.'

So that was it: the gunners on the monkey island were sipping at mugs of steaming hot cocoa, but the only thing was that they were all at action stations, and the only way they could have obtained steaming hot cocoa was for one of the men to leave his post and dash down to the galley. Well, the DEMS gunners were not his responsibility and it was a cold night, and...one could always find excuses. 'No, thanks,' he said, 'mine will be ready on the bridge. Did you sight anything?'

'No tracks or anything, sir. I'd have reported if we had.'

'No, I didn't mean that,' Yorke said, hearing the hurt note in Jenkins' voice. 'I'd be interested if anyone saw anything different from the usual routine. On board the Swede, for instance.'

'No, sir. The only thing was we didn't see anyone moving about. Usually they're careless with cigarettes at night. Light up in the wheelhouse and then go out on the wing of the bridge for a few puffs, and we can see a glow. Not tonight, though, even before the first ship was hit. George commented on it, didn't you, George?'

George removed the cocoa mug from his lips and tried to stifle a belch. 'S'right, sir.'

Back on the bridge Yorke found Cadet Reynolds holding two mugs of cocoa and doing his best not to spill them as the ship rolled. He gave one to Yorke, and Captain Hobson said: 'Another fifteen minutes and we'll stand down. No point in keeping the lads at action stations all night.'

'None,' Yorke said. He felt like adding bitterly that despite the night's destruction the ASIU knew no more now than it did before Lt Yorke left the Citadel. This convoy was likely to end up being another docket. The twelfth convoy docket giving inconclusive details of an insider attack. So far a Swedish ship had broken down, it was blowing hard, three ships had been torpedoed, and the cocoa was too sweet. No doubt Uncle would tell the Second Sea Lord's department that Lt Yorke was now available for sea service and, depending on Uncle's report, he would find himself back in destroyers if good or, if Uncle considered he had made an even worse mess of the ASIU job than expected, then Yorke would find himself NOIC in some improbable small port in the Tropics where the humidity was about 98%, the temperature around 100° and his neighbours would be Somerset Maugham characters peering blearily over their whisky which was poured straight from the bottle into greasy chipped glasses.

'Where's Yorke?' they would ask in the clubs in London. 'Oh, he's Naval Officer in Charge at some place on the Red Sea.' 'Indeed?' Raised eyebrows would show that the inquirer was far too polite to ask what Yorke had ballsed up to warrant such a posting...

CHAPTER FOURTEEN

Next morning Yorke spent only fifteen minutes writing an account of the previous night's attack on the convoy. He had a convoy diagram and it took no time to work out where the U-boat had been lying: she had been at right angles to the convoy course between the commodore's fourth column and the *Marynal's* fifth. The German had definitely fired a bow tube at the second ship in the commodore's column, and the single torpedo from his stern tube had hit the ship ahead of the Swede. Then the *Florida Star*, third ship in the commodore's column, had come into his sights. And, with three ships hit, the U-boat must then have dived clear.

The German would have guessed that he was safe until he heard the fifth merchant ship in a column pass overhead: then he would expect the frigate or corvette crossing back and forth across the stern of the convoy and know her Asdic might pick him up. So he would have gone deep and then stopped, probably knowing exactly where there was a cold layer of water.

The *Penta* had behaved perfectly. Apart from the breakdown and an earlier tendency to be careless with glowing cigarette ends, the ship had done exactly the right thing. She had not used her radio transmitter, she could not have signalled to any U-boat, she had done nothing that could be criticized or arouse the slightest suspicions in a bloodhound with a persecution mania.

Yorke put down his pen impatiently. It had taken one night, one attack by an insider, to show his theory about Swedish ships was nonsense; it was all one of those enormous coincidences (circumstantial evidence was probably the phrase) that at first arouses suspicion but which logical examination by a clear brain eventually shows up as just coincidences. Even if Yorke's brain had been a little muddled, there had been the clear brains of Jemmy, the Croupier and Uncle... All right, so they too were mistaken.

He walked over to the handbasin to shave, and as he lathered his face he knew that what was annoying him at the moment was not so much that the Swede theory had fallen down with a crash but that he personally was going to have to stay in the *Marynal* until the convoy arrived in Freetown. Admittedly it would become a nice cruise once the convoy began to turn south towards the Tropics, leaving astern the grey seas and grey skies of winter in the North Atlantic and replacing them with the blueish-purple of the deep ocean, the startling blue skies, and the night never really dark because of the millions of stars and the Milky Way like an artist's wash across the sky. Providing, of course, the *Marynal* stayed afloat that long.

He seemed to surface to find he had showered, shaved and dressed without conscious effort, and went down to the saloon for breakfast. A weary chief officer and a cadet had just come off watch and were eating fried eggs and bacon and grumbling that the toast was hard. The coffee was hot and strong. In fact the good food, Yorke reflected, was one of the compensations of Merchant Navy life: the wise chief steward bought plenty of whatever was available in a foreign port: a year's supply of currants and raisins, sugar, ham and bacon, chocolate, butter, cheese...all were stored on board, so that wherever the *Marynal* happened to be, alongside the Queen's

Dock at Liverpool unloading a cargo or steaming in a convoy heading for Freetown with supplies for the Eighth Army which would be ferried across the Sahara, the men on board at least ate well: last night, just before the attack, Yorke had eaten a large wedge of currant pie, an inch or more deep, and containing more currants than he had seen for a year or two.

After breakfast, and after a quizzing by the chief officer, who seemed to assume that Yorke had in some mysterious way solved the insider problem by watching three ships sink, he collected his thick duffel coat and went up to the bridge. It was a cold, grey day with low cloud, but the wind had veered and although he had seen neither barometer nor barograph he guessed the depression was passing north. Unless it was trailing secondaries or there was another depression close behind, the weather would certainly get no worse for the next couple of days and might even improve.

The third officer and Cadet Reynolds were on watch, their binoculars searching the horizon all round. A periscope, a drifting lifeboat or a raft – a wooden crate built round empty oil drums and which floated a foot or so out of the water, giving survivors something in which to sit, and containing food and water – were the only manmade objects they were likely to see. Occasionally there would be planks and baulks of timber spread over many hundreds of square yards; either wreckage from some sunken ship, or dunnage thrown over the side to get the deck clear. Dunnage – a curious word and probably an old one, and particularly suitable to describe timber used to wedge or protect cargo in the hold. Usually there would be a few gulls balancing delicately on the planks like old ladies paddling on a pebble beach. Many a distant ship had gone to action stations because the sun reflecting from the white of gulls' feathers in the distance made them look like a long metallic object.

Yorke nodded to Reynolds and stood at the forward side of the bridge. Always he felt this curious sensation that the ship was standing still and the ocean rushing past, the same impression a fisherman had standing in a fast-flowing mill stream. All the other ships in the convoy seemed stationary, too, because they stayed in the same position relative to the *Marynal*.

Now there were the gaps. Always after a night attack one waited until daybreak and looked for the gaps. It did not identify the ships that were hit but merely showed how many had been lost, because the gaps had usually been shifted astern: a ship would move up into a gap ahead and her next-astern would move up too, like the ripple of thuds made by the wagons when a goods train started. There were only three ships remaining in the commodore's column to port this morning; the last ship was now abreast the *Marynal*, although the rescue tug was still following and abeam of the *Flintshire*.

As he had done almost every morning since the first day of the war, because he had served continuously at sea until he was sent to hospital after the *Aztec* sinking, Yorke looked slowly round the horizon the moment he reached the bridge. Out there, probably watching the convoy through its periscope, was a German submarine. Hunter and hunted. Which was which? The U-boat was the wolf that raced into the flock and killed a few victims before running off. The convoy steamed along slowly, the ships as much a flock as the goats being herded by wandering Arabs across a desert, but it was a herd protected by wolfhounds: the frigates and corvettes that were hunting the U-boat. A wag in the ASIU (he could imagine Jemmy saying it) might accurately describe the situation as an insider being hunted by a pack of outsiders.

The *Marynal*'s third mate was a plump and spotty young man who had obviously worked hard on his diction to lose his Newcastle accent and who had made it clear from the beginning that he was not going to be impressed by a Royal Navy lieutenant, even if he was wearing the ribbon of the DSO. The youth's attitude was unnecessary and boring, and Yorke kept out of his way. As the third mate traditionally kept to the port side of the bridge, leaving the starboard side to the cadet, it was interesting to see that the captain seemed to prefer the starboard side too; clearly he found the third mate's fawning manner was too much, particularly since it was often interrupted to bully young Reynolds, most frequently when a senior officer could hear.

The third mate was a particularly poor lookout, apart from having a panicky manner, whereas Reynolds had sharp eyesight and, it was quite clear to Yorke, very sensibly only reported things to the third mate when action was needed: reporting to him a sighting of something not connected with the *Marynal* would usually provoke a spasm of near panic, recrimination and needless shouting. The risk that Reynolds ran was that the third mate might subsequently sight something and bellow across in front of the wheelhouse (thus ensuring that the captain in his cabin on the deck below would hear), pretending not to hear Reynolds' reply that he had already sighted the object and decided not to report it. However, Captain Hobson was not the man to be impressed by the third mate, Yorke realized, but for the sake of discipline there was nothing he could do about it.

The DEMS gunner acting as additional bridge lookout and watching the *Penta* reported nothing unusual. He was a careful man and took out a notebook and read the entries to Yorke: an officer had walked out to the port wing of the bridge and read the log, like that in the *Marynal*, which was streamed from a boom amidships with a repeater recording the distance run at the inboard end; an officer and someone with the four stripes of the captain had gone up to the monkey island and, with binoculars, had inspected the ships in the convoy. That was all.

Had they shown an interest in any particular ship, Yorke asked.

'No, sir; looked to me as though the captain slept late, then came up to the bridge and had a look round with the officer o' the watch to see who bought it last night.'

'Any interest in the escorts – their positions, that sort of thing?'

'No, sir, I was watching for that 'ticularly. Neither looked at 'em nor ignored them. Just about what one would have expected, sir.'

'And no garbage?'

'No, sir, I've been watching for that, too.'

In the course of a day a ship created a great deal of garbage: eggshells from, say, forty breakfasts, and odd scraps of bread, often a few mildewed loaves, empty jam and marmalade tins…on top of them, as the day progressed, there would be potato peelings, the outside leaves of cabbages or cauliflowers, chunks of white fat cut from pieces of meat. All had to be disposed of in the sea, the universal dustbin, but standing orders for merchant ships said it was not to be thrown over the side until nightfall. Under no circumstances was it to be thrown over in daylight. Submarine commanders, Allied and German, were skilled detectives where floating rubbish was concerned: from half a dozen bad oranges, a few leaves of cabbage or a sodden loaf, a submariner could tell how long it had been in the water. The line in which the rubbish floated on the water – usually the cook's mate had two or three drums to empty – could show the ship's course (or its reciprocal).

A submarine commander examining a few sodden bits of garbage could, if he recognized that it had been in the water for, say, six or seven hours, know for certain that within forty miles or so in one direction or its opposite there was a convoy. In little more than two hours on the surface at fifteen knots he should sight it... So rubbish was thrown over as night fell, things like the big tins used for jams and marmalade were supposed to have holes pierced in the bottom so that they sank, and bottles were to be broken, but cooks' mates had little imagination, and rooting round in old oildrums – the usual dustbins – was something they would do only if the chief officer was standing over them. As it was, throwing over the rubbish at nightfall gave a short enough margin – twelve hours of darkness, and during that time a six-knot convoy would be lucky to have steamed seventy miles. A zigzag or two might throw off a pursuer, but zigzags, as Jemmy was only too keen to point out, were only zigs to one side and then zags to the other of a straight line from Point A to Point B, and because the whole book of zigzag diagrams was given to every neutral ship sailing in a British convoy, it was obvious the German U-boat commanders had copies, too, so finding point B was not too hard.

No messages from Johnny Gower, so there were no ideas from the escorts. And, he reflected bitterly, no messages from him to Johnny Gower either. Sailing in the *Marynal* was a crazy idea, and one he would never have had except that he was getting desperate. A contented mind might be a continual feast, but a desperate mind is a fertile ground for crazy ideas. Now he was stuck for weeks in this damned convoy. If only one of the frigates – better still one of the corvettes, because that would not weaken the escort too much – developed some defect that required her to go into Londonderry, or anyway return to the British Isles – then he could cadge a lift back and report to Uncle.

It was hard to guess what Uncle's reaction would be. Perhaps patient and accepting that the only way to be sure the Swedes were not up to some nonsense was to sail in a convoy and watch them. He might be irritated, having had second thoughts himself soon after Yorke left London. He might be under great pressure from Downing Street, in which case Yorke would receive a monumental bottle, and Uncle was just the kind of man – quick tongue, fluent command of the language – to be good at handing out bottles to errant lieutenants.

Well, standing up here on the bridge looking astern, like a seagoing Wellington surveying the lie of the land at Waterloo (well, perhaps not a battle that later rated a railway station; maybe one of his defeats. Or just staring down from the heights of Torres Vedras was more like it) was achieving nothing. He had some old copies of *Horizon* to read – it was always amusing to read that bunch of Spanish War poets and writers patting each other on the back and saying how wonderful they were, even if several had fled to the safety of America, shouting across the Atlantic how freedom must be defended at any price. He went down to his cabin, knowing they would irritate him so much he would end up reading a pre-war *Blackwood's* again – there were several left in the bookcase.

He had been reading for less than half an hour when Cadet Reynolds came down to report that the *Penta* had just received permission from the commodore to complete her repairs. Yorke put on warm clothing and went up to the bridge, where Captain Hobson was standing inside the wheelhouse, examining the Swedish ship with binoculars.

'She's swinging out now and reducing speed,' he said. 'It's what he told the Commodore last night.'

'Doesn't seem to be smoking much,' Yorke commented.

'Aye, but I had a word with our chief engineer. He says the smoke yesterday could have been just the normal sooting up, and what the Swede actually stopped for might have been something quite different.'

Yorke went back to his cabin and tried to forget about the *Penta* until, an hour before nightfall, he watched her rejoining the convoy. There was the same high speed approach from over the horizon, the same slowing down two or three miles astern, and the same leisurely return to her position in the convoy.

He commented to Captain Hobson: 'That's just how we'd do it. And he hasn't called up the commodore so I suppose all his repairs are completed.'

CHAPTER FIFTEEN

Wind force six to seven from the south-east, ten-tenths cloud, attack began at 1955, the first three ships in the sixth column torpedoed. The second of them had been abreast the *Penta*, the third abeam of the *Marynal*.

As an angry and baffled Yorke sat in his cabin and wrote the details of the second night's attack in his notebook he was still looking for patterns. In the previous night's attack when two ships had been torpedoed in column four and one in column five, the two ships had obviously been hit by the U-boat's bow tubes and the single by the stern tube. Assuming the U-boat was firing single torpedoes, the first night's attack had cost him three fish.

Tonight's attack had been much simpler: the German had not used his stern tube: he had probably stayed in the same place between columns five and six and fired single torpedoes as the first, then the second and then the third ship in the column passed across his sights. Three ships were hit within a hundred yard square. The second had probably been hit before she had time to swing clear of the first; the third was hit because the U-boat turned slightly. That much was clear from the timing of the explosions and the positions – the third one had been abreast of the *Marynal* when the torpedo hit.

Three torpedoes probably used up tonight, three last night, six in all. Eight more left. Or perhaps the U-boat had missed one ship. That would make seven, but no one was likely to see a miss because the Germans were using electric torpedoes.

All of which meant that this insider still had seven or eight torpedoes. By now he was probably many miles away from the convoy, surfaced to charge batteries. He might even be sending the brief signal to Kernevel, telling Doenitz of his success.

The signal need only be brief, giving the grid square of the convoy and its course and speed, and that the U-boat had sunk six ships (and the *Oberleutnant* would probably guess at their total tonnage). Or he might wait a day or two until he could add that he was returning to base. In this weather, with a following sea, he could probably make fifteen knots on the surface – a cold, wet and wild pitch-and-roll ride but no one would mind because they were heading for home after a successful operation. They would cover a good three hundred and fifty miles a day until they came into the range of Coastal Command; then they would have to be wary, probably moving submerged in daylight. But in three days they would be in somewhere like Brest or Lorient, St Nazaire or La Pallice, perhaps Bordeaux. No action damage to be repaired and cockahoop at having sunk at least six enemy ships without having one depth charge dropped by the convoy escort...

Yorke found himself writing:

1 Has the Ted skipper eight fish left?
2 Will he attack tonight and still firing singly?
3 Why would he risk another attack, having sunk six ships? Answer. He should be confident in view of lack of opposition.
4 So it is probable that if he has fish left, he'll attack again tonight.

5 If the *Penta* drops astern again today and there is an attack tonight will that be significant? Not really, on present evidence.

He looked again at the last few words '...not really, on present evidence.' It was as simple as that: there was nothing that linked the *Penta* to the insider, and that was that.

The whole thing made as little sense out here in the North Atlantic as it did in the ASIU's underground room at the Citadel. The question then was the same as it was now: how does the bloody insider get inside?

The escorts made the convoy into a box open at the top (but U-boats couldn't fly) and the bottom. So the only way for a U-boat to get inside the convoy was through the bottom – by approaching submerged. That much was obvious, even to an imbecile.

How many times had he gone over all this before leaving London? The U-boat could get ahead of the convoy, dive, hide beneath a cold layer of water where the escorts' Asdics would not pick it up, and then come up to periscope depth after the leading escorts had passed and the convoy was steaming above, like someone popping his head out of a manhole to say 'Boo' at the passing ladies. So far, so good, for the insider. All very practical, and nothing even an escort commander as smart as Johnny Gower could do about it, providing the Ted captain found the cold layer.

Now for the *but*. It was a large-sized 'but' and one on which the waiting-ahead-of-the-convoy theory sank in a flurry of foam. It was a fact of German U-boat life (and confirmed by trials made in the U-boat recently captured intact by the Royal Navy) that although it could make nineteen knots on the surface using its diesel engines, once it dived and had to use its two electric motors, its speed and range were limited by its batteries. It could make nine knots for an hour before its batteries were flattened, or it could stay under for three days (in an emergency) making one or two knots. In other words the batteries contained only so many ampere hours, and the captain could use them up at a rush by going fast for a short time, or eke them out by going slowly. Like an alcoholic with a bottle of whisky – empty it in an hour, or make it last three days.

What the U-boat could not do was make six knots submerged for days on end… Unless he was making only a knot or two, he had to surface every twenty-four hours and run his two big diesels so that the generators recharged the batteries.

How is he escaping from the convoy box after a night's attack so that, out of sight of the escorts, he can run on the surface and charge his batteries? We have answered that – he just dives deep and lets the convoy pass over him. And he stays down until he knows he is out of sight of the convoy, then he surfaces, starts up the diesels, gives the lads a breath of fresh air, and lets in the clutches on those big generators, so that the batteries start getting a charge for the next night's operation.

All well and good: Yorke had gone over the sequence enough times in the Citadel, with Jemmy and the Croupier joining in. There was no set time required for charging the batteries – obviously it depended how much current the electric motors had used the previous night. Perhaps five hours; maybe ten. Jemmy had been emphatic that three days submerged would leave the crew in a poor state because of lack of oxygen and humidity, and probably flatten the batteries. Such a long dive was usually the last resort, when a hunted U-boat was trying to sneak away from an attacker who had the time to stay around and pursue the search.

How did the bastard get back into the box?

That was the question that stumped them in the ASIU headquarters at the Citadel; and now he had seen a convoy attacked by an insider on successive nights, he still had no idea. Captain Hobson had decided that the U-boat simply got ahead of the convoy again during the day, submerged, and came up to periscope depth at the right moment among the columns.

Hobson had been quite sure of that until Yorke scribbled a few figures on a pad. The convoy attack had stopped by 2100 on both nights, so they could assume the U-boat dived deep at that time and an hour later was somewhere astern running on the surface, already charging batteries. By daylight next day, about 0700, he had nine hours' charge in his batteries.

At daylight he could – if he wanted to take the risk – still see the convoy, but if he was running on the surface and able to see the convoy, then one of the escorts was just as likely to spot him, or pick him up on radar, even though the sets the frigates had at the moment were crude.

The important thing was that from 0700 until the German attacked that night was at least twelve hours. During that time the convoy had made about seventy miles, and zigzagged at least once, probably twice, and perhaps thrice. It was quite impossible (even if he had the zigzag diagrams in front of him) for the U-boat to race ahead of the convoy and submerge at a point up to fifty miles away where he knew the convoy would not just pass, but pass immediately overhead. From one side of the convoy to the other was only 1200 yards. The first two attacks had been made on the fourth and fifth columns. That meant not only was the U-boat picking a spot across which a convoy 1200 yards wide would pass, but two columns only 200 yards apart.

The Ted could tear around for half an hour at nine knots submerged so he could change his position by, say, five miles (leaving himself some juice in the batteries to manoeuvre for the various attacks), but if he moved on the surface or submerged then Johnny's escorts would find him: the two frigates were crisscrossing ahead of the convoy all the time, night and day. Yesterday Johnny had put his third corvette right in front, only a few hundred yards ahead of the commodore, and no Asdic had produced an echo, that much was obvious. The U-boat, Yorke had demonstrated to Hobson, was not entering the convoy box that way.

Finally, almost cross-eyed with fatigue, Yorke shut his notebook. It must be black magic, an old recipe kept in an ancient sock by a charcoal burner's great-grandmother in the depths of the Hartz mountains, levitation, knowing which form to fill in or which bureaucrat to bribe...what other explanations were there? He undressed and slid into his bed. If the weather worsened he would envy those with bunks – the only way he could stop himself sliding out of this well-sprung bed as the ship rolled would be by lying spread-eagled on his back.

Years of watchkeeping meant Yorke could waken within a few minutes of the time he set himself, and he woke just before a cadet knocked on his door, telling him it was nearly noon. After a brisk shower and a shave – during which time he could see through the porthole that the weather had improved slightly – he dressed and went up to the bridge. The *Penta* was missing.

Captain Hobson said he had called the commodore about eleven o'clock, and from the commodore's reply it seemed the Swede was claiming engine trouble again. He had, just like the previous two days, pulled out of the column, slowed down and let the convoy draw ahead. Yorke could see for himself that the *Penta* was now out of sight astern, and the convoy had altered course at eleven thirty according to the zigzag diagram.

Grey ships steaming along on a grey sea under a grey sky; a long grey swell rolling in from the west. There had been no hint of the sun at noon, so there had been no sights; the barometer was staying the same. Yorke walked into the chartroom to look at the chart. Hobson had put a pencilled cross, with the time and date, showing the noon position by dead reckoning, and the convoy's zigzag progress across the chart was so slight he had to use a sharp pencil. Six knots – Columbus' little ships must have crossed to the New World at about that speed when running before the Trade winds. Six knots. A man walking briskly made five. The convoy from Liverpool to Freetown was going the whole way at slightly more than the speed of a man walking to church on a Sunday morning with a nip in the air. That was the speed at which most convoys crossed the Atlantic, simply because six knots was the speed that most small merchant ships could guarantee to maintain…

Suddenly in his imagination he saw astern, out of sight just below the curvature of the earth, the *Penta* and the U-boat. He saw them stopped close to each other, the U-boat rolling and pitching uneasily in the swell, a grey cylinder, tiger-striped with rust, the waves slopping and squirting through the gratings of the deck plating. Did the Swede lower a boat and take across fresh bread and other comforts? Pass across special hose and pump over diesel fuel?

He found himself sketching the two vessels lying close together, using the pad left for the navigator's rough calculations. Neither merchant ship nor submarine would dare get too close to each other because even a slight collision could sink the U-boat. But if the Swede passed a cable and took the U-boat in tow at slow speed, a hose could be passed without any trouble and without any risk of collision.

In fact the *Penta* could tow the U-boat back to within sight of the convoy.

Or, more likely, the Swede could chase the convoy at full speed, say fifteen knots, with the U-boat on the surface astern of her, charging batteries at the same time... From the high vantage point of the *Penta*'s monkey island they could keep a sharp lookout for the British escorts, knowing the *Penta*'s bulk would hide the U-boat from radar, and once they were close, within three or four miles, they could slow down – as they had done before – and the U-boat could dive at the last moment.

The U-boat would still be outside the convoy, outside the box with three corvettes and two frigates circling round it, Asdics pinging, the sound waves radiating out with sensitive receivers waiting to catch even the hint of an echo from something solid. And the hydrophones, like old men's ear-trumpets, listening for unusual noises, the sound of a U-boat's electric motors and the swish of the propellers. But the hydrophones were useless when very close to a convoy, deafened by the pounding of the pistons of the merchant ships, whether they were steam or diesel... The effect would be the same as a quavery old lady trying to make herself heard to someone using an eartrumpet as a brass band marched by thumping out a lively 'Colonel Bogey'.

Captain Hobson was leaning over the chart table beside him and Yorke suddenly realized the Yorkshireman was staring at him open-mouthed. 'No one would expect what old lady to compete in what?' a startled Hobson asked, and Yorke realized he had spoken his thoughts aloud.

'Hydrophones,' he said lamely. 'They're like an old man's eartrumpet. Sound carries fantastically under water. Very effective, a hydrophone, providing the operator is well trained. Some chaps get a sort of sixth sense. Of course, you can't chase something at high speed, or your own noise deafens the hydrophone operator.'

'What about the old lady?' Hobson asked.

Yorke was embarrassed at trying to explain his thoughts to this down-to-earth man.

'I was thinking that an old lady wouldn't try and compete with a brass band by shouting into an eartrumpet...'

'I should hope not,' Hobson said. 'Mind you, eartrumpets have gone out of fashion now, you know. Haven't seen one for a long time. Nor a brass band, come to think of it. Still plenty of old ladies around – *competing* old ladies, too.'

'That bloody Swede,' Yorke said. 'I was thinking of her meeting the U-boat back there, over the horizon...'

'Aye, I'm glad you've got round to thinking about that,' Hobson said with an about-time-too note in his voice. 'I've been thinking of them passing over bottles of schnapps and tins of Stockholm tar. And saucy postcards – you'd be surprised what those Scandinavians get up to. I see you've been sketching it,' he said, pointing at the pad.

'And fuel, too,' Yorke said, tapping the chart table with his pencil.

'Aye, that'd be a help; but I still don't follow what you meant about the old lady and the eartrumpet.'

'I'm not too sure myself,' Yorke admitted.

'I don't know about competitions, but an old lady would have to be very stupid to try and shout into someone's eartrumpet if a brass band was going by,' Hobson said doggedly.

'You'd think so, wouldn't you,' Yorke said, smiling sheepishly. 'In fact if it was your eartrumpet you wouldn't even *expect* the old lady to say anything until the band has gone by. Or if you were the old lady you'd keep your mouth shut until the band passed, then you'd say your piece.'

'Aye, that makes sense,' Hobson agreed. 'Doesn't seem to have much to do with wars and Swedes and U-boats and things, but it makes sense. Are you worrying about some old relative who uses an eartrumpet?'

'No, nor anyone who plays in a brass band, but for an eartrumpet, substitute the hydrophone in an escort, and an Asdic, too. The brass band is a merchant ship. The old lady – well, she's quiet, so let her be a U-boat. Where does that get you?'

Hobson thought for a minute or two. 'Absolutely nowhere. A picture of an old lady playing a hydrophone in a brass band, maybe. Where does it get *you*?'

'A Swedish ship rejoining the convoy slowly, twin screws and two engines thumping away merrily, almost deafening the hydrophone operator in an escort, and a U-boat running almost silently on electric motors just underneath her. All the hydrophone operator hears is the thudding of the merchant ship's pistons; the Asdic appears to ping off the merchant ship's hull – no one thinks there could be a U-boat under there. Like a double-decker bus, or a hen with a chick under her wing. Or an old lady singing *Deutschland Uber Alles* as she trots along in the middle of a brass band which is playing "Land of Hope and Glory"'.

'Well, I'm buggered,' Hobson said, his eyes wide. 'You've got something there, lad. It explains the Swede slowing up for the last few miles. And the ships torpedoed are always round the *Penta* – in this convoy, anyway. The murderous bastards. What do you do now?'

CHAPTER **SIXTEEN**

The first thing was to have a word with Johnny Gower. And it had to be a word, a hail, not a flag signal or a radio conversation. The *Penta* was by far the best candidate for the crown of villainy, but it might still be someone else; someone steaming along in one of the columns and guessing that the Swede was the prime suspect. Therefore Johnny Gower had to have a good reason for coming close alongside the *Marynal* with the *Echo*, close enough for them to be able to talk with loudhailers – luckily the *Marynal's* gunnery control Tannoy was loud enough, if the loudspeaker on the monkey island was turned round to point over the starboard side.

Getting Johnny close alongside was, fortunately, one of the situations they had visualized in Liverpool: in the list of signals was one where, when the *Marynal* hoisted the 'W' flag or flashed it in Morse to the commodore (it meant in the International Code 'I am in need of medical assistance'), he immediately passed the signal by Aldis to the senior officer of the escort because the *Echo* carried a doctor, and she would immediately close the *Marynal* – a perfectly normal manoeuvre. All ships would have read the signals; all seamen could hazard a guess at what might have happened – someone in the *Marynal* had a suspected appendicitis, a seaman had broken a limb, or was running a high fever... Something beyond the capacity of the ship's chief steward who traditionally acted as a merchant ship's district nurse, finding the symptoms in a medical handbook and opening up the medicine chest for medicaments. His usual job in the *Marynal*, from the teasing that Yorke had heard, was painting on gentian violet in the usual fight against what the French called *papillons d'amour* or butterflies of love, but the more prosaic British called crabs.

A few words of explanation to Hobson, and a moment later the cadet had dragged the 'W' flag with its pattern of blue, white and red inset squares from the pigeonhole flag lockers, clipped it to the flag halyard, and hoisted away. With the flag streaming in the wind and the halyard made up on the cleat the boy picked up the Aldis lamp, aimed at the commodore, and started calling up, flashing the dot dash of the letter A, repeated until the commodore answered with the dash standing for T, and then for good measure flashed 'W'.

Watkins reported to the bridge with a set of spanners and was sent up to the monkey island to adjust the gunnery loudspeaker. The one and only microphone, Yorke discovered, was also on the monkey island, so he would have to stand up there for his conversation with Johnny. Muffled up in a duffel coat he would pass for one of the ship's officers.

Yorke then went into the chartroom. With the wind on the port bow and Johnny coming up to starboard, on the lee side, it was going to be easier for Johnny to hear him than for him to hear Johnny. Still, he was forgetting the power of a frigate's loudhailer, and the main thing was to get his ideas across in as few words as possible.

The cadet put his head round the door. 'Commodore's calling up the *Echo*, sir.'

'Very well; tell me when the frigate gets within two columns of us.'

Johnny had imagination and, knowing him, he would by now be furious at losing six ships with not one depth charge dropped on a U-boat: this was his first experience of an insider attack, although in Liverpool Yorke had spent a couple of hours discussing with him all that was known about them. It had taken only fifteen minutes to give him the whole background, but Johnny was fascinated and let his imagination run. In the end he had come back to Yorke's original idea, which he dubbed Yorke's Law of the Recurrent Turnip, out of deference, he explained, to the neutral Swedes, who had given their name to a similar vegetable.

Swedes, turnips, insiders, torpedoes... Eleven dockets representing eleven previous attacks...and now they were watching the Swede, to be honest, because Clare had phoned him one morning.

If she had not telephoned, he might not have noticed that there was always a Swedish ship on the list of an insider convoy. What was Clare doing now? On board the *Marynal* it was half past noon; in London it was mid-afternoon. Clare would still be on day duty. By now the ward would have been cleaned, dressings changed, physical exercises completed by the patients, lunch eaten, grumbled about and by now almost forgotten.

Those allowed up will be sitting round those still bedridden, playing cards, glaring at chessboards. Some will be reading; others will have gone to sleep listening to the wireless, the earphones askew over their heads. There will be grey clouds at the windows because yesterday's depression will be passing north of the United Kingdom today and reaching down as far as London. Clare will be writing up reports, perhaps even snatching a moment to write a page or two more of a letter to him.

Her skirt, so lightly starched, a sort of white pinafore thing, the little bonnet pinned at the back of the head, the polished and flat-heeled black shoes, the black stockings (perhaps with a seam crooked), her wristwatch with the large dial and figures in Roman numerals which was consulted as every patient's pulse was taken, her fountain pen clipped into a pocket, a severe black pen with a gold clip and a wide gold band round the cap. He could see so vividly the cool and calm Nurse Exton, who could quell an almost apoplectic commander with a chilly stare, bring a hush to a ward full of unruly men with a quiet, 'Gentlemen!' Nurse Exton, whose eyes and mouth at the height of passion were the essence of all love poems and songs. Clare, the cause of him being on board the *Marynal*, the cause of him wishing he was in London.

'The *Echo*'s just coming through the second column from us, sir,' the cadet said. 'Must be making full speed.'

Yorke did up the toggles of his duffel coat, pulled the scarf tighter round his neck and went out on to the wing of the bridge, where he found Hobson and the cadet watching the *Echo* cut across the stern of the fourth ship in the sixth column, head across towards the *Flintshire* and then gradually turn to starboard to come up on the *Marynal*'s starboard quarter. Once again Yorke was startled at the difference in size; he had the feeling that from the bridge of the *Marynal* he could lob a cricket ball down the *Echo*'s funnel.

He trained his binoculars on the *Echo*'s bridge. There was Johnny Gower, one of the few clean-shaven men. His first lieutenant had a bushy red beard, a modern Barbarossa, there was one grey beard, probably some three-badge AB, one of the men who formed the backbone of the Navy, highly skilled at his job (he was probably a signalman), always grumbling, up to all the tricks of avoiding work, with more than twelve years' service (one good conduct badge for every four years), and who had refused all promotion: not for him the questionable delights of being a petty officer, eating in the

PO's mess. It all meant responsibility and only fools became involved with that. The fact was that very often many first lieutenants faced with a difficult job would sooner put a three-badge AB in charge than a petty officer, because the petty officer was often a young and ambitious man with much less experience.

The *Echo*, like her captain, was paying the price for efficiency; because the lieutenant (E) was the kind of engineer who understood his machinery like a good conductor his orchestra, the frigate rarely had to go into the dockyard for the kind of repairs that were almost routine for other ships, so that the officers rarely managed to get leave. Johnny and his first lieutenant never had a day's illness, so they missed sick leave. All of which meant that most of the officers in the *Echo* had been at sea in the North Atlantic almost continuously since the day the war began. They had been serving in a small destroyer, but the moment the *Echo* was ready for commissioning they were transferred to her so that the destroyer could go into the dockyard for a long-overdue modernization.

Yorke now understood the physical and psychological effect of such prolonged active service at sea because he too had been at sea continuously up to the time the *Aztec* sank. It was not until he was lying in the hospital bed at St Stephen's with his hand and arm fixed like a broken spar that he realized his nerves were wound up tauter than an overtuned violin: another fraction of a turn, it seemed, and something would snap.

The Royal Air Force lately seemed to have come to terms with it, after that bad patch when the senior officers at the Air Ministry who had not flown operationally for twenty-five years had lashed out at air crews who were at the end of their tether through sheer strain. Those that collapsed were branded as LMF, a description dreamed up by men flying their war at safe desks and standing for 'lacking in moral fibre'. Cowardice, in other words. This infamous label was often stuck on men who had flown thirty or forty bombing raids over the most heavily defended targets in Germany, showing that the worst wounds were inflicted by one's own side. *The coup de grâce* usually came from some faceless low-grade individual in the Ministry of Pensions striking a blow for freedom by gipping a man ten shillings a week from his pension. Fortunately some of the younger doctors now in the RAF were men who understood the psychology of the air crews. Because they knew that in peacetime a businessman trying for months to stave off bankruptcy might step over the edge into a nervous breakdown, or a wife nursing a sick husband and struggling to make enough money to buy food and medicine and pay the doctor's bills might well collapse. These doctors finally managed to persuade the Air Ministry that air crews were not supermen: they were ordinary young men who, night after night, spent a quarter of the twenty-four hours waiting for an anti-aircraft shell or a burst of cannon fire to blow themselves and their aircraft to smithereens. They did not sit there in fear and trembling: on the contrary, they flew, navigated, stood by their guns and aimed their bombs, but they knew they might not get home again. Most calculated the odds against them. So many hours flying time, so many raids left before the odds turned against... The worst part probably came in the hour or two before take off in the early evening. The village pub where they met on the nights they were not flying and played darts and sang and flirted was just down the road. For the older ones there would be rented houses nearby where wives lived, hearing the planes taking off and counting them as they returned before dawn. LMF. Every man was a coward, if he had the slightest sensitivity. A man without fear was a menace to himself and his comrades because, lacking in imagination, he could not be trusted to react sensibly to anything except an absolutely routine situation.

Now the *Echo* was less than a ship's length away on the *Marynal*'s starboard quarter and Yorke scrambled up the iron ladder to the monkey island, where Jenkins waited with the microphone of the loudhailer.

Yorke nodded to the seaman. 'How would you like a year in one of those?'

'We were all saying this morning, sir, how we're just waiting for them to call for volunteers.'

Yorke raised an eyebrow questioningly. There was a certain ritual to be followed when a leading seaman made a joke to an officer.

'We'd make sure we didn't step forward, sir!'

From the day a sailor joined the Navy he was warned by his mates never to volunteer for anything. 'You volunteered for DEMS work,' Yorke reminded him.

'Yes,' Jenkins said frankly, 'an' we get the finest grub there is, and discipline is sort of relaxed. More chance o' getting the chop, I suppose; but I'd sooner take my chance in a lifeboat than in one of those Carley floats.'

Yorke took the microphone and looked across at the *Echo*.

'*Marynal*. What are the symptoms?'

Johnny Gower's voice wvas unmistakable, despite the distorted bellowing of the *Echo*'s loudhailer. He saw Yorke standing up on the monkey island and gave a cheery wave.

Yorke pressed the transmit button. 'Feverish but will survive. Listen, have you noticed how the Swede comes back to the convoy at high speed until he's three or four miles off, then slows down to about seven knots?'

'Yes. Couldn't be sure he wasn't nervous and trying to get back into position without bumping someone. Can't see very well from the other side of the convoy. Parallax and all that nonsense.'

'He's not nervous. Listen, Johnny, when he rejoins this evening why don't you go close alongside and ask if he needs any help? Say you're worried that he's had to leave the convoy. And have your Asdic going.'

'Right ho, Ned: I'll switch with one of the corvettes and probably stay in that position for a day or two. I'll report to the commodore by lamp so you can read the answer. If anything crops up tomorrow, ask for medical assistance again. Anything else? Very well, toodle-pip.'

Yorke went back down to the bridge to find Hobson waiting for him.

'You didn't say anything about a U-boat moving underneath the Swede,' Hobson said. 'Do you think young "Toodle-pip" will guess?' Hobson made no effort to conceal the doubt in his mind.

'Don't worry about the "toodle-pip"; he's been saying it to my certain knowledge since he was eight years old. When we left Liverpool he was second highest scorer on the list of U-boat killers.'

'He has a very flippant manner, though,' Hobson said, almost primly. 'I noticed it at the convoy conference before we sailed.'

'Don't let that put you off,' Yorke said and smiled as he remembered something. 'Once his last two depth charges forced a U-boat to surface, so he rammed him. A few moments before they hit Johnny warned everyone on the Tannoy by bellowing: "What ho, she bumps!" '

'Yes, very funny, I've no doubt,' Hobson said, 'but…'

'It was his fifth U-boat,' Yorke said, but did not add that Johnny had in fact deliberately rammed the after end of the U-boat, hoping to damage her hydroplane so that she could not dive again, and that the Germans had abandoned ship so quickly that a boarding party from the *Echo* managed to get below, turn off flooding valves which had been opened, and (thanks to previous training) find and disconnect two explosive charges. The *Echo* had then towed the U-boat back to Scotland and most of Doenitz's secrets – particularly codes and ciphers – had been discovered. But the whole thing was so secret – the U-boat now had a British name and few people knew that the submarine doing trials was telling the Royal Navy even more about U-boats – that Johnny's well-earned DSO had not been gazetted, and every man in the ship's company at the time had been sworn to secrecy. The first Yorke knew of it was when Jemmy had described the vessel. Toodle-pip. Yes, Johnny was flippant. In Nelson's day the sour Lord St Vincent would have disliked his manner, but perhaps recognized a man whose brain worked twice as fast as most of those listening to him.

Yorke could tell Hobson nothing of the capture but wanted to reassure him about 'Toodle-pip'. Then he realized the gulf between someone like Johnny Gower (who would describe working twenty-four hours a day as being 'a touch busy') and Hobson (who believed firmly in calling a spade a spade) was too vast, even though both men put the same effort into a job.

By the time the Swedish ship came into sight over the horizon, the convoy escorts had switched round: one frigate was ahead of the convoy and another, the *Echo*, astern; there was a corvette also ahead, beyond the second frigate. The weather was improving, the seas easing down into the usual long ocean swells without wind waves superimposed on them. During the late afternoon the cloud had begun to break up – not showing 'enough blue to patch a Dutchman's trousers' according to the old proverb but indicating that by midnight a star or two might be seen and sun sights would be possible tomorrow. The day after that the convoy's course would begin to dip south towards warmer latitudes.

Yorke stood with Hobson at the after side of the bridge watching with binoculars. Again there was the almost uniform grey of the sea with flecks of white as a wave crest broke. The *Echo*'s grey camouflage paint blended well; only the straight outlines – stem, bridge, guns – stood out. Beyond her the *Penta* was lifting over the curvature of the earth: first the stubs of her masts, then the funnel and bridge section; a few minutes later the fo'c'sle came into sight, followed by the stem, and then the bow wave could be seen creaming away in a broad, whitish moustache, reminding Yorke inconsequentially of the Lord Kitchener posters of the last war, a pointing finger and the Field Marshal's stern face with the caption 'Your country needs you.' To irreverent eyes twenty-five years later the worthy peer looked more like an irate company sergeant major detailing a dozen men to 'Clean the officers' latrines!' Anyway, more to the point was that Kitchener had a fifteen-knot moustache, comparable to the bow wave of a fully-laden merchant ship of about eight thousand tons.

The *Echo* turned almost lazily as she reached the last column and began her sweep back across the stern of the convoy, her turn making a broad, smooth patch in the sea and reminding Yorke that a cruiser made a wide smooth patch among choppy waves by doing a high-speed turn so that her floatplane, previously catapulted off for a reconnaissance, could land in the flattened crescent and then be lifted on board by crane.

'She's still making fifteen knots,' Hobson grunted. 'Would she dare come in like that with a U-boat on the surface astern of her?'

'As long as she's between the U-boat and the *Echo*, what's there for her to worry about? The U-boat's about two hundred feet long, but not much of that shows above water. Only the conning tower, really. Providing the Swede steers straight for the convoy and doesn't let the *Echo* get too far to one side or the other, the U-boat sits there like a child hiding behind his mother's skirts.'

'And she'll slow down to let the U-boat dive just before the point when the *Echo*'s lookouts can see astern of her,' Hobson commented. 'If that's what they're up to they're cool customers; you've got to admit that.'

Yorke, remembering some of the tricks that Jemmy had played with his submarine in the confined waters of the Mediterranean, simply nodded, and then could not help himself adding bitterly: 'It's like stealing money from your mother's purse. She trusts you and never counts the coins.'

'Aye, you're right. We should never trust neutrals. We should make 'em sail on their own and take their chance. Haven't the Germans offered them a safe passage?'

'Yes, the "Philadelphia Route" they call it. Steam with navigation and accommodation lights on at night and either the name or the flag painted fifteen feet high on the side and illuminated at night... Trouble is that in daylight a ship's a ship, and in overcast weather very few of these U-boats can be sure of their position within fifty miles. So a few days of cloud without a sun or star sight and the merchant ship gets north of its assumed position and the U-boat south, and they're together. A quick look through the periscope shows a merchant ship – no hope of seeing the name or flag on the side if it's a bow shot or visibility is bad. And Berlin gets an angry protest over a torpedoed neutral, Doenitz gets a kick, the U-boat commander gets a kick...so neutrals prefer Allied convoys: much safer – the figures show that. And anyway most of them are making their money by chartering to Britain or America.'

Yorke's arms were aching and he was just going to lower his binoculars when he saw the *Penta*'s bow wave begin to grow smaller. He glanced at his watch, looked again until there was only the hint of water swirling at the stem, and noted that the Swede had taken three minutes to slow from fifteen knots to seven.

'Anyone would think he was a cruise ship,' Hobson said sourly. 'Slow down gently so you don't upset the passengers...'

'Would you expect him to slow more quickly?' Yorke asked.

'Of course. Doubt if they're using engine-room telegraphs – none of us are these days. Simply pick up the phone and tell the engine room to drop to whatever revolutions you want for the speed. But she must be dropping a few revs at a time – sort of thing you'd do if you were towing and wanted to keep a strain on the cable. Seems daft to juggle around like that: I could just imagine what our chief engineer would say!'

The *Echo* was continuing her turn in a great circle that would bring her up on the Swede's starboard quarter. Yorke could imagine the binoculars in the frigate which would be trained on the *Penta*; he could almost hear the monotonous 'Ping...ping...ping...ping' of the Asdic and soon, as she slowed down, the reports from the hydrophone operator of 'H E', which meant 'high explosive' to the Army, but to the Navy meant 'hydrophone effect', or what grandpa heard through his eartrumpet.

The frigate going close alongside the bulky merchant ship looked like a sleek greyhound loping alongside a St Bernard –

and Johnny was taking it close, risking the curious suction effect that drew ships together when they were steaming close on the same course.

Johnny was busy – but he would probably leave conning the ship to his first lieutenant while he talked to the Swedes on the loudhailer, listening all the while to the Asdic pings and the hydrophone operator's reports... Although the Swedes would not know it, the guns' crews would be closed up ready for action, depth charges would be ready for the quick lob that started them on their way down to the depth where the pressure of the water on the pre-set hydrostatic valves sent them off.

Now the *Echo* seemed to be slowing down. Johnny was dropping astern to round up on the other side with the minimum underwater disturbance to upset the Asdic operators, and then coming along the Swede's port side before swinging away as if quite innocently continuing his sweep back and forth across the stern of the convoy.

Now a shout from the radio cabin, and Yorke ran across to listen. Johnny was reporting to the commodore using the radio-telephone on low power. He had asked the ship if she needed engineering assistance and been assured it was only dirty fuel clogging the filters and blocking the injectors. The problem would recur until the ship could pump out and take on fresh bunkers. The commodore acknowledged himself: Yorke recognized the clipped voice and the question; 'Anything else to report?' and Johnny Gower's unambiguous, 'No, sir.'

As a bitterly disappointed Yorke turned away he bumped into Hobson, who had been listening to the exchange and said ruefully: 'Looks as though we were wrong, eh?'

Yorke was thankful for the tactful 'we'. Had it been anyone else but Johnny Gower he would have suspected the Asdic and hydrophone operators were asleep or, more likely, improperly instructed.

'When the Swede saw the *Echo* coming,' Yorke said slowly, thinking aloud, 'could she have tipped off the U-boat so he stopped and dived deep? So that when the Echo came up alongside the Swede the U-boat was in fact a mile or so astern and two or three hundred feet down?'

'Could be,' Hobson said. 'No trouble at all, I should say. But if he was stopped and dived a mile astern would the *Echo's* Asdic pick him up?'

Yorke shook his head and continued to think aloud, hoping Hobson would be able to help. 'Not with that damned Swede's twin screws and bulk so close. But how could the Swede have tipped off the U-boat to dive deep and stop?'

They'll have a way,' Hobson said. 'It can't be too difficult, the way noise travels under water.'

'Yes, a couple of thumps on the hull with a big sledge-hammer – they'd hear that in the U-boat. The only way we'll ever find out what's going on is to get on board the *Penta* for a few hours.'

Yorke looked up to find Hobson staring at him. 'Aye' the Yorkshireman said, 'that's the only way. They do say the best way of proving your wife's adultery is to catch her in bed with the other bloke.'

The *Penta* passed slowly – she was making only a knot more than the convoy – until she regained her position ahead of the *Marynal*; then she turned a few degrees until she was back in her position, midway between the *Marynal* and the leader of the column, and slowed down.

Then Captain Hobson ordered the cadet to hoist the 'W' flag for medical assistance and call up the *Echo*, which was making a sweep over to the starboard side of the convoy.

Yorke in the meantime was in the chartroom drawing up a list of men's names. There was no need to call for volunteers from among the DEMS gunners, and the two men he needed from the *Marynal* (actually only one was needed; but he was proposing to ask for the young cadet, Reynolds) would be chosen by Hobson.

It seemed only a moment later that a cadet was warning him that the *Echo* was closing fast and Yorke snatched the page on which he had scribbled a few notes and ran up to the monkey island, taking the loudhailer microphone from Jenkins.

'We'll soon be known as "Typhoid Mary-nal" sir,' Jenkins said poker-faced.

'Yes,' Yorke said. 'I'm so worried about you all catching it that you'll probably leave the ship tonight.'

Yorke turned from a flabbergasted Jenkins to look down at the *Echo*, to be greeted by Johnny Gower's voice booming: 'Rub Gentian violet on it, Ned, and take two aspirin.'

'That patient is dead,' Yorke said into the microphone. 'You didn't see or hear any congestion of the lungs, I presume.'

'Absolutely nothing. Any more ideas?'

It took Yorke less than three minutes to describe what he was going to do, and another minute while arrangements were made for the times of a listening watch on the lifeboat radio frequency. Finally Gower gave a farewell wave, with the warning: 'All bets are off if there's no attack tonight… Anyway, toodle-pip for now.'

In the chartroom with the door shut Yorke went over his plans with Hobson, who was torn between admiration for the plan and a genuine fear for the lieutenant's safety.

'Now, lad, what do you want from me?'

'The motor lifeboat and whichever engineer you can spare to make sure the motor keeps on working; Cadet Reynolds is not important but he's a lively lad and could be useful to me; what revolvers you have; and a fake boat built during the night so that no one notices tomorrow that the motor lifeboat is missing from the davits. That is, if there's an attack tonight.'

'And if we're not one of the ships hit,' Hobson added gloomily. 'Very well, I'll have the boatswain check over the boat; fuel, water, food…'

'And flares,' Yorke interrupted. 'Lots of flares. A Verey pistol if you have a spare one, plenty of smoke flares, and some five-star red rockets.'

'Pass that pad,' Hobson said. 'I know better than to rely on my memory.' He wrote for a minute or two. 'The boatswain must work with the cover still on the boat, otherwise the Swedes might see him,' he said to himself, 'the carpenter can fake up a boat with battens and canvas and a coat of grey paint. We can use the same canvas cover. By the way,' he said, looking up at Yorke, let me have the boat back if you can. I don't begrudge it, but it's all the bloody paperwork afterwards that gets me down. Now, I've only got four revolvers. Rifles are no good, I suppose?'

Yorke shook his head. 'No, we're survivors, don't forget, not a boarding party! The revolvers must be hidden in our pockets.' Suddenly he remembered Jenkins' warning about the Captain's fascination for the grenade projector. A projector must have grenades to project, and a Mills 36 grenade fitted into a duffel coat pocket without making a great bulge. 'That grenade projector… I'd like to have some of the grenades.'

Hobson's face fell. 'Well, yes, I suppose…but can I get them replaced in Freetown? I don't like having a projector and no grenades. Never know when we'll get air attacks.'

'How many grenades have you got on board?'

'I don't rightly know. A couple of cases, I think, however many that would be.'

'I'll make sure you get four cases when we reach Freetown.'

'Aye, they'd be much appreciated. Pity we haven't more revolvers for you.'

'Well, if you can let us have those four. I have one, both my signalmen have them, and the DEMS gunners might have some. We could do with some knives, though. Nice sturdy ones that'd work like bayonets.'

'The Chief Officer will see to that: we've got just the thing in deck knives. We had a gross delivered just before we sailed. They'll need sharpening, of course; they're not supposed to be stabbers.'

'And the lifeboat radio.'

'Yes, Sparks can check that over and show one of your chaps how it works. Not very complicated, it has the instructions in the lid. It's fitted into a special floating suitcase, you know.'

'Old clothes for me. If one of the mates has an ancient jacket that fits. It isn't that I mind getting my own clothes wet, but they have the wrong sort of stripes...'

Hobson looked at him critically. 'Not old enough to be a chief officer yet; promotion's slow in the Merchant Service. Second mate would do. Yes, Second Officer Yorke. You're about the same build as the second mate, and he can give you a spare uniform coat. You'll have to buy him a new one sometime, but he's more likely to shop at Gardiner's than Gieves.'

'Gardiner's?' Yorke inquired, puzzled at the reference.

'They fit out more Merchant Navy officers than anyone else. I bet half a dozen kids a day arrive there straight from school to be fitted out as cadets to join their first ship.'

Hobson read out Yorke's list and then said: 'You're relying on the DEMS gunners to handle the boat. They're worse than useless with oars. And you leave me with very few gunners.

Why don't you take some of my chaps? Some of them are handy with their fists.'

'They might get killed.'

'They might get killed if the *Marynal* is torpedoed. I think the thought might have crossed their minds. Should I ask for volunteers? How many?'

Yorke thought quickly. Five DEMS gunners, with Watkins and Jenkins, could handle the small arms and grenades. Seven, and Reynolds and himself made nine. The engineer ten. Supposing he took four merchant seamen? That made fourteen. 'Let me have four, Captain. Mix up brain and brawn!'

'Launching the boat,' Hobson said. 'It's going to have to be done at the rush if you don't want that Swede to notice us slowing down too much.'

'He's bound to notice,' Yorke said, 'and I don't fancy launching a boat half full of DEMS gunners while the ship has any way on. Lowering the boat and then boarding it down a rope ladder will take too long. It'll be a dark night so when the attack is finished (if there *is* an attack) you can haul out between the columns. Remember there are only four ships in the next column now, and you can weave around and pretend your steering's gone wrong. Then stop with the ship broadside on to the wind and sea so we have a lee on the port side. And of course the *Marynal* hides the boat from anyone in the convoy. Once we get that damned little engine started we'll clear off and you can get back into the convoy while the carpenter spends the rest of the night making the fake lifeboat.'

'The marine superintendent wasn't joking when he told me you might have some odd requests,' Hobson said amiably, obviously enjoying the change in routine. 'Anything else?'

'Yes,' Yorke said with a grin, 'a few thermos flasks of hot cocoa in the boat, some fifty tins of Player's, the round metal ones that are sealed, and some boxes of matches in a screwtop jar.'

'And a case of Scotch?'

'No,' Yorke said firmly, 'no booze. The cocoa will keep the lads warm and so will rowing.'

CHAPTER **SEVENTEEN**

As soon as it was dark fourteen men assembled on the boat deck a few feet abaft the *Marynal*'s single motor lifeboat while several other seamen removed the canvas cover, let go the gripes and swung the boat out on the davits so that it hung over the water, ready for lowering.

Yorke, bulky with two thick jerseys over the second mate's uniform coat, had stuffed his duffel coat under a thwart with his revolver and a small canvas bag of cartridges in one pocket and a couple of grenades in the other. Now he checked off the men.

First, the junior fourth engineer. Mills was plump, cheerful, and outwardly just an overgrown schoolboy, complete with acne and little need to shave. In fact he lived for engines and, the chief engineer had confessed, the smaller the better: when one of the small water pumps, driven by a temperamental two-stroke engine, gave any trouble, the shout went up for Mills. One of the last jobs he had done before the ship left Liverpool had been to strip down and reassemble the lifeboat engine, test run and remount it. The fuel filter had been replaced, the fuel tank topped up and an extra can lashed down in the bow. Mills had £28 in bets with the men that the engine would start first time.

Mills came with a bonus: he had an automatic pistol of his own and three spare magazines (and, he told Yorke, more than a thousand rounds of ammunition, bought when the ship was in the United States two trips ago) and was probably the ship's champion grenadier. He had been a keen member of his school OTC and a regular winner at the coconut shies in travelling fairs, and when Yorke had seemed doubtful that this qualified him for a couple of grenades he had slipped into the saloon, selected an orange from the fruit dish, and returned to ask Yorke where he wanted it lobbed. They were standing on the main deck at the time, abaft and below the radio room on the deck above. Yorke saw an open port and pointed at what seemed to him a difficult throw, let alone using the overarm lob needed for a grenade. A minute later the radio room door flung open and a startled and furious third sparks came out, holding the orange as though it was going to explode.

'Pistols, spare clips, lifejacket, no papers showing you come from the *Marynal*, and a couple of grenades?' Yorke asked Mills.

'Haven't got the grenades yet. That DEMS gunner chap is just opening the box.'

Yorke looked round to see Jenkins levering the lid off a wooden crate. 'Are the fuses in those things?'

'No, sir; I've got them here.' He gestured to a small metal box. 'I'm going to prime 'em as I issue them out.'

Cadet Reynolds had heard Yorke checking Mills and began: 'Pistol and two spare clips...'

'Where did you get the pistol from?'

'Lecky lent me his, sir,' Reynolds said apologetically. 'He showed me how to work it.'

The *Marynal* seemed to be a floating arsenal. 'Very well, but don't cock it until you want to use it. And remember the safety catch.'

'Yes, sir. No papers identifying the *Marynal*. Lifejacket. Deck knife. Torch and extra batteries.'

Slowly Yorke worked his way through the remaining men, less because there was any particular need to check their equipment than because he needed a brief chat with each of them. He wanted to hear each man speak and equally important he wanted the seamen to hear him when he was talking quietly. Once on board the *Penta*, much might turn on a whispered order or response.

Finally Jenkins came up to him, and handed him two grenades. 'Pity we can't take that projector with us, sir, and drop it over the side,' he murmured.

'Don't be nasty to the projector; without it we'd never have these grenades.'

'I'm a bit doubtful about them, to tell you the truth, sir. These Maritime Regiment chaps are all right, considering they're pongoes, but they're mortal clumsy with their hands. We finished the last trip without a china mug left in the mess, all because they was cack-handed washing up.'

'Don't worry, we're not throwing mugs this time. Now I want you and those other DEMS gunners to forget I'm RN and think of me as the second officer of whatever ship we choose.'

'Fact is we don't pay much attention to second officers, sir,' Jenkins admitted frankly. 'Chief officers is what we have more to do with. The mate in this ship's an 'oly terror.'

'Any chief officer in a ship with DEMS gunners needs to be a terror, holy or otherwise,' Yorke said unsympathetically. 'Now, where's Watkins?'

The signalman was up in the lifeboat, cursing with an unimaginative monotony as he lashed down the large and heavy suitcase that represented the lifeboat transmitter.

Yorke looked over the thwart. 'What's the matter?'

'Oh, just lashing this set down again, sir. That bloody third sparks secured it right against the compass, sir. The south end'd point north if we switched on to listen to Vera Lynn on the distress frequency. Never heard of deviation, that bloody third sparks.'

Yorke realized that as far as Watkins was concerned, the man's name for evermore would be 'that bloody third sparks', and no doubt when he was with the other signalmen he would refer to 'your mate that bloody third sparks'. Mind you, Yorke admitted to himself, any third sparks lashing a radio transmitter within a few inches of a compass had only himself to blame if he lacked friends... That kind of thing could have a boat heading for the north pole when the compass showed it was steering for the south and the worshipful company of penguins.

Now for the long wait. Would the insider attack tonight? It should, if the Swede was part of the plan. Would the *Marynal* be hit? If she was, then there was going to be a squeeze in the ship's three other lifeboats because Hobson had already offered to let the present plan stand should the ship be hit.

It was now seven o'clock. If the insider stuck to his regular routine he would torpedo his first ship at eight o'clock. It was all becoming very Teutonic. It may have worked well the first time – attacking at eight o'clock (or twelve or four) meant catching every ship as the watch was changing. In theory there might be a certain amount of confusion, but if the *Marynal* was anything to go by there was very little: the cadet on watch left the bridge fifteen minutes earlier to rouse the cadet who would relieve him, the mate who would take over from the one on watch, the radio officer and the new quartermaster. The DEMS gunners arranged for their own relief. With the new watch roused the cadet returned to the bridge and waited.

The new mate would come up (by tradition five minutes early) and be told the course and speed (course really, the speed was usually the same), and anything else of importance (like 'The old man's turned in'). The new cadet would arrive and be told nothing, and the quartermaster be given the course by the man he was relieving. And that was all. In a warship it was more complex because there were more men doing more jobs, but anyway, when the insider had hit the first ship on the first night he had no doubt visualized vast confusion and panic, so he had repeated it the second night. Being German he would probably do it again tonight.

Yorke could just see the time by the polished brass clock in the wheelhouse which was screwed to the bulkhead just behind the quartermaster at the wheel in a position where the dim light from the compass binnacle was just sufficient to light up the hands. It also showed the thin black metallic circle outside the numbers on which electrical contacts could be adjusted so that a buzzer sounded at predetermined times – the times set out for the zigzag diagram and warning of the precise moment when the wheel had to be put over on to a new course. He held his wristwatch against the binnacle light. A few seconds' difference from the clock, which was checked daily against the chronometer. Two minutes to eight o'clock. Was that *Oberleutnant* at this very moment lining up the dark shadow of a ship in the graticules marked on the lens of his periscope?

He walked out of the wheelhouse, feeling his way round the armour-plating and on to the wings of the bridge. The cadet and the DEMS gunner were dark figures, impressions rather than people, as his night vision slowly returned.

The now-familiar opening of the furnace door and the hollow boom of it slamming shut lit up the whole convoy for a long moment and Yorke saw that the commodore's ship had been hit. A few moments later he heard Captain Hobson, who had been standing out of sight outboard of the two Hotchkiss guns at the end of the bridge, say, 'I hope the old Admiral's all right.'

Yorke pictured the U-boat waiting submerged, the *Oberleutnant* now watching through his periscope, his men holding the firing levers of the other three torpedo tubes, and waiting to see which way the second ship in the column would go: whether she would pass to port of the commodore's ship – using her as a shield, because the torpedo burst on the starboard quarter – or blunder along the starboard, giving the U-boat another target. Yorke realized the U-boat might have fired at the commodore's ship just after she had passed, so that a slight alteration of the U-boat's heading would bring the second ship into the sights before she started to pass one side or another.

Now a second red flash, this time on the bow of the second ship and showing the commodore stopped and sinking fast fifty yards ahead, revealed that that was what the Ted had done. Would he now turn even farther and get the third ship?

The captain of that merchantman had a few moments only to make one of three choices – turn to starboard (trying to increase speed and head straight for the U-boat, gaining the advantage of surprise and presenting only his beam instead of his length as a target), turn hard a'port to steer the reciprocal directly away from the U-boat (and risk hitting the third ship in the third column), again having the advantage of surprise, or keep his position, just altering course enough to port to avoid the two sinking ships ahead of him.

A third flash from abreast of the *Marynal* lit up the two sinking ships and showed the insider had hit his third victim of the night and the ninth in three days.

'He's not using his stern tube,' Yorke told Hobson, who had scrambled out of the gun position to stand beside him.

'How d'you know?'

'We'd have been hit a minute or so ago: he must have been right between us and that last one. The *Somers Island*, wasn't she?'

'Yes. Bad payers, the owners. Always having crew trouble.'

'Somers Island was the old name for Bermuda, wasn't it?'

'Believe so,' Hobson said, and both men knew they were whistling in the dark because it was still not too late for the U-boat to fire its stern tube. 'At least the rescue tug is in the right column,' he added. 'In fact...' he broke off.

'Yes,' Yorke said, 'the tug's the only vessel left afloat in the fourth column now. The vice-commodore will have to close up the gap as soon as it's daylight: we're a six-column convoy, now, not seven.'

'Bert James is a steady enough fellow,' Hobson said. 'He's the vice-commodore. Leading the second column, isn't he? He was rear-commodore in a convoy we were in last summer. Comes from Aberdeen. Teetotaller, too. Signed the pledge and all.'

'We're out of range of that stern tube now,' Yorke said. 'I think it helps us being close to that Swede.'

Hobson sniffed doubtfully. 'The ship ahead of her was hit the first night, don't forget.'

'Maybe we're in a lucky spot, astern of her.'

'We'll see,' Hobson said. 'By the way, where are you from?'

Yorke almost answered 'Kent' without thinking, then realized the reason for Hobson's question. 'The *Somers Island*, I think: the rescue tug should pick up everyone so there's no chance of a mix up. It was Sir George Somers, by the way: I've just remembered. He was on his way to Virginia sometime around 1605 and ran into a hurricane which wrecked him on Bermuda. That was how it was settled.'

'Hurricane, eh? Well, it blew him off course all right. Hope you have better luck. Say when you're ready.'

Hobson was a cool chap, Yorke noted thankfully, but the U-boat had just made the Yorkshireman's job easier: apart from the tug, which must be stopped and picking up survivors from the *Somers Island*, the whole of the next column had been wiped out, so the *Marynal's* turn to port to lower the boat would be much easier.

'I'm just going down to tell my chaps where we're from, but you can start having steering problems whenever you're ready. I think that U-boat's finished his work for the night.' He shook Hobson by the hand. 'Thanks. Keep my cabin reserved for me!'

Yorke felt the ship heeling as he scrambled down the companionway to the boat deck, and he could picture Hobson's quiet helm orders called through the doorway to the quartermaster as he watched to make sure he didn't ram a wreck in turning to port out of the column: the commodore's ship might still be quite close.

The lifeboat team was squatting down between the two drums round which the ropes of the falls of the lifeboat were wound. 'Cup o' cocoa, sir?' Watkins asked, standing up with a big jug in his hand. Yorke did not want his bladder bothering him for the next half an hour so refused and said to the men briskly: 'That third ship to be hit, the one abeam of us, was the *Somers Island*. We're from her. You can remember her various positions. *Somers Island*, although it's pronounced "summer's", is spelled s-o-m-e-r-s. I'm told the owners have a bad reputation for pay and conditions. The owners are the Hunter Shipping and Trading Company, known to some of you as the "Hungry Hunters". Somers Island, by the way...' he felt the ship begin to heel and the rumble of the engine eased slightly as Hobson reduced the revolutions, 'is another name for Bermuda. And Bermuda is a tiny island standing by itself five hundred miles or so north of the Caribbean. The *Somers*

Island is or was, rather, 6800 tons and carrying a mixed cargo. Under charter to Elder Dempster and the United Africa Company. Engines for fighters and bombers in crates, tents in bales, boots for the Army in wooden crates, a good deal of webbing, tropical uniforms, rifles and Bren guns also all in crates...no explosives, you'll be glad to hear,' he concluded and was glad to hear the men laugh.

Now the *Marynal* was rolling heavily: for the past few days she had been pitching, with only a slight roll, the seas hitting her fine on the port bow. Now Hobson had turned her to port she was lying with the wind and sea on her starboard side, her port side making a lee. Or a comparative lee, Yorke thought as he looked down into the inky-black water. The waves were rising and falling some fifteen feet; once it was lowered and before the falls were cast off, the lifeboat would be like a run-amok lift.

The boatswain and a dozen seamen were ready to lower the boat once the team had scrambled on board. Usually the boat was lowered with only two or three men in it, and it was held alongside while the rest scrambled down a rope ladder, but that took time and Yorke had decided to lower the boat with all his men in it. There was a considerable risk that she would be so heavy that the boatswain's men would not be able to hold her, the ropes of the falls racing through their hands. In that case the lifeboat would drop with a crash, probably upending because one fall would probably run faster than the other, tipping all the men out and then landing on top of them. The alternative was to raise the Swede's suspicions – quite apart from leaving the *Marynal* stopped for many minutes, during which time the U-boat might spot her and line up for a shot at a sitting bird.

'Ready, bosun?'

'When you are, sir.'

'Right men into the boat with you. Mr Mills, I hope you're all ready to start the engine!'

Yorke counted the men as they scrambled out into the boat and followed the last one, sitting at the aftermost thwart, ready to take the tiller.

He glanced down over the side. He was just noting *Marynal* still had some way on when he felt rather than heard a sudden spurt of vibration. Hobson was giving the propeller a final touch astern to stop the ship. Then he heard the boatswain calling that the ship was stopped and a moment later heard the shrill note of a whistle sounding from the bridge: a police whistle, the type the Merchant Navy were given to lash to their lifejackets. It was Hobson's signal that the way was off the ship.

'Lower away, bosun! Handsomely now! And don't let her run!'

And slowly the boat deck seemed to rise and the lifeboat was lowered. Now the main deck was passing, and a couple of seamen standing there waved. They were holding heavy motor tyres, and Yorke realized Hobson had remembered that if the ship was rolling violently the lifeboat might slam into the side and be damaged. The motor tyres would help absorb the shock. The Yorkshireman was a natural seaman.

Now the main deck was disappearing into the darkness above and a shower of spray whipped across the boat. The bow seemed to dip for a moment, then the stern lifted, and a moment later they were afloat, the huge double blocks of the falls tilting over as the boat began its wild yo-yo movement.

'Cast off aft and hold on for'ard,' Yorke shouted. 'Now Mills, get that damn thing started! Oars! Fend off!' Fortunately the *Marynal* in fact still had a knot of way so the lifeboat was being dragged through the water by the remaining forward fall. This in turn meant that the boat had steerage way, so instinctively Yorke pulled the tiller towards him and the boat began to sheer away from the ship. Yorke bellowed: 'Cast off forward!' and saw the big double block with the hook beneath disappear into the darkness.

Simultaneously the lifeboat began leaping up and down like a runaway horse and the great bulk of the *Marynal*, a darker patch in the night, disappeared as the boat dropped into troughs.

Yorke was just going to give the order for the men to start rowing when he felt rather than heard the 'Whhuupp... whup...whup' of the *Marynal's* great propeller starting to revolve. Then a clatter and a roar from near his feet showed that Mills had managed to get the little engine started. The triumphant engineer shouted above the noise: 'Say when I should put her in gear!'

A total of fourteen men, a standard Board of Trade lifeboat, and a few revolvers and automatics, a couple of dozen hand grenades, a lifeboat radio transmitter...the Admiralty was going to war against the insider...

It all seemed a long way from the Citadel, Yorke thought as he crouched over the lifeboat compass, lit by a tiny paraffin lamp. Now they had to head for a precise position astern of the convoy from where they could follow along in its wake so that even if they lost sight of it – as they almost certainly would – they could be sure of sighting the Swede later. He shivered and remembered the loneliness after the *Aztec* sank, a feeling that was worse in daylight than darkness.

CHAPTER **EIGHTEEN**

At ten thirty-five next morning Cadet Reynolds suddenly stood up, holding on to the shoulder of the seaman seated in front of him to keep his balance, and said quite casually: 'There she is, heading away from us!'

The Swedish ship was far enough away that she could only be seen as the lifeboat rose on the crest of a wave. Yorke envied the matter-of-fact way the cadet had reported: for himself he was scared because, in the fifteen minutes around dawn when the black of night turned into the grey wash of the start of a new day, he realized he had forgotten something that could get them all killed: if the lifeboat accidentally surprised the Swede actually with the U-boat, either vessel would simply ram the lifeboat, destroying all evidence that could incriminate them or interrupt the insider attacks on the convoy.

It was vital, therefore, that Johnny Gower and the convoy knew what was happening, and the best way he could think of for doing that was for the lifeboat to start calling up the *Penta* by name, using the lifeboat transmitter on the distress frequency. This would mean that the Swedes would not then dare do anything but pick them up. The Swedes would know that other ships in the convoy listening on the call and distress frequency would hear the transmission, and the fact that the survivors broke the rules by mentioning the ship's name…as far as Yorke was concerned, it was a justifiable form of blackmail, and the thing that desperate men might do if they were a bit panicky.

He looked round the boat. His men were on the verge of looking like pirates: those with beards looked unkempt; those normally clean-shaven had bristly faces. All were wearing woollen caps or balaclava helmets and they seemed shapeless in duffel coats which were becoming sodden from the almost constant spray sweeping the boat as it butted into the waves, pushed on by the little engine. Mills occasionally lifted the wooden casing and looked inside, then turned aft and winked at Yorke as he lowered it again and secured the clips. At this distance it was unlikely the Swede had yet spotted the lifeboat.

'Finish up the cocoa in those vacuum flasks,' Yorke said, 'then puncture them and toss 'em over the side so that they sink. Take what concentrated chocolate and Horlicks tablets any of you want, then screw up the food locker.' The men were shivering with cold; their hands had the dead white skin of a woman who had spent the morning scrubbing the laundry.

He watched the compass carefully as he steered the lifeboat and after three or four minutes was fairly certain that the Swede was in fact lying stopped. She was still heading on the convoy course, but this was probably because it reduced the rolling.

Soon the ship was in sight most of the time, not just on the top of the crests. Now was the time to announce the presence of the *Somers Island*'s lifeboat.

'Watkins, are you ready with that transmitter?'

'Aye, aye, sir: just want a couple o' chaps to hold my duffel over the set to keep the spray off.'

'Very well. When I give the word, just transmit this: "SOS SOS SOS to *Penta* from lifeboat 25 degrees on your starboard quarter distance three miles." Keep on repeating it even if she answers until I tell you to stop.'

Watkins repeated the message twice, to make sure he had it correct, and began to hoist the kite aerial. Then Yorke turned to Jenkins. 'Are you ready, Guy Fawkes?'

The seaman grinned and tapped the bundle of flares and rockets he was holding across his knee, wrapped up in an old black oilskin coat, and then pointed at the two seamen who, with duffel coat hoods up to protect their faces, would hold a length of piping that Jenkins intended to use as a rocket launcher.

'Fine. I want Watkins to get his message off at least twice before we start our display.' Then, because many of the men must be wondering why he had not sent up rockets the moment the Swede was sighted, he decided to explain.

'Transmitting an SOS and calling up that Swede by name isn't because we want to talk to the Swede: he'll see us anyway because of the rockets and flares. I want the Senior Officer of the escort in the *Echo* – and everyone else in the convoy listening on the call and distress frequency – to know we've sighted the Swede. That's an insurance policy against him running us down. If he doesn't pick us up he'll have a lot of explaining to do. So as soon as we've used the SOS to tell the *Echo* that we're in contact, we should have roused the Swedes anyway: they'll be keeping a radio watch. The radio officer will warn the bridge and they should just then sight one of Jenkins' rockets popping out five red stars.'

'Do you want me to keep the engine running?' Mills bellowed, deafened more than the others because he was sitting on the casing, which kept him warm at the cost of his hearing.

'No,' Yorke bawled, 'not when we start transmitting – it'll cause interference.'

Yorke looked once more at the *Penta*. She was definitely stopped. As the lifeboat seesawed over the crest of a wave he stood up and looked carefully. There was no sign of a surfaced U-boat.

He signalled to Mills to stop the engine, and as it gave a final gasp said: 'Right, Watkins, start transmitting!'

The seaman disappeared into the tent of the duffel coat, and very faintly Yorke could hear the muzzled squeaking of Morse. He looked across at the *Penta* and beyond. If the lifeboat had been making three knots then the convoy would be about thirty miles away. Certainly no more because it would not have been making more than six knots during the last twelve hours and the lifeboat was probably making more than three.

Watkins emerged from the coat. '*Penta*'s answering, sir. Came up after my first transmission.'

'Send it twice more. Is she transmitting full power?'

'Yes, sir. Bustin' my eardrums.'

Again, molelike, he burrowed back to his set as Yorke looked warningly at Jenkins.

Finally, when Watkins emerged to say he had transmitted it twice more and the *Penta* was now answering for the second time, Yorke said: 'Acknowledge and say you're standing by. Now, Jenkins, let drive with one of your five-star reds!'

The seaman pulled one of the rockets from the encircling oilskin, slid the stick part into the tube the two seamen were holding and ripped off the base which formed an abrasive striker. He wiped it briskly across the base as though striking a match and turned away. The rocket hissed and crackled for a moment and then launched itself upwards with a whoosh and a trail of sparks which showed up well against the grey of the clouds. Just as it reached the top of its trajectory it dropped a red blob, followed a few moments by another, a third, fourth and then a fifth.

'Now a red hand flare.'

Jenkins stood up holding a wooden handle which continued into a cardboard tube like a short broomhandle. He ripped off the abrasive striker, rubbed it across the end and as it began fizzing held it out at an angle over the side. A dull red glow gave off thick reddish smoke which drifted to leeward and quickly dispersed. Then, as suddenly as it started the flare sputtered out and Jenkins tossed the wooden handle and charred cardboard tube into the sea. 'Useless bloody things,' he said. 'Board of Trade approved, no doubt. Used to have better ones on Fireworks Night when I was a kid.'

Watkins' left hand was waving from under the duffel coat. A seaman leaned over to hear what he wanted to say and passed on the message to Yorke: 'The *Penta* says she saw the rocket, sir and...' he turned back, listened to Watkins and then added, 'and the flare, sir.'

And, thought Yorke, thanks to the radio Johnny Gower would now know for certain: the lifeboat was in effect insured. Even if this lifeboat transmitter did not have the range to reach the *Echo*, certainly the *Penta*'s powerful transmitter would be heard on board the frigate. Johnny would have heard the *Penta* answering the SOS, and then he would have heard she had sighted the rocket and the flare. Hundreds of miles away Admiralty wireless operators at radio direction-finding sets would probably have picked up the *Penta*'s signals too and by now would be working out her position. They would be puzzled because they would not have heard the lifeboat's message. They were always alert, but particularly for one of the new wartime prefixes which were used when appropriate instead of SOS. There was RRR, for example, warning of a ship being attacked by a surface raider, or SSS, which reported an attack by a submarine.

Again Watkins' arm was waving from under the coat and a seaman bent down to listen, passing back the message word by word as Watkins read the Morse: 'The *Penta*, sir...says...she's...putting cargo net...over...portside...will... turn...to...port...to make a lee...we should...come...up to her...that's all, sir.'

'Very well, acknowledge and say our engine will prevent us using the wireless set any more.'

Mills, his hearing partly restored, looked inquiringly and as soon as Yorke saw Watkins emerge from the coat and start putting the lid on his suitcase transmitter, he gave the engineer the signal. Mills wound at the starting handle and the hot engine fired almost immediately. As Mills pushed forward the stubby gear lever Yorke felt the tiny propeller start to bite and the boat began responding to the tiller. The seamen stowed their oars along the thwarts with no sign of reluctance.

Yorke stood up, still holding the tiller, and shouted to his men. 'Cargo net makes it much easier but you've got to be quick. The net will be hanging down the port side, probably amidships, and I'll nose up to it and try to get alongside. Our *starboard* side. Once alongside you can just step off and grab the net and climb up. Remember to take your turn. Don't all crowd to the starboard side or you'll capsize the boat.

'Now, make sure those revolvers and grenades are secure and out of sight. Don't leave grenades in the duffel coat pockets and then hand the duffels over to the Swedes to take away and dry. Remember, we're survivors from the *Somers Island* and the fellows in the *Penta* are our friends and rescuers. Be grateful. And watch out for the booze. They'll probably want to pour schnapps into you. If any man gets drunk, he'll answer to me. Booze loosens tongues.

'Any careless talk and we'll have wasted our time, even if we escape with our lives. But if the Swedes are up to any nonsense and suspect any one of us is a menace to this insider business, then we'll be quietly dropped over the side. The fact the *Echo* heard those transmissions won't save you: the Swedes need only report that the lifeboat capsized and everyone was drowned as they tried to get us on board. So watch it, my lads; there'll be booze aplenty when we're back on board the *Marynal*, that I promise you, and I'll be signing the chits.'

He suddenly felt frightened: until he heard himself speaking the words he had not consciously thought of the Swedes having a perfect alibi for drowning them: certainly the lifeboat capsizing alongside would be an excellent excuse…

It took nearly an hour to get up to the *Penta*, the lifeboat being like a tiny crab making its way over rippled sand towards some distant objective: the slide down from a crest meant a wearying plunge into the trough and an even more wearisome climb to the top of the next crest. The wind and sea were fine on the lifeboat's port bow, a direction which ensured the boat's bow sliced the top from each wave and flung the spray over the men crouching in the boat.

Mills sat four-square on the engine casing, grinning cheerfully to himself and occasionally blowing the salt water from his lips and wiping his brow with the back of an oily hand. Yorke wondered whether the unique situation where the engineer found himself in complete control of his engine and almost touching it, yet out in the fresh air (very fresh and plenty of it, with spray as well) was not so exhilarating and remote from the normal heat of the engine room that Mills hardly noticed he was soaking wet and cold.

The rest of them sat facing aft, many with the hoods of their duffel coats over their heads and seeming like rows of cowled monks undergoing some dire penance, the quilted kapok lifejackets they were wearing over the duffel coats giving them a faintly Chinese appearance. Chinese Franciscans accounting to the cardinal for their misdeeds.

Now the *Penta* was just moving, making a slow turn to port so that she would lie broadside to the wind and waves but without moving ahead. As she swung Yorke could see the cargo net already hanging down the port side, like a square fish net. The net would be made of thick rope, strong enough so that when used for cargo the net could lift a couple of tons or more.

'Do you think they'll try something, sir?'

The questioner was Cadet Reynolds, and the shine in his eyes showed more excitement than fear at the prospect. Yorke had intended his earlier warning to put the men on their guard, and he could see the nearest were listening for his answer.

'The chances are fifty-fifty, I should think.'

'What are they likely to do?'

'They might try to capsize the boat as we go alongside. Either make up our painter and then go ahead so that each wave slams the boat alongside her until it smashes up, or just go ahead as we come alongside and leave the quarter wave to swamp us.'

'There's not much we can do about any of that, is there, sir?' Reynolds commented ruefully.

'Not much, but we can take some precautions. You have a deck knife? Right, I want you up in the bow. As soon as we get alongside the net, don't pass the painter up to them: instead get a turn through the mesh to hold us just long enough to jump on to the net. As soon as each man is on the net he must climb like a mountain goat to make way for the next one. Don't grab and hang on – the next roll of the ship will dip you into the water, and you could be crushed by the boat. Leap, grab and climb! Now, you get forward with your knife and as you go make sure everyone understands the instructions. If you see they're trying to tow us, cut the painter, we can take a sheer away – I'm not stopping the engine until the last moment.'

There was nothing else that he could think of. Keeping the engine running until he was sure there would be no monkey business meant that Mills could shut it off or leave it to run until the fuel gives out. Anything else for the men? Nothing until they are on board the *Penta*: the lifejackets, like padded waistcoats, will stop the grenades falling out of duffel-coat pockets. They would also stop anyone getting one out, or extricating a revolver… And everyone in the boat was wearing a standard Ministry of Transport lifejacket.

He looked up to find the *Penta* very close: he had kept her in the corner of his eye as a grey mass ahead but while his mind raced on, trying out all the permutations of what might happen, he had not been examining her. Only a year or two old judging by the smoothness of the hull plating, built with a cruiser stern, a low squat funnel, the bridge section streamlined, and all the accommodation below it, instead of having the seamen berthed in the fo'c'sle, as they were in the *Marynal*. Swedish flag, no gun on the poop, topmasts removed, both lifeboats on this side fitted with engines so presumably the two the other side had them too. No framework of piping for fitting tropical awnings so the *Penta* probably had not been to the tropics before, although she would need some awnings this trip or else those blond Swedes would go bright red with bad sunburn. Two officers were standing out on the wing of the bridge watching the lifeboat approaching, with a dozen or so seamen standing on deck along the top edge of the cargo net.

He signalled to Mills to throttle back a little as the lifeboat came into the lee of the *Penta*, which was making a great wind shadow with the sea calmer as though they had suddenly arrived behind a breakwater.

There were now three Swedish officers out on the wing of the bridge, and Yorke thought he recognized the captain and the near albino he had seen at the convoy conference. Now the lifeboat was level with the *Penta*'s stern, heading in at forty-five degrees for the patch of the cargo net almost amidships abaft the bridge. Anyone out on the wing could look right down into the boat.

What had begun with Clare telephoning him at the Citadel, had finally led to this, to a Swedish ship hove-to 800 miles out in the Atlantic astern of a convoy and Lt Yorke, RN, about to try to board her with a motley crowd of 'survivors' who had grenades stuffed in their pockets just as schoolboys might have apples after a scrumping raid on a neighbour's orchard.

They were almost alongside the net now: Mills was obeying the signal to throttle back even more, Yorke had the tiller over to port to keep the lifeboat's bow nosing to starboard, nuzzling into the *Penta*'s side, the men along the starboard side were standing up, reaching over to the net as the boat leapt up and plunged down the ship's side, lifting on a crest, dropping in a trough. A moment later half a dozen men were on the net and climbing, with more following as soon as there was no chance of their hands being stamped on.

More men slid across the thwarts from the port side and made the jump to the net and by then the first men were near the top. In what seemed only moments the lifeboat was almost empty. Four, three, two seamen...and now himself,

Mills and Reynolds left. He signalled Mills to stop the engine and go up the net and was startled by the sudden silence as the noise died but was equally suddenly replaced by the whine of wind and the sucking and sloshing of the sea between the lifeboat and the ship.

Finally Cadet Reynolds at the bow was looking aft to Yorke at the stern. Yorke scrambled forward, shouting at the boy to get onto the net, and began untying the painter, but Reynolds stayed on the net and, instead of climbing up to safety, helped Yorke. He had tied a couple of half hitches using a bight of the rope, and the end caught in the net. Finally Reynolds handed Yorke the deck knife and Yorke sawed through the rope, climbing on to the net a few moments before cutting the last strands. Almost at once a wave caught the lifeboat's bow and gave her a sheer away from the ship. Yorke began to scramble upwards, cursing the bulk of lifejacket and duffel coat. When he paused halfway and looked down at the boat, it was already twenty yards away and, with its grey paint, almost indistinguishable among the grey waves.

He scrambled over the bulwark and on to the *Penta*'s deck and for a few moments felt dizzy because suddenly the merchant ship seemed as stable as a rock compared with the tossing lifeboat. He found himself automatically balancing against violent pitching and rolling which no longer existed. Already several of his men had been led away and a young Swedish officer was waiting for him to recover before speaking.

'You are in command of the boat, sir?'

Yorke nodded. 'Second Officer Yorke.' He held out his hand and as the Swede shook it diffidently said with the kind of hearty manner that the British were always portrayed as using by those who did not know them: 'Were we glad to see you come in sight!'

The Swede, unsmiling and without any expression in his voice, said: 'You will come to the bridge.' He sounded, Yorke thought, like a 'Speak your weight' machine at one of the railway stations.

'My men…?'

'They will be given hot food and dry clothing. Come.'

Kom. It was an order, not an invitation; but Scandinavians tended to be abrupt when they were nervous. The English was good; he could not really remember a Scandinavian accent in English well enough to distinguish it from good English spoken by the Dutch – or Germans, for that matter.

His shoes squelched, and for the first time in twelve hours he remembered that they were full of water. The movement of walking made the sodden material of his trousers chafe on his knees. 'Get yer knees *brarn!*' was the ultimate scornful remark in the tropics to a newly-arrived sailor trying to throw his weight about. Legs in general and knees in particular were always the last parts of the body to get, tanned. What the devil brought *that* to mind? The handrails of the *Penta* were painted a functional grey; there was none of the fancy ropework, the Turk's heads, sewn and scrubbed canvas, that distinguished the *Marynal.* The ship had all the warmth of a frigid woman.

The bridge and accommodation of the *Penta* was like a small block of flats: once through a door there was little feeling of a ship – panelling in light-wood veneers, modern prints framed in bare wood. Stairs led upwards and Yorke followed the young officer. The stairs had carpets, and his shoes were leaving wet footprints all the way to the wheelhouse. Every piece of nonferrous metal was chromed. It looked smart and hygienic. Not one square millimetre of polished brass, not even the clock (with its inner circle for the contacts of the zigzag buzzer) or the boss of the wheel. The wheel itself was a circle of stainless steel with four spokes, not the varnished and carved wheel of the *Marynal*. The quarter-master did not lift his eyes from the compass; his round hat was on square and he looked ready for an inspection. Yorke followed the officer to the chartroom. The officer stopped on the threshold and yelped (although obviously he had intended to bark): 'Second Officer Yorke, sir,' and left. Yorke went in to find himself facing two men whom he recognized at once. The nearest was Captain Ohlson, once again hatless, his blond hair brilliantined flat on his head, the skull cap of omelette which had been so noticeable at the convoy conference, the nose large and the ears sticking out like jug handles. Four gold stripes on the sleeve of his jacket showed he was the captain.

The man beside him had also been at the conference, the officer who was almost an albino, his hair cut *en brosse*, and so blond it was almost white, and the impression at the conference that he had no eyebrows had been correct. The face was almost gaunt, cheekbones high, lips as thin as Rizla cigarette papers. The eyes were the pale blue of glaciers and crime-novel murderers. Three gold stripes showed he was the chief officer.

Yorke knew they would not recognize him; at the convoy conference in Liverpool he had been smart and clean-shaven in mufti; now his face was bristly and dirty, his hair sodden, like a wet mop. No peaked cap, no uniform showing, only the kapok lifejacket and the dripping duffel coat.

He pretended a hearty thankfulness. 'On behalf of myself and my men, Captain, I...'

'What ship?' the other officer interrupted.

Yorke ignored him. 'I'm Second Officer Yorke, sir,' he said to Captain Ohlson. 'To whom am I...?'

The Swede nodded his head. 'Ohlson, master of the *Penta*.'

'And this gentleman?'

'The chief officer, Mr Pahlen.'

Pahlen gave no sign that anyone else had spoken. 'What ship, Yorke?'

Yorke deliberately looked at Ohlson. A provoked man often said more than he intended, and now was as good a time as any to start provoking Pahlen who, Yorke guessed, had the power in the *Penta*, even if not officially referred to as the master. Power or influence or something else that made Ohlson pay attention to him.

'Excuse me, captain,' Yorke said, with the stolid determination of a man unable to absorb more than one idea at a time: 'My captain and my owners would want me to be sure to thank you on behalf of – '

'Yes, yes,' Pahlen interrupted, 'we understand and…'

' – my men and myself for the way you handled the rescue,' Yorke said, as though Pahlen did not exist. 'It's not every day men get torpedoed, and to be rescued within twelve hours or so is either good luck or a good lookout on the part of the rescue ship, so thanks for the good lookout.'

'Very well,' Pahlen said abruptly, 'now tell us your ship.'

Yorke raised his eyebrows, still looking at Captain Ohlson. 'Captain, it beats me why your chief officer should be so concerned with the name of our ship. There's no secret. She can only be one of three or four. But what the hell does he keep harping on it for? He sounds like the bloody Gestapo to me.'

Yorke's eyes flickered to Pahlen in time to get his reaction to the word 'Gestapo' and saw that he was now eyeing Ohlson and clearly puzzled by this Englishman. Ohlson seemed to stand more erect – or was it Yorke's imagination?

'Mr –ah– Yorke, I much appreciate your expressions of thanks, on behalf of your owners, your captain and your men. You misunderstand Chief Officer Pahlen – he has a very direct manner. We are very concerned about our – well, our shipmates in the torpedoed vessels, and we like to know which of them we have saved.'

Yorke pretended to be mollified but said in what he thought would be Captain Hobson's most direct manner: 'Aye, well, you know the names of the ships hit so far; it just sounds funny to me that the chaps that rescue you are more concerned with the name of the ship than how many were drowned or killed, or whether there are any more lifeboats bobbing around out there full of men.'

'Quite,' Ohlson said hurriedly, 'how many in your ship were in fact killed or drowned?'

'I haven't the foggiest idea,' Yorke said with suitable bluntness, 'I had enough trouble getting my own boat away. My point is this, that it would have been nice if you'd *asked*, instead of all this Gestapo sort of yapping about the name.'

'You don't know how many of your friends are left alive?' Ohlson said sympathetically. 'Well, Chief Officer Pahlen has to record this episode – that is correct, no? Episode? – in the ship's log so we need to know the name of your ship. That is, of course, the only reason for his interest.'

'Aye, well she was one of the "Hungry Hunters" – poorest paid, poorest victualled ships in the Merchant Navy. The *Somers Island*, owned by the Hunter Steamship and Trading Company. You spell that s-o-m-e-r-s-, not with a "u" and only one "m".'

'Good, thank you. Now, we are very short of accommodation and I counted fourteen of you in the boat. How many officers?'

'Me, the 4th engineer, the cadet.' Suddenly he realized he wanted Watkins with him and took a chance that the Swedes would not stark examining papers because although none of the men was carrying anything that would give away the fact that he was from the *Marynal*, Watkins was not in the right uniform. 'And the third radio operator. The rest are seamen.'

'Four officers – you'll have to share one cabin. The seamen I shall put aft; there is a large cabin there. They'll have to sleep on mattresses on the deck, but there are tables. And of course it will be only for a few hours.'

'It'd be easier for you, sir, if we all stayed together, wouldn't it? I'd like to be with my lads to keep an eye on them. They're a bit wild. You know what seamen are.'

Was it relief in Ohlson's eyes? He said, almost too quickly, 'Very well, that suits me – because of the shortage of accommodation, you understand.'

But I don't follow what you mean about "only for a few hours", sir,' Yorke said, trying to look as obtuse as possible. 'We won't be in Freetown for a month!'

'Oh, quite,' Ohlson said. 'But as soon as we rejoin the convoy this evening – once our engineers have repaired this fault that keeps on troubling us – you will be transferred to another ship. Your men will want to be among English-speaking shipmates.'

'Oh, don't you bother about that, sir: as far as I'm concerned you've got a dozen extra hands – watchkeepers, rust-chippers, painters, riggers; whatever work you want done, just tell me, and I'll make sure the men do it!'

'Most kind,' Ohlson said, 'but it is not possible. The commodore will give instructions tonight. The vice-commodore, rather.'

No one was going to give him the chance of being provoking; the Swedish captain was too polite. So far his comments and explanations made sense: the *Penta* was a Swedish merchant ship with engine trouble which would be rejoining an Allied convoy by nightfall: there was nothing that gave the lie to that…

CHAPTER NINETEEN

As Yorke clattered down the iron ladder to the large cabin in the poop he thought that the officer who had escorted him there and slammed the door shut once he had passed through had in fact then locked it. As he did not want the Swedes to guess that he had any suspicions about anything, he continued going down, deliberately not trying the handle, just in case the officer was waiting outside and watching.

His men were already making themselves comfortable: each had a mattress, which had obviously just been issued by the Swedes, and there was a pile of trousers, jerseys, wool shirts and socks which they had also provided. Most of the seamen had already stripped off their wet clothes and towelled themselves down and were now picking through the pile to find clothes that fitted. There was a good-natured babble as they exchanged shirts or jerseys which proved too large or too small, and the pile of wet clothes was mounting and smelling of damp wool.

Reynolds, already rigged out in grey flannel trousers and a garish woollen shirt in what some Swedish weaver obviously thought was a Scottish tartan, met Yorke at the bottom of the ladder.

'I've put a set of dry clothes to one side for you, sir. Jenkins is sitting in the head – it's through that door there, lavatory, handbasin and shower, including hot water – cleaning the

311

revolvers and wiping off the grenades. None of the grenades got really wet and he reckons the fuses will be all right.'

'Who put Jenkins in the head?' Yorke asked out of curiosity.

'I did, sir. The guns and grenades needed wiping off and we couldn't risk the Swedes coming down and finding us all sitting round doing it, but the one place where a man can reasonably lock himself in is the head, so Jenkins volunteered. The Swedes have given us some tins of food and loaves of bread (they're preparing a hot meal) and Jenkins took a tin of margarine to give the guns a wipe over. Is that all right, sir?' the cadet asked anxiously.

'Splendid, Reynolds. You've done just the right thing.' He looked round the cabin. 'Where's Mr Mills?'

'He's helping Jenkins with the grenades. They fascinate him. Says he's going to use that small bin there for lobbing practice. Like clock golf, he says; you get twelve throws. The man who lobs the highest number of grenades into the bin gets the prize. Seems dangerous to me, but…'

'Clock grenades are forbidden, Reynolds. Cards or uckers are all right, but any game your grandmother would not play is strictly forbidden.'

Reynolds' face was so serious that Yorke held back a grin. A quiet word with Mills would be sufficient to stop a new game developing – one which deserved to be called Swedish Roulette.

The Swedish officer would have gone by now and Yorke told Reynolds: 'Go up and see if the door is locked. Just turn the handle once; don't rattle it. You'll probably find it is.'

He walked over to the table on which stood the pile of clothing Reynolds had put out for him, and Watkins helped him off with his lifejacket and the duffel coat. 'I'll take the grenades to Jenkins,' the signalman said. 'And your gun, too, sir: let him give it a wipe over.'

Yorke stripped off his clothes, shivering violently, and towelled himself vigorously. He was just wondering how long Jenkins would need the head to use as an armoury, so that he could have a hot shower, when Reynolds returned, disconcerted and obviously unsure how to report to a naked naval officer.

'It's locked all right, sir. Who did that? Supposing we're torpedoed – we'd be trapped!'

'A grenade hung on the handle would probably open it for us, but don't worry: obviously the Swedes don't want us wandering around on deck, which means that they probably have something to hide…'

As Yorke mulled over the first piece of real evidence he had against the Swedes, tiny as it was and even then perhaps an accident, he pulled an dry underclothing, a thick tartan shirt – he recognized the lumberjack style – grey flannel trousers and heavy woollen socks. Several boxes of what were obviously tennis shoes had not yet been opened; the seamen were sitting round rubbing their feet, now clad in thick socks, warming them before trying on shoes. Yorke looked through the boxes for his size, remembering the Continental number system, and pulled out a box just as Cadet Reynolds knelt down to help him find the right pair.

Now he was rigged in dry clothes and no longer shivering, although his unshaven face felt like a toothbrush, Yorke wondered how to get his duffel coat dry. He was looking around at the array of piping which ran round the cabin like continuous Pan pipes when he saw three or four coats already wrapped round them at the forward end of the cabin.

Reynolds saw where he was looking. 'They're all steam pipes, sir: Mills thinks it's part of the ship's heating system for when she's up in the Baltic in the winter. I'll hang your duffel up.'

Yorke saw a chair at the far end of the long table which offered a little isolation and went over and sat at it. Beneath his feet he could feel the deck trembling slightly: below, two great thick propeller shafts, each probably the diameter of a man's chest, were turning slowly; occasionally as the ship gave a bigger pitch than usual and brought them nearer the surface, the propellers speeded up slightly, slowing as the stern sank down again and put them back in deeper water.

He waved towards Reynolds. 'Ask Mr Mills if he can spare a moment, please.'

The fourth engineer arrived with a broad grin on his face, smelling of margarine, his hands greasy and holding a grenade in one and a margarine-stained cloth in the other.

'Ha, Mr Yorke, how did things go on the bridge?'

'We're not welcome guests,' Yorke said. 'In fact we're locked in at the moment, though we're not supposed to know it.'

'One of these would make a good key,' Mills said, waving the grenade. 'Just show me the door.'

'There's no rush: we just act stupid for the time being. Now, what do you reckon the ship's engines are doing at the moment?'

'Both are just turning over at enough revolutions to keep the ship head to wind, I'd say.'

'Does there seem to be anything wrong with either of them?'

'No! I was commenting to that chap Jenkins not above five minutes ago that they were running very sweetly.'

'The reason this ship gives for dropping out of the convoy every day is that she has engine trouble.'

Mills shrugged his shoulders. 'I suppose she might have originally, but she hasn't now. Keeping big diesels like these turning over at low revolutions brings out any roughness, and you can hear for yourself, they're running like sewing machines.'

Most of the seamen were asleep after an enormous hot meal brought down by a trio of cheery Swedish cooks and stewards when Yorke felt the ship begin to vibrate and a moment later heard the rumble of the propeller shaft increasing to something approaching a whine. The gentle but deep pitching became sharper and quicker as the ship increased speed, but there was little rolling: she was staying on the same course, for the time being anyway.

Yorke stood up from his mattress and scrabbled about in his trouser pocket for his pencil and little notebook. It had dried out now though the paper was crinkled. He looked at his watch and wrote: '1415 – increased speed.' Mills was awake and looking up at him. 'What do you reckon we're doing?' Yorke asked.

'Going up to near full speed. Fifteen or sixteen knots.'

' "Estimate 15-16 knots," ' Yorke added to his note. 'Course unchanged.'

Two hours later they heard the *Penta*'s engines slow down and once again the ship resumed the gentle pitching, only this time there was a slight roll, too. Either she had come round to starboard a few degrees to bring the wind and sea more on to her port bow, or the weather was changing. Again Yorke made another entry in his notebook. The facts themselves might be relevant or they might not, but he knew his memory was bad and if he survived this present nonsense without finding the answer to the 'insider', the notebook entries might help put an idea into someone else's head. Or be needed as evidence at his court martial.

Watkins sat up on his mattress and groaned. 'Four thirty – time for a cuppa. But no chance of char in a ship like this. Or if there was it'd taste like a Whale Island gunnery instructor's love song, weak and salty.'

The signalman's movement showed that by now most of the men were awake, lying on their mattresses because there was nothing else to do. For months they had stood regular watches at sea or painted gun shields, stripped and greased guns in port, and kept their mess deck clean. Now they were passengers; dunnage, even, as Jenkins grumbled. The Swedish cooks had brought down three packs of cards, but, Jenkins added, the 'square heads' weren't up to uckers yet.

Yorke spent the next half an hour trying to think what he should be doing now while on board the *Penta* and ended up deciding that apart from breaking open the lock at the top of the ladder and searching the ship with a revolver in his hand, for the moment there was nothing he could do. He had to investigate but not raise suspicions; and he had to do something which would put an end to further attacks (on this convoy, anyway) while trying to avoid causing a diplomatic incident. Britain needed the ball-bearings made in Sweden of the special hardened steel; needed them so desperately – no engine of any sort could run without them – that high-speed boats like MTBs went to fetch them. No diplomatic incidents: Uncle had been most emphatic about that.

His orders had come from Downing Street and were (as one could expect from the Prime Minister) brief but explicit: if you have absolute proof, act; but relying on guesses and outward appearances would lead to a diplomatic incident and Sweden cutting off the supply of bearings, which Britain could not afford. 'Proof, proof, proof!' the old man had said, slapping his desk and then lighting a cigar, offering one to Uncle and cursing because he could not find his matches. Yorke could hear those three words, even third hand, because Uncle's description had been vivid and ended up with the

316

warning: 'No medals if you're right but if you're wrong expect a court martial, excommunication, castration and a rude commemorative rhyme scribbled on the wall in one of the men's toilets in the House of Commons. And a Parliamentary debate in secret session, of course.'

'That might be fun,' Yorke had said, 'providing I'm allowed a seat in the Distinguished Villains gallery.'

'You'll be chained to the railings in the Members' car park,' Uncle had said grimly, 'and then hanged, drawn and quartered while the Naval Estimates are being debated.'

In Uncle's office at the Citadel it had sounded funny enough; the very remoteness of it even happening added to the humour. Now it was here; the diplomatic incident was only as far away as Omelette and Cornflower the names by which he found himself thinking of Ohlson and Pahlen. What was going on out there? In half an hour it would be dark and by now the *Penta* had probably caught up with the convoy – the slowing down three miles astern, the slow creep up into position – and yes, Mills had noticed it too: a further slowing down, very slight but noticeable to an engineer or someone like himself whose nerves were on edge. Mills walked over to him.

'Dropping only a few revs. Maybe a knot in speed,' he said, anticipating Yorke's question and watching as Yorke wrote down another entry in his notebook against the time, 1711.

In London it would be dark already; office workers would be folding up their four-page evening newspapers and squeezing out of trains in the suburbs, queueing up for buses, fumbling for their pennies while the conductresses tried to issue tickets by the light of small blue bulbs… Some people would be setting out early to see a film, wives cooking suppers, children trying to find excuses for putting off doing their homework or going to bed. Clare would be off duty by now unless there had been another change which put her on nights. She would probably have supper at the hospital and perhaps go round to Palace Street to see his mother.

Curious that he never felt any jealousy. He had noticed some men going through agonies when they thought about their girlfriends, fiancées or wives, afraid they were out with other men. More than 'out with', all too often 'in bed with'. Real love had to be based on trust; anything else was just a physical attraction or a one-sided affair. Perhaps that was not fair to all those lonely women: he was sure of Clare because she had suffered, and had thought never to fall in love again. Now she had done so (there was no conceit in stating that) it was ridiculous to suppose she would be unfaithful. At least, he supposed it was ridiculous. She was a beautiful woman and any man could be forgiven…he turned to Mills with a question which would stop that train of thought.

'Engines still seem to be running smoothly?'

'Sewing machines,' Mills said. 'The chief engineer of this schnapps bottle must be a happy man. Probably pretty cross at being stuck in a six-knot convoy when he can make sixteen or so and probably with an economical cruising speed of twelve, but still…'

Suddenly all the lights went out. Yorke was just registering that there had been no explosion when he realized what was happening. 'Someone's opened the door,' he called out to the men, who were scrambling up from their mattresses, and a moment later the lights came on again and Yorke looked up at the narrow grating at the top of the ladder and saw the young officer who had greeted him at the top of the net.

'You!' the Swede shouted, pointing down at Yorke: 'To the bridge!'

'Keep talking,' Yorke told Mills, 'it's time this fellow was taught manners.'

'Aye, he's a cheeky booger,' Mills agreed. 'Treated us like sheepstealers being transported when we were brought down here. I took him to one side and said that if he ever wanted to see Stockholm again he'd better ease down.'

'What did he say?'

'Said he came from Malmö. He was serious, too. But he got the point.'

The Swede had repeated his shout while Mills was talking but no one looked up at him and a minute or two later Yorke heard the clatter of leather shoes on the steel rungs of the ladder. Then he felt a hand pulling at his shoulder. He turned his head and looked up at the Swedish officer. Two gold bands on his sleeve, face flushed with anger, a heavy gold ring on the ring finger of his right hand elaborately carved.

'You, English, up to the bridge!'

Yorke looked at the man's hand and suddenly stood up, facing him, and said quietly: 'It is a long way to the bridge and it is dark out there.'

'You're not afraid of the dark, are you, English?'

'No,' Yorke said evenly, 'but you will be, in a minute. Have you ever fallen over the side at night in bad weather with the ship making six knots, you can't call for help and you're not wearing a lifejacket?'

'No, of course not!' But the voice was less sure now, and the man slowly looked round. Every man in the cabin was standing round in a ring and watching him, their very silence a menace.

Yorke waited a full minute while the Swede realized that the only noise was the *Penta*'s engines and the hum of her propeller shafts, and that he was alone at the extreme after end of the ship with fourteen – strangers.

Yorke reached out and suddenly chucked the Swede under the chin as though he was a child. 'Imagine that that was a fist, and now you are unconscious. Two of these men carry you up on deck and drop you over the side. How long before you are missed? By then, what will you care, because you will be dead.'

'*Gott im Himmel!* My apologies, sir,' the Swede blurted. 'The captain is angry and wants you on the bridge at once!'

'My dear fellow, you should have said so,' Yorke said amiably. 'Now, let me find my coat and I'll come with you. I'll just have to visit the head a moment – the lavatory, you understand?'

The jacket he had borrowed from the *Marynal*'s second officer still felt a little damp but it was warm from having been tucked between the heating pipes. Pulling it on, Yorke went into the head, took his revolver from among the five or six nestling between the folds of a towel in a locker over the handbasin, checked that it was loaded and tucked it into the front of his trousers. Then he pulled his jacket straight and did up the buttons. The gun did not show in the mirror on the back of the door. He did not really need to carry it, but that it made him feel braver.

Omelette and Cornflower were both in the chartroom and but for the fact that it was now dark and the light went off and on as the door was opened and closed, neither man appeared to have moved since he had left them several hours earlier.

Ohlson was obviously angry but, dazzled by the lights in the cabin, Yorke could not for a moment see the expression on Pahlen's face. Ohlson began speaking immediately.

'Your vice-commodore,' he said accusingly, 'will not allow us to transfer you to another ship.'

'I'm not surprised,' Yorke said, resuming his placid, second-officer manner. 'It'd mean stopping the convoy in the dark, because it'd be dangerous to stop only one or two ships. Still there's all day tomorrow.' That, Yorke thought, should start something.

'Tomorrow!' Pahlen exploded. 'We are supposed to take you all the way to Freetown.'

Yorke shrugged his shoulders. 'Sorry about that. We didn't ask to be torpedoed.'

'And we didn't ask to pick you up!' Pahlen snarled.

'You did, though. Brotherhood of the sea, you know. Might be you one day. Leaving a lifeboat full of men to die of starvation and exposure is reckoned bad luck.'

Pahlen snapped something at Ohlson but the captain shook his head violently.

'Look, old man,' Yorke said, adopting the voice of sweet reason, 'yours isn't the only ship in the convoy carrying survivors. Nine ships sunk so far means nine sets of survivors. An average of fifty men per ship means 450 men distributed on board the remaining twenty-six ships. That works out at seventeen men per ship, mister, and you've got only fourteen. Supposing you get your lot tonight – how are you going to feel if some British ship's master says he doesn't want you on board, eh?'

'That won't happen to us!' Pahlen said angrily and a moment later obviously regretted his hasty words and tried to correct himself. 'I mean, no British ship would refuse to have us. It's not the British tradition. Play the game you chaps, what-ho, by jove, chin-chin, bad show. You see? I know the British!'

'Aye, I can see that,' Yorke said stolidly. 'And now it seems I'm getting to know the Swedish tradition. What is it you want? Money? The British Government will pay for our victuals. I didn't bring any money with me as there was a bit of a rush, you see.'

His sarcastic tone made Pahlen go even whiter: the harsh overhead light threw shadows over his face from his high cheekbones, so it seemed even more cadaverous; a skull over which bleached parchment was stretched.

'You talk too much!' Pahlen snapped.

Yorke took a step towards him and spoke very slowly, as though to a child or a backward adult. 'You called me up to the bridge. You told me the vice-commodore won't let you transfer us to another ship. If I had been you, mister, my pride would have kept my mouth shut because what you wanted to do isn't the usual way of treating survivors. Yet you told me. Still, you're a neutral so we'll let it slide. But what the bloody hell do you mean by blaming me for it? If the vice-commodore has to remind you what's the honourable and decent thing to do, don't expect *me* to wipe your eyes or congratulate you.

'Come, come, there's no need for us to lose our tempers,' Ohlson said soothingly. 'Mr Pahlen and I are just worried about your comfort: fourteen men stuck in that miserable accommodation.'

'We're comfortable enough, captain,' Yorke interrupted dourly. 'It's a lot more comfortable than a lifeboat, and providing we don't get torpedoed tonight or any other night we'll have no complaints.'

'Ah, well, then let's hope we have a good trip,' Ohlson said with the heartiness of a doctor comforting the widow of a man who had just died because of his wrong diagnosis.

'Aye, we can live in hopes,' Yorke said, adopting a Yorkshire accent, 'even if we die in despair.'

Ohlson paused a moment, working out what had been said, and then he smiled. 'You English, you have these wise sayings.'

'Ah, there are plenty more where that came from: "He who hesitates is lost!" ' Yorke said, and a moment later could have bitten his tongue, but Ohlson merely nodded in agreement, and Yorke said goodnight to both men and left the cabin.

The young officer was waiting in the darkened wheelhouse. He was alone, but Yorke wondered if others were waiting below on the maindeck. The officer led the way down but once they were on the maindeck motioned Yorke to lead the way along the starboard side, which was the lee side. Instead Yorke turned, as though misunderstanding him, and ducked round the hatch and made his way aft in the darkness along the weather side, arriving at the door of the cabin a good minute before the other man, who arrived puzzled and out of breath.

'Why did you go that way? I am your escort.'

'I needed the exercise,' Yorke said as he waited for the Swede to undo the door.

He went down the steel ladder as the men, alerted by the opening door extinguishing the light, were looking up at him, and he heard the door slam shut behind him and sensed that the Swede had not come inside. The men looked worried. Mills and young Reynolds obviously wanted to ask questions, but had learned the hard way that one did not question superior officers. However, it was better that the men knew exactly what was happening; there was nothing secret about it, and he had learned one thing in the war so far: men were usually frightened only of the unknown. Once they knew what threatened them, they were not scared. Fear was a question mark, and a good leader gave the answers as soon as possible.

He gestured to the men to gather round and brought them up to date, describing both visits to the *Penta*'s bridge and the attitude of the Swedish officers. He did not mention

Cornflower's comment that torpedoing 'won't happen to us' –
the man might have been one of those incurable optimists
that believed only his neighbour's car crashed, never his own.

The seamen seemed almost bored, and when Yorke
finished and asked for questions, there was none; only a
comment from Jenkins.

'That door, sir,' he said, gesturing to the top of the ladder. 'I
had a look at it while you were gone. Any time you want it
opened, just pass the word.'

Yorke looked surprised. 'I didn't know you were a
locksmith.'

'I'm not, sir, but locks have to be fitted. That one, like most,
is intended to stop anyone breaking *into* this cabin, which
means it's screwed into the wood from the inside, with no
fastenings showing on the outside. I just have to undo four
screws on our side and the lock either falls off or moves
enough to open the door. The Swedes haven't realized that!'

Yorke grinned with pleasure. Like most people (including
these Swedes) he tended quite wrongly to regard a lock as a
lock, thinking that whether you were standing on one side of
the door or the other when you turned the key, the door was
locked and that was that. But of course a lock could be
smooth only on one side: the outside of the front door of a
house but the inside of a cell door in a jail.

'Screwdriver ready?' He was only joking, but Jenkins held
up the remains of a deck knife and Yorke saw he had broken
the blade so that only a narrow sliver near the hilt remained,
where the metal was thickest.

'I took the liberty, sir,' he said apologetically, 'but I 'ad a
word with Mr Mills first. I've just "started" all four screws on
the lock. Nobody'll notice and I haven't scratched the paint,
but it means I know all four will come out. Otherwise you risk
getting three out and the last bleeder sticks like a limpet.'

Yorke thought of Ohlson and Pahlen, the Omelette and the Cornflower, both secure in the knowledge that 'the English' were locked down below. The best laid plans (whatever they were) of those two villains might yet be brought to nought because they forgot which side their lock was screwed.

But what *were* their plans? There was nothing on board the *Penta* that they felt had to be hidden from the eyes of the English officer: he had walked up to the bridge and back and it was obvious the escort was only concerned to fetch him and see him back to his quarters. There had been no attempt to hide anything on the bridge: he had seen the wheelhouse and the chartroom. So what could be done? There was no point in unscrewing that lock and turning the lads loose so they could take over the ship. He realized, with a sick feeling, that he was going to have to hear tonight's attack on the convoy – and surely there would be one – from his prison and there was nothing he could do about it. The *Penta* might have something to do with these insider attacks, but it was damned obvious that whatever it was they did did not occur during the night: it must happen, over the horizon, in broad daylight, when no one from the convoy or escort could see the *Penta*.

CHAPTER **TWENTY**

Yorke and his men had nine wristwatches between them and they differed by a maximum of eleven minutes. Yorke was fairly certain of his own which gained about twenty-five seconds a day so they all set their time by his. Now it wanted five minutes to eight o'clock or, as Yorke wrote in his notebook, 1955, and beside it: 'Team waiting for usual night attack to start.' He had talked with all the men in the hope that one of them had seen something or had an idea which would provide a clue to what the Swedes might be doing. None of them had seen anything and all, like Yorke, felt a cold but blind fury and they might be able to stop the night's attack – if only, as Mills said bitterly, they 'had the second sight'.

Either Yorke's watch was a minute fast or the *Oberleutnant* commanding the U-boat was late, but the first torpedo hit was noted as 2001, and in the *Penta*, where their cabin was below sea level, it seemed as though they were inside a big drum which had been struck lightly: a reverberation rather than an explosion, the. shock waves coming through the water and reminding Yorke of the ripples of heat rising from a road on a hot day. A minute later he was not sure whether or not he had heard the waxed-paper crackle sound of a ship breaking up.

Three minutes after that there was a similiar reverberation, followed a few moments later by a tremendous explosion which they heard through the plating of the hull above them as well as through the water. Yorke found all the men looking questioningly at him.

'The *Hidalgo*, he said. 'At least, I think so. She was the only one carrying that much ammunition. Torpedo warheads, bombs, shells…'

'Where was she?' Mills asked.

'Third ship in the third column.'

'That's the column which must have moved over to take the place of the commodore's column,' Reynolds said. 'The old fourth column.'

Would there be a third torpedo hit? The men were still watching him, not because they expected him to say anything but because they too must be waiting for the third hit…and the minutes dragged. Finally it was nine o'clock.

'That'll be it for the night,' he said.

'Only two hits,' Mills said.

'Perhaps he fired three and missed with one.'

'More likely the blast from the *Hidalgo* cracked the lenses in his periscope,' Watkins said bitterly. 'I hope the bloody thing drips all over him.'

The men began to stretch out on their mattresses. Four of them squatted round on one mattress and began a game of cards, Mills went off to the head and Reynolds dozed in a chair, his head sagging on to the table.

Eleven hits meant eleven torpedoes and perhaps twelve. Perhaps more because there was no way of telling how many had missed. The U-boat carried fourteen, so probably had two or three left. Watkins' explanation was likely to be close to the real reason why the U-boat had broken off tonight's attack: the sheer enormity of the *Hidalgo*'s explosion could have started rivets or damaged gear in the U-boat. And a U-boat commander, seeing such an explosion through his periscope, might well decide that that was enough for the night. Don't push your luck, Jack: the German Navy must have a similar expression.

Yorke took off his jacket and put it down on the deck beside his mattress before stretching out flat, staring up at the deckhead with its network of automatic sprinklers sticking out like metal sea anemones growing downwards. Perhaps three torpedoes left: that could – almost certainly did – mean another attack tomorrow night.

So, with eleven ships torpedoed by an insider, what did he know for certain, having watched most of it? What would be acceptable evidence in a court of law? Well, the *Penta* dropped back every day before an attack and rejoined just before nightfall. How significant was that? Possibly very, because she had not dropped back once before the attacks started. So that was one thing.

The other was that this insider always attacked ships in the next column to port of the *Penta*'s column. How significant was that? Not very: probably just a quirk of this particular *Oberleutnant*. Perhaps he was left-handed, or his periscope would not train to starboard, or his port propeller had a chipped blade so that he tried not to turn to starboard... a dozen different explanations. It could be just a coincidence that the column usually attacked was the one next to the *Penta*.

In fact, if he was honest Yorke knew that so far coincidence could explain everything. Coincidence that dirty fuel (the explanation given to Johnny Gower) kept plaguing the *Penta* so that her daytime stops were genuine and a night's running was long enough to block them again; coincidence that this convoy was being attacked by a U-boat commander who liked attacking the fourth column. It was a safe one anyway because he could see the escort dare not start depth-charging inside the convoy itself.

Coincidence. Diplomatic incident. Melodrama. Lack of detachment. Dreaming up a theory and then trying to find the facts to prove it. They all seemed to fit. But, he told himself angrily, they did not help. So...after the *Hidalgo* blew up, that bloody U-boat would have dived deep and stopped all machinery, lying at two or three hundred feet like a sleeping whale until her hydrophone operator could report that the convoy had long since passed and there was no sign of an escort. Then what? By tomorrow night she will have to catch up with the convoy again. Will she do that by following in the *Penta*'s wake?

Yorke sat up on one elbow and found he knew what he had to do. Or, rather, what he was *going* to do. Tomorrow afternoon, about two o'clock, just as soon as the *Penta* increased speed: that would be the time for Jenkins to work on the lock with his new screwdriver, so that the door could be opened just enough to let Yorke look astern, along the *Penta*'s wake. It was fortunate that the after side of the *Penta*'s poop was curved so that opening the door a fraction gave a good view over the stern. Yorke yawned and looked at his watch. More than sixteen hours to wait. One glance through the partly open door should answer all his questions one way or the other.

At seven o'clock next morning the Swedish cooks and a steward opened the door and brought down a stainless-steel pail full of steaming coffee and several containers of sliced bread, marmalade, jam, butter and sugar, plus a flat baking tin piled with fried bacon and many fried eggs.

Watkins, helping to place the containers on the table, looked at the bacon and sniffed disparagingly. 'Very fat. In fact it's all bleedin' fat. Don't you have no lean up there?'

Neither of the cooks spoke English but the steward translated and gave the answer: 'We Swedes like fat bacon. You English like the lean. In Denmark they breed special lean pigs to make lean for the English – in peace, of course.'

'Yes,' Watkins growled, 'that's what makes me cross, the idea that those bloody Jerries are eating up all those nice lean rashers. Here mate,' he added, having been briefed by Yorke, 'who was hit last night? Torpedoed,' he said; when he saw the steward did not understand 'hit'.

'Ah yes, the name of the first one I do not know. The second ship in the next column to the left exploded. The *Hidalgo*. No survivors, I think. The ship vanished in the flash.'

'What about the *Penta's* engines? Are they still giving trouble?'

The steward paused as he was taking the lid off a container of sugar and looked puzzled. 'I don't know what the engineers do. It seems dangerous to me.' With that he said something in Swedish to the two cooks and together they left the cabin, the steward tapping his watch. 'Next meal at noon,' he said. 'You have containers washed ready for us. The box,' he pointed to a small cardboard box at the end of the table, 'has the soap powder. You wash good, eh?'

The door slammed shut at the top of the ladder and Jenkins went up to check it, coming back to report to Yorke that it was locked. Reynolds and Mills were serving out the eggs and bacon as the seamen stood in line with their plates.

Mills handed a plate to Yorke. 'Two eggs each. We can't complain that the Swedes are starving us!'

Yorke remembered pre-war visits to Scandinavia. 'By Swedish standards, they are. Most Scandinavians are trenchermen.' He saw the puzzled expression on Mills' face. He probably thought the word meant homosexual. 'Most Scandinavians are great eaters.'

'Aye, and drinkers too,' Mills said. 'I've seen a couple of Scandies full of booze pull out knives and clear a bar in ten seconds. Must remember to ask that steward to get us some fags. Wonder how we pay for them.'

'Sign chits, I suppose,' Yorke said, sitting down and reaching for a knife and fork. The bacon was very salty. He preferred breakfast on board the *Marynal*.

The morning had dragged. Just before eleven o'clock they had noticed a slight reduction in the engine revolutions followed an hour later by another drop, with the *Penta* resuming the previous day's slow pitch and slight roll. Mills was certain the propellers were turning at just enough revolutions to keep the ship heading into the wind and sea.

When the Swedes brought the midday meal, Watkins had teased the steward. 'Good job you cooks and stewards don't have breakdowns in the galley, otherwise we'd all starve,' he said. The steward took a few moments to absorb the complex sentence and then said sourly; 'The engineers like to sit comfortable and play the cards.'

The seamen had drawn lots to take it in turns to wash the plates and cutlery, and it was all clean and stacked away, with the men sitting round playing cards or gossiping, by two o'clock. Yorke and Mills sat at the table, both listening to the whine of the shafts and the steady, low rumble of the engines. Five minutes past two, quarter past, twenty past…

'Perhaps that steward misunderstood Watkins,' Mills said. 'Maybe we haven't left the convoy. The vice-commodore may have reduced speed.'

Yorke shook his head. 'No, the steward understood, and anyway we altered course slightly.'

'A zigzag?' Mills said hopefully.

'Too small an alteration, only five or ten degrees. It was just…'

He broke off as the engines slowly increased speed, the propeller shafts beneath them increasing their hum and the ship beginning to vibrate. He looked at his watch and took out his notebook. '1425 – ship increased speed to estimated revolutions for 15 knots.'

Jenkins was sitting on his mattress, alert, the deck knife-screwdriver beside him.

Give them time out there to do whatever it was they were doing. Don't rush, Yorke told himself: don't be impatient. But he knew he was not fighting back impatience; on the contrary ho was having to force himself to set a time for the signal to Jenkins.

How should he signal? Point upwards nonchalantly with his right index finger? Point up to the door with his hand? Just speak a few words? Stand up himself to lead the way, gesturing to Jenkins to follow?

He was deliberately wasting time, and he was prepared to admit it was nerves. The few moments following Jenkins unscrewing the lock would be the climax of his appointment to the ASIU, perhaps the climax (or end) of his career in the Navy. All those hours. spent going over those bloody dockets had been steps on a path which ended here and now on a grating at the top of a steel ladder on board the *Penta*: one glance aft the moment Jenkins removed the lock, or loosened it, or whatever he needed to do to allow the door to be opened a fraction, that glance would be enough. If there was nothing, then he was wrong, very wrong, and wasting everyone's time. He pointed upwards and led the way.

Jenkins worked to a system. First he slid a knife into the seam nearest the lock between the thick planks of mahogany which made up the door, and told Yorke to use it as a hook to keep the door pulled inwards, so that it did not swing open when the lock came free. Then he took out the deck knife and undid one of the screws, putting it away carefully in his pocket. Then he undid the second, and then the third.

'Right sir, now really keep the door pulled in: one big roll and it might swing out, in spite of you, so be ready to reach round and grab the edge.'

With that he crouched down over the lock again and turned the knife. Yorke watched the screw turning, as though growing up out of the brass plate of the lock. Jenkins glanced round at Yorke to warn that the moment was approaching, slid the knife into his pocket and undid the screw the rest of the way with his fingers. After putting the screw away safely he gently slid the lock sideways less than half an inch, just enough to disengage the metal tongue from its slot on the door jamb. Quickly he seized the knob, then turned to Yorke. 'It's all right, sir, no chance of it swinging out so you can let go of the knife. Perhaps you'd like to have a look out!'

Yorke grasped the knob and gently pushed the door open a fraction. There was no one standing between the door and the taffrail. The *Penta*'s wake streamed astern, a white, swirling path of lace in the sea made up of whorls and eddies typical of a twin-screwed ship.

The U-boat was slicing along on the surface about two hundred yards astern, and for a moment it seemed the *Penta* was towing a slim but rusty iron cigar, a giant paravane. Three men were in the conning tower. The green slime of marine growth covering parts of the conning tower and deck seemed symptoms of some oceanic leprosy: dull, reddish rust streaks looking like dried blood. The U-boat was simply steaming along in the *Penta*'s wake, using her bulk to shield it from any radar beams ahead, and presumably relying on the men standing on her high bridge to act as lookouts – from their height of eye the Swedes could see several miles further over the horizon. One 88mm gun forward; two 20mm cannon in a mounting abaft it for use against aircraft.

CHAPTER TWENTY-ONE

His mattress was becoming the equivalent of a fakir's bed of nails. It had all the discomfort but, he thought ruefully, it did not seem to help provide the answers even after much contemplation. The U-boat was surfacing during the day and proceeding on the surface (in the Navy no ship or person ever 'went'; Their Lordships preferred the word 'proceed') in the shadow of the *Penta*. Fifteen or sixteen knots (from what he remembered of conversations with Jemmy) would give the best charge from the U-boat's generators and top up the batteries as quickly as possible while economizing on diesel fuel. It was also by a convenient coincidence (perhaps not such a coincidence) the best speed for the *Penta*, so the two in tandem caught up with the convoy.

That was why they used to watch from the *Marynal* and see the *Penta* come over the horizon from astern like a dose of salts, then slow down three or four miles away. At that point the U-boat dived, and somehow got into the convoy, passing the two escorts weaving back and forth across the rear of the convoy.

He had guessed all that before leaving the *Marynal*, so there was no point in wasting time lying on his bed of nails and going over it again. The important question was simple enough: how did the U-boat get from the *Penta* to the middle of the convoy?

It was a good question; a waffling counsel in the Law Courts could spend thousands of pounds of a client's money arguing about it without having a single fact, or, indeed, the slightest knowledge of the subject. A bureaucrat could conduct an official and inconclusive correspondence about it for years, keeping himself busy until he was ready to retire on a comfortable pension, when he would hand it over to another younger man travelling the same road to superannuated obscurity.

Yorke, by his own unaided efforts, had manoeuvred himself into the position where unlike a lawyer or a bureaucrat he had to provide an answer, or else... Civil Servants in high positions were in the happy position of having what one politician had quite wrongly attributed to the Press: 'Power without responsibility, the prerogative of the harlot through the ages.' The press had little or no real power; the upper-level Civil Servant, on the other hand, was all-powerful; he encouraged or thwarted ministers who generally took his advice and resigned if the resulting uproar proved it wrong.

The bureaucrat, however, took neither blame nor responsibility; indeed, he usually denied ever having given 'advice'. What he did, he claimed, was to outline 'the alternatives' open to the minister. No bureaucrat could be sacked unless he committed some criminal offence. If he was incredibly and consistently stupid, the only way of getting him out of a particular job was to promote him. Some of the highest Civil Servants owed their rank to sheer incompetence. Had they been a little brighter they would have reached retiring age in quite a lowly post.

Though true, none of this helped Yorke's present problem. There was a diplomatic incident lurking at the foot of his mattress, a dereliction of duty charge was on the left side, a negligence on the right, while under the pillow was straight failure, with a job waiting for him as naval officer in charge at Calabar, or some other collection of mud huts up some tropical river in Africa. And none of it mattered a damn if he could stop the sinkings.

He decided to look at it through the eyes of the *Ober-leutnant* commanding the U-boat. The *Penta* gave him a way of approaching within three or four miles of the convoy in daylight and on the surface. It was still daylight and he was within three or four miles and now he had to dive to avoid the British Asdics and hydrophones. What did Heinrich do? Bark out the question in the best Erich von Stroheim manner, monocle screwed into the eye. Hurry, hurry, Heinrich, the Tommy frigates are racing towards you! What are you going to do?

Well, sir, I will dive and get right under the *Penta*, so close that the top of my periscope (housed) is nearly scratching the barnacles off her bottom, and I will be running on the almost silent electric motors, and I will rely on the appalling roar of the *Penta*'s two diesel engines, and the heavy thump-thump, or whoomp-whoomp, of her twin propellers to deafen the frigates' hydrophone operators. The vast bulk of the *Penta*'s hull will send the probing sound fingers of the Asdic bouncing back without the Tommy operators realizing that the *Penta* whale has a lethal remora on her underside.

Leave that idea to soak in for a while and then come back and have another look at it, Yorke told himself. Stay with *Oberleutnant* Heinrich who has just been given his first command. A new boat, 770 tons, strong enough to dive to four hundred feet without damage, twin diesels giving 19 knots on the surface, and a battery capacity of nine knots submerged for an hour or three days at one to two knots.

Repeating what Jemmy had said parrot-fashion reassured him that he had remembered it correctly.

There you are, *Oberleutnant* Heinrich, this is your new boat: no dents, newly painted, no kinks in the guardrails, no rust, no slime… You board at the Tirpitz Pier in Kiel and way up above you on the side of the hill is the Navy war memorial, commemorating the dead of the First World War, those who perished for the Kaiser in those early and crude U-boats, or who died at the battle of the Heligoland Bight, which the Tommies called Jutland…

You probably know your first lieutenant, who will be your right hand, and perhaps your second officer. The ensign, equivalent to the Tommies' sub-lieutenant, will probably be a stranger. If you have any sense or enough influence you will know your chief engineer. Fourteen electric torpedoes will be stowed below, fuel tanks will be full, batteries topped up with electrolyte, the latest signal books and the settings for the cipher machine will be on board…

Your orders would come from the Senior Officer, West, a procedure which (although you do not know it) has the Tommies baffled, because Admiral Doenitz's U-boat headquarters at far away Kernevel, near Brest, will give you your tactical orders.

So now the time has come to leave the Tirpitz Pier: best uniform for you, with medal ribbons worn. You might have an Iron Cross, too, and perhaps other decorations slung round your neck. A Navy band standing on the jetty is thumping and blowing as you ease 75 metres of boat (most of which cannot be seen because, like an iceberg, the bulk of a U-boat is under the water, even when technically surfaced), and you take a spin round Kiel Bay. Before the war you sailed some of the Navy's yachts across these waters, beautifully-kept 50-square metres that slept six or eight men and were fast. The

Olympic Games yachting was held here just before the war. The big Navy ocean racers were here that took park in the race across the Atlantic before the war began and had romantic names like the *Roland von Bremen* and *Wappen von Hamburg*...

Back to Kiel and then up to the locks opening into the North-East Sea Canal linking the Baltic and the North Sea in an almost straight line. The Tommies do not seem to understand the importance of the canal because they have not destroyed the locks either at the Kiel end or at Brunsbüttelkoog, where they opened into the River Elbe below Hamburg, nor bombed the sections where the high sides would tumble down into the water and block the channel.

The trip through the canal is like a cruise through Dutch canals or a cycle ride through sunken lanes with hedges on either side. Here a village, with old men fishing in the canal waters; there passing under a bridge where, high above, cars and lorries stop so their drivers can look down admiringly at the U-boat on its way to the Atlantic.

Out of the locks at Brunsbüttel and down the Elbe, fast flowing with long sandbanks which constantly shift position, something of a nightmare for poor *Oberleutnant* Heinrich, who can imagine his fate if he puts his new command on to a shoal before reaching the open sea. 'Open sea' means the North Sea, with the North Frisian Islands to starboard, scattered along the Danish coast as though protecting it from the winter storms, and the East Frisian Islands on the port quarter, scattered along the north German coast; islands with names that are fast becoming part of German naval history: Borkum, Juist, Norderney, along to Wangerooge, protecting such ports as Emden, Wilhelmshaven and Bremerhaven. No Zeppelins now at Wilhelmshaven, of course, but everyone honours Graf von Zeppelin, a man who turned dreams into the reality of enormous silver flying cigars filled with highly explosive hydrogen because the Americans would not sell the inert helium to foreigners.

All of which is most interesting, but Yorke and his alter ego, *Oberleutnant* Heinrich, are still lying on the mattress of nails.

The *Penta* is now back in the convoy making six knots. Less in fact because the convoy rarely actually made six knots 'over the ground'. *Oberleutnant* Heinrich stays beneath her while she passes through the area being covered by the frigates, and perhaps remains there until she is back in position as the second ship in what was the fifth but is now the fourth column.

Once there, Heinrich was safe because he knows the escorts do not come inside the convoy. However, there was no reason why he should not stay beneath the *Penta*. He could go deeper, of course, so there was less risk of him bumping his periscope against her bottom, but he would always be able to recognize her because of her two diesel engines, which had been made in Germany anyway.

Now what does Heinrich do? His batteries are well charged. He only used them for that run at a little over six knots for less than half an hour which was necessary for the *Penta* to get back into position. It is now 6 p.m. and he likes to wait until 8 p.m. before attacking, which means another two hours at six knots submerged. An hour's slow manoeuvring while he sinks his quota of merchantmen. Sometimes it only takes half an hour and by 9 p.m. at the latest he is diving deep and stopping while the convoy passes overhead. Later he can surface and begin charging the batteries again, slowly following the convoy until he sees the *Penta* on the horizon.

Oberleutnant Heinrich knows the Tommies will never guess how he gets into position and as soon as he has used up all his torpedoes, he will steer for Brest and a good leave, after sending a brief report to Admiral Doenitz. The man the German submarine service call 'The Lion' will be delighted. Eleven ships sunk so far, and with three torpedoes left Heinrich can hope for at least two more. Thirteen ships with fourteen torpedoes; thirteen ships sunk on one patrol. That should mean oak leaves to go on his Iron Cross.

Yorke now knew all about how *Oberleutnant* Heinrich operates. I've just looked through the crack of a partly-opened door, and discovered the secret. Now I've got to destroy you, Heinrich old boy, and between us you and I could well cause one vast, enormous, gigantic diplomatic incident, even if you have just drowned at a hundred feet and your U-boat is lying like a crushed biscuit tin on the bottom of the Atlantic.

It might not work, but it was the best plan he could contrive after what seemed to be hours of thinking. He refused to look at his watch, but then realized that he had to know what the time was to see how much of it was left before they set to work.

At half past five the *Penta* had slowed down and as Yorke had. scribbled the fact in his notebook (*evidence* now, he hoped) he knew he had two and a half hours to go before the U-boat would fire its first torpedo. It would be dark in less than half an hour.

'Gather round and make yourselves comfortable,' he told the men. They sat on forms, perched on the edge of the table or stood leaning against the nearest bulkhead. Mills had not shaved and even though plump he would look a desperate fellow clutching a grenade in one hand and a revolver in the other. Cadet Reynolds was still too young for a couple of days' growth of beard to do much more than show faintly in a bright light. The bearded seamen had the same sort of faces that must have been familiar to Francis Drake or Edward

Teach. They all looked ruthless and tough. Within an hour they would look desperate as well, because they would *be* desperate.

'Listen carefully,' he told them. 'When you were boys playing games at school I expect you played pirates. The legal definition of piracy is depriving the rightful owners of the possession of their ship. You, gentlemen, will soon be pirates.'

Watkins looked across at Jenkins and winked, making a gesture with his right hand as though cutting someone's throat.

'Yes,' Yorke said, 'it might come to that too.' He looked at his wristwatch with some deliberation, then round at the men. He saw he had all their attention. No gunnery instructor at Whale Island or battery sergeant major at wherever the Royal Artillery trained its gunners had seen men more alert. They reminded Yorke of high divers poised to leap.

He said in a carefully controlled voice: 'In forty-five minutes' time we capture this ship.'

No one showed the slightest surprise or excitement. Yorke suddenly felt like a boy who had scored the winning goal only to find that all the other players had gone home. Eventually Mills scratched his left buttock. 'Aye, that's a good idea,' he said conversationally. 'I thought it'd get down to that in the end. We're going to be a bit short-handed in the engine room, though.'

Yorke looked at his watch, 'You've forty-one minutes to train four volunteers to be engineers, or electricians, or greasers, or whatever it is you want.'

'You want me to keep the ship running for an hour or a week?'

'An hour. Perhaps less.'

'Good, because I'd need more men if we have to stand watches. Now I can make do with three.'

Yorke looked round at Cadet Reynolds. 'What are you like at the wheel?'

'All right, sir. Never steered a twin-screw ship, but I'll be all right.'

He pointed at Watkins. 'You two signalmen will take over the wireless cabin. Get the Swedes out, or secure them there, guard the door, and don't let anyone damage the transmitter. If you can tune the receivers into the *Echo's* working frequencies, do so and keep the bridge informed of anything concerning us.'

Yorke stood for a minute or two staring into space, collecting his thoughts. Then he noticed that Jenkins and most of the other seamen were sucking teeth, scratching their heads, clicking finger joints or giving signs that any petty officer would recognize as displaying disappointment, impatience or resentment. Tooth-suckers of the world unite! Yorke thought.

'The rest of you,' he said casually, 'have to do the fighting. Half a dozen will seize the rest of the ship, but particularly the bridge. I don't think you can manage it...' he saw enough resentment showing in their faces to know that the challenge had worked, 'but we've no choice.'

'Now first of all, the ship's saloon. That's going to be the temporary jail. Any Swede who surrenders goes down there. There may be two doors leading into it, there usually are in most ships, one from the corridor on each side. Lock one. Then once we have prisoners I want one of you standing guard just inside the other door juggling a couple of hand grenades. These Swedes haven't fought anything more dangerous than hangovers for many generations, but they'll recognize grenades. Any trouble, toss in a grenade, step outside and lock the door: you'll have time.'

'So don't worry about killing 'em sir?' Jenkins asked.

'If they try to kill us, or resist what we're doing, we kill, yes, because we don't have enough time to argue the toss. At 8 o'clock that U-boat will attack again. He's got three or four torpedoes left. Four British or American ships, fifty men on board each. He can kill a couple of hundred of our chaps unless we stop him, and we can't stop him if any Swedes interfere.'

'Ah,' Jenkins said, taking an appreciative suck at his teeth. 'A grenade in the saloon... What a bang! It's going to take a lot o' soap and water and O-Cedar to clean the Swedes off the panelling.'

'Right now, remember the saloon is a sort of refuge as well as a cell. What I'm hoping to do is this.' For the next five minutes he sketched out his plan, conscious that he was overworking phrases like 'I hope by then that we'll...' and 'by then the *Echo* should...'and 'providing the Swedes don't...' Phrases, phrases...they had a meaning, but so did notices on the gate like 'No hawkers or circulars', 'Stirrup pump kept here', 'Beware of the Dog', or the list of Sunday services on the church notice board with, next to it, the rota for the Home Guardsmen who nightly stood guard in the tower, armed with a motley selection of weapons (usually their own 12-bore shotguns) against a German airborne invasion.

CHAPTER **TWENTY-TWO**

Six o'clock. It would be dark outside, pitch dark because it was a no-moon period. Yorke signalled to the men to get ready, and ten of them trooped through to the head, where Jenkins issued them with grenades and, for the lucky few, revolvers and automatics. Reynolds agreed that his automatic should be given to Jenkins; Mills had decided that only he would carry grenades to the engine room. 'Give me a couple,' he said. 'I know when and where they can be thrown. I don't want some keen type chucking a grenade into a whole lot of copper fuel lines. Nothing like that for stopping the lorry on the level crossing.'

At two minutes past six Yorke was at the top of the ladder with Jenkins undoing the second screw of the lock.

'Don't bother to put the blasted things in your pocket', Yorke snapped impatiently as the man finished unscrewing it with his finger. 'We won't be needing them again.'

All the men were on the ladder or standing in a crocodile at the foot of the first step, holding the shoulder of the man in front. The moment the door opened the cabin would be thrown into darkness by the automatic switch.

As the third screw came out Jenkins went to put it in his pocket and then tossed it over his shoulder, producing a prompt, "Ere, watch it Jack, bloody near 'ad my eye out!'

'Can't do anything right,' Jenkins grumbled.

'You take the Swedish captain,' Yorke reminded him. 'Four stripes, hair blond and like a Brylcreem advertisement. Leave the albino with three stripes to me. He'll be on the bridge.'

' "In the King's name!" That's what I'll tell him. Those buggers boarding the *Altmark* used up "The Navy's here!" '

Jenkins had a sense of history – providing all this worked. If it did not, then the proud shout repeated at the court martial following the diplomatic incident was going to cause giggles and then outrage. Yorke could hear the disapproving sniffs from the presiding admiral (he was sure he would get an admiral, if only to satisfy those lemons at the Foreign Office who would be telling the ambassador in Stockholm what to say to grovel to the Swedes) for letting the King's name be brought into it. Mind you, if it all worked the Chief of Naval Information (not to mention the present First Lord and the other proud former First Lord now in Downing Street) and the whole of Fleet Street and the BBC would fairly trumpet the four words that Jenkins, exasperated by four small screws, had just uttered.

'Last one, sir,' Jenkins said, tucking the makeshift screwdriver into a pocket with one hand while he undid the screw with the fingers of the other.

Yorke looked down at the men behind him on the ladder. 'Shut your eyes, all of you; start getting your night vision. You too, Jenkins: you can open the door with your eyes shut.' He shut his own eyes and at once became conscious for the first time for an hour or more that the propeller shafts were still spinning below them; that outside the sea was hissing its way past and below a U-boat was gliding through the water like the Swedish ship's shadow. By now the electric torpedoes would have been slid into the torpedo tubes, *Oberleutnant* Heinrich (he might of course be a *Kapitänleutnant*) would have chosen his targets for the night, and whatever happened a number of men had only a few hours of life left – either the German crew of the U-boat, or men in Allied merchant ships.

He found he had little sympathy for the U-boat men. Too many naval officers regarded hunting U-boats as a sort of sport, where the Teds were alternately the hunter and the hunted, but anyway keeping to some sort of rules. In fact that was rubbish; it had been almost true at the beginning, but the *Athenia* had been sunk within an hour or two of the war starting, and had been packed with children. By now there were far too many authenticated reports of lifeboats run down by U-boats to kill trained officers and men when a single ship had been torpedoed; too many cases of U-boat captains tossing grenades into lifeboats full of survivors – dozens of boats had remained afloat so that a frigate on passage, or even a fast merchant ship sailing by herself, spotting a lifeboat on the horizon, had raced up to rescue the survivors – and found it full of the remains of dead men, many blown to pieces by the grenade. Occasionally, but all too rarely, a man had been left alive who could identify the U-boat, and presumably somewhere in the Admiralty a file was being kept, giving numbers, positions, and dates, so that when the war was over the U-boat commanders could be traced and brought to trial. The Ted of this war was a different bird from the Ted of the last war: too many of the present ones were fanatics – not fanatical Germans, which was understandable, but fanatical Nazis. Many Germans seemed to have two loyalties, to the Fatherland and to the Party. The Fatherland tended to be the same vague patriotic focus that the British had, except that a Briton would be embarrassed if anyone started talking about 'the Motherland' and the more vulgar would make some wisecrack about pregnant girlfriends, but from the German prisoners he had seen, and from intelligence reports he had read, the real Nazis were killers: they could, and consistently did, bomb open cities – he remembered watching Canterbury burn one night, praying that the Cathedral would be saved – and their fighter planes could and did blaze away at shot-down RAF pilots as they drifted down with parachutes. He had seen that happen too during the Battle of Britain: the parachute began falling faster and faster, sometimes catching fire and sometimes twisting up as a distraught woman might wring a handkerchief, and the black speck at the end of it would hit the ground at near terminal velocity, a bloody mass of jelly.

He had night vision by now. 'Open the door,' he told Jenkins. He felt the man wrestling with something, and then the door was flung open, putting the light out. He opened his eyes to see the doorway as a grey rectangle, a patch that was not quite so black as the rest. Those flecks and blurs were the crests of waves. Beyond them, where he could not see her, the *Marynal* kept station astern of the *Penta*.

His knees felt like weak springs. One grenade was clinking in one jacket pocket, a second bulging in the other, and his revolver was a hard lump held in place by the waistband of his trousers. Now he had his men under control, but the moment he gave the word they would split into three parties, and the failure of one could mean the failure of the whole affair.

Silence and surprise were their only allies. If one of his men gave an excited shout, one started running so that an unsuspecting Swede became alarmed, it would spoil everything. They had to creep, open doors quietly, gently prod a dozing Swede with the blade of a deck knife...

As his night vision improved he could see more details: the swan-neck pipe sticking up from the deck aft there, ventilating some tank; the stanchions of the rail through which he had seen the waves swirling. He turned and said down the ladder: 'Right men, let's get started.'

Jenkins was clipping the door in the open position so that it did not slam back and forth as the ship rolled, and Yorke stood to one side as Mills came out. The engineer found Yorke's hand and shook it. 'Best o' luck. Use the engine-room telegraphs for orders if need be, but give me a buzz on the phone when you can: it'll be nice hearing your voice.'

'Listen for the ring in about ten minutes!' Yorke said with a heartiness he did not feel. He counted the three seamen following Mills. Each was holding the next man's jersey: Mills was taking no chances that seamen who might well have never before been into an engine room would get lost in the approach.

Now Watkins and the other signalman. Both were carrying deck knives: the blades were dull but unmistakable in the darkness. Suddenly Yorke thought of night vision again.

'Watkins!' he hissed. 'Listen. When you get to the wireless cabin, just open the door. That'll put the lights out. Then wait. Count thirty seconds. Then the pair of you nip in and shut the door. The lights suddenly coming on again should dazzle the Swedish operator as much as you, so you start off equal.'

'Thanks sir,' Watkins muttered. 'And a moment later I'll have my knife at his throat.'

Six men on their way. Now a seaman accidentally brushed against Yorke so that the grenades in his pocket clinked. He was the first of the next six, who were coming with him and Jenkins to secure the captain and the bridge.

Yorke led the way along the starboard side and felt Jenkins, as instructed, grab the tail of his coat. They all walked slowly, like a crocodile of schoolgirls keeping close against the wall in heavy rain as they made their way from one school building to another.

Clear of the poop and up to the coamings of number four hatch. It's a damn dark night; not even a poacher's moon.

Now the mainmast, the derricks sprouting out of its base and stowed flat, two across the top of number four hatch, two lying forward over number three hatch. Toe stubbing against something, probably a ringbolt. A glance to starboard to see, distant and almost ghostly, the ship abeam in the next column, ploughing along silently, no sign of human life, just smothers of white at the bow as she shouldered her way through the waves. Now level with the square shape of a liferaft stowed at an angle against the mainmast shrouds, tilted and held by a single wire and toggle so a clout with a maul would send it toppling into the sea.

Past number three hatch and there's the after end of the accommodation and bridge section, a rectangular black box stretching from one side of the ship to the other. At the forward end the bridge with the squat funnel just abaft it, and the wireless cabin a tiny square box just abaft that, by itself with aerials reaching up to the triatic stay between the masts, out of the way so that there was no risk of anyone touching them while the transmitter was working.

And here was a companionway. One way to the bridge was to enter the accommodation through one of the doors on this level and walk forward along the passageway until directly under the bridge, and then go up one of the internal companionways, passing the captain's accommodation one deck below. Or up this first ladder on to the top of the accommodation, which was the boat deck, and along it, passing the wireless cabin and approaching the after side of the bridge. And that was the way they were going: it meant that if necessary they could give Watkins – who should be ahead of them – a hand at the wireless cabin, and there was almost no chance of meeting anyone. The danger of walking through the accommodation, on the other hand, was that someone, perhaps on his way to the toilet, would take one look at a bunch of hairy seamen tiptoeing through the accommodation and let out an almighty bellow.

Up the ladder and pause at the top while Jenkins caught hold of his coat to re-form the line of men. Ahead was the wireless cabin, where Watkins and his mate should be in control. Still the slow shuffle. The eye usually spotted a sudden movement but rarely saw anything moving slowly. This trudge was bad for the nerves – his nerves, anyway. He could usually steel himself for a quick dash but hated the slow build-up. Abreast the wireless cabin now. He pressed Jenkins back a little, the signal to stop, and broke away to tiptoe over to the big steel box. No one outside the door and no shouting inside. Watkins was in control, he could be sure of that.

He turned back towards Jenkins and was pleasantly surprised to see how little the group of men showed up in the darkness. Against a dark background, a bulkhead for example, they would be invisible.

The bridge was one deck higher, up that steel ladder. Captain Ohlson's cabins were here, in the section just below the bridge, on the same level as they were standing. Yorke again stopped; nudged Jenkins and pointed to the door into the cabins. 'Count to ten and then go in!' he muttered as Jenkins and another man glided away.

Yorke began pulling himself up the steel ladder, Reynolds and the rest of the men following him. He paused for a moment to reach under his coat for the revolver tucked into his trouser band. He cocked it carefully, and although the clothing muffled the click it sounded very loud. Very loud indeed to someone with his thumb on it who was half scared that the tug of a piece of clothing would result in the gun firing, with dire results to his manhood.

He pulled out the gun and put it into his jacket pocket, found a grenade in the way and pushed it down the front of his jacket, not daring to risk banging it against the steel ladder if he held it in his hand as he climbed. The top of his head was level with the top rung, and he paused a moment, finishing his count…eight, nine, ten. Jenkins would be opening Ohlson's door now.

A few steps up, his right hand reaching for his gun as he cleared the top, left hand dipped into his pocket for a grenade.

On the forward side of the bridge, hunched over with his elbows on the bridge rail, concentrating on looking at the ship ahead, was the Swedish officer of the watch and Yorke recognized him as the one who had met them on deck when they had climbed up the scramble net and escorted him to the bridge. Yorke tiptoed over to him and then paused for a moment, feeling foolish: did you knock out someone using the butt of a revolver, gripping it by the barrel, or just hold the gun in the palm of the hand and give him a good clout with the side of it? What a hell of a time to have to decide. The gun was cocked: a sudden jar and it might go off.

He stuck the gun back in the top of his coat, returned the grenade to his pocket, tapped the Swede on the right shoulder with his left hand and hit him on the jaw with a wild right-handed punch as the startled man turned to look over his shoulder. The man gave a mild grunt as he slid to the deck and for a moment Yorke felt he had smashed every bone in his hand.

'Starboard side of the bridge secured,' he reported to himself ironically and turned to go into the wheelhouse. Now he needed the revolver and he reached into his coat, conscious that someone behind him was pushing impatiently.

He stepped into the wheelhouse from the wing of the bridge and the impatient person passed him, proving to be Cadet Reynolds making for the wheel. Another seaman took his place and walked across to the helmsman who, almost hypnotized from concentrating on the dimly-lit compass bowl, was slow to react. As he walked across the wheelhouse to go out to the other side of the bridge, Yorke saw the seaman jabbing his revolver into the helmsman's ribs and pushing him away to make room for Reynolds at the wheel.

There was one man standing out there in the darkness, a thin man whose shoulders were slightly hunched and who, like the other officer, was looking forward with his elbows resting on the bridge rail.

'Mr Pahlen,' Yorke said softly. 'Good evening.'

The officer swung round with a muffled curse. 'English? Yorke is it? What the devil are you doing up here? And who are these people with you?'

Yorke moved to one side to let the two seamen immediately behind him get out of the wheelhouse.

'Stand back from the rail,' Yorke said sharply, remembering that the button for the action-stations alarm would be fitted close to the binocular box on the after side of the coaming.

'Don't you dare give *me* orders!' Pahlen snarled, then stepped back quickly as one of the seamen cocked his revolver with a click which in the tense atmosphere sounded like a steel bar snapping.

'*Kapitänleutnant* Pahlen,' Yorke said calmly, 'we've taken the ship. You are a prisoner of war. However, since the Swedish Government will never admit you were on board, nor will the German Government, we are free to toss you over the side, dead or alive, without anyone shedding a tear. Go to the chartroom. One silly move and I doubt you'll even feel the splash...'

The two seamen bundled Pahlen back into the wheelhouse and then to the chartroom. Yorke, left standing on the port side of the bridge, was congratulating himself on trapping

Pahlen. The man had not protested that he was Swedish when Yorke had given him a German rank and told him he was a prisoner of war. Suddenly it occurred to him that he was alone on the bridge. No one was keeping a lookout and if Reynolds was a few degrees off course, there would be an almighty collision with one of the ships in the next column to port or starboard.

Reynolds was obviously wasted at the wheel; he would have to be the officer of the watch for the next half an hour or so. Yorke hurried back into the wheelhouse, found one of the seamen capable of acting as a quartermaster, and told Reynolds to go out to the starboard side of the bridge to keep a lookout and make sure the young Swedish officer was still unconscious.

'We've got 'im 'ere,' one of the seamen said, gesturing into a dark corner of the wheelhouse. 'That chap wot you 'it, sir. Still asleep, 'e is. We've tied him up with electric flex that Watkins sent along.'

They all froze for a moment, then Yorke realized it was a telephone, not buzzing but giving a sharp, urgent, high-pitched ring. A seaman passed Yorke the receiver. Where the devil was the call coming from? He grunted into the mouthpiece, a word which could be 'Ja' if you were expecting a German to answer or 'Yeah' if you were English.

'Is that you, Mr Yorke?' The alarm in the voice was palpable.

'Yes, Mills: how are things down there?'

'Fine. Got 'em all bundled up, no one hurt very much. None of us, anyway. Same revs?'

'Yes, we're staying in the convoy for the time being. I'll use this telephone for passing orders, not the telegraphs.'

'Very well, sir,' Mills said. 'How are things on the bridge?'

'Fine – we have it. Wireless cabin secured. I'm just waiting to hear from Jenkins that Captain Ohlson is locked in the lavatory like the three old maids, then we'll secure the rest of the people.'

He put down the telephone to find Jenkins grinning at him. 'That's just where he is, sir. So surprised he never spoke a word. I've left a man watching the door.'

Yorke glanced at the compass bowl, saw the seaman was keeping a good course despite the sea coming in on the port bow, and said to Jenkins: 'You're absolutely sure you can get the rest of this ship's company out of their cabins and into the saloon?'

'How important is it that we don't kill any of them sir?' the seaman asked carefully.

'It does not matter now, because the *Penta* isn't a neutral: at least one of the officers is a German. Still, I don't want you acting like a lot of wild cowboys down there.'

He paused as the second signalman came into the wheelhouse. 'Message from Watkins, sir,' he said as soon as he saw Yorke. 'Wireless room secure, operator tied up, one receiver tuned to the *Echo*'s working frequency, and a transmitter and receiver on the distress frequency.'

'Good, so Watkins can be left?'

'Yes, sir, he told me to report and then lend your chaps a hand. He's got a phone. Ah, that'll be him,' he said as a phone rang. He picked up the instrument. 'Bridge here, that you, Watkins?' He listened a few moments, said 'Yes, and I'm sure he sends his love, too,' put the receiver down and said: "That's the phone to the wireless cabin, sir. Second one along.'

'Right. Now Jenkins, I need a guard for Pahlen, and you've left one with Ohlson, so you've got...' he counted them up in his head, 'four.' Not many, to capture perhaps twenty men. Unarmed and sleepy men, admittedly. 'Is that going to be enough? Wait, bring Captain Ohlson up here and put him in the chartroom: that'll give you the guard as an extra man. Five and yourself.'

'That's enough, sir,' Jenkins said cheerily. 'A bullet ricocheting down the steel corridor will be worth a dozen men, if I have to fire one. If you'll take the man you want as guard for here, I'll get Captain Ohlson up and start sorting out the bastards below.'

Yorke knew that for a guard he needed an unimaginative man who was not squeamish. 'Leave me Baxter. Warn any Swede who speaks English that the bridge and engine room are already under our control; they can telephone the bridge to confirm...'

As Jenkins went down to fetch the Swedish captain, Yorke gave Baxter his instructions for guarding Pahlen and Ohlson in the chartroom. 'Watch the one who looks like an albino. He's in there already. He's dangerous, but I want to question him in a few minutes, so don't...'

'I won't, sir,' said Baxter, 'but the captain...?'

'Not so important.'

'And the officer outside that we wired up with flex?'

'Just check from time to time that he's not getting free.'

Out on the starboard wing of the bridge Yorke found Reynolds keeping a sharp lookout with a pair of binoculars – obviously appropriated from the binocular box – slung round his neck.

'Can you see a signal lamp anywhere?' Yorke asked.

'Yes, sir, I kicked the box just now. It's a sort of Aldis, smaller than ours. Already plugged in, so watch out for the flex. Ah,' Yorke heard wood scraping against wood as the cadet dragged the box out of a corner, 'here it is.'

Yorke picked it up, pressed the glass against his body and touched the trigger. 'That's lucky, it has a blue shade on it. Now, look round with those binoculars of yours and see if you can spot the *Echo*. She'll be over on the starboard quarter of the convoy.'

As the Cadet looked, Yorke heard a shuffling and grunting but did not look round: Jenkins was bringing Captain Ohlson up to the chartroom. Captains that pass in the night.

Half the job was done. No perhaps a third. Capturing the *Penta*, providing Jenkins and his men managed to secure the rest of the Swedish crew, had seemed a difficult enough task when they were all locked up in the cabin aft, but it was only a small part of the hunt for the insider. Just how small was shown by the fact that he was now standing on the *Penta*'s bridge, for all intents and purposes in command, fairly certain there was a U-boat underneath him, and still utterly helpless; as helpless as if he was sitting astride a wooden horse on a runaway merry-go-round. Helpless, that is, until he found out from Pahlen what was going on, and passed the word by signal lamp to Johnny Gower in the *Echo*. Even so, if he found there was definitely a U-boat beneath the ship, what the hell could he or Johnny do? There was no way of destroying the U-boat without blowing up the *Penta* at the same time...

'You've got about ten minutes to spot the *Echo*,' Yorke said. 'In the meantime keep a good lookout ahead and astern and watch the revolutions: use your own judgement. Don't drop back so the *Marynal* rams us or I can imagine Captain Hobson's comments!'

'So can I, sir,' Reynolds said with a shiver, swinging his binoculars astern. 'She's there all right, on station.'

Yorke walked back into the wheelhouse, getting a confident grin – that was all the binnacle lamp illuminated – from the man at the wheel, and pushed open the door into the chartroom, going through and shutting it quickly so that the light came on: it was the moment of darkness that might give Ohlson or Pahlen a chance to try to escape.

Pahlen was lounging on the settee at the after side of the chartroom, Ohlson standing against the bulkhead on the other side from the door. Baxter made the apex of a triangle joining the three, a cocked revolver in his right hand and a grenade in his left. Baxter had a heavy piece of line round his waist. At first glance it seemed to be keeping his trousers up. Then Yorke saw it was a lanyard which he had tied through the ring on the safety pin of the grenade. Baxter had only one hand for the grenade yet throwing was usually a two-handed job: a finger of the left hand went through the ring and pulled out the safety pin while the right hand kept down a safety lever until the grenade was flung. Baxter's method was excellent: he had only to jerk the grenade and the safety pin would come out, letting the lever spring up as it went through the air. Baxter was, in the confined space of the chartroom, a one-man army.

Yorke took out his own revolver as he said to Baxter, 'All quiet?'

'That bloody light going out when the door opens, sir: we need some warning.'

'Tell the man at the wheel to warn everyone to knock and wait a few moments before they come in. And…' he saw a long chromed tube on the chart table, 'pass me that torch.'

He switched it on and said to Baxter: 'Right, tell the helmsman now.' He kept the beam pointing at Pahlen and made sure that as the door opened the torchlight also showed the revolver.

Baxter returned, shut the door and the chartroom was once again fully lit.

'English,' Pahlen said, almost casually, 'you might just as well put that revolver away because you'll never use it. It's not sporting to shoot an unarmed man.'

'You've been reading the wrong books about the British,' Yorke said quietly. 'I'd sooner shoot you than offer you a cigarette.'

'Rubbish,' Pahlen said, as though talking to a child.

'Hit him, Baxter,' Yorke said. 'Just once, hard.'

As the big seaman walked back to the chart table, Pahlen gasped painfully for breath and then bent over, clutching his stomach. As soon as he was sitting upright again Yorke said briskly, 'I have three questions to ask. You will answer them all.'

'I answer nothing!' Pahlen snarled.

'You'd better listen to the questions. First, is the U-boat still beneath us? Second, what time does she leave to get into an attacking position? Third, an alternative: does she go when she feels like it or do you make a signal?'

'I don't answer,' Pahlen said.

'Baxter,' Yorke said conversationally, switching on the torch, 'just put your head round the door and tell the man at the wheel to warn Mr Reynolds not to be alarmed when he hears shots.'

The chartroom plunged into darkness except for the torch; then the lights came on again.

'Now, Pahlen, answer the first question.'

'You'd never shoot!'

Yorke aimed at Pahlen's leg, glancing at the watch on his left wrist. 'In one and a half hours that U-boat is probably due to make its first attack. Fifty British or American seamen might be killed. Then it will torpedo a second ship, killing perhaps another fifty. And then later it might get a third. One hundred and fifty Allied seamen might die. Unless, Herr Pahlen, you answer some questions correctly.'

'It is war, English!'

'Yes,' Yorke agreed, 'it is war, and I'm afraid you're the next casualty. I'm short of time. The first question please. Is the U-boat still beneath us?'

'Would you shoot an unarmed man, English?' Pahlen sneered.

'Yes,' Yorke said. 'I'll count to five. Remember, a hundred and fifty of my people will die within a couple of hours if you don't answer.'

'For God's sake,' Captain Ohlson screamed. 'The Swedish Government will protest! This is a neutral ship. I am the master. I order you to get out of here and let my men take over again.'

'Do you?' Yorke said politely. 'Very well, I've made a mental note if it. But don't interrupt again, please; your turn will come should *Herr* Pahlen not survive his questioning.'

The flicker in Pahlen's eyes showed Yorke that the German was beginning to get worried because he must already have realized that Ohlson was a weak link. Ohlson would talk to save his life. It was just because Pahlen was so typically a Nazi that Yorke was going to make him talk first.

'Pahlen,' he said, 'I told you we don't have much time. Baxter here can give you what they call in American gangster films "a roughing up", but it takes five or ten minutes. I want answers in a few seconds. I'm going to count five. If you haven't answered that question by then, I'm going to shoot you. One...two...three...four...five.'

The explosion in the confined space seemed to blast his eardrums and Baxter, as a precaution, had already half turned to face Ohlson.

Pahlen's high-pitched scream was the first noise to get through the ringing in Yorke's ears and the man was crouched down grasping his left foot. His hands were slowly turning red as blood dripped from the torn shoe.

The German stopped screaming and looked up at Yorke. 'You…you shot me!'

'That's the first one,' Yorke said crisply. 'Sit up because I'm going to count to five again, and if you haven't answered I'm going to shoot you a second time. Only this will be the last and in the stomach. I can't risk deafening myself, you know. Deuced noisy things, guns. I wish this one had a silencer. Now – one…two…'

As Yorke counted he hoped desperately that Pahlen would answer. He knew he could not shoot the man in the stomach in cold blood but shooting him in the other foot would tell the German that the 'English' would not kill him.

The German broke at four.

'He's still underneath us!' he shouted. 'Where else do you think, you fool!'

Yorke nodded, and Baxter looked at him admiringly. This lieutenant was a cool one. That Jerry ran it close: another second and the Lieutenant would have shot him in the stomach, that's for sure. Now he still has two other questions to answer.

Baxter kept an eye on Ohlson, but the Swedish captain was white as a sheet and from the look of it, pressing himself against the bulkhead to stop himself from fainting. Now Mr Yorke was talking to the Jerry again, coolly, conversationally almost. Not even almost – it bloody *was* conversational. More to the point, though, if that bleedin' Jerry did not answer quick and Mr Yorke continued shooting bits off him, they would all be deaf before he used up all the cartridges in that gun.

'The second question, Mr Pahlen, which I'll repeat in case you've forgotten it: when does the U-boat go off to her attacking position?'

Answer, you bloody fool, Baxter thought; Mr Yorke's going to save 150 of our men so you don't count for a puff of smoke. He's cocking the gun again. It's a double-action job but the heavier pull needed means that for accuracy it's best to cock it, reducing the trigger pressure to a couple of pounds or so.

'I'm going to count, Mr Pahlen, because unless you co-operate at once it will be quicker to get the answers from Captain Ohlson. So this is your last chance and in case you decide not to answer...' Baxter saw Yorke give a slight bow, 'we'd better take our farewells now. One...two...three...'

Come *on*, Baxter tried to will the man; talk, because that bloody gun makes such a bang!

'...four...'

'Stop!' Pahlen flung himself sideways and crouched, his hands over his stomach, his left foot waving in the air and dripping blood.

'Well?'

'I tell you,' Pahlen gabbled, 'but don't shoot me in the stomach...'

'Tell me, then,' Yorke said coldly. 'Tell me all about it.'

Just like a headmaster determined to hear all about some pupil's villainy, Baxter thought, and swishing a cane in the air as he spoke.

'The U-boat, he leaves us about 1930, half an hour before he attacks.'

'You make no signal?'

'Yes, yes!' Pahlen said, hastily, sitting upright, his eyes fixed on Yorke's revolver and quite oblivious of the blood now dripping from his torn shoe. 'We reduce the revolutions on the port engine for half a minute – applying corrective helm, of course. That tells him that no escorts are inside the convoy – or within sight, anyway.'

'How many revolutions do you drop?'

'Twenty-thirty… The chief engineer just slows the engine when we telephone down to him. That answers both your other questions.'

Yorke nodded. 'Most obliging of you, but they raise others. Supposing you do not make the signal…?'

'He would stay in position beneath us.'

'What does he do once he's completed his attack for the night?'

'He dives and stops and waits for the convoy to pass clear.'

'And then?'

'Once he's sure… I'm feeling faint, can't I get this leg bandaged?'

'You're alive,' Yorke said unsympathetically. 'The convoy passes clear. Then what?'

'He surfaces when he's sure it's safe so that he can run his diesels and charge batteries. Then next day we drop back…'

'Come on, come on!' Yorke suddenly snarled.

'Well, we drop back and meet him, and he follows us on the surface so we block any radar beams from the escorts until we get close, then he dives and stays under us. We rejoin the convoy slowly so he does not have to use up much of the electricity in his batteries.'

'Is this a German ship?' Yorke asked suddenly.

Pahlen shook his head weakly. Baxter saw that shock, pain and the bleeding were beginning to take effect, but he knew the Jerry was going to have to try deep breathing or something, because Mr Yorke was going to get all of the story that he needed. In the meantime, though, what the hell was he going to do about that U-boat underneath them?

'She's Swedish then – but under charter to some fake German-owned company?'

'Yes, she is.' The answer came from Ohlson. 'All the papers are in that safe – or enough for your purposes: charter party, and all the rest of it. There are only two Germans on board the ship – him, and the second officer, the one who met you when you climbed up the net. Everyone else is Swedish.'

'You bastards,' Yorke said bitterly. 'You hide in a British convoy and help the Germans sink the ships. And you get a double profit – the British pay you for carrying a cargo, the Germans for chartering them the ship so they can put naval officers on board.'

At that moment Yorke knew he would have no trouble in shooting a man in the stomach, only it would be Ohlson, not Pahlen. Pahlen was fighting a war. Ohlson...

Baxter was thankful when he saw the lieutenant stuff the pistol in his pocket: for a moment he was sure Mr Yorke was going to shoot Ohlson: he had gone dead white, as though he could see those torpedoed ships – like the *Florida Star* which had burned, and the *Hidalgo*, which had blown up last night – and he had realized that a double-crossing neutral was even more to blame than a German.

'Sit the two of them together there on the settee, Baxter. If they move, shoot 'em.' Yorke turned to Ohlson, hoping his voice had sounded fierce enough. 'Is that safe locked?' When the Swede nodded, Yorke said: 'Open it, now. Key or combination?'

'Both.'

Yorke picked up a notebook and pencil. 'Write down the combination.'

The Swede wrote, and Yorke ripped off the page and said: 'Now dial the combination as I watch you.'

The Swede turned the dial back and forth four times, to numbers corresponding to those he had written down. 'Now you use the key,' he said.

'Use it, then.'

The Swede took a key from his pocket, unlocked the safe and pulled the door open.

'Give me the key,' Yorke said. 'Now sit back there. Baxter, keep them away from that.' He pointed to the safe.

'But you can't leave it open!' Ohlson protested. 'All those papers are secret!'

'They *were*, but not now. However, if either of you so much as point at the safe, Baxter will shoot you. Don't forget, I know all I need to know, and I have the evidence. Your lives…' he snapped a finger and thumb. He turned to the seaman. 'Here's the torch. If anything happens, these two must not escape alive.' Then he bent over the chart table, writing hurriedly on the pad, which he took with him.

Out on the starboard wing of the bridge Cadet Reynolds said: 'I've spotted the *Echo*, sir, but I don't think I'll ever be able to point her out to you. Do you want me to pass a signal?'

'Yes, it's long and I'll read it out word by word. Call up the *Echo*.'

The blue light from the signal lamp was ghostly: its flickering lit the planking of the bridge deck and Yorke saw it was newly scrubbed. Dot-dash, dot-dash, dot-dash: 'A,A,A,' the Morse letter for calling up another ship. A tiny blue pinpoint in the distance, a dash, the letter 'T'. 'They're answering, sir,' Reynolds said.

Yorke stood where he would be able to read from the notebook by the flickering light of the signal lamp. 'Right, I'll just read the signal word by word, as you transmit, beginning now:

Lancaster I have seized *Penta* stop submarine beneath which departs to attack only on *Penta* signal stop submit you drop charges shallow setting closest possible across my bow while I go astern with helm hard over so submarine overshoots stop because usual attack begins figures 2000 suggest you attack soonest Yorke end message.'

Reynolds lowered the signal lamp with a sigh. 'Phew, that's the longest I've ever sent, sir.'

Yorke noticed that there had not been one hurried sequence of dots, the 'E E E' standing for 'erase'. 'You didn't make a single mistake. Good work. But stand by for the reply.'

He could imagine Johnny Gower now reading the signal. He would be holding the pad against the dim red light over the chart table, his eyes going back and forth across the hurriedly-written pencilled message. This would be the first news Johnny had that the *Penta* definitely had a U-boat under her and the first news he would get that Yorke had actually seized the ship, instead of continuing to pose as a survivor. Blast, Johnny must know one more fact which he had forgotten to include in the signal.

'Quick, call him up again!'

There was the tiny blue flash and Yorke began dictating:

Lancaster have secured *Penta*'s German officers prisoner Yorke end message.

He could imagine Johnny's sigh of relief. German officers were the justification for everything: for Yorke seizing the ship and for the *Echo* trying to sink the U-boat and risking the *Penta*. He had just told Baxter that it did not matter if he shot them, but to hell with it. There were papers in the safe that were probably far more important as evidence.

He saw the blue pinpoint of the *Echo*'s signal lamp. Yorke could read it but preferred to have Reynolds speaking it as he wrote in the dark:

Yorke on my way stop switch on navigation lights lancaster.

'Christ,' Reynolds exclaimed, 'all the electrical switches are marked in Swedish.'

There was a clattering on the companionway ladder behind them. 'That you, sir?'

Yorke recognized Jenkins' voice. 'Yes, what's happened?'

'Nothing, sir,' Jenkins said composedly. 'Absolutely nothing.'

'Do you mean that...'

Realizing he had been misunderstood, Jenkins explained hastily: 'No sir, we're holding everyone in the saloon. I meant there's been no trouble. One door's locked, and a couple of chaps are juggling grenades at the other. The Swedes are all lying down flat looking like a bunch of wogs when the muezzin sounds off and the old codger calls 'em to prayer.'

'Have you any spare men?'

'Yes, sir, I thought you'd need 'em. Me here, and three seamen waiting at the bottom of the ladder.'

'Send a man with a revolver to help Baxter guard those two in the chartroom. The rest of you stay here. No, send one man over to the other side of the bridge as a lookout.'

He turned and went back into the chartroom. Pahlen was trying to tie up his bleeding foot with his jacket, watched by an alert Baxter and a completely unhelpful Ohlson who, from the look on his face, was regretting, on behalf of himself and his owners, ever getting mixed up with the German Navy, or whoever chartered the *Penta*. Presumably several other

Swedish ships were involved because there could be no doubt now that the *Penta* was only one of a squadron of neutrals helping to play the insider trick in different convoys.

Yorke found the ship's log on the chart table and then bent down and took out the papers in the safe. A hundred or so pages of different shapes and sizes, some with wax seals and looking like contracts, all typewritten, and here at the bottom of the pile signed letters from addresses in Stockholm and a German firm in Berlin. Presumably some apparently innocent company set up by the German Navy.

There was the usual canvas bag for secret papers at the back of the safe, open at one end with brass eyelets and a drawstring, and a lead bar inside. Yorke took out the lead bar, slid the papers into the bag with the log, tightened the drawstring, and put the bag on the chart table. That would be all the written evidence needed, he hoped.

The *Echo* would be working up to full speed now, cutting through the lines of darkened ships in the convoy, watching for the one that carried something rarely seen in wartime – navigation lights. Red on the port side of the bridge, green to starboard; a white light on the foremast, another several feet higher on the mainmast, and a stern light. They would all help the *Echo* see exactly where the *Penta* was. Johnny was going to have to get it right the first time with his depth charges; there would be no second chance for anyone.

There was a knock at the door and Baxter switched on the torch as the door opened and then closed again. A red-bearded seaman, Barbarossa's cousin, if not a younger brother, stood there with a revolver in one hand a knife in the other. 'Jenkins sent me, sir.'

'Help Baxter guard these two,' Yorke told him. 'Shoot if necessary,' he added, more to discomfort Pahlen and Ohlson than threaten them. He pointed to the canvas bag on top of the chart table. 'The pair of you guard this, too. In an emergency, that's all we need to save.'

'The evidence, sir?' Baxter asked.

'Exactly.' He gave Baxter a wink, knowing neither Ohlson nor Pahlen could see it. 'We don't need these two prisoners as long as we have the papers.'

Yorke turned to Ohlson and pointed to the red-haired seaman, Harris. 'Go with this man and switch on our navigation lights.'

'Lights?' Ohlson repeated incredulously.

'Port, starboard, masthead and stern lights. Hurry!'

The helmsman was shouting through the door that Reynolds wanted him.

The frigate was signalling but just as Yorke's eyes adjusted to the darkness and could see the blue light, he read the Morse letters 'AR' and saw the reflection of Reynolds' single-letter reply, 'R'. Message ended, message received.

Reynolds put the signal lamp back in its box and said: 'The frigate asked us to light up our bow at the right moment, sir, if we can. That's not the exact wording but it's what he meant'

'Very well.'

Damn and blast it, why hadn't he thought of it himself? But how? The light would have to be kept inboard just in case the U-boat looked through its periscope while submerged and saw above it an eerie green light – that's how a floodlight would look from, say, fifteen fathoms down. Floodlights! The arc lights merchant ships used in foreign ports where there was no blackout so that unloading or loading could go on through the night. They were like huge inspection lights on long leads with a wire mesh across the front to protect the bulb.

There was only one man who could get a couple of arc lights out of the store and plugged in in time and that would be the *Penta*'s electrician. He turned and hurried back into the wheelhouse, where Ohlson was turning switches.

'Christ, the navigation lights are coming on!' yelled a seaman.

'That's all right; they're supposed to be,' Yorke answered. Then to Ohlson he said: 'Are they all on?' When the Swede nodded, Yorke said: 'This seaman is going to take you down to the saloon. There you must find your electrical officer and order him to get two arc lights – floodlights you understand, like you use in the holds – on to the fo'c'sle and alight within five minutes. Look at your watch, and you too, Harris. If they're not alight in five minutes, Harris will shoot you, Captain Ohlson.'

The Swede bolted for the wheelhouse door, followed by Harris, who had seen Yorke's wink. He seemed to be winking a lot tonight; but he was having to make these bloodcurdling threats to keep the Swede and the German tractable. Tractable was a nice word and it was the right one. Nothing like the threat of a bullet in the stomach to make a man tractable. And did Jenkins send that fellow Harris on purpose? Harris was in fact an amiable ox of a man, immensely strong, and his red beard stuck out round his face like the petals of a sunflower. His laugh, though, was fantastic. When he chuckled he sounded like a mass murderer doing away with his hundredth victim. Yorke suspected that the man would have to steel himself to shoot a pigeon; but at the moment this did not matter. Ohlson and the rest of those prisoners in the saloon, including the electrician, would see only a smiling swashbuckler with a gun in one hand and a knife in the other and a laugh that sounded like a thousand corpses rattling down a ramp to eternal damnation.

He went back outside to the starboard wing of the bridge. 'Call up the *Echo* and say we'll have the bow lit up within ten minutes.' The extra five minutes might be needed, and it would be five minutes of agony for Ohlson and seem like an extension of life. It also left it to Johnny whether he slowed up and waited for the light before he attacked. It was a godsend that he had known Johnny for so many years. Johnny's extra half stripe meant one had to put the odd 'submit' or 'propose' into a signal, but Johnny knew him well enough to accept without question what must be one of the most bizarre signals made so far in this war. Not dramatic, just bizarre. 'I have a U-boat at the bottom of the garden *de ma tante.*'

Johnny would come whistling up the starboard side and then turn hard a-port across the *Penta*'s bow: close enough, no doubt,' to risk a glancing collision. At that moment the *Penta* should be almost stopped. Dare he risk explaining to Mills on the engine-room telephone what was needed, or should he bring the engineer to the bridge? He would try the phone to start with.

He picked up the telephone and pressed the button. Almost at once he heard Mills' cheery, 'Engine room here!'

'Bridge here. Listen, Mills, this is Yorke.' Quickly he brought the engineer up to date with the events of the last fifteen minutes and explained that the *Echo* was coming up fast, and what was needed from the engine room.

'No trouble,' Mills said. 'You use the engine-room telegraph. You know they need a double pull, so when you're ready just tweak one and then the other so they ring and I'll go full astern on the port engine, full ahead on starboard and pray. If you bung the wheel hard over at the same time we'll go bolting down a side road like a lame pickpocket.'

'Listen, Mills,' Yorke said, 'if anyone makes a mistake, you're going to get blown to pieces…'

'Yes, you said that just now. But some bugger's got to stay down here and spin the wheels and it has to be me. I recognize 'em, but all the dials are labelled in Swedish. I need one man to help me.'

'Ask for a volunteer.'

'You look after your end and I'll look after mine. We've got a good volunteer poker game going down here. I'm five quid ahead at the moment.'

'I'll try and give you three or four minutes' warning on the phone,' Yorke said.

'That'll be a help; it'll give us time to gather up the winnings. Don't forget the "left hand down a bit" with the helm – she'll take a minute or two to start turning with the screws: Much longer than you destroyer folk realize.'

Then Yorke remembered with a shiver that he had not warned Mills about reducing revolutions, and he passed on Pahlen's description of the signal to the U-boat.

'Aye, it's damned lucky I didn't just juggle about with one engine and then the other. Still, he'll only have a few seconds warning down there when we do our fancy two-step; not enough time for him to say *Donner und* whatsit.'

When Yorke put down the receiver he turned to the seaman at the wheel. 'Did you hear what I just said to Mr Mills?'

'Yes, sir.'

'So when I give the word, you put the wheel hard aport. Watch that telemotor indicator. There, the red pointer. That shows how much rudder you have on. Get it right over so the rudder is helping to stop us, as well as turning us.'

Out on the wing of the bridge, Reynolds pointed over on the quarter and Yorke saw a pinpoint of blue light. It did not wink and seemed to be moving. There was a greyish blur just forward of it and Yorke realized that the *Echo* was using it as a fighting light. She had slowed down and was abreast the fourth ship in the next column, obviously waiting for the lights to appear on the *Penta*'s bow.

Yorke looked round the convoy. Ahead of the *Penta* was one ship, the leader of the column. Astern, just visible as a bow wave, was the *Marynal*, with the old *Flintshire* the last in the column. The next column to starboard still had five ships, with the *Echo* on the far side. A sensible position, Yorke noted, because it meant that all those merchant ships' engines masked the sound of the frigate's approach until the last possible minute.

A night like this showed what the devil of a job the U-boat had. The Teds must rely on sound to an almost incredible degree, because even standing up here high on the *Penta's* bridge, fifty feet or so above the waterline, it was hard to see more than three or four of the nearest ships in the convoy. Imagine trying to spot one through a periscope which stuck up briefly only a few feet above the water, frequently covered by the odd wave. About like trying to drive a car at night through heavy rain without headlights or windscreen wipers.

There was no putting off answering the next question: those Swedes in the saloon. Did he allow them up on to the boat deck, in case something went wrong? He had forgotten to ask Jenkins how many there were, but he had only three or four sailors to guard them. A determined rush by the Swedes and they would recapture the ship and the whole operation so far would have been a waste of time.

The answer was that the Swedes had to stay where they were. There was time to send a messenger down to tell the guard to let one of the Swedes out to collect all the lifejackets needed for however many prisoners were there. Yorke turned and gave instructions to Jenkins.

There was a flicker of harsh white light on the fo'c'sle, then suddenly a powerful lamp lit up the foredeck. Yorke looked down over the rail and saw the forward part of the ship, with its hatches and stowed derricks, was a complex maze of shadows. A second arc lamp came on and he saw three men on the fo'c'sle, two adjusting the lights and one standing back watching them, close enough to shoot them with a revolver, too far off to be suddenly dazzled. Harris was wide awake and wary.

'Mr Reynolds, call up the *Echo*. Make "Tally-ho". Just one word; don't bother with a hyphen.'

A fo'c'sle of blazing light played hell with night vision but made it easier on the bridge: he could see the engine-room telegraph clearly now, a tall brass pillar waist high with what at first glance looked like two clock faces on top, a dial to the left and another to the right, with a lever on top of each one. One dial was for the port engine, one for the starboard, each with various orders – stop, slow, half and full ahead, and the same for astern, plus finished with engines… And each lever, or pointer, showed the order the bridge was transmitting to the engine room.

Yorke stood behind the telegraph and experimentally held the levers. It would not matter a damn where the pointers stopped as long as he did the quick back and forth movement that made sure the telegraph bell rang in the engine room to attract attention. Not that Mills would need waking up.

And there was the *Echo* increasing speed, the grey blur of her bow wave becoming more pronounced in the black of the night and from the look of it she was crossing the bow of the fourth ship in the next column.

Yorke snatched the binoculars from Reynolds. Johnny was taking that merchant ship damned close, just shaving her stem. Now the *Echo* was turning back to starboard and slicing across the ship's bow a second time. Then she was hidden by the ship again – Johnny must be slowing down almost alongside her. Here he comes now, first the bow wave, then the blue light – and a great swirl of water just ahead of the merchant ship as her bow wave hit the frigate's.

Johnny was making dummy runs at various speeds across that poor beggar's bow. Must be scaring the wits out of the officer of the watch of the merchantman. Johnny would probably have called him on the loud hailer to give him a friendly warning.

Now he was turning again, now dropping back out of sight, hidden by the merchantman. Now appearing in yet another wild dash across the bow, the Echo seeming tiny against the bulk of the merchant ship.

Yorke hurried into the wheelhouse, pressed the button on the telephone to the engine room. 'Three or four minutes to go' he told Mills. Pack up your playing cards, pay your debts, and tighten your brassiere straps. And once you hear the telegraphs and have spun all the wheels and valves, get out of that engine room fast!'

'We're really waiting halfway up the ladder already,' Mills said: 'Me and my volunteers.'

Yorke chuckled, buoyed by Mills' cheery manner. Going out on the bridge again he bumped into Captain Ohlson being brought back by Harris, whose features, now lit by the reflection of the arc lamps, looked quite diabolical. 'I put that 'lectrical chap back in the saloon with his mates, sir,' Harris reported. 'The sentry said to tell you they all had lifejackets now.'

Yorke nodded and turned away to see a blue light flashing a series of dot-dash, the letter A, from the commodore (the former vice-commodore who had taken over when the old Admiral's ship was sunk) who must be wondering what the devil was going on – Johnny was probably too busy to report, or was keeping radio silence.

Then a signal lamp began blinking from the *Echo*, calling the *Penta*. Reynolds was acknowledging almost before Yorke had time to speak. 'One five knots end message,' he said. So the Echo would be doing fifteen knots when she made her run... Johnny hadn't hit the practice ship – but he hadn't been juggling with a lot of high explosive, either.

He must warn the *Marynal!* Blast, he seemed to be forgetting half the things that mattered. 'Reynolds – call up the *Marynal* and tell her to disregard my movements. Hurry now!'

Reynolds moved quickly to the after side of the bridge and while Yorke watched for the *Echo* he heard the brisk clacking of the signal lamp trigger and mirror. He was a sensible lad, Yorke noted; by going as far aft as possible he kept that flashing blue light out of Yorke's eyes.

This was all unreal, like a half-remembered nightmare: here he was standing on the bridge of a merchant ship in the middle of a convoy with navigation lights on and the bow and forward part of the ship lit up like a peacetime cruise liner. All the ship's company were under guard, and there was a U-boat underneath blissfully unaware of what was going on a few feet above him... He still had grenades in his pocket and a revolver stuck in the front of his jacket. None of his men seemed to have any lifejackets... Too late to worry now: Johnny was on his way!

The *Echo*, a dark blob beneath the blue fighting light with a smudge of grey showing where her bow wave was curling up, was cutting across the next column halfway between the fourth ship, which he had been using for practice, and her next ahead, and heading diagonally across the gap between the columns towards the *Penta*, second in the next column.

'Quartermaster, stand by!'

He walked over to the engine-room telegraph and put a hand on the handle of each indicator. The metal was cold. The throbbing was his heart beating, not the *Penta's* diesels. A few seconds too late or too early and he would wreck everything: perhaps hit and sink the *Echo* and she would go down with all those depth charges set to explode shallow.

The forward side of the bridge helped hide the glare from the arc lamps, but although the *Penta* must look an extraordinary sight, Johnny would see the stem black and sharp like the edge of a cliff, the *Penta* herself towering over the frigate. He looked over his right shoulder–time was slowing down and the black blob with a grey smudge under the blue light was now recognizably a frigate racing along in the darkness, slicing wavetops into sheets of spray. Johnny would be under that blue light, standing on the bridge, peering up at the *Penta* which was now broad on his bow. It was, Yorke thought inconsequentially, as if the *Penta* was an express train thundering down towards a converging level crossing with Johnny driving a small sports car along the road and trying to cross the track before the engine could hit him.

The *Echo* now seemed almost bows on, with the glare from the arc lights sending out flecks of reflection from her bow wave and making it seem she was chasing a swarm of fireflies.

Men were grouped round her forward gun and the reflection of the lamps began catching the front of her bridge; Yorke imagined he could see a row of heads, Johnny Gower in the middle. More men were crouched aft, by the depth-charge throwers. Johnny had a hell of a responsibility. If he got it right he blew up a German U-boat; if he got it wrong he blew up a Swedish ship and killed everyone on board.

And, for God's sake, blew up all the evidence! If Johnny got it wrong they would crucify him at the Admiralty for suddenly going mad and sinking a neutral. The *Echo's* signal log recording the brief messages from the late Lieutenant Yorke would not help; they were too brief, and gave no proof that the late Lieutenant Yorke himself had had any proof – or even that he had sent the signals...

Here she comes, like the sports car at the level crossing, her bow abreast the *Penta*'s stern, overtaking at nine knots.

'Quartermaster!' he shouted, 'hard a-port!' and as he shouted he gave the double jerk on the two telegraphs, one forward, one back, he heard the ring –and the ring in reply. Now the *Penta*'s bow would turn to port and her stern would swing out to starboard – would Johnny allow enough distance for the swing?

Suddenly the *Penta* began vibrating; a heavy shuddering as though a blade had come off propeller: what the hell was going on down there in the engine room? Jenkins was shouting 'What ho, she bumps!' with Reynolds screaming with excitement, 'Just look at that!'

Yorke looked back hurriedly at the *Echo* but she was not there – she had vanished. No, the *Penta* had turned sharply so the frigate would be...

A great booming thunderclap seemed to come up from the depth of the ocean, followed by a greater double boom and then a single one: the *Echo* had dropped a diamond pattern of depth charges where the *Penta* would have been had she not suddenly swung to port. On where the unsuspecting U-boat should be, unaware until the last few seconds that anything untoward was happening overhead.

Over on the starboard beam Yorke saw a great flat, boiling mass of water at each of the four points of a diamond and, even as he watched, each spurted up a great column like wet volcanoes.

Suddenly he thought of the *Penta* heading for the ships in the next column to port.

'Quartermaster! – hard a-starboard,' he yelled as he felt Mills bring the revolutions back to normal and looked back on the quarter where the *Echo*'s searchlight was now lighting up the area of boiling water as she desperately tried to turn back to get over it.

The searchlight caught the *Marynal*, lumbering along; still in her correct position in the column and about to pass through the mass of disturbed water.

Then Yorke saw it, just ahead of the *Marynal*: like a black log in a millstream to begin with, then surfacing like a whale, and a few moments later high enough in the water so that he could see it, was the U-boat.

Several streams of tracers suddenly tore across from the *Echo*, but Yorke saw that she dare not fire her bigger guns in case she hit the *Marynal*. Now red lines of tracer were darting from the *Marynal* as her machine-guns and twin 20mm cannons opened up on the U-boat. The *Echo*'s searchlight lost the U-boat as her bridge section masked the beam in her desperate turn to get into position for another attack on the submarine, which had obviously been forced to the surface and could not dive because of damage.

Yorke noticed a thin trail of sparks rising diagonally into the sky from above the *Marynal*'s bridge and then curving over, bursting a moment later into a brilliant 'Snowflake' parachute flare, perfectly placed right above the U-boat, its harsh light dramatically white against the dull red of the streams of tracer below which were bouncing off the U-boat's hull and then richocheting at crazy angles from the waves in a cobweb of childlike squiggles.

Yorke sighted the *Penta*'s next ahead in the column and shouted a course correction, then looked over the quarter again at the U-boat, black and evil in the magnesium white of the flare, and which now seemed to be moving slowly ahead out of the great pond of white froth. The *Echo* had her helm hard over to avoid a merchant ship; Johnny Gower would now have to do a figure of eight before he could get back to the U-boat. And that bloody fool Hobson was getting well off course with the *Marynal* – he would block the way if and when Johnny ever got the *Echo* round again.

What was Reynolds shouting about? Yorke checked that the *Penta* was more or less back in the column and not likely to hit the ship ahead and then ran to the after side of the bridge, where Reynolds was dancing up and down with excitement and yelling 'He's going to ram the bugger! Oh do look, sir, he's going to ram the bastard! Oh, do look…' while Jenkins was cheering like a drunken football fan.

The *Marynal* was increasing speed: the light from the Snowflake flare showed her bow wave getting bigger, the dark water at her stern now curling up and over into a white moustache – a hundred yards to go, probably less. And there's a trail of sparks from another flare going up from the *Marynal* – Hobson had seen that the U-boat's one hope of escape was to get out of the circle of light from the first one into the safety of darkness.

'Those bloody Snowflakes,' Jenkins snarled angrily, 'we've carted 'em halfway round the world and now the first time we use 'em I ain't even on board!'

'You're getting a better view from here,' Yorke said unsympathetically, looking forward again and just managing to spot his next ahead's stern as the second Snowflake flare exploded in an almost blinding white glow beneath its parachute.

'We don't need those arc lights now,' Yorke told Jenkins. 'Get them doused.'

The seaman walked to the forward side of the bridge, rested his revolver on the rail, and started firing. It took three shots to put out the first one but he missed with the rest.

'Send someone down to pull out the plug,' Yorke said impatiently, his ears ringing. 'Look sharp, there's a war on!'

He turned back to watch the *Marynal*. The Snowflake lit up the whole merchant ship, the portholes on the forward side of the accommodation looking like the reflection on rows of buttons. There were two or three black figures on the bridge. Spurts of flames were coming from the Hotchkiss machine-guns at each end of the bridge and from the twin Oerlikons on the monkey island and turning into tiny red darts of tracer. It was curious how tracer seemed to start off slowly and then speed up as it approached the target. That burst from a twin Hotchkiss ricocheted off the conning tower, the tracers scattering like sparks from a blacksmith's anvil. They may not be doing any damage but the Teds would hardly dare put their heads up for a look around.

The *Marynal* ploughed on, a great lumbering elephant determined to crush a wounded black serpent.

Would Hobson remember he did not have to go for the conning tower; that a U-boat was like an iceberg, most of it beneath the water?

Hell, the old *Marynal* must be making twelve knots already and still increasing speed. The chief engineer must – then Yorke saw that the chief engineer most certainly would not be pleased: the *Marynal*'s funnel was squirting sparks like a Roman candle as the sudden increase in speed blasted out all the loose carbon accumulated in the past few days of six knots...

Forty yards to go, perhaps less. The *Marynal*'s stem was now very close to the submerged after section of the U-boat. The *Echo*'s searchlight suddenly came on but Yorke saw that it was blinding old Hobson on the *Marynal*'s bridge. Just as suddenly as it came on it went out: Johnny Gower had spotted that too.

The Snowflake was swinging on the parachute and dropping fast. It was dimmer, too, and the magnesium was dripping, as though weeping red tears.

'Bloody things,' Jenkins swore. 'They've only got two launchers: I've argued time and time again to get two more fitted. That's the last – Christ!'

The *Marynal's* stem hit the U-boat just abaft the conning tower. The ship seemed to stop for a few moments, the bow reared up a fraction and then she ploughed on, having cut the U-boat in half, and in the dying light of the flare Yorke saw the U-boat's forward section point up in the air and then vanish, looking like a Christmas cracker torn in half and thrown away. Then the flare died and the *Echo's* searchlight came back on as the frigate approached from astern, looking for survivors.

'Reynolds,' Yorke said, 'get on the phone to the engine room and tell Mills what your captain has just done to that U-boat.'

'He deserves a medal,' Reynolds said jubilantly as he headed for the wheelhouse.

'He'll get one, I expect – once they've repaired the *Marynal's* bow.'

CHAPTER TWENTY-THREE

Johnny Gower leaned back in one of the two metal-framed chairs in his cabin and reached up into a black, lacy brassiere swinging over his desk to take a round tin of fifty Players out of one cup, and a box of matches and an ashtray from the other. As he lit a cigarette he said to Yorke: 'So you are certain this chap Pahlen is a German?'

'Yes, regular German Navy I should think. And I'm sure Ohlson is German too, even though he claims he's a Swede. More likely to be a reserve officer – probably served his time in the German mercantile marine and has a master's ticket. Just the man to put in command of the *Penta*.'

'Wouldn't the Swedish owners insist on a Swedish captain?'

'That depends on the terms of the charter. Probably a bare-boat agreement – just the hull and machinery, with the charterer responsible for maintenance, crew, insurance, and so on. And you can bet your life,' Yorke added, 'there's a clause saying the owners aren't in any way responsible for anything done by the charterers.'

'What the hell do they think the Germans are going to do, then?' Johnny demanded. 'Use it for those "Strength Through Joy" cruises they were running before the war begun?'

'Blockade running, probably. Though if the crew really are Swedes, I suppose the Swedish owners would know what she's being used for. If they're German, then I'd be prepared to believe they didn't. But the Swedes chartering the ship to the

Teds shows they'd sooner be on the Spree than on the Thames.'

'On the spree?' Johnny asked. 'What's that got to do with it?'

'The Spree is the river on which Berlin stands.'

'Oh yes. Thanks for trying. Well, the Swedes are more Jerry than anything else; most of their trade is with Jerrylanders. I suppose they think they're backing the winning side.'

Johnny reached up to put the cigarette tin and matches back in the brassiere cup. Noting Yorke's amused glance he explained, 'A gimballed smoking kit. Swings back and forth and summons up brief memories. More important, if you leave a tin of cigarettes on the desk you can be sure it'll roll over when we heel. The lid comes off and you have forty-nine cigarettes strewn across the cabin. Anyway, I like the nostalgia. Captured and unstuffed in Rio.'

So Johnny had recovered his interest in women again. His former wife had been described to Yorke as fitting perfectly the strictest specifications for a wife for Johnny Gower. She was a good tennis player, loved classical music and was a good violinist, had a private income, was striking to look at rather than beautiful and had copper-coloured hair. She could twist misogynist admirals round her little finger and had ordinary seamen offering to mow the lawn. And she had loved Johnny so deeply that she had had a nervous breakdown because of the eternal wait for him to come back alive. She had left him for a man in a safe job. She had stayed sane – but some people reckoned Johnny had gone round the bend: he just stayed at sea and hunted U-boats.

'You'd better write me a full report,' Johnny said. 'That starts it off "through channels". I'll cover the *Echo*'s side in another report. We'll have one from that wild man in the *Marynal*,

Hobson. And another from you describing the interrogation of Pahlen and Ohlson.'

'I'd like to finish off the interrogation – they should be ready in the wardroom by now.'

'I'll come too,' Johnny said. 'You'd better have a witness who'll say you didn't use violence.'

'I've already shot one of the bastards in the foot, don't forget.'

'He was trying to escape.'

'Oh no,' Yorke said. 'I shot him in the foot because he wouldn't talk, and his silence could have cost us one hundred and fifty lives. I'm all ready for the court martial on *that* one.'

The wardroom had been specially prepared: even though it was broad daylight outside, the ports were closed with deadlights. A seaman complete with boots and webbing gaiters, a revolver in a webbing holster at his waist, stood on guard just inside the door. Pahlen, his foot heavily bandaged, sat side by side with Ohlson on the settee, which was a miserable piece of furniture notable for its broken springs and the fact that it was made several inches too low. Sitting on a straight-backed chair in front of them was the *Echo*'s master-at-arms, a broken-nosed former boxing champion who was holding a golf club – his favourite weapon for breaking up fights in shore bars.

As the two men were being transferred from the *Penta* to the *Echo* last night, Yorke had been startled to discover that they had not understood what had happened to the U-boat: the solid mahogany door to the chartroom had prevented all the excited shouts of young Reynolds and the rest of the men from reaching the prisoners: all they knew was that the *Penta* had suddenly gone astern on one engine for a few moments and that there had been depth-charging and a lot of shooting. And that was all.

The sentry at the door sprang to attention and the master-at-arms came to his feet as though his limbs were springs and, to Yorke's surprise, looked as smart as a Marine drill instructor as he stood to attention with the golf club held like a sawn-off lance.

'At ease,' Johnny murmured, and said to Yorke, 'Perhaps you should introduce me?'

Pahlen and Ohlson both looked up for the first time.

Yorke made an off-hand gesture towards Pahlen. 'This fellow with the bandaged foot is *Oberleutnant* Pahlen – that may not be his real name – of the German Navy, and the other one's name I don't know, except that it's not Ohlson.' Yorke watched him carefully. 'He's a naval reserve officer from the German mercantile marine.'

Ohlson's eyes flickered and his shoulders seemed to slump; he had the appearance of a man who had played his last ace and seen it trumped by a three of clubs.

'This gentleman commands the frigate,' Yorke told them.

'This gentleman,' Johnny said casually, 'had a sister who was a nurse killed in the *City of Salisbury*...'

Both Pahlen and Ohlson went white; they stared down at Johnny's feet, and Yorke saw beads of perspiration beginning to form on Pahlen's upper lip and brow.

'You've heard of the *City of Salisbury*?' Johnny asked Pahlen, who nodded without raising his eyes.

'It was a mistake,' Ohlson whispered.

Big red crosses painted on a white hull, bright sunshine, the Swiss government gave you her exact route and the times she'd pass along it...yes, I can just imagine how easy it would be to make a "mistake"'.

'I was not involved in it,' Pahlen said suddenly, still not looking up, and Johnny swung round and stared at him.

'We'll find out about that,' he said in a quiet voice. 'Our intelligence people now know the number of the U-boat and the names of her officers. There's a file in our Admiralty. We check every German naval officer we capture,' he added, 'just in case...'

Both Yorke and Johnny sat down in armchairs and stared across at the two Germans without speaking. The master-at-arms saw a gesture by Johnny and sat down in his chair again, the golf club across his knees. The man had one of the more extraordinary broken noses Yorke had ever seen; once clear of his eyes it dropped vertically like the edge of a cliff.

After a good two minutes' silence Yorke, who was carrying a small pad, took a pen from his pocket and unscrewed the cap. He scribbled a few words and then looked up at Pahlen. 'I have a report to write and I find there are some gaps so I have more questions to ask.'

'I've nothing to say.'

Yorke nodded to the master-at-arms, who rapped Pahlen across the unwounded shin with the golf club. 'A prisoner of war is required to give his name, number and unit.'

Pahlen shook his head.

'Very well,' said Yorke, 'no one knows you've been taken prisoner, so we can lose you over the side whenever we want. Your naval friends are all dead, by the way.'

'My *naval* friends?'

'The U-boat underneath the *Penta*. She was sunk last night.'

'Those depth charges...that gunfire?' Pahlen whispered, obviously badly hit by the news.

Yorke shrugged his shoulders. 'Depth charges, ramming, gunfire... Once we knew what you people were doing, it wasn't too hard to stop it. There will be no more insider attacks on British convoys. You had the honour of taking part in the last one. The twelfth.'

'Yes, twelve,' Pahlen sneered, recovering himself. 'It took you long enough to find out...'

'It didn't actually,' Johnny Gower said. 'This officer was given the job of finding out what was going on. He read all the papers concerning the previous eleven attacks. And here you are, caught on the twelfth.'

'Tell me,' Yorke said, 'are the ship's company of the *Penta* all German? Or are some Swedish?'

'Ask them,' Pahlen said.

'There's no problem – just that we don't have any Swedish translators in the convoy.'

'So you eventually sank the *Penta*,' Ohlson said regretfully. 'She was a good ship.'

'She still is,' Yorke said. 'She is just ahead of us, towing a damaged merchantman and carrying her original crew under a heavy guard.'

'Where are we bound, then? To Freetown?'

'Not now. This frigate is escorting the *Penta* and her tow back to Liverpool, or perhaps the Clyde. Now Pahlen, and you, Ohlson, the questions. First, which...'

'I'm not answering any questions,' Pahlen said sharply.

Yorke stood up slowly, almost casually, and walked over, steadying himself against the *Echo*'s roll, until he was looking down at the two men.

'Those buttons on your uniform,' he said conversationally, 'what are they?'

'The buttons of the shipping company, of course; the Eskjo Shipping Company.'

'The same as your cap badges?'

'Yes,' Ohlson said, almost eagerly, as if pleased to be able to supply information. 'You see – ' he reached down for his cap, 'it is a map of Sweden surrounded by laurels.'

'And your papers, of course, your identity cards and passports, describe you as Swedish nationals; the master and the chief officer of the *Penta*.'

'Well, yes,' Ohlson said. 'Of course. We needed them when we visited Britain and other countries.'

'So your uniforms and papers are of Swedish mercantile marine officers – I expect the uniforms are even tailored in Stockholm.'

Ohlson grinned. 'The Swedish have good tailors – and good cloth. No war there, making shortages. Socks, shirts and shoes, too.'

'I wish I could visit Stockholm,' Yorke said enviously. 'It's impossible to get decent cloth in London now, and you can see what's happening to this uniform.' He pointed to stains down the front. 'Now, to get back to these questions. I…'

'You said yourself that we need give only name, number and unit,' Pahlen said.

'Name and rank, I imagine, since you are both officers,' Yorke said.

'Very well,' Ohlson said, 'I give mine: Hans Lauterwasser, *Oberleutnant*, German Navy Reserve.'

Yorke looked questioningly at Pahlen.

'All right,' the man said grudgingly, 'Heinrich Pahlen, *Kapitänleutnant*, German Navy.'

Yorke nodded and smiled. 'Thank you. The witnesses to what you have just said are Lieutenant Commander Jonathan Gower, Royal Navy, myself Lieutenant Edward Yorke, Royal Navy, and these two men, the master-at-arms and a leading seaman, whose names I will give you in a moment.'

'Why all this formality?' Pahlen demanded suspiciously.

'You have just confessed to being spies,' Yorke said evenly, 'and spies are hanged – after a proper trial, of course.'

'Spies?' Pahlen exclaimed, sitting bolt upright, his foot wound forgotten. 'But we've just told you our names and ranks in the German Navy!'

'And you've just admitted you are wearing Swedish mercantile marine uniforms and badges and you were carrying papers "proving" you are Swedish officers.'

Pahlen was the first to recover and, eyes narrowed, wiping the perspiration from his face with his sleeve, he said angrily: 'I'm warning you, Yorke: you'll have to answer for this when we've occupied England! We have long lists of names; we know who our friends are, and who are our enemies.'

Yorke nodded affably. 'When Germany has occupied Britain the four of us will give ourselves up. We'll go to the Admiralty and ask for you. Except of course, whether or not Britain is invaded, you'll be dead. Hanged as a spy, if we decide to hand you over to the authorities. Drowned by us if we don't. Now; about these questions…'

With that he sat down again, the notebook open on his knee. He looked directly at Pahlen. 'How many Swedish ships are chartered to the German Navy, and what are their names?'

Pahlen looked round at Ohlson who, his hair damp with perspiration so that he looked like a wet Siamese cat, nodded vigorously. 'Tell him, or I will.'

Pahlen gave eight names, which Yorke wrote down, asking for two to be spelled out.

'How does the U-boat rendezvous with the convoy and find the right ship?'

'The Swedish ship informs the Swedish Embassy when the convoy is due to sail. That is quite routine; the Embassy does not know it is being used. It informs the Swedish owners through the Swedish Foreign Office. U-boat Headquarters knows almost at once, works out when the convoy will be out of range of British air cover, and sends a U-boat to rendezvous.'

'And finding the Swedish ship?'

'There is no trouble about that – you saw for yourself, the ship pretends to have engine trouble and drops back to bring the U-boat into the convoy.'

'And just one U-boat is assigned to a particular convoy – another does not take over when the first runs out of torpedoes?'

'No – by the time we've sunk twelve ships or more in a convoy there's not much of any value left.'

'Why did the Swedish ships not supply extra torpedoes and fuel?'

'The same reason – after a U-boat has sunk a dozen ships, the survivors are usually carrying cargoes of little importance... And it was too risky for a neutral ship to be carrying the German electric torpedoes, apart from the problem of transferring them in bad weather.'

'What other neutral countries are chartering ships to you people?'

'None. Only Sweden.'

'Why not Spain?'

'The Spanish government will not take the risk.'

'The *Penta*'s crew – let's go back to that question. Are they Swedish or German?'

Pahlen shrugged his shoulders. 'You want me to convict them as spies, but I suppose you will question and trap them. They are Germans but they speak Swedish as well. Usually they come from mixed marriages, like Ohlson and me. We have hundreds of such young men in Germany. In Sweden we can pass for Swedish, in Germany we are German.'

'The pure Nordic type,' Yorke said.

'Ah – yes,' Pahlen said, not detecting the sarcasm in Yorke's voice. 'Perfect specimens.'

From the bridge of the *Echo* Yorke and Gower watched the *Penta* towing the *Marynal*, the long curving cable occasionally straightening like a bar when the heavily laden British ship was momentarily slowed down as she butted into a swell wave. Gower read the message from Captain Hobson, just received by Aldis lamp and written on a signal pad, and passed it to Yorke.

'Detailed survey shows bow damage confined to flooded deep tank,' the message said. 'Consider speed can safely be increased by two knots.'

When Yorke handed back the pad, Johnny tore off the page and wrote a short signal. 'Make that to the *Penta*,' he said to the signalman, explaining to Yorke: 'If Hobson's happy making another couple of knots, that suits me. The sooner we get back inside the range of Coastal Command the better.'

The *Echo*'s first lieutenant, Fenwick, said: 'It doesn't do to think about them being hit. An extra 360 survivors and prisoners in the two ships.'

'Think of it another way,' Johnny said. 'The *Penta* has three sets of deck officers and three of engineers, quite apart from seamen. You stand a four-hour watch and then take a day and a night off. A luxury cruise.'

'I suppose that technically the *Penta* is a prize,' Yorke said. 'Probably the first ship captured by DEMS gunners and merchant seamen!'

'An interesting legal point,' Johnny commented. 'A neutral ship chartered to one belligerent is captured by another belligerent. Does the charter party, or whatever the document is called, give her temporarily the nationality of the charterer?'

Fenwick said: 'If we chartered a Spanish ship and she was captured by the Germans, I reckon we'd compensate the Spaniards.'

'I can't see the Jerries being so kind-hearted,' Johnny said and, looking ahead, commented: 'Ah, that looks better – the *Penta* has turned up the wick. And I do believe the *Marynal* tows better at that speed.'

'I don't think anyone should ever mention this tow to Hobson again,' Yorke said. 'When I went on board this morning he was just about foaming at the mouth.'

'Why? He sank a bloody U-boat, didn't he?'

'Yes, and he's pleased enough about that, but having that chunk of U-boat wreckage knocking a blade off his propeller and bending the shaft – that was too much! He expected trouble at the sharp end when he rammed but having the U-boat cause trouble at the blunt end too seems – to him anyway – the sort of damned unsporting thing a Ted would do.'

'By the way, Number One, any news from Bennett about the wreckage we picked up?'

'Yes, sir. Bit of luck with the papers – there's the deck log, half the signal log, various letters belonging to seamen, a book of ciphers Bennett can't understand – hardly surprising – and the usual training manuals. He's drying out what matters but doing an immediate rough translation of the last entries on the log. He should have it ready very soon.'

'He's being careful not to damage it, I hope.'

'Very, sir. Ah, here he is.'

A thin, sallow-faced RNVR sub-lieutenant came on to the bridge, and Johnny said to Yorke: 'You haven't met Bennett. He's one of DNI's bright boys – codes and ciphers. Speaks German like a Berliner – which is hardly surprising, since he was born there.'

So Bennett was not his real name: he was a Jewish refugee, brought over by his family when it was still possible to get out of Germany.

'You were right enough, sir,' Bennett said to Yorke, 'it's all in the log. He left Brest for a routine patrol, received fresh orders from the Lion – that's Doenitz – four days out directing him north and, a couple of days later, giving him a position where he'd probably sight the convoy. Not a position but a fifty-mile patrol line.'

'The dates all coincide?' Yorke asked.

'Yes, he actually sighted the convoy a day before the Swede first dropped back, and stayed submerged in daylight – the log entries show they're getting scared of Liberator attacks – and caught up at night.

'The log notes everything in detail after that – very wordy and bureaucratic, the Germans. I speak,' Bennett said with a grin, 'as a naturalized Briton. Every entry is signed by the officer that made it, just as the regulations say. How they came up astern of the *Penta* for the first time – they actually name her – exchanged signals and information about the individual ships in the convoy, the general route, the zigzag diagram numbers used so far, size of the escort and so on. I haven't checked the signal log yet for the exact wording, but the details are in the general log.'

'Any names of officers?' Johnny asked.

'All of them, sir. She had been undergoing a long refit in Lorient and had a completely new ship's company. The names of all the officers and warrant officers were noted as they joined. Anyway, this is my rough translation of the entries – I've omitted routine things,' he said handing over several handwritten pages. 'Just the details of Operation Cuckoo.'

'Cuckoo?' Johnny exclaimed.

'Yes, sir, that was the German name for it. There's a number following it that I don't understand, but – '

'Is it twelve?' Yorke asked.

Bennett glanced at him and grinned. 'Yes, perhaps you'd explain it to me, sir, then I can get some sleep. I've been working on the log most of the night but that twelve was so intriguing I knew it would keep me awake!'

'Let's adjourn to the chartroom,' Johnny said. 'You'll have to wait for your sleep, Bennett.'

Once in the chartroom, Johnny turned to Bennett and said: 'You work for the Director of Naval Intelligence, so you can tell me this. I don't trust our cipher tables. If the Jerries don't know we've caught the *Penta*, there's a chance they'll try some more cuckoos in the nest, and we'll nab 'em before they do any harm. But if there's a chance they are cracking any of our ciphers I'd sooner wait until we get into port and report to the Admiralty by landline, using a scrambler phone, rather than make a signal now in cipher.'

Bennett looked embarrassed and Johnny, misunderstanding the reason, said: 'No, sorry, it's not up to you. I meant I wanted your opinion on the chance of the Germans reading any signal I might make.'

'I hesitated, sir,' Bennett said, 'only because not many others in DNI agree with me. I think the *B-Dienst* – that's the radio-intelligence branch of the German Navy – have penetrated a number of our ciphers. That's just a feeling I have – a hunch – and it's impossible to prove one way or the other. But if you were asking me,' Bennett said carefully, 'whether I thought there was a chance that the Germans would decipher any signal you could make to the Admiralty from this ship, using the cipher books we have on board, I would say they could read it as clearly as if you sent it in plain language.'

'Thanks, Bennett. Officially I haven't heard a word you've just said. And I've decided to maintain radio silence.'

'Coastal Command,' Yorke said suddenly. 'We'll have a Sunderland or a Liberator noseying round in a few hours. As soon as a plane spots three strange ships about which it knows nothing it'll very quickly investigate. If we have a signal ready we can pass it by Aldis with strict instructions that it must be sent to the Admiralty as soon as possible by landline but not transmitted by wireless and likewise they shouldn't report having sighted us until they land.'

'That's it,' Johnny said. 'I'll draft the signal now. Their Lordships will probably slap my hand, but...'

'I'm requesting you officially not to pass information by wireless about capturing the *Penta* and the U-boat sinking,' Yorke said formally. 'That means... I'm not sure what it means, but I'm supposed to be the outsider trying to catch the insider, and you had written orders to cooperate with me...'

'Thanks Ned, but I'll take the responsibility. We're heroes, not villains,' Johnny said philosophically. 'Either we're heroes for catching the cuckoo and Hobson gets a gong for carving up that U-boat, or we'll be sent to sew mail bags in Aden for bringing Sweden into the war against us. As the Foreign Office will decide, I've no idea which it will be, but we'd better practise our herring-bone stitch.'

The scrambler telephone had a curious echo but it was such a clear line that Yorke could hardly believe that Uncle was sitting in the Citadel in London, several hundred miles from the Clyde, and not in the next room.

'Telephone me at ASIU at noon,' the signal had said and because the time had seemed important, Yorke had gone to a lot of trouble to arrange it.

'Gower's signal and yours caused quite a stir when they arrived,' he heard Uncle say, the satisfaction showing in his voice. 'We bunged copies to our friend round the corner – to Downing Street,' he explained when he remembered he was talking on a scrambler telephone, 'and the Foreign Office panicked. They called for an immediate conference with the Vice Chief of Naval Staff, Assistant Chief of Naval Staff (U-boat Warfare and Trade), Director of Naval Intelligence and myself ordered to attend, to draft an apology to the Swedes and decide where you and Gower were to be shot.'

'Where was decided?' Yorke asked.

'Ha, there are times when the wicked prosper. We were in the midst of this special meeting, with these senior Foreign Office wallahs sitting round with long faces and saying smugly that both of you would have to be "sacrificed" to placate the Swedes, when our friend round the corner – I'd called on him just before I went to the Foreign Office – came on the phone to the chief FO wallah and squared his yards by ordering him to send the Swedish Embassy a copy of that U-boat's log and the *Penta* charter agreement… That shut up the FO people and we all – the Admiralty boys, that is – went out and had a stiff gin.'

'I'm catching the next train with all the documents,' Yorke said.

'You come by train because the man round the corner wants to see you at once, but we're laying on a special car and escort for the documents. That log is considerably more valuable than a ton of gold. How's your arm, by the way?'

The sudden change of subject caught Yorke by surprise. 'Bit painful, sir. I haven't been doing the exercises, and the weather's been cold.'

'You haven't been doing your exercises and the weather's been cold?' Uncle repeated. 'Oh dear. You're in trouble. I suspected that and sent for your medical adviser, who's waiting now. Hold the line.'

'Hello, darling,' she said, 'you're back early.'

'I love you. I'm catching the night train down to Euston. Can you get some leave?'

'Captain Watts says I have some sewing to do,' Clare said, as though she had not heard him. 'Another ribbon and a half stripe for you, and tell Johnny Gower he's getting an immediate award as well.'

DUDLEY POPE

GOVERNOR RAMAGE RN

Lieutenant Lord Ramage, expert seafarer and adventurer, undertakes to escort a convoy across the Caribbean. This seemingly routine task leads him into a series of dramatic and terrifying encounters. Lord Ramage is quick to learn that the enemy attacks from all angles and he must keep his wits about him in order to survive. Fast and thrilling, this is another highly-charged adventure from the masterly Dudley Pope.

> 'All the verve and expertise of Forester'
> *Observer*

RAMAGE'S CHALLENGE

The Napoleonic Wars are raging and a group of eminent British citizens have been taken captive in the Mediterranean by French troops. The Admiralty traces their location and sends the valiant Lord Ramage to effect their release. As Ramage and his crew negotiate the hazardous waters off the Tuscan coast, they soon begin to doubt the accuracy of their instructions. Ramage comes to realize that in order for his mission to succeed he must embark upon a fearful and highly dangerous escapade where the stakes have never been higher.

Ramage's Challenge is another action-packed naval adventure from the masterful Dudley Pope.

DUDLEY POPE

RAMAGE AND THE GUILLOTINE

As France recovers from her bloody Revolution, Napoleon is amassing his armies for the Great Invasion. News in England is sketchy and the Navy must prepare to defend the land from foreign attack.

Lieutenant Ramage is chosen to travel to France and embark upon the perilous quest of spying on the great Napoleon. His mission is to determine the strength of the French troops – but his discovery will mean the guillotine!

'The first and still favourite rival to Hornblower'
Daily Mirror

RAMAGE'S PRIZE

Lord Ramage returns for another highly-charged and thrilling adventure at sea. Instructed with the task of discovering why His Majesty's dispatches keep unaccountably disappearing, Ramage finds himself involved in a situation far beyond his expectations. Based on true events, *Ramage's Prize* is another gripping story from Dudley Pope.

'An author who really knows Nelson's navy'
Observer

DUDLEY POPE

THE RAMAGE TOUCH

The Ramage Touch finds the ever-popular Lord Ramage in the Mediterranean with another daring mission to undertake. He soon makes a shocking discovery which dramatically transforms the nature of the task at hand. With the nearest English vessel a thousand miles away, Ramage must embark upon a truly perilous and life-threatening course of action. With everything stacked against him, he has only one chance to succeed…

RAMAGE AT TRAFALGAR

Lord Ramage returns to fight in the most famous of Britain's sea battles. Summoned by Admiral Nelson himself, Ramage is sent to join the British fleet off Cadiz where the largest battle in naval history is about to take place. Finding himself in the front line of battle, Lord Ramage must fight to save his own life as well as for his country. The result is a thrilling, hair-raising adventure from one of our best-loved naval writers.

'Expert knowledge of naval history'
Guardian

OTHER TITLES BY DUDLEY POPE AVAILABLE DIRECT
FROM HOUSE OF STRATUS

Quantity	£	$(US)	$(CAN)	€
ADMIRAL	6.99	11.50	15.99	11.50
THE BIOGRAPHY OF SIR HENRY MORGAN 1635–1688	10.99	17.99	23.99	18.00
BUCCANEER	6.99	11.50	15.99	11.50
CORSAIR	6.99	11.50	15.99	11.50
DECOY	6.99	11.50	15.99	11.50
GALLEON	6.99	11.50	15.99	11.50
RAMAGE	6.99	11.50	15.99	11.50
RAMAGE AND THE DRUMBEAT	6.99	11.50	15.99	11.50
GOVERNOR RAMAGE RN	6.99	11.50	15.99	11.50
RAMAGE'S PRIZE	6.99	11.50	15.99	11.50
RAMAGE AND THE GUILLOTINE	6.99	11.50	15.99	11.50
RAMAGE'S MUTINY	6.99	11.50	15.99	11.50
THE RAMAGE TOUCH	6.99	11.50	15.99	11.50
RAMAGE'S SIGNAL	6.99	11.50	15.99	11.50
RAMAGE'S TRIAL	6.99	11.50	15.99	11.50
RAMAGE'S CHALLENGE	6.99	11.50	15.99	11.50
RAMAGE AT TRAFALGAR	6.99	11.50	15.99	11.50
RAMAGE AND THE DIDO	6.99	11.50	15.99	11.50

ALL HOUSE OF STRATUS BOOKS ARE AVAILABLE FROM GOOD BOOKSHOPS OR
DIRECT FROM THE PUBLISHER:

Internet: www.houseofstratus.com including author interviews, reviews, features.

Email: sales@houseofstratus.com please quote author, title, and credit card details.

Hotline: UK ONLY: 0800 169 1780, please quote author, title and credit card details. INTERNATIONAL: +44 (0) 20 7494 6400, please quote author, title and credit card details.

Send to: House of Stratus Sales Department
24c Old Burlington Street
London
W1X 1RL
UK

Please allow for postage costs charged per order plus an amount per book as set out in the tables below:

	£(Sterling)	$(US)	$(CAN)	€(Euros)
Cost per order				
UK	1.50	2.25	3.50	2.50
Europe	3.00	4.50	6.75	5.00
North America	3.00	4.50	6.75	5.00
Rest of World	3.00	4.50	6.75	5.00
Additional cost per book				
UK	0.50	0.75	1.15	0.85
Europe	1.00	1.50	2.30	1.70
North America	2.00	3.00	4.60	3.40
Rest of World	2.50	3.75	5.75	4.25

PLEASE SEND CHEQUE, POSTAL ORDER (STERLING ONLY), EUROCHEQUE, OR INTERNATIONAL MONEY ORDER (PLEASE CIRCLE METHOD OF PAYMENT YOU WISH TO USE)
MAKE PAYABLE TO: STRATUS HOLDINGS plc

Cost of book(s):_____ Example: 3 x books at £6.99 each: £20.97

Cost of order:_____ Example: £2.00 (Delivery to UK address)

Additional cost per book:_____ Example: 3 x £0.50: £1.50

Order total including postage:_____ Example: £24.47

Please tick currency you wish to use and add total amount of order:

☐ £ (Sterling)   ☐ $ (US)   ☐ $ (CAN)   ☐ € (EUROS)

VISA, MASTERCARD, SWITCH, AMEX, SOLO, JCB:

☐ ☐ ☐ ☐ ☐ ☐ ☐ ☐ ☐ ☐ ☐ ☐ ☐ ☐ ☐ ☐ ☐ ☐ ☐

Issue number (Switch only):

☐☐☐

Start Date: **Expiry Date:**

☐☐ / ☐☐   ☐☐ / ☐☐

Signature: _____

NAME: _____

ADDRESS: _____

_____

POSTCODE: _____

Please allow 28 days for delivery.

Prices subject to change without notice.
Please tick box if you do not wish to receive any additional information. ☐

House of Stratus publishes many other titles in this genre; please check our website (**www.houseofstratus.com**) for more details.